Niamh and the hermit

To Suzanne Mary Travers —
Hope you enjoy! God bless,
Emily C.A. Snyder

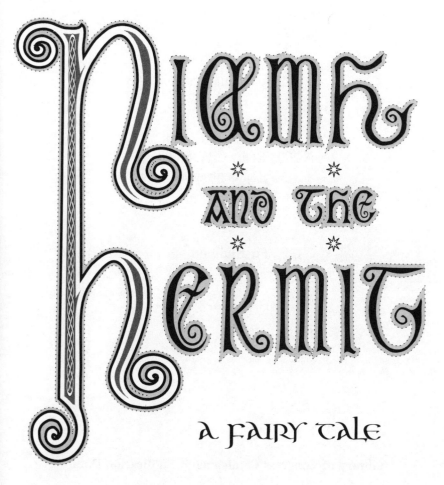

Niamh and the Hermit

A Fairy Tale

by

Emily C. A. Snyder

Arx Publishing,
Bristol PA

Arx Publishing LLC
Bristol, Pennsylvania

First Edition

ISBN 1-889758-36-1

Library of Congress Cataloging-in-Publication Data

Snyder, Emily C. A., 1977-
  Niamh and the hermit : a fairy tale / by Emily C.A.
Snyder.-- 1st ed.
      p. cm.
  ISBN 1-889758-36-1 (pbk.)
  I. Title.
  PS3619.N93N53 2003
  813'.6--dc21

                                                    2003006526

For my family, who supported me,
for my friends, who inspired me,
and most of all for Peter,
without whom the Twelve Kingdoms would not exist.
Deo gratias!

CHAPTER 1

The daughter of a Fairy and a King, the Princess Niamh was glorious fair, so that just as once her father could not see for his christening curse, so others could not look upon Niamh for her beauty.

And when the ten remaining Fairies came for the newborn Princess's christening, even *they* were blinded and shielded their eyes.

Niamh grew in size, age and wisdom, the constant delight to her parents, and to those who learnt to turn their eyes just *so* and at least converse with her. As she grew, so did her beauty, until even to sit near the Princess seemed like passing through a fire. Her parents alone could touch her when she came to age sixteen, for King Gavron himself was saintly, and Queen Rhianna doubly so.

But as the days wore on, the counsellors grew fearful, for although they dearly loved their Sovereign and his Lady, and as much as they cherished Niamh—who could be brought to marry her? There were no nobles' sons good enough to withstand her radiance, nor were there any other princes—for this was before the kingdoms split, and Gavron had no male heir. Even among the honest burghers, the mayors' sons or the chandlers', none were found to even withstand an hour in Niamh's company. And it was not long before all the land trembled in fear.

"What a quandary is this!" one Duke, Llewellyn by name and most senior of all the nobles, said to his fellows. "We thought it bad when King Gavron could not see, but he set forth and was cured in ways miraculous to tell. But the Princess needs no remedy. This time it is *we* who lack.

"And who shall rule after her?" he pressed, when the room grew silent with sullen rebuke. "For if none of us and none of our get are worthy of her beauty, then we are neither worthy of the crown."

"It is easy for you to speak," a Count called forth, "for you are old and married and have often said that you prefer your country home to any palace. But there are those of us with sons a-bed, raving sick for a year and more now from having touched her hand; and those who have killed themselves for want of her. For there is no denying that she is a terror, no matter if you bespeak her through a veil betwixt—she burns, and we have suffered for it."

1

"You would have her defiled because your son left her side in holy raptures and renounced his right for a heavenly crown?" the Duke exclaimed.

"I would send her to a convent, where she will harm no man further."

"And set yourself as King, no doubt?"

"I should not hide within my country home, smug, surrounded by my married sons!"

"There is one," a lowly squire, Ewan, cried when it looked as though the Duke and Count might come to blows, "who might marry her."

His Knight, Lord Mackelwy, who had raised his hand to box the squire's ears, stopped and permitted the youth to speak on.

"I am from the far countries," said the youth, "north and west of this land. And there lives a man, a Hermit, who is well respected by all his neighbours, far flung though they be. I myself have made pilgrimage to where he lives, and through his instruction came I to my lord's service. I have never seen this man, but it is said that he has the head and tail of a lion, and the arms and wings of an eagle, those double marks of valour and of savagery, and is terrible to look upon. I know not how he came to that unhappy state—whether through birth, curse or sin—but it is this which has sent him to the life of a Hermit. Although I have never laid eyes on him, I know he has a soul equal to the King's own, and it has been rumoured that he has performed miracles, and thus may be a fitting bridegroom for the Princess."

Upon hearing this, the counsellors all agreed that they could do no better nor worse than to beseech the King to parlay with the Hermit. To King Gavron they went, where Ewan again recited his tale. So simple was his telling that it moved the hearts of many with hope for Niamh—and more, with curiosity to see such a wonder as this Hermit.

"Hath he a name?" King Gavron asked, when the squire paused for breath.

"If he has a name," Ewan answered, "I do not know it. But we all call him Duncan, for his hiding in shadows."

"And can any substantiate thy claim that such a man existeth?"

"You have only to ask any man who has travelled to the north and west, Majesty, below the Ice Giants, beside Loch Corraigh."

With that the King dismissed his court, and leading his lady to their chambers, he asked her if she had ever heard of such a man.

"I have not," Rhianna said, shaking her sunglory hair. "Although those of my kin may. I shall ask Maelgwenn, who guardeth those lands—although I must admit myself disposed to believe the squire's tale without my cousin's word. For I have lived now five full centuries, and attended christenings of every sort, and have seen much stranger things than this!"

"Aye," Gavron said. "How well we know, beloved, the wonders and terrors of the Dark Wood, from thy sad banishment there and from my many sallies upon its border. A battle with a manticore wouldst convince many a stonier heart than mine what wonders are in this world.

"But what concerns me, beloved, is from whence these abnormalities spring. If from a source outside himself, then I can well forgive him. Shouldst he prove himself a good man and true, gladly shall I give him crown and daughter. If, however, he brought his misfortune upon himself...."

"These things," his wife urged, "may not be divined by speculation. Let us amongst ourselves agree to send for this Duncan, and see what manner of man he truly is. We can do no more this even."

The King acquiesced to his wise wife's words, and soon messages were sent to the Hermit, and also to Maelgwenn: the first a summons, the second an inquiry. From both returned missives. From the Hermit came a request to know for what cause he was summoned, for he had not left his solitude for fifteen years. The letter, written in an elegant hand and intelligent, although not overly proud, greatly impressed the King and Queen—an impression only deepened by Maelgwenn's own correspondence.

> "*My dearest cousin,*" wrote he, "*how glad am I to receive word from thee, since last we spoke was too long ago. I lament, even now, the misfortunes thou suffered at our fallen cousin's hand—although how well I wont thy present happiness. It is a selfish lament, I concede. When once thou wert full one of us, I mean, with thy wings, how much more quickly such matters as these might be resolved! For thou mightest have flown to me, then, and so inquired over nectar and ambrosia, but thou hast chosen a mortal path, and so I fumble with mortal pen and mortal parchment, and spill the ink like footprints.*
>
> "*In the question put to me, I reply in fashion suitable to a Fae. Yea, I know the man after whom thou seekest. But on his past, I shall not speak. It is as dark as it is mysterious, and shalt come to light in given time, God willing. (Sure! And I must be out of practice to mangle my prophecies so!) As to his character, for that I will doubly vouch and more. But hear me now: as thou lovest thy daughter, do not delay in sending for the Hermit. Nor delay their marriage by courtship, or even by an hour, lest they never marry, and thy proud line dieth with thee.*
>
> "*Alas that I cannot think to end this note on hilarity, as I am*

3

wont to do. Thy concern, Rhianna, is the concern of us all. But be thou assured, that shouldst thou or any who calleth on thy name approach me for aid, I shall readily give it, though it cost me all I am."

So the heart of Rhianna and the heart of Gavron were appeased and worried all at once, for if Maelgwenn, the trickster of all the Fairies, thought the matter weighty, how much more dire must the matter be! So promptly they sent once more for the Hermit, with full and lengthy entreaties, calling upon every manner of persuasion and appeals to duty at their command. Long, then, must they wait for answer—for even by swiftest messenger and fastest horse, their hope could not arrive until the first heavy Harvest Moon at the earliest, and this was just recent Lent.

Of Niamh's would-be suitor, Gavron and Rhianna agreed to acquaint their daughter with all that *could* be told, for the half-year of waiting must suffice for a courtship. The Queen found her daughter coming from the chapel, fully veiled beneath a white mantilla and clasping her cherished gold-leafed prayer book. Behind her trailed two of her Handmaids, Gwendolyn and Magdwa, golden haired both, whispering between each other like two senseless butterflies wafting in the breeze. When they caught sight of the Queen, they gasped, swept low curtsies, and drew away respectfully. Thank God they did, for Niamh smiled joyfully beneath her veil, and her glorious eyes lit with an inner dancing flame, causing all around her to turn their heads and cross themselves. How dearly Niamh longed to embrace her mother, but how well she knew that to reveal her face would blind the only retainers willing to follow her. So the Princess allowed herself to be drawn away to her rooms.

There the Queen revealed all that had closeted her and the King within their council chambers. But Rhianna's heart sunk when first she told Niamh of the Hermit's demeanour, for the Princess, always the best of daughters before, grew agitated and paced about the room, wringing her hands.

"What can this mean," she cried at last. "That I am so strange that none can bear me but a monster? I am not so good as to be ignorant of my effect upon the others who have courted me. And, although I weep for joy that some leave my side to take up Holy Order, still, it is hard when I hear other tales of those who have slain themselves or gone mad when they but approach the castle!"

"So it *is* hard," her mother said. "But thou must not take the blame upon thyself, or that which Heaven endowed. Those who come here have had their mettle tested, and some have been found wanting. Weep then for them, and for their souls, but not for thine own beauty."

With this must Niamh content herself, and no more word was spoken against the arrangement. Young Ewan was oft called in to recount what he could of the Hermit, although perforce always through a chink in the wall, and even that proximity to the Princess burnt like a hand held in the fire.

Yet, as the squire was heard to say as the weeks wore on, "Twas, at first, so strong as to make a man faint, like the full force of the sun at noon. But after a time the pain lessened, until a man felt almost cold upon leaving."

Other travellers, too, were prevailed upon to give any witness of the Hermit's character, and these were carefully written down and given to the Princess for her perusal. But though the testimonies spoke always to the Hermit's favour, Niamh could not quite bring herself to believe all the wondrous tales attributed to such a strange creature.

It was said by some that he had raised three sons from the dead when they had been brought back on shields to their widowed mother. Another account claimed that he could converse and rule the animals, being one himself. Or still another that he had foretold a husband's return, whom the wife had thought lost. The husband, for his part, said that a stag had led him home—surely sent by the Hermit. Nor was the Hermit without justice, for a band of marauders, coming upon a maid, had suddenly turned to swine at his approach, and at another time a notorious gossip had gone mute for a year when once she spoke ill of him.

Mercy he possessed likewise. One humble Baker recounted how, when a youth, he had stolen bread from the Hermit's small fire and had been surprised by the master of the house. Rather than death, he found himself a guest of honour, feasted until his gaunt belly was full and then sent on his way to apprentice at a bakery, "Where thou mayest steal from thyself, and likewise serve thine own punishment!"

From this Baker, indeed, came the only clear account of the Hermit's countenance although even this was wrought with trembling pen and much hesitation. "He had a kindly face," the Baker's story ran, "though 'tis no denying the tawny mane, nor yet the wicked teeth. But his eyes are kindly and a fairer blue than you've ever seen. They are not the eyes of a cat—although that is little comfort when he yawns. His arm, indeed, was leathery and taloned, like an eagle's, though deft enough to serve a guest. Only one arm saw I, so only one arm can I vouch for. As for wings, I saw none, but he wore a cloak, and may have concealed them and his tail within it. His voice was low and deliberate, and his speech refined like a gentleman's. I dared not ask him how he came to that unhappy state, nor did he volunteer to tell me, but I saw about his thick-furred neck a golden chain, much like hounds wear in mimicry of their master's chain of state. I wondered at it, for it clearly chaffed him, and nothing else he wore or owned was half so fine."

Tales of the Hermit's past abounded, each conflicting so violently as to make Niamh throw up her hands and disregard them altogether.

Come spring the sudden well of accounts ran dry, and Niamh was left to review old bits of speculation and testimony, or else to conjure up dreams of might-bes for solace. "Perhaps," she thought, while gazing out the window at the wheeling stars, "he is *not*, after all, grotesque as rumour hath him. But—so may it be!—he is indeed a magician, and thus adopteth a vile glamour to preserve his solitude. Why, perhaps it is his collar that maketh him appear so. And *if* so, then perhaps he wilt not wear it when he cometh."

This excuse, Niamh's favourite of all she had conjectured thus far, served for but a little time; for nearing the vernal equinox, when all the court arrayed itself in gaiety, news came that the Hermit had been seen on the road.

"Fearful big, he was," one farmer's wife reported. (She had herself received the news from her neighbour's cousin who in turn had it from a reliable pubmaster he had met in his travels.) "Silent as an hunter," a gamesman claimed (who had the story from his brother's youngest son, and that son's friend, who had been caught laying snares for rabbits). All confirmed the bizarre appendages, most particularly his fearsome head. "I have seen a griffin once," a woodchopper told, "and had he not walked upright, I should have thought him a sort of griffin. And who knows? He may yet be—slowly resolving himself into a man, and not the other way around."

Midsummer's Eve came and passed with much merry-making, gay banners and buntings, tourneys and revels of every sort to beguile the court. Within the fifteen courtyards that surrounded the castle, before each of the ten towers, masques of history and myth played. Once more, Titans roamed the earth, the Sun and Moon danced incarnate, dragons soared and fell, the lands were plunged into Perpetual Twilight, wolves and jackals roamed the hills unchecked, and the Lion who was the line of St. Siawn roared.

But one man held himself aloof from the revels—the Count, who had spoken so violently before against the Princess. Anger, envy and pride were his threefold bedfellows, for his ambitions had been thwarted when his son had taken up the cloth and again when the Hermit had been summoned.

What cause for celebration when his son lived, yet lived dead to his rightful inheritance? What cause for celebration when the woman who had beggared the Count's ancient line lived and soon would wed? What cause for celebration when all the world lay bereft of hope?

And yet the Count, ever the courtier, smiled, nodded, laughed when occasion demanded—even sought out the Princess's dance before the Vigil Mass and applauded heartily, politically. In chapel, he received the host. After, he joined his peers for mulled wine and reminiscing. Always, always smiling. When toasts were raised to the monster coming, he smiled. Salutations to the King, he smiled. Happiness to the Princess, he smiled.

Yet when, walking alone in the matin hour he came upon a young lordling from Viviane bleeding in the grass from the light wounds of a foolish duel, he did nothing. Another dead for the Princess, no doubt. He cared not.

For every word spoke of the coming felicity only knit the Count's three shadowy bedfellows more closely, until the Count became a twisted man, consumed by all his vices.

'Twas now a mere four weeks before Harvest Moon and letters from the Hermit himself came to the palace, by messengers most strange and wondrous: twin eagles with white caps and wings and breasts a deep sky blue; the letters tied to their ankles with bits of string. They entered the castle to great shouts and exclamations of joy, as they circled over the busy courtyards, skimming the roofs of the blacksmith and the equerry, until at last alighting upon the chapel's roof. Nor could any coax them down but the King, who bore one on each wrist into the Lyon Rampant.

The letter upon the male was addressed to the King and Queen, assuring them that the Hermit was en route, and eager to meet his Sovereigns and serve the kingdom in whatever way their wisdom chose. The other letter, borne by the female, was addressed to the Princess, and it was with great reluctance that the King delivered the missive unopened to his daughter, for he longed to know what words this man might use in intimacy.

Niamh received the letter much surprised, and at once opened it within her rooms, her heart a nervous flutter with unknowing anxiety.

> "*Lady,*" the letter ran, "*greetings and salutations from one untitled and unnamed to the greatest Beauty the Heavens have formed but one. I fear me that I am, for once, at a loss for words, or how to proceed. How should a creature as I am become make love to a lady? I have no experience that might guide me in this matter nor, apparently, have I eloquence. So I shall write as my poor heart dictates, and pray your heart, if not your eyes, comprehend me.*
>
> "*First know with what surprise I received my sovereigns' summons. So much so that at first I could not credit it. No doubt you*

have been told by this time how I appear. Would that it were otherwise! How well I know what a specimen I am, and for that I hid myself and for that, if I understand aright, I am in part summoned.

"Well I know your beauty, although I did not scry for it as I might. The tales of those who have been honoured to be near you I have heard, even in so remote a dwelling, and must perforce believe. But Princess, I fear it. When so many suitors before me have been found wanting, it seems likely that you shall find no fit match in me. More though, were your beauty all that you owned, I should not come. I have known intimately beauty disassociated from the soul. There is nothing more vile. Your beauty, however, I am sure springs from every faculty of your being— not just your face, nor your mind, but from your spirit too. No wonder, then, that strong men have fainted as you passed them! Who can withstand an angel incarnate?

"In this much, then, we are evened. You revile my appearance, and I cower in your shadow! A poor beginning, to be sure, and yet I have known worse. For it has been told to me that we are to marry—that it has been ordained and may not be gainsaid. But I beg you, Princess, should you find me unworthy, or find yourself trembling in terror or disgust, fear not to tell me. I would in no way desire your unhappiness. Speak but the word to me and I shall be gone, never to trouble you more, no matter how many summons plague me after.

"To close as clumsily as I began, I offer myself as your devoted servant, humbled and grateful and eager to end my pilgrimage at your feet."

Upon reading this, the heart of Niamh softened, and on reading again, it fell in love, and on reading a third time, it urged her to respond equally and with haste.

"Sir," she wrote with shaking hand, *"if you are not eloquent, then I am imbecile. How well you defined my heart and my fears, and how shamed am I to admit that, for all my fears, I never once considered your own. Pray, pardon my iniquity, the first of many you shall encounter. You are also correct in divining the many things I have heard of you—enough to confuse me mightily, for so much has been laid to your doing and yet so little can be recounted first-hand. You sound quite the legend! I am afraid it is as much this seeming myth about you, as well as your*

8

reported aspect, which has caused me anxiety. I have oft tried to picture you in my mind, the better to acquaint myself with an heretofore invisible suitor, but always I imagined you fearsome, silent and serious—never guessing who you truly are: thoughtful, generous and kind. (For I trust your letter does not lie.)

"Be sure, as you journey these last long miles, that I pray for thee and await thee anxiously, that we may come to know one another better. I shall say no more lest I say too much. Believe that thou shalt find a kindred heart in me."

The Princess sent the letter post-haste by the eagle, much to the surprise of the King and Queen, who had been waiting anxiously without her door all afternoon. Beyond that their daughter *had* sent a letter, and did not appear flushed or indignant upon sending it, the King and Queen could learn no more of what had passed between Niamh and the Hermit. They could only hope that what they witnessed were the symptoms of love.

Not five days passed before the eagle flew again, this time whilst Niamh and her handmaidens sat in the solar, embroidering the sleeves of the guards' tourney garments. For although only the Knights were allowed to compete for points of honour and their lady's favour, yet the guard must be present to prevent any real disputes from becoming bloody. And what better protection than the touch of the Princess herself? So the Handmaids broidered the cuffs with dainty chains of ivy, borders of saffron knots, and—as they had been gently teasing the dark eyed Findola since breakfast—golden bands of matrimony.

"They are but rings like mail," Findola protested, her dusky cheeks blushing red. "Like the protection the Princess patterns on all the cambric."

The other girls—Magdwa, slender and still more child than lady; Gwendolyn, older than all and promised to proud Gwrhyr who had no sooner won his spurs at Easter than sued for Gwendolyn's hand; and Elowen, laughing and always merry—bent their heads over their needlework and cast knowing glances at each other. The Princess too smiled and bent her head over her own handiwork, murmuring, "I do but stitch crosses, not rings, Findola."

And, when her Handmaids could not help but giggle as Findola, flustered, pricked herself on both sides of a stitch, 'twas the Princess who quietly said, "I'm minded of when Gwrhyr first beheld a lass, and she, that very even, before terce could be rung, began to fill a chest with finest linen, broidered—or so methinks—with roses and with daffodils?"

Now it was Gwendolyn's turn to colour, and turn the fold of the dainty handkerchief upon her lap away from the mirthful sight of the others.

"Very well," Elowen cried, threading a knot. "But you, Princess, shall have no such chest if you insist on stitching crosses to *these* shirts!"

Niamh laughed merrily, for well she loved Elowen who feared nothing. "How should I prepare for so strange a bridegroom? How shouldst *thou* instruct me, when thou hast a chest full of good men's hearts—and they, none of thine?"

Elowen sighed at that, and leaned back into her chair. "I would gladly give them back, but that their owners all refuse them. Poor hearts! But what of your Highness? Does your heart still beat within your breast? Or is it tied to an eagle's leg?"

"I hardly know," Niamh replied, dropping her work into her lap, and glancing out the window, where the gardens gave way to the broad Gwyrglánn, along whose paths the Hermit must surely come.

And as she watched through her spangled veil, the eagle she had sent back only the day before alighted just beside the Princess, stretching forth its leg as though bowing. Magdwa, ever timid, gasped and drew back. Even Elowen blenched for the suddenness of the arrival. But Niamh reached down and removed the letter from the eagle's leg and Findola searched in her shawl and found three biscuit crumbs and offered them to the eagle—for she was from Cadwyr and knew much of the wilds.

"What does it read?" Findola asked, stroking the proud bird's head.

But no one said more—even Gwendolyn, whose lips were pressed close with silent disapproval at Findola's whispered question. For the Handmaids all wondered at the change that had overcome not only the Princess, but also the whole court, thanks to the rumour of the Hermit. And some, like Gwendolyn, wondered at a man of such reputation, wooing through birds; while others, Magdwa first among them, thought it romantic, like a story of legend, like the wooing of Elena—although far less disastrous. Still others, intimates of Niamh, gay Elowen among them, concerned themselves solely over the practical happiness of such an unlikely match. Only a few, such as Findola, took the squire Ewan's word for truth. But then, only she broidered rings on his cuffs.

No answer did Niamh give but to ask her Handmaids to remove themselves for a space, and Findola to care for the eagle in the falconry until such a time as she called for it. And when once her handmaidens had withdrawn with many backward glances, the Princess opened the letter again, and threw back her veil with a great, shuddering sigh. For thus the letter ran:

> "*Madame,*
> "*Little can letters suffice for discourse. Tonight, if it please you, send for the eagle, and through it I shall speak and listen. Should it please you not* [and here the script faltered and trembled], *then do but send the eagle to me, and I shall know I have been too forward.*"

Niamh let out a sad laugh upon this second reading, and rested her warm cheek against the cool stone lattice. "Ah, Elowen! I fear I have indeed sent my heart by wing. And more, I dread, to me this eagle beareth another too large for my small breast."

That evening, as the stars ignited, Findola brought the eagle, who hopped courtly onto a high-backed chair before the fire. Elowen accompanied the Cadwyr lass, and because Elowen was distant kin and the daughter of Donell, the Captain of the Guard, she pressed the Princess's shoulder through the light cloth, braving the burn upon her fair skin. Then they withdrew.

Niamh remained where she stood, upon the white-furred rug, twisting a strand of flaxen hair within her dainty fingers. The eagle clacked its beak and shifted on the carvings of twining leaves and fruits. With the movement, Niamh remembered her station. She dropped her hands, drew herself erect, and crossed to stand before the fire so that she seemed to glow herself. Her veil she let hang upon her arms. Lowly, she said, "Speak."

But no change came over the eagle. Nor did any word it utter. Niamh clutched her veil in both her hands, fearing that perhaps she had spoken wrongly, or at the wrong time—a moment too soon or late—or that, perhaps, the Hermit had heard her and disdained to answer, liking not her voice. Some whole minute crept on, with no sound save the crackling fire—ever dwindling, eating its own nourishment. The eagle blinked its massive eyes. The fire snapped. Below, the high clear voices of the pageboys hailing each other as they scurried to the kennels and the stables sounded, mixed with bursts of lovers' laughter in the labyrinthine gardens of a far earlier age. But still the eagle did not speak.

"I have failed," Niamh whispered into the chilly night. She smiled and pulled her veil about her like a shawl. "Poor bird," said she, sitting on the rug before the hearth with her knees drawn to her breast. "I have roused thee from thy well-deservèd slumber for naught. I know not whether thy master shalt thank me for my ill-treatment of his messenger. But I suppose," with a sigh, "I shall never know. For surely he shalt never come now, and my father's proud line—all scions of Siawn Shieldbearer, first set upon throne by my mother and her kin at wise Aldhairen's sad bidding—all, all shall die in me.

"Look not so sternly at me, bird! I do not ask thee for thy pity. What canst thou care for the dealings of mortal men? Should we all perish, thou shouldst only prosper. Far-sighted thou art, and perhaps thou canst see already the day when we—and all our petty worries—shall pass on. But I have not thy sight, nor do I desire it. For man was not made to know all things, good and evil.

"Come," said she, rising to take the bird upon her wrist. "I shall carry thee myself to thy rest and trouble thee no longer."

But the proud eagle refused to step onto her arm and although Niamh wooed it with gentle words and crumbs, still it would not move. "Alas for thee, poor creature!" she cried, with a laugh. "Well then perch, if thou wilt, where thou likest! In the morn mayhap, thou mayest come to thy senses!"

Smiling and shaking her head in wonder, Niamh left the eagle and made for her bed, undressing herself unaided. She had but let slip her veil and removed slipper and stocking, when a voice called out, "Princess!"

Niamh

Niamh started and looked about her for the source of the sound. But no man found she who might have spoken thus, and the eagle's blue back was turned towards her.

"Who speaks?" she asked into the darkness.

"One who has been too long silent," came the reply.

Niamh let the folds of her velvet gown fall the little way to cover her toes. She felt, without seeing, that she knew to whom the voice belonged.

The eagle did not move, but she heard, "I am he."

Niamh's breath caught. She thought she might faint. She thought she might fly. But all she could think to say was: "Hast thou seen me?"

"I have, lady," came the reply. "Although I did not mean to look."

"And thou hast taken no harm?"

"I have taken the gravest harm, lady—a wound to the heart. But I am not like to flee or run mad, if that is your fear."

"It is my deepest fear and sorrow. It is that which I feared delayed this meeting."

"And so it did. No—I pray, do not come closer!" when the Princess moved towards the eagle. "It is not meet that I should see you before we are betrothed. It is, at present, unjust. For I may see thee, but I am veiled to thy sight."

"Yet we may converse?"

"It is my fondest hope."

"Then thou shalt not be twice disappointed. Here I am. What wouldst thou?"

A laugh, relieved and merry, resounded through the room. Had the Princess looked then into the eagle's eyes, she might have seen a weary figure

12

seat himself gratefully upon a stone and cover his strange face with stranger shaking hands.

"Now the moment is upon me," he said, "I do not know what to say. 'Struth, lady, I did not think thou wouldst allow such a strange assignation."

"I would not know if this were strange. No man has ever dared to tryst with me by day, much less by night."

"Much less by eagle."

"No," with a laugh. "Well, good my brazen lord, may I know the name of he who is to wed me?"

The eagle shifted upon its perch, as though uneasy. At last, the warm voice said, "Wouldst thou had asked any other question, lady, I should have readily answered. But thou wouldst know my true name, which few now remember. There is power in names, as well I know—and who knoweth what other ears may be listening?"

Feathers ruffled and beaked clacked as the eagle shifted again. Niamh, still with veil about her shoulders, pursed her lips and thought that perhaps she had, indeed, asked too much. But then she thought, *How could I go to the arms of one whose very name is a mystery?* And so she kept her peace and let the Hermit wrestle with his own doubts.

Until, very softly, the Princess seemed to hear his voice again, whisper, "Gethin. Gethin."

"Gethin," she whispered in return. And perhaps she dreamed it, but the very air seemed to lighten with the sound. "And I," said she, "am Niamh, simple Niamh, henceforth Niamh, Gethin's love.

"But, since I have been so bold in my questioning thus far," and truly, she felt it was quite a mad night something out of a tale—and that someone else spoke for her, someone who feared no one and nothing, "I shall ask another thing, and mayhap it will be answered me. Thou hast said that the reports of thee do not lie, but no one canst tell me how thou camest to withdraw from the world of men?"

If the voice had been warm before, with trembling and hoping and longing all in one, it was only bitter now, as a lion when he snarls. "Let us speak plainly, lady. Thou wouldst know what sins are upon me."

"I did not say so."

"Thou questionest to the quick." And that was their first argument.

"Then I shall tell thee something of myself," Niamh said, drawing herself erect and regal again. "What wouldst thou know? The same that I have asked of thee? I shall tell thee: it is nothing great. My beauty is not of my own doing. There are those who will say that one of my godparents—now Viviane, now Maelgwenn—gave me my face at my christening, but I know all the gifts I was given and beauty cannot be counted among them.

"And now that long years have passed, and only few can bear me, I hear whispers—although my Handmaids do all within their power to keep these rumours from me—that I am no beauty at all. That I am hidden within the palace with some deformity; that I am a monster, a basilisk, a dragon—terrible and lovely to look upon. I have even heard that there is a minstrel who hath made so bold as to write a song about me, in which I am Cináedd of the fires, reborn to revenge her murder, luring men into her bed, thinking each her traitorous lover.

"Another mayeth find heart within herself to laugh at these petty stings and arrows, but well I know my lineage, and we have each of us earned the crown, or lost it, within a breath of fate. Some nights I have wondered—before Ewan made bold to speak to my Father—whether the songs and the whispers were not true. For I have not looked in a mirror for many years now—ever since the first man died for love of me—and all tell me that I am lovely, and who am I to know whether they flatter? Or if their eyes see me so because they love me, or are merely accustomed to me, or have forgotten my aspect hidden beneath my veil?

"It is all folly and vanity to linger longer on my face. Could I become plain, I should rejoice and never fear again to smile lest I blind a poor retainer. But thou hast seen me and mayest judge for thyself. And truly, canst thou think that I, of all in the land, could judge *thee*?" She sighed and sank upon the rug, laying her golden head upon the bear's.

The world was very silent—even the most ardent lovers had left the gardens, and the stableboys had at last drifted into sleep. The uncertain flames cast a golden light over her ivory features, and the Hermit, daring to turn the eagle's head and glance only briefly at his bride, felt all anger drain from him and stronger more certain love fill his breast. He desired to hunt down the root of the vile rumours and silence them. He longed to gather the Princess within his arms and protect her from the whispers of the world. He wished she would ask him some impossible task so that he might do it. He wished she desired his life; he would give it. He wished she would ask him again the most painful question; he would answer it until every truth lay strewn like rubies at her feet.

But she did not ask him again, and so he called her name, until she turned her lovely eyes upon the eagle. With a gasp, she saw that he regarded her, and made to draw the veil over her face, but he stayed her, saying, "No, do not fear. But if thou hast the courage, take the eagle upon thy arm—she shalt not harm thee—and look within her eyes. Thou shalt see me, although darkly. It is but a little that my magics may do."

"I have the courage," said she, although she breathed very deeply. Rising, the Princess approached the chair and put out her bare arm beside the eagle. Carefully, it stepped forward. And so large the eagle was, Niamh did not need to raise her arm to look within its eye, although she might have, for the eagle seemed to weigh no more than the least of its feathers. Very dimly, like things seen just before dawn, Niamh could see a cowled figure sitting within the forest upon a stone. The figure stood and removed his cowl, and looked, so it seemed, directly at her. Perhaps it was a trick of the light or the result of deep magics or of deeper mysteries, but although Niamh could discern the fabled lion's head, grim and fierce, she saw more clearly another face within that one, of a young man, handsome—although not unnaturally so—likewise grim, but also wonderful.

Then Niamh smiled, fully and with her heart held in her eyes, and all about her glowed more brightly for it. And within the eagle's eyes, she saw her betrothed press his claw and not-claw to his breast and bow, and through the eagle's beak she heard him whisper, "I am Gethin, Niamh's love."

chapter 11

The next morning broke to wails and lamentations for Gwendolyn, going to wake her mistress, had fallen as though dead, several steps from the Princess's door—so great had Niamh's beauty become, merely conversing with her beloved. The guards rushed to the handmaiden's aid when they heard her fall. But they had not come even to the corridor, running up the steps two at a time, when the first among them also fell—although not into sleep—toppling backwards onto their brothers. By this time, the Knights had been roused by their squires, and pages had been sent to wake the King and Queen, and the other handmaidens had come—but all no further than the bottom of the stairs.

"What new devilry is this!" one guard demanded of Elowen, who had shoved and pushed her way to the front of the crowd, until she could just make out Gwendolyn's slipper.

"No devilry," she replied. "But we had best none of us go up there, saving only, perhaps, their sovereigns or the priest."

She had no chance to explain herself, however, for almost immediately new shouts were heard from below, and the sounds of scuffling and blows. Cries of "What is happening!" and "Stand aside!" clanged together like two winds in the belfry, discordant and battlesome of their own. "It is Gwrhyr!" someone shouted upwards, his voice echoing like a drowning man's last plea. "It is Gwrhyr!" The call resounded from lip to lip, eddying upward even to Elowen's ears. "Let him through!" and "Keep him back!" followed after like bubbles.

At last one voice rose over all the clamour below, with a dreadful bellow. "Stand aside! Stand *aside* for the love of Christ!" But even this followed, as some from the southern countries claim the Hydoemi echo all the whispers of the sea, "Before God, Gwrhyr, if you move more, I shall cut you down!"

A new rumour arose almost at once, "Donell! Donell is come! The King cannot be far behind. It is the Captain!"

"Father," Elowen whispered, before elbowing her way to the banister and shouting down, "Father! Let him through! If on his word of honour he wilt be guided by his betrothed's companion."

Far below, Elowen saw a familiar helmed figure raise his hand to his brow to block out the rising morning light from the high stained glass window. "So be it," he answered. "Do you so swear, Gwrhyr?"

Another figure, brawny and sweated already, with hand on the pommel of his sword, nodded.

"Then let him through. And woe betide you, Gwrhyr, should you be the cause of any further grief."

The young Knight strode upwards, and the people parted before him, many drawing away as though afraid of his touch. He paid no heed to them, but kept his eyes ahead, always ahead, until his gaze rested on Elowen. "Lady," said he. "Let me pass."

"Thou hast promised to be ruled by me, Gwrhyr," Elowen said. And in that beam of light, with her dark locks unbound and her white gown still on, she looked very majestic and terrible. Many a youth's heart she collected, merely standing there. "In such a rage and with the passions in thy breast,

Gwrhyr

thou shalt get no further than the topmost step before thou fallest."

The young Knight's face flushed with rage and all remembered why some called him the Bull upon the field. "But who shalt care for my love?" he demanded, blowing hard through his nose. "Thy mistress hath wrought this! Stand aside and let her answer me!"

"Thou standest upon a knife's point, Gwrhyr!" Elowen cried. "Speak no ill of the Princess, lest thou fallest where thou art!"

But Gwrhyr would not listen, and bowled up the stairs, and even reached Gwendolyn before he too fell, and lay like slain Night with his arms wrapped around his dead love. No sound made he, except for the shiver of his sword as it slid upon the stone. Nor did the assembled dare to speak, but ever and anon echoed that dread silence.

Elowen herself stumbled against the banister and onto the step, her hands covering her mouth to keep back the rising bile. Already, she could seem to hear the whispers that would arise: *The groom came to his bride in the night, and turned her into a beast like himself. He came to her in the night and slew her, and liking the taste, now gorges on victims the King feeds him. He came to her in the night, her own handmaidens brought him to her, and then they slew her for jealousy, and slew their fellow handmaiden—loveliest of all the Princess's house—when she discovered them, and that is beauty's poison.*

Would they call her mistress Cináedd now, openly? Or would they remember other myths, dredge up memories of Day's lust for his niece within these very halls? Would they say that Titan's shame lay upon them all, still? Would they call her Malinka's child, and so slander the King, claiming that fallen Fairy for Niamh's mother? Would they call her sorceress, succubus, dragon, abomination? For Gwrhyr's words still rang through all their minds: *Thy mistress hath wrought this! Thy mistress hath wrought this!*

But Elowen could only whisper, "I have done this," and curse that ever an eagle came to them.

As for the Princess, she slept soundly enough, whether because of some magics—or more likely, because of a night long spent in conversation and a bed sought only with the horizon's lightening. If she heard the cries and shouts without her door at all, she thought them only the calling of eagle to eagle, or the senseless howling of wolves after the moon. As for herself, she dreamt she walked within the forest glade, always looking—although, not fearfully—for Gethin, and always sensing that truly he was close at hand, no more than a breath away, calling her.

She could have stayed happily in that dream and never woken until he bade her, but that she heard her mother's voice within her ear and felt her mother's hands upon her arms, gently shaking her.

"Niamh! Niamh! Rise, gather thy things, and come with me. Evil, ever jealous, is afoot, and bringeth sorrow in his wake."

The Princess immediately awoke and heard the clangourous cries outside, and heard her own name used in curses, and wondered at it. "What hath happened?" she cried, turning to the Queen.

To her surprise, her mother flinched and raised her arm, as though to ward away a blow—so lovely had Niamh become. Quickly though, the Queen regained herself, smiled, and kissed Niamh upon both cheeks, saying, "We shall speak of it anon. Come, I shall play thy Handmaid and help thee dress."

Long minutes passed, but the shouting outside the door only grew. And now Niamh could hear her father's voice, answered by terrified wails and yips and barks, as though his hounds and not his court crowded on the stair. Like cries in a storm, tattered and confused, the voices came to the Princess's ear:

> *The King! The King!*
> *The King is come and all is well!*
> *Take her from me.*
> *She lives! See, she stirs!*
> *Ah, Gwendolyn! Fairest of all the maids!*
> *Elowen, run, find—*
> *Ah, God! Too late! Gwrhyr! Gwrhyr slain!*

Brave Gwrhyr! Gwrhyr of the Bull! Gwrhyr of the Golden Spurs!
Elowen! Elowen! To Father Cadifor—quickly!
These fools speak nonsense....
Gwrhyr slain! Gwrhyr, Gwendolyn's love!
Here, your Majesty, lean on me.
No, no. I shall walk among my people.
Gwrhyr dead! And Gwendolyn fallen!
Black deeds done in sunlight!
Evilness beget by beauty!
They shall rend thee, cousin!
Where is the Princess?
They are but fearful. They will not harm me.
Where is the one who has done this?
Let her answer us!
Let her answer Gwrhyr!
Let her speak of Gwendolyn!
Bring her forth!
Way, way for the King!
Show us the monster!

And all the while, Rhianna bedecked her daughter, plaiting her hair with sapphires and rosebuds, arming her daughter with the daintiest torques and bangles, as though they were breastplate and shield. Niamh had no need now to ask what had happened—the answer brawled at her very door.

"I shall see them," she said gravely, opening her eyes to stare at her mother's cool reflection in the glass. She dared not look at herself.

Rhianna only shook her head and continued weaving the strands of her daughter's hair. "They do not know what they ask for. Do not go seeking danger, Niamh."

"But I shall wear my veil."

"Thy veil no longer shieldeth thee."

Then Niamh did dare to look at herself for the first time in long years, and when she looked her heart grew light, for she did not see an awful glow about her, as she had that night so many years ago when the castle mourned the loss of one of their sons, but a pleasant face, well-formed, pleasing to many no doubt, but not the terrible beauty she remembered. Alas that she could see herself only within so thin a glass—for her beauty had not diminished but grown *deeper.* "My prayer is answered!" she exclaimed, clapping her hands to her cheeks to feel if they were real and pinching her fingers for the same. "I am less lovely! I shall not need a veil! I may greet Gethin as his bride, in truth!"

She turned to her mother joyfully and the radiance so filled the room that Rhianna cried out and buried her face in her arms. Niamh rushed to her moth-

19

er's side to help her to her feet, but the Queen pulled away saying, "Do not touch me, yet, Niamh!" The sound outside grew faint before Rhianna found, like when the eyes accustom themselves to light, like the low, dark passage to a glittering feasting hall, that she could see the Princess again. She wondered that she ever cowered before her own daughter.

Twin tears coursed down Niamh's face, like the twin rivers of the Suirebàir and the Rhún. And Rhianna seemed to see her daughter, as she had not for many years: lovely, but no more than lovely. Little did Rhianna know that she, herself, held the faint glory of Queenship about her. They embraced, sharing tears like diamonds upon each other's breasts.

The clamour outside had eased and ceased and only the sounds of the wind and bell and dirgeful psalm soughed throughout the castle. The air was new and damp, like the best spring mornings, rich with earth and growing things. Niamh's tears had all dried; her whole body felt gritty and hot as she lay in her mother's arms, listening to the lullaby of her heart.

"What shall I do?" she asked at last.

"We shall repair to the Lily Spire. But as befits our station, and not like beggars in flight."

So saying, the Queen paced to the door and opened it, gesturing to the Captain of the Guard and those few of his men he trusted. "Come," Rhianna said to Niamh. "We shall both walk unveiled and bravely through our home."

The guards walked ahead by a full two rooms, and so cleared the path for the Queen and the Princess. And not another human did Niamh see, saving only her mother and her father when they could be spared, for all that long imprisonment in the tower.

That night the court scurried hither and yon, glancing fearfully towards the small rectory where Gwrhyr and Gwendolyn lay under the ministrations of Father Cadifor, or with a biting hatred towards the Lily Spire, which shone more brightly than ever the Southern Lighthouse, where the Queen once dwelt. But Findola stole upwards to the Princess's own chambers, with a letter in her hand. The room was dark and cool, as an ancient mausoleum. The only movement was the fluttering of the light-gauze curtains, rustling with the twilight wind.

She whistled into the shadows, half-afraid that the eagle might have already flown away to its master, but a hoarse screech replied and Findola breathed easier. Deft fingers that the day before had embroidered rings, now tied the letter to the eagle's leg, and lips whispered, "Fly straight and true." The eagle clacked its beak once and nodded its proud head, then flew out the window, soon no more than a speck against the stars.

Below within the chapel choir, a strange council was being held a few doors away from the fallen lovers.

"We cannot *hope* upon such a strange chance," the Earl Marshall, Gwrhyr's aging uncle cried, addressing the few others assembled there including Elowen with Magdwa asleep on her breast. "How can you tell me a beast for a bridegroom—a beast for a *King*—will ease our burdens? My nephew is *dead!*"

"He does but *sleep*," Duke Llewellyn retorted, hardly pausing in his pacing to and fro.

"He is dead—and by that witch!"

"Witch!" Elowen exclaimed, shaking Magdwa from her slumber and setting her to crying again. The youngest handmaiden's tears were not alone— many of the other ladies had assembled there and were also weeping. Elowen could not spare time for tears and so shouted, "Dare you name the Princess a witch? If the King heard you now...."

"He would have pity on a man's grief!"

"Remorse, yes. Pity, no. No pity for a slanderer of the fairest maid...."

"Fairest? Thinkest *thou* she is the fairest? Paugh! She hath thee within her snare! Gwrhyr is...."

"*Sleeping*, cousin!" the Duke bellowed. "And thou art mad to speak against me!"

"I'll have thy blood to purge that slander! I see her poisons hath seeped deep in thee."

"This is no day to bleed," the Duke replied, but he loosed his weapon, too.

"What devilry is this within the house of God!"

The combatants whirled as one to see Donell within the doorway that led to the courtyard.

"Captain," the Marshall said, lowering his weapon. The Duke gave way likewise.

"Before God," the Captain said, in a voice very low and dreadful, "I never thought to see the day when *you*, my lord Marshall, should draw steel in a holy place. And you, your Grace! You are ever the most temperate of men! What grieved words has he dropped into your ear, to take away your senses and goad you on to greater grief? Gentlemen, sheathe your weapons. You will have no need of them anon. The King sends for you to his council chamber."

"I would not leave my nephew," the Marshall said, lowering his head in very imitation of his Gwrhyr in rage.

"You can do nothing for him here," Donell replied. "Elowen shall remain and if any change occurs, she shall send word." Then looking at his daughter, alone tearless amongst such a flood of woe, he raised his own fist to the sky, and cried, "By Heaven, I would give my sword to have one man with as much sense as she! For today, I have been shamed to see what lunacy can possess our sex when the passions are upon us. But I'll no more. My lords, if you will. The King is most anxious you attend him."

They departed then, leaving Elowen within that house of mourning. And she thought, even as the wails rose and fell and naked hands beat the floor and breasts for solace, that villainy made fools of all.

The case was brought before the court, with much braying and banging of fists upon chairs before any sense broke through.

"Good, my lords, you will *cease!*" Gavron roared, standing himself and throwing his sceptre down. "Full well we know the complaint you bring against our sovereignty. Full well do we also know what perjuries you have brought against our blameless daughter's name. We have heard you worry the issue, like a dog with his favourite bone, never reaching the marrow of your argument." Then, falling onto his throne with a mighty sigh, Gavron raised his hand and said, "Squire Ewan, arise and stand before us. Thou hast seen the stricken?"

Ewan's cheeks were very pale, but he did not tremble and his voice rang clear and sweet. "Yes, your Majesty."

"And thou hast spoken with Father Cadifor?"

"Yes."

"And he hath revealed his mind to thee?"

"He has, your Majesty. They breathe yet. He has hopes that the lady may recover within the hour."

"And young Sir Gwrhyr?"

Ewan's fingers clenched and his vision swam before him, remembering his friend's bloodless face. But bravely he answered, "He—he is not dead, your Majesty. But he does not live."

"He served Lord Mackelwy with thee, did he not?"

"He did, your Majesty. And was ever in the best of health. I—I have never seen—never seen him fall, my liege. It is as though, having warded away Malady all his life, it has grown more powerful, like an enemy who is quiet and now seizes him...." Ewan swayed and nearly fell. But one of his fellow squires ran forward and guided Ewan to his seat, where the youth collapsed into a faint.

While all watched the young men, one voice raised again, calling, "And still you will not name another to come after you, Majesty? You do not see the danger?"

"Well we know thy voice, oh Spite," Gavron said, turning his eyes upon the Marshall who had leapt to his feet. "Wouldst *thou* greet this Hermit when he cometh, and tell him his bride is fled? Hath been sent away by her own King and Father? 'Struth, I am glad to hear all ye speak openly to me at last. Did you think we were still blinded? Or have you forgot the star, which hangeth unmoving over our anointed head? Or do you contend against God Himself, and *His* governance? Well, then, go! And find His dwelling place, and bring your complaint against Him and what He hath wrought! But I'll no more of your single, selfish note tonight. I had hoped the squire's words might comfort ye. But now I see you do not long for any comfort, except the sound of your own braying! For the love of Christ! Make of me demands that I might bear, proudly, before the greater Judge. If one man amongst you haths sense, let *him* speak!"

Then the hearts of the King's men grew shamed and humbled, and even the Marshall sat once more and wept into his hands and felt sorrow for his liege. No man spoke. No man dared to cross the King in his ire. No man was *quite* fool enough for that.

But the Count, who had for many long months remained silent, and so holding his tongue for the better part of the year had gained the aura of wisdom, stood, and bowed, and begged leave to address the King and the assembled.

"Your people," said he, with eyes downcast and hand upon his breast, "are not monsters, Majesty, nor are they devils to despise. Yet, what else can the people believe but the rumours we all name vile. They have only the stories—and stories will be twisted until they become myth—for that is the only way the people understand things that are above them. But, Majesty, as much as it grieves us all, we must give them *some* answer to satisfy their myth-riddled minds."

"What answer?"

The Count demurred, murmuring humbly that he was only a courtier, not a king.

"Had thy king a better wit, we should all be a-bed, dreaming. Sure, thou hast a thought—we will hear it."

The Count smiled but kept his body slightly bowed. Long had he waited for this moment when all eyes should look to *him* for succour; long had he waited to be the counsellor of the King. Long had he practised and devised his speech, for he was a clever pantomime. But he saw not his heart. Alas, the Count did not know to what depths his deception lay; his acquaintance with his soul skimmed, merely. And while he spoke, his sonorous voice salved his own conscience and that night he believed that all his thoughts were pure.

"First, Majesty, although it grieves the hearts of many, I should advise you to stand firm upon the matter of your daughter, the Princess. Clearly, for her sake, she must remain alone within the Lily Spire—at least until this bridegroom is come, if not longer, should such a creature prove unfitting despite all. In this way, at least, we shall appease the people's fear that they too may be struck down by the Princess.

"I had mentioned the bridegroom, and will utter no word gainst him. But what we here speak, being better acquainted with the particulars of the case before us, is not what our people fear. In their minds, the Princess and the Beast who is brought to wed her are one. The first must be imprisoned because they dread the second. Ever we hear the whispers in the village below us: '*Would that the squire had not spoken! Better his tongue had fallen from his mouth that day, than ever this monster turned bloodlusty eye towards us!*' How shall we answer this, pray? How shall we appease the vile whisper: '*Would the squire had not spoken! Would he had been silent!*'

"And now, good my lords—regard him! See the youth: perjured, faint! How shall we tell him that he must flee the court to keep his life! How shall we acquaint him with his destiny? How shall we inform him that he must share in thy own daughter's imprisonment? Ah, but words fail me. I am overwrought. I must defer to the King. These are my dual thoughts. Do with them what thou wilt."

The King was silent for some time, his mouth hid behind his hand, the full burden of his body resting against the arm of his throne. He did not mark the presumption of the Count's address—his whole thought was bent towards three people alone: his daughter, the squire and the groom. At last he said, "Of our daughter, we have done what we might. She shalt not leave us. She shalt not be banished, cast off to some convent or even set up in state within her own household. Nor shalt she make progress unseasonably. As for the coming groom, we shalt not make judgement until we have met him, but rely upon the prophecy of our cousin, Maelgwenn, whom we honour greatly."

He grinned fondly into his short beard, and looked about the room with much love and sympathy. "It may very likely be," he said, "that all our fears are like children starting at the night wind. I do not doubt my godfather's word, nor do I doubt Niamh's heart—they are neither given lightly. But for the rumour our wise Count relateth...." Turning now his eyes upon the fallen squire before him, he asked, "Is it true? Can our subjects long for such a noble youth's...*banishment?*"

Lord Mackelwy, who had hid his ire at the Count's foul words, looked up saying, "Even if the mewling peasants so demanded, would it be just to acquiesce? Shall Ewan, upon whom I look as kindly as my own son, be sacrificed for a rumour?"

"It hath been known before," the King said with a sad smile, touching the crucifix upon his breast. "Lord Mackelwy, hast *thou* heard such a rumour?"

The lord shifted upon his chair and lowered his head, but could not deny that the whispers were true and the people did indeed resent the day Ewan spoke.

"And dost thou fear for thy squire's safety? Hast thou witnessed hostility towards him?"

"Never in my presence, Majesty."

"But thou hast an imposing presence, my lord. When first thou laid fealty at my feet, I trembled myself and wondered what manner of man begged admittance to the Knighthood of St. Siawn. I have had much cause to bless the day Hugh Mackelwy took up arms beside me, shieldbrother and slayer of the Cadwyr Manticore!"

Despite all, Lord Mackelwy smiled, murmuring, "My King does me too much honour."

"Not honour enough, Hugh. Never honour enough. But let us inquire of others, who might better answer us. Squire?"

"Pwll son of Pwll, Earl of Branmoor, your Majesty," the squire who had caught Ewan said.

"Ah, yes. Our apologies and greetings to thy noble parents. Well we remember the Lady Imelda when she wast a Countess in our court. How doth Islendil suit her?"

"The Golden Valley is too bright and the Spires of Sunset too slender. In short, she is as ever, Majesty."

Gavron laughed at this, throwing his head back, lost in memories. So do we ever seek to find joy even in sorrow. Too quickly he sobered and asked the Squire Pwll to relate his tale.

"When first I came to your court, Majesty," Pwll began, "as page to his Grace, my grandfather, much did I think of myself. Much did I think I had cause to, for my father sent me with a train of riches and I myself came arrayed as though already Knighted in azure and in ermine. The first soul I met while still

Ewan

on the road was the Squire Ewan, riding with only one manservant and one packhorse and himself in gear suitable to the hardships of travel. Little did I think of practicality—and being a spoiled youth, told him so outright. I have no recollection of my exact words, for they were no sooner out of my mouth than I lay flat upon my back with laughter all about me and blood down my doublet. I had only struggled to my elbows, when I felt myself being heaved up from the ground and ministered to by the very boy I had insulted. As he daubed my nose, he spoke—but again my memory fails me, or else I never really heeded what he said, which is as likely. *As he spoke, I felt a strange stirring within my breast*—shame, humility, gratitude, and love.

"I am, as your Majesty may know, my parents' only child. I have never had a brother. But Ewan took me in, tamed me, taught me proper bearing—for which I am sure my grandfather is the most grateful. In short, Ewan is closer to me than any kin and not one word is whispered about him, good or ill, but I know of it."

"Thou hast learnt rhetoric at thy mother's knee, I think," Gavron said merrily. "For I am well instructed, but not yet answered."

"If I answer not at once, that is your answer also, my King."

"I amend, good Heir Branmoor: thou hast learnt diplomacy in abundance from thy grandsire, I perceive!"

At this, the Duke stood and bowed. "I have oft told my grandson that he shalt make a fine bard, for many's the day I despair he shalt ever win his spurs!"

"All things in time," the King replied, and then said sternly, "And time and past to know what hath been said."

Pwll, who had even to this moment been bearing the burden of his fellow, now lay Ewan upon Lord Mackelwy's breast, rose, and knelt before the dais. A change fell over all the assembled as the squire bent his head and pressed his hand to his heart. And when Pwll looked up at the King, all saw a change had come over him too, as thought the customary mask of urbane mirth lay discarded on the bench beside his friend.

"Majesty, your Grace, Lord Mackelwy, and all my lords, I crave your pardon for what I am about to reveal. Pardon for what I have done, and what I have not told before.

"On Easter morning, I drew blood from two ostlers who had heard fearsome stories of the Hermit and who threw mud at Ewan as he passed from chapel to feasting hall. Of this fight, brief and base, none but we four knew. As an ostler's nose might beak from a bucking steed, it was never reported.

"I thought the matter settled until the first sightings of the Hermit came and the rumours began again. On Midsummer's Night, Ewan stayed me from challenging a lordling—I shall not name him unless your Majesty requires it—to a duel. But even Ewan could not stay my hand when that petty cur and a few of his lackeys saw fit to ambush us as we escorted ladies from the revels. I believe two broken arms, a fractured rib, a sprained ankle, and several teeth count among the casualties that night."

"We had heard of that," Gavron said, stroking his beard. "But we had attributed it to an excess of wine."

"As did I, Majesty. And may have been right to do so. But that since the eagles came, I have come very close to slaying five men and one page who dared to do more than spit and grumble as Ewan passed. So you see, but for Ewan's presence, you should have a smaller kingdom."

"It seemeth thou makest a silent plea to be sent whither we send young Ewan."

"If he must be sent at all. I beg rather you should rule to keep him here, lest no one rule my sword. But it is not only for myself I plead. The Lady Findola...."

"The handmaiden, Majesty?" the Count interrupted, stepping forward once more.

But Pwll would not give way and keeping his eyes fixed on the King, said, "The Lady Findola is beloved of Ewan and would not see him go."

"In times of war," the Count explained patiently, "women send their husbands to the field with only a kiss. The handmaiden may do the same."

"This is not war, Majesty," Pwll said, turning to stare angrily at the Count. "Although it may come to that if you send him into the very heart of the hostility you would shield him from!"

"Thou speakest freely before thy betters, Pwll son of Pwll," the Count said.

"I have not spoken a tenth of what I might."

"Peace, good sirs!" Gavron cried, raising his hand. "The judgement rests with none but my Lord Mackelwy, to whom the Squire Ewan is bound. My lord, thou hast heard the arguments. What dost thou request of us?"

Lord Mackelwy did not move from where he sat, cradling the squire as though a newborn babe. When he spoke, he seemed three times his years. "What I truly desire, Majesty, you cannot give me. Nor were it within your power should I ask it. But the safety of Ewan, son of Ioan Ys, Lord of Houndshelm, I may address. I cannot send him away, even for his own safety— I cannot do it. But I may take the example of my King, and lock him from the world for a time, although it break my heart."

"So be it," Gavron said. "And perhaps it shalt not be too long before this Hermit is come, and all is set to rights. As for thee, Squire Pwll, whom we perceive still stubbornly kneeleth before us, as thou begged our pardon, now we beg thine. Thou shalt not share in Ewan, son of Ioan Ys's fate, lest the people fear that thou shouldst release him. But as thou hast the noble care for his heart, so we entrust the Lady Findola to thee, until her love mayeth walk freely. Use thy sword on her behalf, as ever thou didst for thy friend."

Pwll bent his head once more. "I shall be ruled by my King."

"Then go now, and seek thee our daughter's handmaid, and be thou her champion from this moment on. Let her command and temper thee, as ever a sister may."

Pwll thumped his breast, did honour to the King and then to his grandfather, the Duke, and left the council hall. When once the doors of oak and brass closed, Lord Mackelwy begged leave to remove the squire to Father Cadifor's aid and from thence to ill-named Magpie's Nest, where Ewan would remain captive. As that good lord left, assisted by two others, Elowen entered, held brief conference with her father, and then fearlessly approached the throne.

Curtseying deeply, she said in voice loud enough for the whole court to hear, "The Handmaiden Gwendolyn is recovered, Majesty."

"Thou comest with the best news of all this long day, cousin," Gavron said.

"Canst thou speak to young Gwrhyr's condition?" the Marshall whispered urgently.

"Nothing, my lord, but that he is no better nor worse than when you last left him. The good Father believes he too shall come to his senses in time. Fear not."

"I shall have cause to fear, lady, until he standeth before me."

Elowen shrugged. "Grieve as you will, then. It alters not his condition. Majesty," with another low curtsy, "the news I bring should be told to my mistress's ear. I cannot think what she suffers, alone and friendless. I beg you, as King and kin, to give me leave to visit her with these tidings."

"Gladly would we allow this," the King said, rising, "but that we can ill afford thy level head amongst all this tumult. We shall tell our daughter ourselves and bring to her thy love."

"As you will, Majesty," she said, sweeping one last courtesy—curt and militaristic. "Pray give her the love of all her maids. Her imprisonment is ours as well."

"And now, gentlemen," Gavron said, taking up sceptre. "Bid you good night, good dreams, and prayers for a happier tomorrow."

With that, the King descended and swept forth from the Great Hall, followed by all his courtiers. Elowen wandered slowly after gazing ever towards the heavens, lost in thought and contemplation.

Even as they spoke, an eagle flew silently northward, following the star-shimmered Gwyrglánn, itself barely a reflection in swift flowing waters. Three days it flew, resting only when its wings could bear no more. Then on the fourth night, it circled down, letting the wind eddy gently beneath its wings, until it landed with a small rustle of leaves upon a gnarled oak. A hand, silent and dark like a branch itself, reached out for the eagle's leg and took from it a letter.

Two breaths later, another eagle climbed the sky paths. And some looking up that late night, as the harvest moon teetered at her zenith, swore that no eagle flew but a lion.

chapter iii

espite the King's command, few slept well that night. And so as the sun rose, a lovely shimmer of blue-white blooming outward like a lily, Elowen found Findola sitting in their mistress' old perch, within the broad window overlooking the river. Findola did not move as Elowen approached but said, "I have heard. I have heard it all thrice over already."

"It is criminal," Elowen whispered vehemently, joining Findola by the window. "Why does no one say, 'Let us imprison Gwrhyr, since he was ass enough to defy his warnings?'"

"That was unkind, Elowen."

"Unkind! Too kind by half! And I wonder at you, Findola, sitting like a monument to martyrdom. How can you smile so? Have you not anger within your breast? Have you no feeling? Your love lies captive while those who slander him walk free! Is that justice? Is that cause for silence? Is that reason for *kindness?* No! Oh!" she beat her fist against the wall. "Had I a man's office, I should have done well by your love. Were I my father's son, and not his mere daughter, I should have spoken on his behalf. But I was left to comfort the cheerless, and you were barred withal from your love's fate!"

Still Findola was not moved, and would only and anon look out the window. Tears threatened to wend their way down Elowen's cheeks—travesties upon such a face accustomed to mirth and boisterous laughter. She sat beside her friend and grasped her arms. "Ah, dearest, dearest sister!" she cried. "Canst thou not even shed one tear for him? Is thy love so shallow, a plaything of the moment, that thou sittest complacently within this very room? Canst thou convince me that thou art *happier* with him gone? Thou mayest say thou art relieved that our lady lies under the same lock and key! Oh, Findola, where is thy heart?"

"It lies safe and secret, awaiting the day when a ring binds it forever to my love's bosom. When the Hermit comes...."

"*'When the Hermit comes'*—how oft have we heard that phrase this past six month!"

"Not often enough, if you do not yet credit it."

Elowen whirled at those words, and scowled when she saw who had said them. "What do you here? Have you not a commission from his Grace Llewellyn? Some lordling to hawk with this fine morning? Some several dozen assignations with painted ladies? A hunt or feast to attend upon? Armour to polish or mirrors to kiss?"

"I have none of these, lady," Pwll said, stepping forward into the room with a curt bow. Then to Findola, "My Lord Mackelwy sends word that he would be honoured by your presence, lady, at his table this morning."

Elowen sniffed, "A small compensation. Is Lord Mackelwy banned from the King's table now, that he dines alone?"

"Do you require an answer or merely a scratching post?" came Pwll's polite retort.

"I should be honoured to join Lord Mackelwy's table," Findola said, touching Elowen on the arm. "Pray tell him that I shall attend him and his lady within the hour."

Pwll kissed Findola's hand, bowed sternly to Elowen, and left.

Before her companion could say anything, Findola turned to Elowen and said, "I shall not hear one word against him. He is Ewan's dearest friend, and now my sole consolation whilst these hardships visit us. Thou art distressed and thou hast neither slept nor eaten and th'unnatural fast doth thee only ill. Let me converse with my lord and let thee show some civility to my champion, for it was not many seasons ago that you looked fondly upon each other."

Elowen sighed, and slumped against the wall. "I shall sleep, and forage for some bread and wine, if thou wilt. But we can neither command each other's hearts, it seemeth, for thou wilt not cry and I cannot reverse time."

Smiling, Findola leaned forward and pressed a kiss upon the handmaiden's brow. "It is enough for now. When the Hermit cometh, thou shalt find all well again. I am sure of it. And," she gazed anxiously out the window once more, "I do not think it wilt be long before he cometh. Wait but a little—thou shalt see it all come right."

They smiled, then, and clasped hands against the morning.

A week passed in scurrying.

And Gwrhyr did not rise.

Gwendolyn remained ever by his side, blue-eyed and silent. Magdwa was sent away to her aunt's estate in Dalfínn, bundled up with nursemaid and guard as though a little Princess herself. Elowen spoke no more of Pwll, but busied herself with the dangling duties of Niamh's abandoned household.

Thus another care was added to Findola's heart. And oft she looked at the Magpie's Nest for a glimpse of her beloved—for she could not meet with him, even with guard attendant, nor could she write him or sing beneath his window. But oftener still, she looked to the sky and waited for eagles.

"My lord! My lord!"

Donell glanced up from his report—as one of the few lettered men in the court, his duties as Captain included those of a scribe—and started as he saw who had entered.

"Liam! What hath happened? Here, here, take my seat and catch thy breath. There is nothing so pressing it requireth thy expiration!"

The fair-skinned youth sat, heaving in huge gulps of air like a man atop a mountain. He shook his head as Donell tried to ply him with a glass of wine, instead bringing forth from his breast a letter and thrusting it into the captain's hands. "It came…it came by eagle."

Little did Niamh know what transpired beneath her, for none now visited the Rose Garden or the great Labyrinth—having neither the desire for more beauty, nor the inclination for wooing. The Princess's glow paled but a little as she paced the alabaster room, too perfect for much comfort. That Gwendolyn was recovered and Ewan imprisoned she had heard—but no more, for matters of the court kept both King and Queen ensnared.

How to while away the hours, never knowing how many hours remained to her captivity? Some few articles had been brought her—ink, quill, and parchment; thread, knit, and board; prayerbook and bestiary, the whole of her collection—and all fell short of companionship. Stories she told herself, rosaries she prayed, songs she sang—and all incompleted, for the Lily Spire also looked over the Gwyrglánn, and that waterway contained all her salvation.

"Ah me!" she cried, throwing aside a bit of tapestry and leaning out the narrow window, as though she might fly upon white wings. "I shall run mad! Gethin, where art thou?"

"This is foolishness," Donell opined, tucking his helm beneath his arm and shaking out his damp hair.

"It is pageantry," Gavron corrected gently. "That which my Court loves best of all. To speak truth to them will not convince as well as to announce truth grandly."

Donell sighed and squared his shoulders. A signal to the Heralds on the Lesser Hall's Gallery sounded a fanfare unheard for twenty years and more, since Gavron returned with his bride, preceded by a star.

Whispers of "What is happening?" and "Who is come?" quickly gave way to the stomp of feet and rattle of latches as those able gathered in the courtyard between the halls.

31

"Behold!" the King cried, when the main court thronged. His voice echoed off the surrounding walls, fell back on itself, and drifted into wordless sound as it approached the Princess's prison. "The Groom is come, is even now standing at the city gates. Who shalt parlay with him and prepare our way on the morrow?"

"I, sire," Donell said, standing forward and kneeling. He wore full riding garb already, the chain of office gleaming upon his breast. One of his men held his horse by its argent bridle.

"Then take thee this our seal and this our greeting and God speed thee to our hope!"

The Captain kissed his cousin's hand and rose, mounted and cantered through the gates, thrown back a half-hour past. Gavron watched him go, all expectation riding with him. At last he said, "See how well pleased we are with the good Hermit that we do him such honour. Good my friends, we have mourned but shall be merry! Let us feast tonight! Let there be singing and dancing! Let nothing trouble ye; let nothing disturb ye. Light the lights and banish woe! All shall be well anon."

The people cheered—a dutiful hurrah—and set about for the feast. But as they retired, the Earl Marshall only muttered, "Gwrhyr has not risen and the Lily Spire still shines."

To which the Duke replied, "Take heart, cousin. All sorrows cannot last."

Lights glimmered in the Great Hall, bobbed along the parapets, illumined every nook and cranny as thought it were full day—as though to outshine Niamh, pacing restlessly in her prison. The trumpet's sound rang in her ears as though to say, "Beloved, I am come."

Within the Great Hall, the dancers whirled their capes blue and green and musicians sawed with angry determination—a melancholic merry-making. No conundrums did the jesters offer, no riddles from the harpers—the only one that signified had not yet come to court. The Earl Marshall sat with eyes fixed upon the hour candle, an untouched flagon in hand. The Duke spoke of important things to the King, playing his part well. Pwll danced with Findola, but when he offered his arm to Elowen, he received only white pressed lips and silence. And when the hour candle slipped its way to the third rung, the Count politely excused himself from the feast, and made his way to the Lily Spire.

Much is often made of the doings of the court—the rise and fall of Princes, the romances of Kings, Knights' quests, christenings, passions, pride and honour. And much does it benefit us to raise our minds to those greater heights.

And yet, truth be told, it is little that a tournament affects the growth of wheat, or councils full of shouting help to turn the beer.

So it was that in a low, dark tavern, well-kept and respectable, modestly profitable from a happy situation near the southward Pilgrim's Gate, and known commonly as the White Hind, named after Guilian Silverbow's greatest feat, the following conversation took place:

"Ho, there, Brenna Housewife! What hospitality have you? There's a stranger at the gate, won't come in."

The matron addressed turned her ponderous way, carefully through the close tables. "What's that you say, Malcolm Tater?"

The Tater sat, unwinding the heavy scarf from his ruddy neck and accepting a mug as due payment for the tale he brought. He drank deeply, relishing the foam upon his whiskers and the ginger in his mouth.

He took too long about it, though, and so got no seconds free. "Malcolm Tater!" the Housewife chided. "Is my ale so weak, your tongue's not loosed?"

Cowed, the Tater wiped his mouth on his well-mended sleeve and said, "A stranger at the gate, all in black like a priest—or more like a monk for he would not speak to me when I asked him if he would come."

"Then how know you he wasn't deaf, and couldna understand you for your mumblin'?" John Carpenter called, before the Housewife could shush him.

"He shook his head well enough—he heard me," the Tater replied into his cup.

"Enough with you!" the Housewife scowled, flapping her apron at John Carpenter. "You're as witty as wood and I would you were mute!"

"Ah, you've bittered the ale!'

"You've snagged on a splinter!"

"Peace, you two as well!" Brenna Housewife said, rounding to pin the offenders with a glance. The hecklers Nob and Rob, tanners both and twins to boot, hid their grins in foam and said no more. Satisfied, the Housewife turned back to the Tater, asking, "Is he a holy man, think you? Has he come to pray the round, or make genuflection before the crosier?"

"He willna speak—how can Malcolm Tater tell?"

The matron did not bother to narrow her eyes at John Carpenter again, but waited for the Tater to answer.

"He seemed to be waiting for something. Although with barely tempered patience. Like a man too long fasting."

"Was he haggard? Gaunt?"

"He could use some bread and company. He was that agitated."

"Right." She nodded once, and began fumbling with her apron strings. Someone brought her shawl and another her scarf and a third held open the door. As she disappeared into the night, her voice rang back, "If I find the tap and tiller dry, it's thirsty you'll *all* go for a se'ennight!"

33

It was not far to the Pilgrim's Gate, the merest left-turning of the custom's house and skirting of the guard tower to the slotted wooden doors, where she was hailed by one of the sentries.

"Ho! Mistress Barleywine! Where are you out so late?"

Brenna Housewife raised her hand to shield her eyes from the lanthorn light. "Colin Carterson, is it?"

"The same."

"Malcolm Tater says you've a man perishing of hunger you won't let in."

"Have seen no man to speak of. There's a shadow that sent young Liam running for the Captain early this morning."

"Shadow! Fool of a man! It's no wonder they put you on the inward-facing door! If an army came attacking, with a roar up to the King's very ear, you'd claim it was the wind and stop the Knights from facing them! It's sorry you'll be when the guardhouse gets no barrels for your stupid tongue wagging meanly at me! Be off, rudesby and let me through. There's a man out there, say I, and one that I intend to feed and maybe wheedle out his tale, for sure he has one. Saints and sinners! He may be no man at all, but a King or Fairy or sommat greater, as some do say they've et with Angels. And being so grateful for a cup of mead and a bit of cheese and bread, who cannot say, but I might be given sommat in return?"

"Peace, peace, woman!" Colin said, laughing. "For that I'll let you through, for you've surely drunk your own medicine tonight! But being so blind as you say, if you fall on your face running out to will-o-wisps, I'll not catch you. See, here the door, Madame, pass thou by peacefully."

"Thou me no thous, Colin Carterson. I know you from when you were whelped. But for your help, come claim a pint of bitter some chill even."

So she passed and for all her brave words, she still started when the gates closed with a boom behind her. But she gathered courage about her like a shawl and into the dark she said, "I know you are here, although I cannot see you. I have not brought anything with me, but my tavern's not far and is reckoned by many very fine." No one answered her and she felt very foolish indeed, and began wondering how such a tale would sound to the ears of her patrons, much less to the high-and-mighty Colin Carterson. She hoped there were not many about to hear her.

"Malcolm Tater says he spoke with you. I'm no Malcolm Tater, just a harmless Housewife. But the night is cold, and I've a few rooms to lend out, and I've beer rich as butter and good, hardy bread and brown bread and meatpies and two whole rounds of cheese—even a barrel of apples and a few late pears, and it won't take much to stir up some stew with peas and carrots and potatoes and the like in it. I've got corned beef and roast beef, and a whole leg of lamb, off of Farmer Cartwright, who comes in every Lord's Day, looking for a wife among the congregation. He's got his eye on Agnes Baker's daughter, but I know for a fact she's been walking out a nights with Bob Cobbler's bright apprentice. There's that and plenty more talk in my tavern—stuff that might interest you more than our goings on. For we've guards often nip in and out, when no one's watching, and they'll drop a thing or two about high-and-mighty doings, that's good for the telling no matter where you roam."

"What sort of news?" came the reply at last—a low, hungry voice, emerging like a hand into lamplight.

The housewife smiled, feeling that at last she knew where she stood. She knew young men's voices well enough, had known them gestating beneath her breast, and on many a lonely night when the deep purse trickled out in a golden flood of foamy woe. "Well, they say they've locked the Princess up, though Lord knows why. They're queer folk up that way, and always doing strange things for the poets to write verses of."

"Is she well?"

"Lord love you! How should I know? I've never even seen her! For her christening day, I were too busy here, preparing for the merrymakers, to trudge all day uphill to stand in a hot crowd and 'Ooh!' and 'Aah' over a babe no bigger than a speck to my eye. And she never comes down this far into the city— never did, even when she were a child and before she drove her suitors mad. But if you're asking for my guess, well, I'd say I feel hard sorry for her, and'll be glad to hear when the King's come to his senses and let her out.

"They say they've found someone for her—strange things I hear, but I don't credit them, for some'll say anything for a free mug. And if they have, I say God bless him and send him quick and give him a good strong arm and stout heart to deal with the stupidities of the court, say I. For 'struth, I've often said that if only they'd send the Princess down to work for her bread, there should be far less of this to-doing, for I do think that all her wondrous beauty cannot be much more than mystery."

"Oh, no, mistress. The stories do not lie."

"Is it so? You must be a pilgrim with such faith. 'Til I see it, I'll keep my thoughts. And you'd be well to do so, too. No more than mystery, I say, golden chains and needless mystery. She's been locked away one way or 'nother; a tower may make no mind to her. Though all the same, I'm sorry. But will you come? I can have toast and eggs and ham whipped up in no time, and you're like to learn more if you eat slow and keep your ears pricked."

"I thank you, mistress. But I may not enter yet."

"May not! Well, there's a fine to-do! Do you fancy yourself a gentry to speak of 'mays'?"

"I did once."

"Go to! You are a riddle! You're hungry, but not for food; you're gentry and you're pilgrim. I can't say I'm not sorry to miss your tale. But if I can't convince you, I'll save my breath to cool my soup." She turned to leave, then, calling over her shoulder, "Spiced cider? Hot toddy? I've a few drops of mulled wine I keep for gambling lordlings."

"Nothing, mistress, but your orisons."

With that, Brenna Housewife must content herself, and so left to tell the strange tale for many a day after that—for even she heard of the happenings that came after and many's the day she sighed that she had not seen the Pilgrim's face.

Now learn of a curious thing: how well we know that only those pure of heart could even bear to draw near to Niamh's beauty and that those even slightly tainted of soul could not come within the castle walls without running mad. So it is also true—although until now untested—that those with no trace of goodness in them could also approach the Princess. And so blackened had the Count's soul become that, the night before the Hermit arrived, he could come close enough to touch Niamh—for he could not perceive her beauty.

The Count found her pacing in her prison, in such a state of mind that when the Count came boldly into her chambers, she thought it a divine sign of Providence and heartily welcomed him—telling him, as though a confessor, her secret hopes and fears. And when he revealed to her that indeed, the Hermit was at the very gates of the city, Niamh jumped to her feet, clasping her hands and crying, "Gethin! Gethin come! Ah, Lord! That this man, among all men mighteth hold me."

"Gethin?" the Count said pleasantly. "I had heard him named differently."

At this, Niamh coloured and would say no more of the Hermit's true name. Already, her heart told her she had betrayed her love—although how and to what peril, she knew not. Aloud she said, "I fear, my dear Count, that I may strike him down before he even cometh. I have heard no news of Gwrhyr."

"He is the same as ever," he replied.

Niamh hung her head and buried her face in her hair, as she sat upon the bed. "What shall I do, then? How can I ever hope to wed?"

"Why!" the Count said, sitting near her and smiling. "What a simple question! And how easily remedied. If thou fearest that *thine* aspect wilt drive him off, thou hast only to introduce thyself to him in stages, so that he mighteth learn to bear a little at a time until he canst bear all. Consider the man who laceth his comfits with poison. When his enemy seeketh to do away with him by that means, it hath no effect!"

Niamh pondered this in silence for a moment, doubt and anxiety warring in her breast. Never, though, did she think to question the Count's word—for always before those who had addressed her were, of necessity, good and worthy of trust. At last she said, "How shalt this be accomplished? In the past I have spoken to some behind grates and screens and walls. And veils, I have found, hath no effect."

"That is because none of these addressed the true question—that is, thy beauty. Didst thou expect mere distance to be thy shield? If that were so, the sun shouldst not beat so harshly as it doth! But to a man who hath lived his whole life blind, or in a cave—such as the Hermit, of whom no one hath a *clear* account—why, the sun canst only blind him again! It were better to first show him a spark, a tinder, then a candle, then a fire, and so on until he canst squint at the moon, and later stand full in the sun. Dost thou understand, Princess? The light remaineth constant, but dimmed."

"And thou wouldst dim me?" the Princess asked with terrible clarity.

The Count laughed and shifted upon the seat. "I would caution thee only to consider the soul of one thou *seemest* to love so well. Or—dost thou love?"

"With all my heart."

"Then *give* him thy heart—oh, aye, and thy mind, too. But relinquish thy foolish vanity that hath been the ruin of so many!"

At this Niamh stood and paced about the room, running her fingers over the pearlescent walls until she seemed a moving statue, made likewise of marble. "Have I been vain?" she whispered. "Can it be vanity to be born? To live as I was made?"

"What else is it but vanity, child? True beauty wouldst not strike men dead." The Count spoke so well and so sweetly, as though he were her very kin, that Niamh's heart grew convinced of such folly that put the blame upon the good without acknowledging the weakness of the fallen.

"Tell me what I must do!" Niamh cried, flinging herself upon her knees before the Count. "Counsel me against my wickedness!"

For answer, the Count thrust his hand into the very heart of the fire, and gathered a handful of embers from the hearth. "Do penance. Cover thyself with ashes and this wilt be thy shield."

Seizing the ashes from the Count's hand, Niamh smeared them all over her face and arms and every place not clothed. But even as she did, the ashes fell off her and what they exposed glowed more radiantly for Niamh's sincere mortification.

"It is not enough," the Count said, and handed her more ashes. These, too, fell away to reveal skin shining like golden sunrise over the Well at the End of the World.

"It wilt not do," the Count said with slipping patience. "Thou art only covering thy noble parts. All of thyself must be clothed in ashes—thou must go into the fire."

Niamh's eyes widened but she thought of the Hermit, and so she disrobed and stepped into the fireplace and rolled within the burning embers until she was singed and sooty as the night outside. When she stepped out from the fire, the Count came to her and took her hands, saying, "Ah, *now* thou art a fitting bride!" And he kissed her.

At this moment, the King and Queen entered thinking to wish their daughter goodnight, and to assure her of their prayers for the morrow. But when they saw the Count making love to a shadow, they were appalled. At their arrival, Niamh pulled herself free from the Count's loathsome embrace and grasped her father about the knees, calling out his name. But he did not know her—and so he ordered her from his presence. Weeping, she fled.

The King then turned his attention to the Count, demanding to know what unholy demon had inspired the nobleman to desecrate his daughter's rooms the night before her wedding. The Count only laughed, doubled over on the empty bed, gasping, "Ah! If only thou knewest! Why, I have done nothing more than thou hast done thyself! Indeed, I have done better for her, for I embraced her, whilst thou turned thy daughter away!"

At this, Gavron understood and calling his guards, he ordered them to search after Niamh; he himself would settle accounts with the treacherous nobleman. But when he turned back to lay hands upon the demonised, he found the Count had vanished.

chapcer iv

he King's guard were all noble men and true, and thoroughly they scoured the palace and the town beyond—but, although they often passed by Niamh as she cowered within the shadows, they could not see her. She was so changed.

By midday, the hunt ceased. And with heavy heart, the Captain of the Guard—who had been overtaken by the news, even as he rode through the city to the gates—approached the King and Queen upon the dais. Slowly he removed his helmet and all his men did likewise. Slowly he knelt and all his men did too. "I have failed you, Majesty," Donell said. "Twelve hours we have sought and have found no trace of the Princess." So saying, he stood and held his helmet out to the King—but Gavron would not accept it.

"'Twas not thee or thy men who failed the Princess—for I first failed her when she clung to me. Should I require thy resignation, dear cousin, I should require my own. But pray, and all ye men pray! We have all of us been found wanting and unworthy of the treasure granted us briefly. Make reparation and perhaps mercy shall be granted us, and the Princess returned."

"And the Count?" Rhianna asked, when it seemed her husband could speak no more.

"Him we *have* found, Majesty," the Captain answered. "Sitting pleasantly by the fire within his town home, as though he had no weight upon his immortal soul! So cordially did he greet us that at first we doubted his guilt. But then young Liam," touching the shoulder of a fair-skinned youth, no more than Niamh's own age, "he saw a shadow behind the Count—a shadow with eyes of coal, who clung to that man like a lover. So loudly did young Liam shout that we could no longer hear the Count, and at that moment, we all saw the shadow. We immediately laid hands on the villain, who suddenly thrashed about like a rabid dog, and nearly overpowered us. But we eventually subdued him, and even now he lies chained in the dungeon, guarded by my best men."

"Thou hast done well," Gavron said, raising his head from his hand, to reveal a face white with grief and rage. His eyes, which had won him fame, were lined and old and red with unshed tears. "Retain thy place, Captain, and receive our gratitude. To thy men, we reward triple wages. To young Liam, we grant a boon. To thyself, all the Count's estates, wealth and title. As for the demon himself, we shall deliberate and mete justice accordingly."

How dearly Gavron longed to retire then! But Rhianna lay her cool hand upon his wrist, whispering, "Stay. There is one more to see thee." The Queen gestured and the guards stood down. The great doors opened and the Hermit walked in.

Those attendant within the Great Hall strained over their neighbours' shoulders to catch a better glimpse of the creature so long expected and feared. But he approached with cowl fully drawn and hands within his sleeves, so that he might have been no more than a monk with full and tawny beard. Some claimed they saw the tip of his tail as he moved and others swore they saw his whiskers twitch.

"Is it the Lion of St. Siawn," they whispered amongst themselves. "The spectre of Siawn Shieldbearer, come himself to prolong his lineage."

"Nay," others answered, "the Lion is not so base to mate with his own as wolves do. But this creature is a sign that the Great King is with us and has shown favour to the bridegroom."

"He is valorous," one lady whispered to another. "Surely, his prowess and bravery have stamped themselves upon his very outward appearance."

"He is proud," the second lady sniffed behind her fan. "Elsewise he should show his face to us and not spurn us as though we were no more than chaff upon the wind."

"He is humble," the first lady retorted.

"He is a beast," a slit-eyed noble responded.

Of claw, no one claimed special revelation. The Hermit's hands were better concealed than his face. Nor did any man see his wings, although all noted the humps upon his back beneath his plain robes. But later, after the nobles had retired, two serving girls sweeping found long white eagle's feathers upon the marble floor. They said nothing, but tucked the feathers away and revered them after as relics. For they knew, as the nobles had forgotten, that the eagle is by nature good although likewise ferocious.

All saw the chain about the Hermit's neck, just as the Baker had described. But none knew the meaning of this.

"Oh, Lord," Gavron breathed, as the cowled figure approached. "So great wast my sorrow, I forgot th'impending happiness." Aloud he said in formal tones, "Good sir, you find a sorry welcome. So long have you travelled, and now we find our summons vain, for your bride has gone and all is come to naught. Come, if you will, and we shall withdraw and reveal all to you presently."

This they did, and while Gavron spoke, the Hermit neither answered nor removed his cowl. When Gavron had done, the Hermit still remained mute and hidden—like a spectre of death, until the King, overcome by all that had transpired, called out, "*Speak*, man! We would know your mind! Can you think that by your silence you spare me just rebukes? There is nothing you can say that I have not used in self-remonstrance already. Or, if you will not speak, as by your manner you seem disinclined, then show your face that I may know you are flesh and not some dark angel sent for our demise!"

For answer, the Hermit pushed back his hood and withdrew his hands from his deep sleeves. Beneath his black cloak, something twitched and shifted like wings and a tail. One claw extended to catch up a taper and hold it to the monstrous face, so the King and Queen might intimately know to whom

Gavron

they spake. And as they looked, both Gavron and Rhianna wondered if their daughter were not better for having fled.

There was about the Hermit's whole being an awfulness, disturbing to behold, and made worse for the patience in his eyes. As Niamh's beauty sent one quaking with delight, so the Hermit made one's knees tremble with righteous fear. His body, they could see, was strong and he moved with a terrible grace of one who has killed and often. But the black curve of his lip revealed a strange remorse—jarring in such a savage.

"I do not rebuke you," he said.

So soft his voice, Gavron could not bring himself to have heard aright.

"But neither," the Hermit said, replacing the taper and pacing to the window, "do I blame myself—as I might, given…" he gestured to his face, with the shadow of a grim smile. Then, drawing himself erect, so that the tinted light from the window fell almost gently upon him, he said, "Your daughter hath been grievously deceived. She hath been defiled and violated by the man within your mercy. He is indeed a very demon and were he within my power, I fear I should not hesitate to feast on his gullet this moment. It is well he is not within my power. Although it grates to say it, even he might be redeemed, if he allows it. I have…known such a thing." He fell silent for a moment and flexed his claw and sighed. Then suddenly and with a low snarl, he said, "Majesty, I am your servant. Command me."

So rapid were the Hermit's changes of mood, that Gavron was speechless and could only gape.

"Art thou not a magician?" the Queen asked.

The Hermit bowed. "I am. But not damnable."

Rhianna nodded. "Then perhaps thou mayest use thy talents to discover where she is."

"If it *is* possible, I will do so—but if she hath become, as you say, somehow a shadow of herself, then my poor magics may prove insufficient. I am not a wizard to delve into all mysteries."

So the Queen sent for the scrying things, a silver bowl, holy water, and a lock of Niamh's long hair, and gave all these things to the Hermit. He received them gravely as instruments of his art. But the lock of Niamh's golden hair affected him and he hesitated before receiving it from Rhianna's hand.

"Art thou afraid?" Rhianna asked when she perceived the Hermit's discomfiture.

"Awed, Majesty," he replied.

That night, within the chapel, the magician searched—but when dawn arose, he stumbled weary from the altar, as the King and Queen and all the court assembled for mass.

Rhianna saw the Hermit first and ran to him, bravely touching his eagle arm. She lifted her eyes and searched his oddly human ones. Within their depths, she knew defeat.

"There is no hope?" she whispered, pressing her coral lips together to ward away tears.

"There is always hope, dear lady," the Hermit replied. He touched his other hand to hers. The Queen started at his touch, for she saw that his right hand was human, although his forearm was still feathered.

"How cometh this?" she asked, clutching his human hand, when he would pull away. "Tell me *this* is hope, good sir. I am myself bereft of my Fairy magic, but my eyes and mind are sound, and well I know the symmetry of spells. Whence came this new transformation?"

As though suddenly shy, the Hermit withdrew his good hand away and into the folds of his cloak. "Majesty, your wisdom, renowned, humbles me. I..." he stopped and cast his eyes about in indecision. His breathing was ragged and raspy, as though some fire should burst forth from his breast at any moment. But when he touched the Queen again to draw her into the half-light of a side chapel, his touch was gentle, like a nursemaid's upon a newborn.

"Majesty," he began, "pray forgive me any offence."

"It is forgiven," she replied immediately.

He seemed to struggle again for a moment, lost between duty and sorrow. At length he said, "You have lost your wings in your love for the King—and that is your curse and blessing. But I have grown wings so wide that they pain me beneath my cloak. Oft I have used them to hasten me to birthbeds and deathbeds when I am needed, or I have stretched them for the sheer joy of flight. With every use they grow, spreading across my back and arms like a cancer, until I am half bird, half beast. I might have used them to carry me here, too—and who knows now whether it were folly or fate that I did not. But I walked and with every day one feather or one talon fell, until you see my hand—so long concealed!—at last to flesh restored. Yes, Majesty, there is hope, although its cost is dear."

Upon hearing this speech, Rhianna's heart softened, and she thought that perhaps this Hermit was not so terrible to look upon. Smiling, she stepped from the side chapel—but the Hermit did not follow. "Dost thou not attend?" she asked.

From the shadows, in the flickering light of votive candles, she saw the tawny mane shake a silent no. "I set forth to seek the Princess. Before God I have sworn to do so. Before you I likewise swear."

"But thou wilt take no bread for the journey?" she pressed. "Nor avail thyself of aught we can give you?"

Again he shook his head. "I have received neither the host nor the cup these twenty years."

"Nor sought confession?"

"Who would hear me?"

"Then heed *me*," the Queen said, as the Kyrie raised. "Thou hast sworn an oath to God, to me, and to thy King. Thou hast pledged thyself our soldier in this task. Therefore heed me, Duncan, by the name by which thou art called—and if it be not thy true name, yet by God it wilt serve!—from this day forth, thou shalt find neither rest nor reward until thou hast tended to thy soul. And though thou seekest for my daughter, thou shalt find her not, until thou art worthy. This geas I lay upon thee, binding until thou returnest victorious or perish at the price of thine immortal soul. This also do I press upon thee—although bind thee not. Stay until the moon swelleth in a fortnight and see if news cometh, or if our daughter will not return. She—she mayeth not have fled, as the false Count led us to believe."

So saying, the Queen who was once a Fairy left him and rejoined her husband in the pew. Never once did she turn to see whether the Hermit followed, but turned all her burning, tear-stung eyes upward.

The Hermit stayed at the castle, a restless shadow pacing the darkened Lily Spire without reprieve. Few spoke to him besides the King and Queen, although all showed him courtesy for fear of the same and out of respect for their lost Princess.

43

Eagles came and eagles flew, messengers bearing the King's seal rode to all Rhianna's kin, and the guards sent word to the garrisons guarding the Dark Wood.

And all was silent as though Niamh and the memory of Niamh and the beauty of Niamh had turned to ashes. Colour had fled the world. Poetry gave way to prose; music to ceaseless wailing. Life itself drained with her every step away. For when the Princess fell, all loveliness fell with her. When the Count smothered the Niamh who had been, he brought death to all she possessed. The world was forever changed, although the change came slowly. Grace had been given—and who knew if it could ever be restored.

On the third day of the tragedy, the Earl Marshall overtook the Hermit whilst he paced from chapel to the stations. "You have powers, sir," the Earl Marshall said, standing with fists clenched and legs rooted, as though he expected the Hermit to attack him.

The Hermit barely turned his head to see who addressed him. Quietly he answered, "News travels swiftly."

But the Earl did not hear the smile in the words—he may have not heard the Hermit beyond the answer he desired—and so he said, "My nephew was struck down by the Princess. Some have said you might cure him."

"Did he love the Princess?" the Hermit asked, inspecting the fold of his deep sleeves.

Again, the stranger's tone made no dint on the Earl, for he was an honest, straightforward man and for all his years at court, knew little of subtlety. "He was not her suitor. She struck down his love, her Handmaid, and when he went to Gwendolyn's side, the Princess's curse struck him down too. The priest says that he lives, but I cannot see it."

"How long has he slept?"

"It is eleven days now."

At this the Hermit started—no more than a silent hesitation and marked by no soul other than the spit boy who had been hiding in the winery to escape the cook's wrath. The story he brought back to the kitchens spared him double boxed ears, but did little more than season the servants' curiosity and conjecture.

"Eleven days?" the Hermit said slowly, his mind full of Niamh's golden hair strewn upon the floor, the gentle flicker of the dying fire, the hem of her gown weaving itself into shadow, the moment when she saw him and did not blink. Double joy and guilt welled up within him—giddy joy that the night they spoke should have brought a deeper beauty to the Princess, and the awful guilt that by such beauty Gwrhyr had fallen.

"Yes," he said. "I shall come."

44

Father Cadifor's square, lined face greeted the Earl Marshall and the Hermit that evening. "For," the Hermit had explained, "some things are better seen in candlelight." With a long, tight-lipped sigh that spoke more eloquently than any words, the good Father led the way into the room where Gwrhyr lay, clad in shirt and breeches only—pallid and terrible upon the neat pallet.

The Hermit accepted the candle from the priest silently and held it in such a way to examine the body that Father Cadifor felt—for the first time in entirely too long—that perhaps at last someone with sense may have come to tend his unlikely visitor. Encouraged by the Hermit's grave and precise motions—placing human hand thoughtfully upon Gwrhyr's wrist, brow, and throat—the priest volunteered, "He hath not even blinked since three days agone. However his breathing is steady, though shallow. I have tried to pour broth and water down his mouth, but even pinching his nose wilt not make his lips part. So he has somehow remained this whole time—like a kind of living stone."

"Have you seen cases similar to his?"

"I have," the Father answered. "But I have not seen a case so grave now for several years. Most men grow fevered and toss about and wail as though they were tormented by a Hellish fire. And if they do not recover themselves within a week—either to a sort of sadness or imbecility—they die screaming her name. But he...he is cold and heavy as stone and calleth out no one's name. No, not even Gwendolyn's."

If the Hermit took offence at the Father's words, he said nothing, but pulled back the sheet to examine the Knight's feet. The toes were curled and black.

"And when did this?" he asked the priest, passing the candle to the earl.

"This," the priest said, moving to join the strange physician's side, "this began when the first eagle flew. Although the discoloration of the nails were evident as early as Midsummer, on the eve of his third tourney."

Gethin nodded and said, "It is as I thought. They are becoming hooves."

"Hooves!" Father Cadifor exclaimed. The Earl Marshall looked with horror at his nephew's feet, thinking of the pride he had felt only recently when others named Gwrhyr "the Bull."

Gethin only replaced the sheet, saying with face turned into shadows, "There is no cure of spirit for that malady. And even your ministrations, Father, may only go so far if he himself does not turn back in time. Comfort yourselves in this though: your nephew is honest. Most men hide what beast they are becoming.

"But leave me apace with Sir Gwrhyr. I may do something for his unnatural sleep."

Fearfully, the good priest and the Earl Marshall withdrew to the other room. The Hermit waited until the light burned but dimly beneath the door and their voices rose like whispered water, before he pushed back the hood of his robe and rolled up his deep sleeves above his feathered elbows.

45

His human hand was useless. It comforted the human, but held no magic of its own. But the claw was deft and could snatch things invisible from the air—or if need be, cut them. It cut now. Swooping above the youth's chest, above the heart, passing talon between air and air, it severed an invisible string between the Knight and the hand of Death. "Begone," the Hermit said to the voiceless screech that followed. "Thou hast no power here."

His human hand reached for the bowl of holy water at the door and traced the cross upon the Knight's brow, heart and hand. Still Gwrhyr did not stir. The Hermit's great lion's brows lowered. Beneath the robe, the tail swished.

Presumptuous boy, a voice, laden with the past, seemed to say within his ear. *Didst thou think thou hast the holy office?*

For answer, Gethin flicked his tail, and took up the candle to see where else the Angel of Death lay upon the youth. Talons swung, severing air, over shoulder, stomach, eyes, throat, thighs, loins, and brow. But wherever he swung more cords grew, until the Knight seemed fair covered in a cobweb shroud. The shrill cries after each slash ceased, shifted, grew into a sentence, *Thy mistress hath wrought this. Let her answer. Let me pass.* Black threads spat out of the Knight's lips and bound him ever closer to the bed. Talons shot out in reply, gripped a handful of shadow, threw it aside, and reached for another handful, as thought to peel Gwrhyr from the heart of a cocoon.

"What is this place, that all my magics fail me?" the Hermit snarled, even as he ripped a dark swath away from the Knight's belly. The shrieking grew louder and added a low thrum that sounded the Princess's name. A sable maelstrom encompassed the two men, filled the room, and threatened to overflow it. Shooting like a hundred octopedal creatures, undulating for an entrance into Gethin's secret heart, all seemed at a loss. Other voices joined the refrain, mocking the Hermit, borrowing words from his past, words that had rung in his ears since he had left the company of men.

And within that maelstrom one ghostly voice—cultured and gentle, as a long-suffering tutor—rose above them all. *Hast thou learnt nothing? Are all thy woes and disfigurations for naught? When didst thou forget to truly see?*

The Hermit shook himself, his tawny mane shedding shadow threads and scattering them on the floor. His eyes blinked. He rubbed them. He saw nothing but shadow upon the Knight, like a man beneath quicksand. "See?" he laughed, leaning forward to press his palm against his eyes. "Ah, God! How can *I* see?"

Through the sliver of his fingers the shadow ruled, now bent on deepening itself. Gwrhyr's head was lost in it. His body was as black as his toes. But somewhere within that storm, a small light flickered yellow-white-blue, ever shifting like the dawn. Gethin reached out to that light with his claw. It burned him and he drew back. Using his hand he gained purchase and drew the light towards him.

Fingers encountered water and the rough edge of the bowl. Hardly waiting to bring the light closer, he cupped the water and splashed it over his human eyes. Drops dripped down his fur, briefly showing pale human flesh beneath—before the mane drank in the droplets and the deep ingrained lion's face regained its place. Gethin blinked away the holy tears and took a deep, shuddering breath of cool, sweet air.

When he came to his senses, he saw the shadow but faintly—no more than a memory, the remnants of dream upon the wall. Muttering words of power, he stood and crossed to the boy. His human hand touched the youth's lips. His deep, quiet voice said, "Open."

Gwrhyr's bottom lip sagged. The eagle claw reached in and removed the black pearl of Gwrhyr's ill words against perfection—the black pearl that had been the cause of so much woe and Gwrhyr's own downfall. The Hermit set it aside.

One arm lifted the Knight's head up, the other brought the bowl to his lips to drink. Some of it fell in the Knight's mouth—most dribbled down his loose blouse. Yet the bowl still brimmed. The Hermit lifted Gwrhyr until he was almost sitting, his proud head resting against the Hermit's shoulder. This time, the water all went down his throat and made him cough. Another draught, the young Knight stirred; a fourth, he moaned; a fifth, his lashes fluttered; a sixth, his skin grew warm; the last, he smiled—a shadow of a smile—and whispered, "My thanks," before drifting into a natural slumber.

Gethin lay the Knight down gently, backed away, and crossed himself. The pearl he saw in the light of the taper, pulling light into itself. With distaste, the Hermit picked it up and threw it in the bowl where it steamed, shrank, and dissolved. Without, the bells tolled the vigil hour and the turning of night to day.

Had the Hermit known how the news of Gwrhyr's recovery would affect the court, he most certainly would have left that very night. But he had kept aloof from men for twenty years and the common folk had let him go. The court had no such manners. By lauds, long before Gethin—exhausted after last night's battle—even thought to raise his head, several knocks came at his door. Five minutes they pounded and then began to shout, to rattle the latch and at last to make camp before his chamber. When Gethin woke, he found his doorway littered with courtiers and their servants—all with petitions, a few with gifts. He groaned and wiped the sleep from his eyes, which were hot and gritty.

The courtiers drew away at that, murmuring nervously between themselves. Exposed, the Hermit gnashed his wicked teeth and threw back his hood. A few courtiers fled, dropping gifts of precious gems as they went. Still others smiled and looked on him as though he were one of the curios in the menagerie. These made no effort to hide their remarks, commenting on his every aspect indifferently.

"Well?" the Hermit growled, fixing a particularly offensive lordling with his unnatural blue stare.

The lordling silenced at once and bowed his head to hide the sudden pallor of his emaciated cheeks.

The Hermit grinned—an awful sight. "Those of you who would follow me, do so at your own risk. I have not yet feasted." Again the smile, a flash of curved teeth—and then with the swirl of his hem and the flick of his powerful tail he left, striding down the hall with a hundred petitioners running to catch up.

For the next few days, the Hermit was kept busy hearing cases, solving some, and dismissing others. By the end of the first day, word came that the Hermit would make no love possets. Anyone who asked got only laughter for his pains. By morning, they knew that he could not be bought to kill. Those reckless enough to approach him on the matter all carried three light scores on their cheeks as a reminder of their impudence. Slowly the court sorted itself out, until only those with reasonable or sorrowful requests attempted to converse with the Hermit—and these received a kindly welcome.

By the sixth day of the Princess's flight, Gethin took to the Lily Spire for a semblance of solitude.

A week had passed when Findola dared to climb the tower and disturb the Hermit's peace. She walked boldly and if she shivered, only her inner heart knew. How should Findola hope to speak with a legend incarnate? And yet she had handled his eagle without harm, so she approached him.

"My lord," said she, waiting within the doorway of the Lily Spire until he should choose to turn and face her.

The man who should even now be a prince stirred himself, pressed a hand to his brow as though to wipe away the memory of azure sky and stream. "Lady," said he, "forgive me. I had not heard you come. You are…?"

"Findola, my lord. A handmaid."

"Ah, yes. Niamh spoke of you…." Again his voice grew distant, as though pulled back with the breeze of wind to the window, waiting, searching. He shook himself, rising to his height, and causing Findola to catch her breath. "What would you, lady?"

She hesitated only the briefest of moments before rushing all at once, "I have heard you have powers. If so, as it may be, my love Ewan is imprisoned within these very walls—was imprisoned when all thought fearfully of you. It was he who first spoke of you. Perhaps, if you would but say a word in the

King's ear, remind him that all griefs are not yet ended...."

"I see your thought, lady. And yet, I do not think you come on one business alone."

"I do not," Findola said, her dark cheeks blushing roses beneath the skin.

"You have had the courage to make one request—have courage for the other."

"I thank you, my lord. I fear for the Lady Elowen. She is not herself. Has not stirred from our mistress's old chambers since you came. Will neither speak to anyone, nor listen, nor be coaxed out of hiding. I fear, my lord, she will waste into a shadow."

The Hermit was silent for a time, his head bent, and his arms within his sleeves, like a monk at prayer. At last he said, "I will do what I can for your love. But for the lady, I fear her remedy will not lie in me."

"Then she is lost to me, sir. But for any pains you take I am grateful, although I can tender you no more than my devotion and gratitude."

"The care of your heart for the princess is payment enough," the Hermit said. "Well I think I can answer, now, who sent me word when danger first befell Niamh. It is I who owe a debt to you. I can promise nothing, but bring me to your friend and I shall look upon her. Wait for me after this evening's feast."

Findola nodded and left then, even as Gethin turned to look for one more glimpse out the window, to a landscape that did not hold his love.

That evening, somewhere between red wine and broth, the Hermit leaned over to his King and quietly inquired after the Squire Ewan. The next course was not even set before Gavron ordered an attendant to release the squire from the Magpie's Nest.

"Thou hast the right to chastise me once again," the King said, turning to the Hermit. The hours had tolled heavily on his proud features, scoring lines into his face and hands.

"No chastisement, Majesty," the Hermit said. "The Count's words sound like wisdom. They drip a slow venom. But I doubt the youth has come to any harm that the embraces of his lady will not cure. And as for the valour which he showed in the face of every adversity, perhaps his spirits might be greatly restored if, with his freedom, also came his spurs?"

The King smiled wearily. "May God shineth blessings down upon those who brought thee to our court. It will be a happy day when thou art crowned."

The Hermit bowed his head and whispered, "A happier day when I marry, Majesty."

"These are her rooms, my lord," Findola said some few hours later as they came before the door to Niamh's chamber.

The Hermit stopped. He knew this place—although through the eagle's eye. Aloud, he said, "Lead me on, lady."

Findola opened the door and called within to Elowen. All the drapes were closed and the room further shut off by a wall of thick tapestries. Within that darkness, Elowen sat so still that at first Gethin mistook her for another embroidered figure. On the great tapesty behind, a griffin reared as though about to descend bloodily upon her. Within her lap, a unicorn took shape in threads.

"Thus has she been since the princess fled," Findola said, not bothering to whisper. "She will neither speak nor listen. I think she suffers from a sort of madness."

"Her griefs have overwhelmed her," the Hermit replied, nodding. "I have seen such things at deaths of babes or sisters."

"They are cousins, my lord."

"There is a slight resemblance."

Findola looked curiously at him, but kept her peace. Perhaps she suspected such magics.

Gethin pulled at his golden beard. Then kneeling before the handmaid, he said, "Art thou well, lady?"

Elowen did not reply, although her eyes looked long at the Hermit with bitterness and dislike.

Biting back his pride, Gethin touched the edge of the embroidery, wondering what the black, hollow eye of the unicorn portended. But no sooner had he touched the white flank than he drew back as though sparked. The unicorn shifted within the threads and looked upward at him with eyes that reflected the moon. Lightning lanced the sable pool, reflecting past, present or future—he knew not. But he saw himself at a waters' edge, kneeling beside such a wonder as this creature, raising a claw and....

A drop of blood marred the tapestried unicorn's breast. The Hermit flinched and looked upward to where Elowen had pricked herself and then over her shoulder to the simple crucifix upon the wall. His own heart quailed, expanded, trembled between the man and the saint. What innocent blood would ransom the Princess before this tale had done?

Casually, he asked, "What dost thou sew?"

The corner of the cloth twitched away from him and the needle flashed angrily.

"Wilt thou not speak to me? Thou once did me a kindness, when thou didst bring my messenger to my lady."

The scissors snapped the black thread and said no more. Eyes met and saw there both unyielding grief. The Hermit blinked and rose to rejoin Findola.

"There is naught that I can do, lady," he said, bowing.

Findola blinked. She could not bear to look at Elowen. With a sad smile, she said, "Then she is dead to me. But for restoring my beloved, I thank you."

A tear, as black as Gwrhyr's pearl, slid down Findola's cheek as Gethin led her out of the room. They neither saw the same tear wend its way from Elowen's eye to stain the unicorn's eye blue as the boundless sea.

chapcer v

OW when Niamh had fled, she knew not whither she was bound, except away. The King had banished her and every moment spent within the castle pained her. Many times she saw the guards passing by her with lights—all for naught for they could not see her. When she saw the Captain her kin, Niamh called out to him, but he did not hear her.

The castle walls seemed oppressive and like to fall upon her at any moment. Almost she fancied she saw mortar flaking down, like unseasonable snow. So burnt was she that any coolness would be welcomed. She was still naked—but felt stifled in her charred skin. She longed to peel it from her face. She longed to scrape the ashes from her arms. She longed to scour herself until she became as white as bone, until she was naught but bone and far beyond the reach of fire.

Flitting from place to place, Niamh reached the outmost court—bustling with torches and hounds and men, hallooing out her name. To them, Niamh responded and rushed among them and clasped their hands. But they did not see her and they felt her no more than a man feels air.

All night she wandered about the castle, unable to escape until morning came and the gates opened. She caught moments of restless sleep in the swine pen, mud and dung her counterpane. With the dawn she fled, down the road, away from the Gwyrglánn, with no thought but to bury herself beneath the Ice Floes, to drown beneath the Giants' frozen blood and so slip beyond the world's very rim. Her father's star still shone over the Castell Gwyr and by that bright light, Niamh walked away.

Within the city, she tried to beg for food and shelter, but those she addressed seemed to suffer the same maladic virtue as the guards, saying when the Princess spoke, "What an awful wuthering within the chimney is there tonight!" And when she touched, "My, but I *am* cold! What Wydoemi sprite has visited me?"

Even Brenna Housewife thought no more of Niamh sleeping in her stable loft than supposing the boy she employed had been up to mischief. "Well, the young will have their day—and pay for it, as like as not," she said on the second morning of the Princess's flight.

Niamh had not travelled three days before she came to the Gwyrglánn. Her cracked skin recoiled even as her soul longed to reach out and plunge beneath those star-studded waves. "Not yet," she whispered to herself. "I cannot yet." And so she travelled south and west, leaving a wide berth around the castle and town, like a peregrin caught by its jesses. By the seventh day she came again to the Gwyrglánn—and again could not bear to touch the water, although all her heart yearned for its caress. Westward once more, Niamh followed the line of that great river to the Triton's Bridge, the white marble span from Maelgwenn to Cadwyr, whose belly reflected the golden river glow. But days walk slow as years when one has only scraps in one's belly and every cooling spray from the river burns more terribly than a night of fire.

By the end of a fortnight, the dreams began.

The Princess stared down the endless road to the ever distant Triton's Bridge. And before her stood all the men who had died for want of her. Even in death, their eyes shone full of madness as one by one they reached for her. Skeletal fingers plucked her scorched skin, drew out her golden hair, groped for purchase on her body that they might possess even the smallest part of her. And when the last had done with her, the ravens picked at her bones and the earth swallowed even those and the Gwyrglánn rose and washed away all memory of Niamh.

The Princess woke gasping and coughed into the dry earth, as though to rid herself of the dream.

But the dream came the next night and the night after that.

And so Niamh heaved her weary limbs forward and tried not to sleep. One night only she withstood the need to slumber—one day that seemed to bring her no closer to the Triton's Bridge.

When she slept, the dream had changed.

She stood alone on the parapet of Lyon's Paw while the court made merry in the bright-lit Great Hall. Wedding-trumpets sounded, and flutes and drums and viols played their wild dance. The groom was coming—Gethin coming. Niamh turned to look over the garlanded rooftops to the road where her beloved should surely come— but no dark-robed man saw she.

"He is coming! The bridegroom coming!" the minstrels cried each to each and pointed to the sky. Courtiers and servants tumbled from the Great Hall, hung over the balconies and looked upward where Gavron's star shone.

And Niamh looked upward, too, and saw no eagle flying, but her Father's star descending in a blaze of Titan's fury to consume her. She cried aloud and threw up her arms but she felt her breast lanced, as though by lightning. And when she looked behind, floating numbly through the twilit sky, she saw her body lie in ashes and in blood.

The Green Mountains loomed before her now, the tallest peak known as the Falcon's Folly where eyries of those wild birds dwelt safe from men who could not climb so high. The mountains seemed to call to her wandering mind, repeating the Count's half-truths: *"Vanity, vanity. Thinkest thou art as great as we? Hast thou touched the Sun at his zenith, felt his rosy heels brush thy head? Hast thou stood for a thousand years unchanged and unchangable? Art thou godlike, as we? Nay, thou art as like a worm. Blink but once and thou shalt perish."*

Dreams and waking blurred as the days or years or centuries wore on. Niamh subsisted on berries harvested from passing bushes and nuts fallen from the tree. Muddied water could she drink. Oft would she rise with hunger, smelling the morning bread baking or the venison smoking tanged with salt from some distant farmhouse. But though she had fallen, the Princess had not yet lost all herself. She would not yet stoop to stealing.

Not yet. *Thou art a worm.* Not yet.

A month passed before Niamh came to the Triton's Bridge. The dreams had not abated, although they had changed, granting the Princess no respite in which to accustom herself to any one horror. Few were the nights that she slept well—and even those nights she dreamt of times that had been and woke herself with crying. Which the worse? The nightmares were but prolongation of her miserable days. But the memories of laughter left her more bereft than before.

"It is too much for me," she sighed as the last, embattled remnants of the day faded into the night's starry mantle. "Sweet Jesu, it is too much."

That night she did not dream. And when she woke, with the sunrise glinting golden, the waking dream was sweet. Niamh rose and rubbed her eyes. Before her a single rose bloomed on a bush long past its summer season. The rose blushed not crimson nor yet ochre, but a pure and shining white like a sunburst caught and crystalised. Niamh reached out her gaunt arm to touch it and then cried out as her fingers encountered the morning dew that stang more sharply than the wicked sanguine thorns. Dewdrops scattered, bearing within their hearts dreams of things that were and things to come and things that should have been. One pool remained within the very heart of the flower and in this Niamh saw a face and heard a voice that salved her saddened soul.

"The four Hydoemi beneath, they are for the four corners of the world." Lady Marien *spoke, Niamh's governess half a world ago. Her face was lovely, dark, set with shimmering eyes. Her hands were as graceful as a dolphin's spray. She came from Sirena's court and many were the stories she had of the water spirits and their ways.*

In the dewdrop's depths, Niamh saw her own small face nuzzle into her tutor's shoulder and whisper, *"I am sure you are one of them."*

Lady Marien *laughed and stroked her charge's hair. "A Hydoema, Princess?*

You flatter me. But I shall tell you who the four beneath the bridge are. Look at the two mermen on the farther side, north and west. Can you see them? The one on the right, with the great beard flowing over his breast and the bridge held on one shoulder, that is the mightiest of all Day's making. That is Yurë and his coat is Frost. Beside Yurë, with his arms upraised, that is Ydulhain, his brother and Lord of Waterfalls. And the two we cannot see so well, those are ladies, their wives—Sylenn, Queen of Rains, which is why the water flows through her fingers, and Sylvaenn of the Deeps, who looks at her reflection. We shall see them better once we have crossed."

"And the others?" Niamh of memory asked.

"You should know those, Princess. Or else my teaching has been for naught!" Lady Marien coughed into her handkerchief, closing it tightly within her hand to hide the blood. But Niamh had seen, even then, although a girl of seven did not know what it portended. *"But I shall aid you. On the other side are Hintev and Voro."*

"Earth and Air."

"Just so."

"Then these must be Baone and Sylenn again."

"Bravo, well done, my love!"

"Way! Way for the King and Queen!" the herald on the carriage before theirs called, making the dewdrop waver. Niamh of memory poked her nose outside the drapes before her. Already subjects lined the river—both on land and in small boats. Niamh could glimpse her mother's white arm reaching out the window and fancied she could see the Fairy's smile. Her father had ridden on his charger, flanked by Llewellyn and Mackelwy. Donell's guards had surrounded them all. How young they looked!

"We shall be over in a moment," Lady Marien had said. "Are you brave enough?"

Niamh of memory nodded. Lady Marien coughed.

"Are you afraid?" Niamh of memory asked.

"Yes," the Princess of the moment answered.

The Lady Marien only said, *"I am always afraid. But I shall not fear the long journey if I know my brave little Princess will not!"*

And the Lady turned her head and looked at the Princess and smiled all the warmth of a winter morning tucked safe beneath the counterpane.

The image faded, grew dark, and reflected only Niamh. The Princess looked upward to the Triton's bridge, a mile distant. Her heart lifted. She would cross it. She would not fear. Reaching forward, despite the terrible dew that steamed as soon as it touched her skin, the Princess plucked the rose and put it in her hair and set out across the Triton's Bridge.

A Maelgwenn farmgirl who had been courted by Cadwyr forester three years now, saw the white rose lift itself from the bush and float across the Triton's Bridge into the heart of her suitor's home. Pausing only long enough to wipe her hands upon her apron, run inside and ask her Father's blessing and kiss her Mother and seven sisters farewell, she followed the rose across the bridge and to her beloved's house where that evening they were wed.

And when the forester asked which of his charms had finally won her hard-got heart, she replied that no charms of his had won her, but the intercession of the Heavenly.

That evening, curled up beneath one of the innumerable firs that gave the Green Mountains its name, Niamh held the white rose within her hands and gazed into its depths as she trod the border of sleeping and awake.

Niamh turned nine when Lady Marien left. Her governess's dark cheeks had grown pale, and her coughing worse. "I shall cross the Triton's Bridge without you," she had said over Niamh's girlish tears. "And then a longer bridge that even my brave little Princess cannot cross with me."

Findola held Niamh's gloved hand as Donell entered with his daughter.

"Princess," the Captain said—and how careless he looked as he bowed to her! Niamh had only to wear a veil in those days and any might converse with her. "The loss of the Lady Marien can never be replaced. But I hope you may allow your cousin, the Lady Elowen, to join your household. She is a few years your senior and may aid your studies."

Niamh looked to her tutor, as she did with every decision. But Lady Marien shook her head and said, "This, I cannot teach you. You must choose for yourself."

"Then I should be honoured to have thee in my household, cousin," Niamh of memory said, very gravely for a girl of nine, much in awe of her distant cousin, "although thou mightest command one of thine own, if thou desirest."

Elowen, a beauty even at the gawky age of eleven, curtsied deeply, saying, "Believe me, Princess, I desire nothing else but to serve you." And the fierce joy in her eyes had dried a little of Niamh's tears.

As long as the Princess held the white rose, no harm came to her, either waking or asleep. Where'er she walked, the beasts that roamed those mountains kept a distance from her and even timid animals, too—for perhaps they saw with a truer, unfallen sight what the Princess bore with her, or what bore the Princess. Foresters or hunters she passed, even if three miles from her, found their daily work prosperous, and those hardy women who lived upon the

56

sloping foothills found their backs eased as well as their anxieties. Couples newly married—including the Maelgwenn farmgirl and the Cadwyr forester— were blessed with children, and those children themselves who romped through the tangled woods and criss-crossed Niamh's footprints, grew straight and strong and keen-eyed and wise.

Goodness still flowed from the Princess, but sapped now and failing with each step she took. So great a height had she fallen from, that even the descent was graceful, as a man buoyed for a while on warm winds.

But goodness and beauty and safe-keeping from intrusive dreams are not food to fill a starving belly. Niamh, already a fading shadow of the glory she had been, became a shadow of even that, hollow-eyed and wretched in body. Had any been able to see her, they should have thought her a sapling with legs, a monster neither human nor elemental.

Long she looked into the rose's heart, to that pool of water that never fell upon the rich loam ground. Long she looked and saw the sweet and sad and merry of her life. Long she looked and hungered.

"I cannot do it," she whispered one night, doubled upon herself, twiggy fingers caught in snarled hair. "I am not whom once I was. I do not think I can return. I am already dead, have failed my Father. To die in this wilderness were but to make real what is real in truth.

"And," she continued, looking upward at the sky that pulled ever farther from her, "it is a small thing but noble to die without doing greater wrong than hath been done. Is it not?"

The stars did not answer her.

Niamh shuddered and wrapped her arms around her belly. The rose lay before her bony knees, but showed no solace tonight—only Niamh's haggard reflection.

The sweet smell of a wood fire drifted down the mountain like a second fog. The Princess smelt it and her hunger worsened.

"Would that *thou* wert edible!" she cried to the white rose. "Were the flesh of a man offered me now, I think I should eat it. Were blood my only drink, I should receive it."

The smoke bore to her promise of bacon and flat cakes. Niamh covered her mouth with her hands, bit her thumb and rocked back and forth as her soul and her hunger warred. The smell of sweet apples and raisins joined the aerial feast and Niamh stood, groping her way over the rocks and fallen branches, between low bushes and around the sharp-pointed firs, following the scent until she came to the house nestled in the hillside.

Fat pigs trotted within an enclosure beside a shed for roosting hens. Warm, honey-light spilt out from under the door along with the rise and fall of varied voices. A barrel of late apples stood beside the house.

Niamh bit her lip and reached for one of them.

The door opened. A youth, broad and newly-bearded, stepped out and looked at her. Through her. Did not see her.

Behind him, Niamh glimpsed a table modestly set, a father bent over his whittling, a great black dog upon his feet, and a mother, her hair caught up in falling braids, bring a skillet of fatty ham to the table. A daughter scraped the last of scrambled eggs onto the central plate while three other children ran about and laughed. The father scooped up the littlest, a boy of maybe six and blew hard upon his neck to make the child squeal with delight.

Such a sight deepened the Princess's hunger, but not for food.

The youth turned his head to look inside and said, "I see naught. P'raps 'twas some beast slithering through the trees."

The father and mother exchanged a glance and the father whispered, "No. The Wolf would not venture here. We have not tempted him." Raising his voice, the father said, "Then let you come in, Kieran." To which the mother added, "With those apples, mind!"

The youth, Kieran, nodded and ambled down the wooden steps to where Niamh stood, her hand still outstretched. As he neared the Princess, he paused and looked once more at her, although he did not see her. Then slowly, with arms before him like a blind man, he stepped closer and whispered, "Who is there?"

Niamh answered, "One who hungers."

But her words sounded like the last notes of an owl, and so Kieran said again, "Who is there?" The words *I have dreamt of thee* lingered twined within his meaning.

"No," Niamh said and took a step away. Already she saw the hopeless madness spark in the youth's eyes.

Still he advanced, helpless, longing. Niamh took up an apple and threw it so that it crashed against the wooden house. Kieran shook his head and looked after the apple, astonished that one had rolled so far from its barrel. He went to it, stooped, and picked it up from the earth, rubbing the dirt from its sleek sides—heedless of Niamh who ran, an apple in each thieving hand, back to the place where she had left the white rose.

Twigs cracked and branches quivered as Niamh fled, marking an easy path for Kieran to follow. But he did not go beyond the boundary of his land, marked by two grand spruces that stood so close they kissed. He seemed to see a dying fire race between the woods, taking his heart with it.

That night, he went in to his family. The next day, Kieran tracked the land and found a withering white rose petal between two apple cores. He took up the velvet leaf and held it between his callused fingers and from that day forth he wandered.

The moon rose a full world away from that night on. The woods were as dark as those hedged in by her Father and the evenings held no stars. Niamh kept to the high paths, away from the valleys where the people dwelt and rivulets ran from the Gwyrglánn. When she hungered, she followed the fires, like a dog that tracks a scent, and took what she desired. The mountains rose ever upward. The Princess did not. The white rose crumbled in her hand. Its pool dissolved, its petals browned and curled inward. No longer did she dream of whom she had been—she did not dream at all. No longer did she wonder whether she should take, but took with no remorse. Her conscience withered with the rose, browned along the edges. She spoke but seldom now. No man could hear her, she knew. And that which she would say to herself would gall. Her skin fleshed out, grew—if not healthy, then not stick-thin—but her eyes remained hollow. And so she did not see when a shadow followed her on padded feet, through the ancient pines.

"Soot girl! Soot girl!"

Niamh whirled to see who addressed her and found a boy a few years her junior, dressed in bright silk rags with a chipped gold loop through his ear.

"Do you call me?" Niamh breathed, unable to believe her fortune.

"Unless there is someone else as black as sin, I do call thee." And he grinned in such a manner that Niamh remembered her nakedness and curled upon the ground to hide herself, although her skin was so charred that it was like its own clothing, revealing nothing.

"Art thou hungry, soot girl?" the impudent boy asked, holding out a piece of old bread.

"Oh! Yes!" Niamh cried and reached for it.

But the boy danced away, taunting, "Come for it, soot girl! Dance for thy food! Come after me, if thou hungrest!"

So Niamh lunged after, covering her breasts with one arm and reaching for the food with the other, but the boy was always too quick. Downward they danced, into another copse of trees, where a band of the boy's family had made camp. As they neared, Niamh held back, for even in her altered state—or perhaps because of it—she saw that these men were evil.

"Why dost thou stop, soot girl?" the boy asked. "Dost thou not hunger?"

"More than thou canst know," said the Princess and turned on him baleful, starving eyes that shone with something of her former beauty and caused the youth to flinch.

But the moment passed and the boy grabbed Niamh's singed arm and drew her protesting into their band.

"See what I have brought!" he crowed, dragging Niamh before the oldest and most wicked of all the men. His teeth were strong and yellow, like a wolf's, and his eyes were pinpricks of infernal flame.

"What *hast* thou brought, villain? Is she for eating or for whoring? She seemeth well done for the first!"

"She is mine, old man, and I long to feed her and keep her, for she amuseth me—she is so ugly!"

"Wretch! Thou hast made her blush and that fire stirrreth my own. Give her here."

"No!" the boy cried. "For thou hast my pony for thy tent and my sparrow for thy dinner. Wicked man, she is mine!"

So saying, he pranced away with Niamh in tow to the other side of the fire and made her sit near him, so he could touch her. "How thin thou art!" he exclaimed. "I can see all thy ribs! 'Struth! Thou art so thin, I wonder if thou hast any blood within thee. I shall prick thee and discover."

"Without my bread?" the Princess asked.

"If thou canst bleed, I shall feed thee. If thou canst not, I'll not waste my bread!"

Thus withdrawing his knife, he pricked her just between the ribs. Two drops of blood fell down, like twin tears, and the boy gasped in awe.

"Thou *art* flesh!" he yelped.

"My bread!" the Princess cried.

To which he replied, "Tomorrow. Good night, soot girl."

That night she slept alone, outside the boy's tent. The dying flower she held cupped in one hand. Twice she tried to slip away, but there was always a guard before her who shook his inky curls and slid daggers into his hands from up his silken sleeves. When she woke, the boy made her dance for her supper, holding bits of bread always just out of her reach. The people of his band laughed, the old man most of all, as she cavorted and lunged after the boy. Her eyes flit everywhere for a way out but whether the camp woke or slept, wicked looking men, with curved swords at their waists, stood always, always sentry.

On the third day, Niamh woke to the boy's rough hand upon her shoulder. "Take this, soot girl," he said, throwing her the remains of an apple core. "We are going hunting and I am going with them!"

"What do you hunt?" Niamh said, her mouth full of apple seeds.

"What we always do: we hunt people," he said, grinning at her round, horrified eyes. The dagger appeared in his hand and nicked her ribs twice. "I did not mark thee yestere'en, I forgot. But thou hast been mine three days, and I shall mark thee to remember. My goat hath five hundred marks upon her, but her hair mostly covers it. Do not cover thine—I like to see how long I have kept thee. If thou dost not flee, soot girl, I shall not mark thee tomorrow, but wait to give thee two nicks again."

He stood back thoughtfully, pouting his lips and touching the dagger absently to his round cheek. Then, swift as a sparrow, he bent down and kissed her lips. "Paugh!" he cried, wiping them on his dirty sleeve. "Thou tastest like ashes and not sweet at all! For that, I shall mark thee!" and the dagger came down once again, hitting Niamh's upraised arm, and drawing a jagged line across the skin. "I should mark thee twice for that impudence, soot girl. Thou shalt get naught to eat tonight!"

With that, he strode off, and soon after the hunt left, silent as wolves on the prowl. Long time they were gone, but the women—harder than the men, like rocks made to move and talk—proved no less able guards and Niamh found herself battered from one task to another.

"I have wandered into Hell!" she groaned, as another granite fist knocked her about the head.

Flint eyes met hers and did not blink. A voice like gravel said, "More than thou couldst know."

That evening, as the men returned with the spoils of their hunt—salted venison, squared logs, two girls and a boy among the spoils—Niamh huddled hungry, within the shadows, and prayed for death to come.

The old man did not return with the hunt, but came as the darkness deepened—the only indication that dusk had fallen in those oppressive woods. Several dogs, long lanky rangers, lay here and there gnawing on old bones. But one, grey and large enough to be a wolf, slipped in among the fire crackle as stealthily as night stole upon the forest. No sentry stopped him. They stood aside and let him pass and women moved their mountainous forms when he approached. The wolf padded up to the old man's cushion and howled—and as he howled he rose and shifted, until the old man stood before them, the yellow glow of his eyes dwindling to their pinpricks.

"Sleep, all," he said. "Ye deserve your rest and the enjoyment of your goods." The two stolen girls clung to each other, but when Niamh moved to comfort them, the boy's dagger shivered out of its sheath. The old man continued, caring little for the small intrigues of his court. "I shall watch tonight, for I have tasted man flesh and feel the strength of the gods upon me." And his eyes rested on Niamh, with a smile like the moon in waxing.

One by one, the men and women, guards and prisoners alike retired to their tents to sleep. But Niamh thought only of escape—and perhaps her prayers were heard, for soon after the wolf-man wandered away, with never another glance at the fallen Princess. Unsteadily, she stood, slipping a little on the uneven earth, cradling the last few petals of the white rose to her breast. Creeping forward to the nearest lane of trees, she espied within the heart of the dying bonfire a whole blackened loaf of bread.

"I shall take it without payment," she thought, matching her actions to her words. "It is evil to steal, but perhaps not so evil to steal from evil men." Her hand reached through the flames and her fingers closed upon the bread. But before she could pull it out again, she heard a voice behind her speak.

"Dost thou know the price? Art thou willing to pay it?"

Niamh whirled, the loaf in her hand. Her eyes searched the darkness, and at last found the soulless eyes of the wolf-man who had desired her. "I owe thee nothing," Niamh said.

The man shrugged. "I could take thee now, but thou art vile. Take the bread. Thou wilt get no good from it."

Niamh's heart quailed, and she knew not what to do. Even as she clutched the bread to her bosom, she felt her soul shifting to match her skin. The white rose glowed briefly, feebly to combat the powers that pressed upon her. Quavering, she whispered, "What are its properties that thou art eager to part with it to one whom thou despisest?"

He answered, with a flash of his yellow teeth, "However much thou consumest, it shalt never dwindle. But every bite shalt make thee hunger for more. And that hunger shalt drive thee to deeds now abominable in thy sight. That is its price. Do what thou wilt. I care not. If thou fleest, then I shall be revenged upon the boy. If thou stayest, I shall have thee by and by."

Then, suddenly, he was beside her, circling like a hound about a bitch. "Thou mightest have taken thy liberty long ago, Princess. We are ever thine to command, for even we cannot gainsay will."

Niamh started, clutching the bread and rose to her breast like a bit of ragged silk.

The man laughed, not unkindly and touched the marks upon her side and arm. "Didst thou think I could not know, I who roam keen-eared and unseen among men? I who once ruled thy kind? Thou mightest have left us or had us killed hadst thou commanded it, but I see thou art a fool, though not of thine own devising. I shall give thee counsel, Princess, and thou wouldst do well to heed me, though I am a very devil.

"*Trust no one*," he whispered in her ear, with a nip upon the lobe. "We are none of us saints and all comes to betrayal in the end." He leapt back and gave a mocking bow. "But go thy ways, Princess. We may meet anon."

The Princess took a few steps forward, glancing frequently over her shoulder to where the old man stood behind the undying flames. A wail rose from the nearest tent—a stolen girl's pained whimper. Despite her terror, Niamh turned around and said, "Thou sayest I might have commanded in this place and I shall test the mettle of that now. Thy men didst steal three of my subjects today. They shall come with me."

The fire burnt black at its heart, before the old man replied. "Trust no one, Princess, or thou mayest leave by the longest road from which no man retur-

neth." Still, Niamh did not yet flee and so he amended, "We found them all three trysting, Princess. No one cometh to us but those who allow it—not even thee."

The girl's wail went up again and Niamh shuddered but held firm. "Perhaps it is as thou claimest. Perhaps those whom thou hast caught deserve their fate. But though thou art the Devil himself, thou art bound to obey a higher law. What wouldst thou for their freedom?"

"All three? Thy very life, Princess. But for one, the least blameless—that rose which thou hast kept concealed."

Niamh looked down upon the white rose that glowed in slow pulsations. "Thou shalt release her tonight?" she asked.

The Wolf King nodded.

"Then I shall bargain with thee, although it cost my soul."

So saying, she held out the fragile flower that shone as brilliantly as a star within her palm. But before he could take it, to rend it or swallow it or cast it in the fire, a strong wind blew and carried it upwards to the heavens where it remains fixed even to this very day.

The Wolf King snarled. "Thou shalt pay with thy life!" And with that, he crouched and leapt through the very flame, emerging as the wolf on the other side.

Clutching the bread to her bosom, Niamh fled, the laughter of the old man trailing her.

chapter vi

he moon waxed, but no news came of the Princess and the bride-groom grew impatient. And on the ninth day of his stay, the Hermit approached the Queen declaring that he would go.

"Whither shalt thou?" Rhianna asked.

He shrugged, smiling fondly. Already, his features had softened, or so it seemed to the Queen, whose own hope, entrusted so fully to this strange man, informed her sight.

"Where'er the Princess shalt lead me. Only one direction I do not believe she wilt choose—to the West where the sun sets into his earthly bed. For I fear the Count changed more than her appearance, but the very essence of herself. He has planted a briar among roses, although the image is worn and crude. No less so is the Count's vile seed: a canker, that can birth only monster, and claw outwards from her belly in the final gestation.

"This it was which first barred my vision—for we had thought the Count had only altered her skin, not her soul. Recalling her beauty, we forgot her goodness. She hath far to fall, and this hope sustains me: she may be recovered. But I speak to no purpose other than to salve my soul for the trial. Great words are but a little balm."

"And I have worse words ere thou goest: thus speak I in poniards," the Queen said. "Keep vigil. We have late heard from our cousin, the Captain, that his guards who watch the treacherous Count have, despite their wills which are formidable, found themselves lulled into a sort of waking sleep. Were they less than what they are, were they common or foolish, or mercenary as some in straits employ, then should we count them only lazy, or carousers, liars, drunks or cowards, and dismiss them from their posts.

"But the men who guard the Count are the best of all our men. And as none of those men is base, so well you can measure their superiority. Yet they feel their minds grow blank, their vision wander, their ears close, their arms go slack. To all outward appearances, they look as ever, but to speak to one under such a spell hath no effect, although the merest touch may bringeth another out of reverie. And although it gladdeneth my heart to relate that only twice did the guards succumb—and each time no worse conclusion than embarrassment when relieved by the next watch—still it is reported that it groweth harder daily to resist. The guards, sir, must shift themselves upon the hour! Soon they shall run ragged from anxiety and lack of sleep, for as soon as one feeleth even the slightest laxity, he runneth for his relief—and so they are constantly waking each other up."

"While the Count makes not a motion?" the Hermit hazarded.

The Queen nodded. "Thou hast hit upon the very point. The Count aimeth for no less than madness."

"And still the King will not have him killed?"

"Thou saidest thyself a man might mendeth his ways."

"Yet have a care, lady. For 'might' is a tenuous string to lead a hope upon."

"If that were so," said she, "I should wonder at thee going forth at all. For it seemeth to me more perilous than a 'might be.'"

At this the Hermit laughed and took Rhianna's hand in his human one. "Thus am I justly chastened! Sought I to match wits with you, lady? Nay! Let all men beware their pride when near my lady's presence!"

So saying, he bowed over her hand. And it seemed to Rhianna that his tawny mane had grown more thick and golden.

Despite his light words, what Rhianna had expressed concerning the Count and the guards troubled the Hermit greatly—more than he cared to reveal. He asked for an audience with the captive not an hour later although his heart was loath—for he feared that bars would not constrain his ire and that the Count should be found with heart torn out. The seeing did nothing to aid the Hermit. He found the Count resting peacefully on his pallet, his arm thrown over his head, exposing the gentle curve of his neck.

The Hermit bade the guards move just out of hearing, although not out of sight, as a measure against his baser instincts. So he stood, his hands within his sleeves and his cowl pulled over his features. For some minutes they remained thus, silent although taut, waiting for the other to break.

"Do you come for my confession, that you stand so still and shrouded?" the Count said at last with no movement visible but the subtle pullings on his throat's sleek lines.

"Of a sort," the Hermit replied. No more was said, but that the Count rolled onto his back and yawned and some said he winked his eye from under his arm. At length the Hermit said, "I come to learn where the Princess might have fled."

"Ah, sweet bestiality. Such passion. It must make Gavron's girlish heart squeal with pride. Moreso if he knew how well your lusts extended to his harlot Queen...."

But the Count could say no more, for the Hermit rent the bars and was even now advancing on the Count, in time to the guards' shouts of alarm. Catching the Count up by the throat with his human arm, the Hermit did no more but to snarl, his black lion's lip curling upwards to his black nose. In the dim light of the cell, his pointed teeth glimmered and lengthened with every passing minute. Beneath his robe, his wings and tail shifted restlessly, straining against the thin material and poking through at the bottom. "I will hear no more word against their Majesties from *your* foul lips. Where is the Princess?"

"I have already been questioned," the Count gasped. "Ask thy betters."

The Hermit's human hand shifted, the fingertips became leathery, and the blunt nails sharpened to small talons. But the pressure upon the Count's throat did not increase, as though the Hermit fought against himself. He whispered, "You are within an inch of your life."

"Take it."

"Has she gone north?"

"*Take it!*"

"East!"

"Kill me—you long to anyway."

"*South!* Say the word and I shall spare you."

The Count remained mute.

"To the Wood then? Speak, God help you!"

But the Count only grinned affably. "Did you woo Niamh this roughly? No wonder she longed to please you."

It could not be helped. Three scratches scored the Count's pale chest, even as the Hermit's robe split with his mighty wings' *snap*, revealing leonine breast and feathered back. Beneath the kilted tatters of his robe, his tail thrashed so violently as to do harm to the stony walls.

"Get back!" the Hermit roared to the nervous guards. "One step nearer and I cannot account for my actions!" Then turning to the smiling Count, he said, "You proud, stupid, foolish man! See where your vanity has got you! Do you long for a sudden, unshriven death? Do you seek it at *my* weak hands, to bring me down with you? Thank God I've some shred of whom I once was to ward me gainst your promptings. Beware your pride, you wretched worm. It is turning you into a grotesque, although none yet can perceive it."

With that he threw the Count onto the meagre bed and left with a contemptuous swish of his tail. And all the while the Count made not a move, but lay furious impotent on his back, while the Hermit fled to some secluded room and wept blood.

One last observance courtesy required and this the most painful of all, for Gavron could not be consoled and his resolve to bear through only worsened his grief. His aspect haggard and his mien grim, the King greeted the Hermit like a man of legend, standing and bidding the Hermit also to rise.

"Sir, God grant thee grace and every good thing. We are told thou meanest to journey after our daughter."

"I do," said the Hermit in a low rasp. He had been clothed again in a friar's robes by the Queen and his whiskers were sanguine tinged. "I must, for reasons manifold. Although I am not worthy of the task—I pray the task shall make me so."

"It is well and noble to continue the task," Gavron answered. "But we are not tyrants to command for our own pleasures. When first we solicited thee, we requested and did not demand. And when thou asked our reasons, we held nothing from thee, nor did we order thee upon that second occasion. Neither do we lay any burthen upon thee now. Out of kindness, thou humoured thy liege to journey here and once here found thyself, thy bride, and ourselves betrayed. 'Twould be betrayal of another sort to now command thee to put thyself in peril. No contract signed, no vows exchanged, nothing shall bind thee but thyself.

"And," the King said, raising one hand when the Hermit would protest, "neither shall I hear of oaths sworn in the very fist of passion, nor geas laid in the same. I hope," Gavron said with a rueful grin, "I use my power gently and with occasional good wisdom—although the events of ten days argue against twice many years of reign. But not all sorrows must be shared. Therefore, we decree with the full weight of our crown and authority, the breaking of all bonds upon thee in this matter. Duncan, thou are free."

"Bind me once again, sire," the Hermit cried, sinking to his knees. "Or, if you will not, believe that I do take up all cords again. Your daughter's salvation and my own hang in the balance of this vow. I shall not be swayed."

"Peace, friend!" Gavron exclaimed. "Be not too hasty! Consider the road before thee, the dangers and the costs!"

"Full well I know them, sire, and still take upon me this quest. Do not deny me twice."

"How swelleth my heart with gratitude and unshed tears, my mouth refuseth to say." Quitting his throne, the King went on one knee before the bowed Hermit, until they were of a height. "My eloquence abandoneth me, yet my resolve doth not. I speak to thee as a father to a headstrong son and bid thee to heed me. Do not now take vows to bind thee to eternity. Save those words for weighty, joyful matters; reserve them for thy nuptial hour, which thou shalt find more needful when the unseen daily trials come. But if thou must needs vow, then do so daily, and not yet 'til everlasting."

"I shall be swayed," the Hermit said. "And now, having vowed for the day, I shall set forth. Your Majesty is too good, too grief-ridden to know that your grief is shared by all willingly. Now, sire, please stand. 'Tis not seemly you should be so humbled."

"Stand with me," Gavron said. "Thus am I content."

The King and Queen and all the court accompanied the Hermit to the outer gate for their last parting. So it always is with guests whom one loves—although the need be great, the parting brings too much sorrow. So too the King and Queen had a final gift for the Hermit that would guide him well.

"There are songs," said Rhianna, "of such beauty and power that they have been entrusted only to a few and even those have been divided seven ways after being divided thrice within the mystical spheres. Some, sages know from their travels. And these we have heard exist: the songs of wind and water, of the soughing Wydoemi and their frolicsome cousins, the Hydoemi. Dwarves, even, report the songs of the earth—the Vertae. But salamanders are silent and little do we hear of the fire's voice, for their tongue is weird to human ears.

"But I have travelled everywhere and know a stranger truth: that songs may be mingled and their properties translated. The Pyrae have a song of longing, which the fire of all blood singeth but cannot say. The sea a similar song in words of sweeter sentiment. A concoction of these both we give thee—strong yet still diluted—that thou mayest bear it with thee. Sing it and thou shalt be guided to Niamh as long as thy heart is pure. And if she hear it and hath any part of herself left, she wilt answer. If she heareth it and still turneth away, then let us all grieve, for our daughter shalt be dead."

Rhianna

Then Rhianna lifted her voice and sang, high and sweet like water washing on the shore:

> Wander, wander I—
> Over earth and sea,
> Over sea and sky, I
>
> Fly.

Then Gavron raised his voice and sang the lover's part, twined within his bride's song:

> Where hast thou gone, my lady love?
> O, where o'er the earth hast thou gone?
> I have been to the mountains,
> I have delved in the sea,
> I have sung to the air, "Sweet love, come to me."

Rhianna responded, her eyes grown distant with memory:

I have been to the mountains,
I have delved in the sea,
I have flown through the air,
I have not found thee.

I am here, I am hidden,
In the heart of the flame.
Nor wander, nor flee,
Shouldst thou call my name.

Thus they concluded with hands entwined, and eyes more joyful than they had been for a long while. Turning as one to the Hermit, they asked if he could recall the words and tune.

"Aye, both," said he. "But I am frankly amazed—I had thought a song of such power should require complexities beyond my skill."

"The most powerful things are often the simplest," said Gavron heartily. "Hast thou not known when one word overcame a host of babble?"

"But now we have stayed thee overmuch," Rhianna said. "Good Duncan, blessings be with thee, and may it please Heaven we meet again and soon, in happier circumstances."

So saying, she bent forward and kissed the Hermit's brow. After many bows and backward glances the Hermit left, rising upon his mighty wings much to the consternation and amazement of all.

All the court attended the parting save one. The Count lay under lock and key, and two guards attended him. The watch that day had fallen to young Liam, who had proved the least susceptible to the Count's spell, although that resistance felt little enough some nights. With him stood another guard named Ceallach, an older war-horse who had also proved his mettle. They were, while the court followed the Hermit and their Sovereigns to the gates, much tempted by the Count's continual unseen barrage and were even on the point of falling when they heard the Queen's voice and then the King's raised in song.

How beauty affects men's souls! At once, Liam and his companion woke, as though all their lives they had slept and only now thought to blink. They looked at one another in wonder, and strained to hear the joyful chords of King and Queen combined. But the Count, whose eyes had been growing and glowing with a cruel, hungry glee, shrieked and covered his ears and writhed, until the song ended. Then he lay panting, curled and perspiring like a newborn.

Liam could not forbear to laugh and exclaim, "How should you like to meet the Princess *now*, sirrah? That were but a tenth, if that, of the loveliness *you* drove out! But for all that, I cannot help but pity you for it was my burden to see your shadow first."

"Do you speak of pity?" Ceallach said. "Though my heart be lifted now, I can feel none for him. But his judgement is not my doom, so he may have no fear of me!"

"You may fear *him*," Liam said, jerking his thumb to where the sad Count lay. "If you cannot pity him, you will soon dream of retribution—and who is there to relieve you? The Captain and all the men are with the King."

"Warn me of dreams! No doubt you dream of releasing him! Paugh—keep your pity. It weakens the mind against attack."

"Say rather it strengthens me," young Liam whispered, as his companion settled back to his customed position. "Poor fool, he does not know mercy. It is the only dream he does not think to send me."

In twos and in threes the court dispersed their separate ways, their thoughts as varied as their courses. The Hermit's leavetaking sent the last poetry and even all prose with him and the court was left to stutter conversation, to make do with commonplaces, to live no more than human. Together, Findola and Pwll walked to the Lesser Labyrinth, supporting Ewan between them—for he had not wholly recovered his spirits.

"And so our part is ended," Pwll said, helping Ewan onto a low bench bedecked with morning-glories.

Findola took the place beside her beloved, their fingers quietly clasping. "Are you saddened?" she asked.

Pwll smiled and ran his hand through his hair. "Saddened? Aye, a little. For our part is done, yet not *all* is done." And he looked northward, as though he could see through the intervening buildings and to the royal wing where Elowen remained self-imprisoned.

Ewan laughed—a cough, merely. He had been well cared for in the Magpie's Nest, but with the good Father's attention wholly devoted to Gwrhyr and Gwendolyn, the squire's own small fever went all but unnoticed. He had cursed the cold but once upon his release, for he must put off Findola's kisses for a time. Aloud, he said, "My lord is never happy unless he has some quest! Why, I have known him to brave the menagerie when a lady he fancied dropped her handkerchief among the tygers! And that is but one of a number. Indeed, my dear friend, I do wonder if you would rather I were still under lock and key and my reprieve require something greater than a word dropped in the King's ear at supper."

"How are you with the bow?" Findola asked, picking a late white rose in bloom and tossing it to her sometime champion.

"I am no Guilian," Pwll replied. "But truly Ewan, I would not have you suffer again for all the world. *You*, my lord Houndshelm, are the greatest quest a man could desire! Indeed, for such a gentle disposition, you have an amazing number of enemies, the extermination of which allows me ample opportunities for heroics."

"If the women do not claim your blood first," Ewan said. And then immediately repented of it, for both Findola and Pwll now looked northward and it seemed to the squire that the shadow of Elowen clung to both their faces.

"Thou art in the right, brother," Pwll said softly. Unnoticed, the late rose petals sifted to the Labyrinth floor—the simple sign of hope, forgotten.

Within the dungeons, an hour passed uneventfully. Liam and his companion kept silent watch, while the Count slept. But as dusk drew on and every minute took the Hermit further from the Castle, they began to feel weary and knew that the Count had regained himself enough to once again torment them.

"Quick, boy," Ceallach cried, rubbing his eyes, and leaning heavily upon the bars. "Call for relief! If I move, I shall surely fall. Quickly!"

Liam nodded and wrenched his mind into wakefulness with that awful mental crack, like standing up too quickly after drinking wine that is too strong. He tottered down the hall calling for the other guards—but no one answered. Perhaps his voice was too faint, or the Count's will too strong. Perhaps someone greater stopped up the guards' ears—it may be so. Within sight of their quarters, Liam fell to his knees, calling for aid one last time. Alas! Not one head turned towards him— they were all merry from hearing the song. From behind, Liam thought he heard his own named called. Turning, he stumbled back through the corridors, at once resisting and impatient, for every step felt heavy with black sorcery.

When at last he came to where the Count was kept, the young man found his companion fallen and the Count sitting pleasantly upon his pallet—the setting sun warming him, so that he seemed haloed and quite kindly.

But Liam had been chosen for such a moment as this, and squinting he demanded, "Where is your shadow?"

The Count smiled with a twitch of lip and eye. "Foolish boy, dost thou seek it for thyself? What if I told thee I had swallowed it so thou couldst not see it, for it is within me? Or what if I told thee I had sent it for to seek the Princess?"

"Foul man! Well I know evilness begets itself. Nor would it surprise me to learn both are true. You speak doubly, and nothing to the point."

"Very well. What if I said it wast behind thee?"

With a crash, Liam reeled against the bars, tearing at his throat which invisible hands held captive.

"Thou art quite right, young Liam," the Count continued pleasantly, as the boy thrashed before him. "Shadow begetteth shadow and all three my bidding do." He waved his hand and Liam collapsed, panting beside the fallen companion. The Count rose and paced to where Liam lay, shook his greying head and crouched until their eyes met. "Thou alone resisteth me," the Count said, touching Liam's hot cheeks with slim, cold fingers. "Why, I wonder, and how? Hath not Niamh fallen? And she twice thou. Did she not madden my only son? Doth she not grip the boorish Hermit, although he never saw her? But not thou of common birth. Tell me, why didst thou not sue for the Princess's hand? I lief she hadst rather a boy than a monster—and Gavron wisheth too. Come, what is it? Wert thou ashamed?"

"You mistake yourself," Liam spat. "Spare your idle flatteries—you cannot know my faults, nor my sometime victories. But I shall scream now for the guards and even if you stop me, they shall come presently, for our watch ended with the passing sun. You shall not escape again!"

The Count laughed and stood, brushing dirt off his knees. "Thought *you* I longed for escape? No—but for company. We must be alike, you and I, for you do not fall to me. Good! Be *my* companion, and I shall treat you like the son I lost. Will you?"

"I mistrust you," Liam gasped.

"I doubt that not. Yet how can it harm to hear me?"

The Count

At this Liam laughed. "Have you forgot already? Have you forgot I was of the company you tried to seduce with words? I saw through your spell then and see through it now. Speak not with me."

Just then came the sound of laughter, and the shapes of the night guards rounding the corner. The Count bared his teeth briefly, like a flash of mountains against a stormy night, and retreated into the shadows of his cell with a "Think on it" lingering in Liam's ear. When the guards found their comrades—one fallen, one struggling to rise—they rushed immediately to help them. Quickly Liam told them all, reserving only his discussion with the Count—for he knew not what to make of it.

chapter vii

The White Hind flowed in constant conversation, like a tap broke loose or a spring of flowing water. From every city house and all those country farmers close enough to travel, talk and speculation burbled, burst forth, and billowed to the White Hind. Bodies drifted in and out, so that the door was almost never closed. Lights glimmered in a long procession leading to the tavern. And amidst so much welter, one more figure in hooded pilgrim's robes, who took a quiet corner seat and sipped his beer in silence, caused no stir at all.

"Aye!" Bob Cobbler's lithe apprentice said, rushing in breathless from a tavern further in town, where men who preferred brandy to ale usually gathered. The apprentice, James Bobsboy as he was commonly known—since no one quite knew who his antecedents might be, although many speculated he was a cast off from a high dalliance, as he had so much wit and grace about him—wandered over to Agnes Baker's daughter. The other apprentices, who had likewise served as couriers between the several meeting places in the town, also sat with him. Thumping the table, James declared, "He is gone. I thought I saw him flying as I came."

Immediately, a sizeable contingent rushed to the door, gazing heavenward. Shouts of, "I see him!" and "'Tis there!" "'Tis there!" and "'Tis naught," sounded even up to the top of the wall, making the guards look to the sky. In the corner of the inn, Brenna Housewife absently filled the stranger's mug, straining herself to see more of the sky through a window.

"I see nothing," John Carpenter said, stomping back loudly into the room.

"You never did believe aught," Brenna Housewife snapped, swishing her broad hips past the stranger and going to the bar.

"You never *saw* aught," John Carpenter returned. He quieted briefly when someone jabbed him in the side.

In ones and in twos, the observers returned to their tables, warming their hands along the sides of their mugs of spiced cider and licking their lips in thought.

"Where do you think he'll be going?" Agnes Baker's daughter asked, leaning against James's arm.

"Certainly, he is headed home," Farmer Cartwright said, glaring moodily into his mug. He had proposed to Agnes Baker's daughter at the door two hours agone and had not yet the heart to lose what little face remained him by scurrying to his broad and empty hearth while the evening was still young. "He has done his work here and more, for I understand he paid for his room and board by acting the physician at the palace."

"Home!" Brenna cried, entering the fray again with a fresh jug of spirits in her fist. "He is not such a coward! He shall go to the Dark Wood, of course. Where he ought."

"And why there?" someone asked.

"Why not there?" another returned. "It seems a likely enough place. All the old tales come there at one time or another. Even the King's."

"That's as it mebbe," the first answered, shrugging himself further into his patched coat.

"I cannot think of any story to the contrary," James Bobsboy said.

"Well, if *you* cannot, who can?" John Carpenter called across the room. Farmer Cartwright grinned behind his gloved hand. James Bobsboy's way with a story was renown and some said that one of his parents must surely have been a poet.

"He'll have to get past the garrisons, if he goes that path," Nat Younger said, the brother of Colin Carterson and general knowledge-bringer of the doings of the guardhouse. "They say the monsters have been many this year, as have the deaths."

"With his face, they'd shoot him ten leagues back!" one of the tanners called.

"Shame on you and your foul mind!" the Housewife whispered, slapping the offender about the ear. "Belike he should wear a glamour, for they say he's a magician."

"And you believe that crock?" John Carpenter called, dodging Brenna Housewife's sound fist.

"All I say is that if he's a magician, he may do as he pleases—and none may be the wiser. And I didna say I ever believed he looked as some claim, at any rate."

"Claim what you will, you never did see him!" John answered back, skipping behind the tables before Brenna could reach him.

"They do say the garrisons south-easterly are plagued this fortnight," the blacksmith's brawny boy, Bran said in his quiet voice.

Others encouraged the apprentice to explain himself and at length, after much cajoling, he said that he had overheard his father speaking through the hammer sparks to another of his trade who lived in Goewínn about a fell shadow that had lately stalked that countryside. No one asked how the blacksmith conversed over such a distance: iron has its own magics that none dared meddle with unknowingly.

"It is sad, then," someone said, "that your master has not the secret of adamantium to forge anew Deirdre's blade."

"That was his own lament," Bran said. "But I do not know that Deirdre's blade would be much help against this creature. It is not flesh and blood like the Wolf King, and may have no power over shadows, though it be formed from them."

"Do you think it is a ghost?" someone asked.

"Of whom?" another replied.

"Belike it is naught but a nightmare or bansidhe," a third opined.

"Or sommat coloured by this blacksmith's own fears," still a fourth added.

"No," Bran said. "If it is anything, it is what it is said to be—a shadow."

"One from Auberon's court?" James asked with the quirk of an eyebrow.

"Go your ways, Bobsboy!" Farmer Cartwright sneered. "You and your tales!"

"They've paid me well, Master Farmer," James answered genially, before kissing Agnes Baker's daughter.

The conversation lasted well into the night when the stars had shifted their position westwardly across the sky. The stranger had long disappeared with as little notice as his coming had caused. So only Malcolm Tater, coming in late to the White Hind, saw the Hermit flying.

Even eagle's wings are mortal and must tire, no matter how strong or determined their owner. So it was for the Hermit. And though as he flew Gethin softly, almost shyly, sang the hybrid song, twining the lock of the Princess's hair about his human hand, he felt no immediate gain from singing and so this he also quit as soon as his feet touched Goewínn's earth.

Little more than a fortnight brought him to the Garrison of that land—for his wings bore within them not only mortality but something of the Fairy, too. If his wings could not quite cut time, they halved it, beating away the days even as they glided on hours.

At the heart of the world stood the Dark Woods. Every tale, every history began or ended there. Once, when the Titans slept, the woods had overrun the earth, swallowing beasts and men alike. But when the Titans reawoke, when miserly Brigglekin and gentle Östrung lifted the Moon and Sun to the sky paths, the woods had dwindled, beaten back in places where the Titans ruled. And when the Titans fell again, when Day released his fury, the wood lay waiting to reclaim its own. Then the Wolf King ruled—the wildness of the wood well suited him. And once more men quailed, until the Fairies came.

So it had ever been: a war between light and dark incarnate, order and chaos, life and death. Many thought the woods were tamed now, under

Gavron's rule. Few remembered a time before he set up the great wall around its remains; fewer still remembered when he conquered the woods, burning black swaths of seedlings, wrangling the creatures of the night within its leafy border. And some even protested, saying that he had no right to hack and burn and slay. But these voices spoke from the heart of hard-won comfort—they had forgotten in whose debt they lived.

Twelve Garrisons Gavron had ordered built, one each in the Fairies' lands. Twelve Commanders set he, under his banner combatant, with order to keep strong the wall even at peril of death. In twenty years, the Garrisons had prospered. Many men took commission for five years and others for more and these brought their families with them. Thus many of the Garrisons now resembled small castles, some even with more than the keep alone.

Goewínn stood in this half-state, neither guardtower nor palace. But the Hermit was surprised to see, as he landed before the outmost gate, that no workers plied their trade, no stonemasons lifted the abandoned chisels, no carpenters busied themselves with hammer and saw.

A soldier hailed him from the wall's height, crossbow at the ready and well aimed. "What would you? State your name and business!"

Gethin lifted his face revealing his strange features. His cat ears heard the ominous shift of the soldier's finger upon the release. "So please you," the Hermit said, "I am come on the King's command. I seek the Princess who has fallen into shadow and have heard that such a shadow stalks your land."

The soldier hesitated then said, "How can I know you speak the truth?"

The Hermit smiled. "I had thought that my mein would be sufficient truth. Or do you see lions walking upright daily?"

"We see many strange things who guard the woods," came the reply. "But if you can swear by God and by His Name, then I will bring your word to my Commander."

"Then by the Father, and His Son the Christ, and the Holy Ghost, I swear to you I am the bridegroom searching."

The soldier nodded and removed for some time. When at last he returned, it was with his superior, but not the Commander. A similar inquiry was made and similar calls for sacred oaths before the heavy gates swung outward and the Hermit was allowed within, escorted by no less than seven soldiers all with crossbows.

The Commander himself, Séamus mac Tighearnach named in the southern style was the second Goewínn man to rule at that Garrison. He greeted the Hermit cordially and apologised for his soldiers' caution.

"For these are dark days," the Commander explained, "and we none of us can be too careful. News has come to us that you neared Castell Gwyr, but no more than that. The story you bring us is ill news indeed and may cast light on that which haunts our lands. But first, let me put you to the test again so that my men may be appeased and trouble you with crossbolts no longer. They say that you bear also the eagle's nature upon you and your hands are not like men's, but claws."

"No holy oaths?" Gethin murmured.

To which Séamus replied, "Had you refused them at the gate, you should not sit here now. We are honest men in Goewínn and know how to rid ourselves of demons."

So the Hermit pushed back his sleeve to reveal the full terror of his arm and all the assembled drew back in wonder, except the commander who nodded.

"I thank you," said he, "and do not long to humiliate you, or show you any less courtesy than we hold to our Sovereign. If it pleases you to hide your hand, your comfort is our desire."

"You are kind," the Hermit said, folding his arms within his sleeves again, "and I shall do as you suggest. For your men blenched—men who daily contend with stranger beasts than I."

"Prescribed beasts," the Commander said, with a twitch of the lip. "A chimera is terrifying to those who rarely see one. But the chimera of the brain, the beast of imagination, is always more ferocious because it cannot be killed with mortal arms. We garrison soldiers still bear our own chimeras—somewhat tamed though they may be.

"But let me tell you why these fiercest of men blenched and why we questioned you so closely and asked to see your hand. A shadow has stalked this land of late and mothers wailing have lost their bairns from their arms in sleep. My men have removed their families to this fortress, after one of our own number was lost. When you came, cloaked in black, we dreaded that you were the shadow come to speak in fair voice to foul end. We had heard, as I said, of your coming to the court, but not of your departure—whereas every bloody morn brings new sorrow. We have done what we could for the people under our protection, but there are those who refuse our aid until it is too late."

"A woeful tale," Gethin said softly, and his mind grew full of the unicorn's head upon Elowen's lap and the blood pricked upon its white bosom. "Mayhap, tonight I may do something to seek out the creature. When does it strike?"

"At the moon's crest," came the answer. "Some hours distant."

"Then with your leave, I shall rest me, and be roused one hour before the fair moon's zenith."

To this Séamus agreed, assigning a soldier to bring the Hermit to a bunk.

"You will find our quarters not built for luxury or comfort," the soldier said, as they walked. "But we are able to rest there, when exhaustion overwhelms us. And our families have not much complained. And, were it other than it is, you should lay you in the Commander's quarters for, he will not tell you this—but his own girl-child, his only, but a year old and the delight of all, was the first found dead. Do not think he keeps you from your due!" the soldier hastened to add. "But he has given over his quarters to the women and would not disturb their semblance of peace."

The Hermit nodded understanding and thanked his guide for the kindness. But the soldier hesitated by the door, at last saying, "By your leave and without presumption, may I say my prayers and hopes are with you? I am but courting myself and have no child to fear for, but I have a sister, Esyld, lovely in form and face, named so because of her passing resemblance to our fair Princess. She is barely in the first blush of maidenhood. I have nieces, too, in every age from newborn dandling on the knee to laughing lock-wound daisy chain. And if this creature can be killed, if fiends can be torn asunder, I hope you kill it tonight!" With that he coloured beneath his ginger beard, bowed and fled, leaving the Hermit to wonder at his words.

Gethin knew not whether he slept or dreamt or stared unthinking at the swirling stars. The blackness of the unicorn's eye filled all his thoughts. A blackness that turned from inky sky, ever falling and retreating, to the heart of Niamh—twisted and destroyed by the Count's black devices. Memories swirled and mixed, caught up with scraps of legend so that the stars that wheeled within the unicorn's eye were now the Dragon Prince's fire, now the Moon's silver tears, now lights that hung over the Lornloch and caught in the Princess's golden hair. He dreamt of flying, of white roses and wolves at midnight—for he was still Gethin, Niamh's love.

In time, a rap sounded at the door and the soldier who had guided him brought the Hermit down to the gates. The soldier said not a word, perhaps ashamed of his outburst before. But the Hermit stopped the soldier, saying, "For you and for all who dwell here, I shall seek this shadow. Although if it be, as I dread, one whom I hold dear, I may not kill it but hold her fast until she returns. But first, answer me this: does the shadow strike only girl-children?" The soldier nodded yes. "And what girl-child is it likely to strike this even? Who is left? Your kin?" Again a nod. "They are not within the Garrison?"

The soldier could not seem to find his voice and his mouth struggled against his fear. His face reddened in the torchlight, stripping years from his light-wuthered face. Finally he spurted, "They are all within, my lord. All but my parents and my sister. They do not think to fear, for although the shadow has slain thrice many days since the full church bells rang, it has slain only babies to youths waist high. But last night…."

"It is enough," the Hermit said. "Where does she live?"

"On my father's land, north and east, upon the Wyvern's Steep, within its mind, surrounded by the blue pines."

78

"And what is your name, that I may answer when your family asks?"

"Collum, my lord."

"Collum." The Hermit laid his hand upon the soldier's shoulder and smiled—a gesture surprisingly tender, despite the curve of his giant teeth. Then with a swoop, he was gone.

Some have said that the great, spiky hills of Dalfínn and Goewínn, those twin lovers of the hunt, are not hills at all but the long mouldered carcasses of dragons, felled by bold Day and valiant Night, when Titans roamed the earth. Those are tales of pagan years and ne'er has living eye nor living memory beheld a dragon. But the people of Dalfínn and Goewínn, usually so free and merry with their speech, grow close when asked even in jest about the Caves of the Dragon Prince. And so most men hold the tale to be false: a young governess' tale to please her charges, or the story of an old dame of questionable faculty.

Yet of all the twisted beasts that prowled the woods, only one did these eastern men fear—for the knowledge of dragons ran deep in their blood, these age-old sentinels against the Crimson Prince. In whispers while weaving, as the shuttle flew with rhythmic thunks this way and that, they would sing the lay of the Green Wyrm, whose body divided the Fairy twins' land in twain. So long had the Dalfínn and Goewínn sung the songs, so well did children know them, that other lands thought them mere quaint rhymes. And the Fairies said no differently—for Fairies do not tell all they know.

But now, as the Hermit flew above the Wyvern's Steep, he seemed to see the outline of a skull—the sunken nostrils, the hollow eyes, the arched brow, surmounted by promontories like cruel horns. Within those horns, nestled deep at the skull's base, the soldier Collum's homestead lay. The chimney smoked and the windows blazed with light in defiance of the extinguished countryside around it. Yes, here the shadow must strike.

The Hermit slipped to earth, waited in the trees, and watched. Ancient, heathen tales filled his mind—visions of Dawning within fatal Cináedd's arms—and he growled, clutching the collar about his neck. Long time the moon rose while the Hermit waited—for Niamh, for shadow, for golden Cináedd of the fires—he knew not whom he should meet. Memories of his one fleeting glance of the Princess danced before his human eyes, as well as sickening premonitions of how she might be now—this murderous shadow. How should he greet her? How should he offer her harm? What course if this scourge, this child-killer, be his heart's-pledge? What if she had no reason? What if no part of her remained?

He shook his head and breathed deeply, settling himself within his robes.

"Silence, fool," he told himself. "Thirty years *thou* in the making and only ten, perhaps, better spent. While she—mere days. Thou art no scholar if thy fears so easily persuade thee!"

No sooner had he said this, than something moved—the merest unnatural rustle—and giving no more thought to anxiety, the Hermit pounced, landed on air, heard the rustle again, and gave chase. Down through the spiny pines, over root and fallen tree, bramble, bush and acorn path, until burst outward to the grass, the shadow pinned by tooth and claw.

"Niamh," the Hermit whispered, calling her by name.

Beneath him, the shadow grinned, pursed its lips, and disappeared.

With a roar, the Hermit fell upon his hands and knees. His keen nose tracked the foul stench the shadow left and his body followed, winding down the Green Wyrm's neck, between the bony spikes. And as he ran, he did not sing so much as bellow the hybrid song:

> *"Where hast thou gone, my lady love?*
> *Where o'er the earth hast thou gone?"*

But the shadow never stayed, never wavered, and the Hermit's convictions faltered. What beast did he pursue? Once more he batted at the shadow's diaphanous form—but the creature eluded him with a tinny laugh. Within the house, the lights went out, and the chimney smoked in a trickle stream.

"Thou shalt *not*," the Hermit cried, leaping forward—and as he did so, he felt a shift upon his sandaled feet as they lengthened, became lionesque. On all fours he ran; every time his feet touched earth, he felt them change, solidify, bend in odd places. The golden chain jingled on his breast, mocking his transformations, even as the lock of Niamh's hair that hung in a posset from his neck warmed the place just above his heart, recalling him to humankind.

The homestead door swung inward on its hinge and all lay dark beyond. But the Hermit could smell the shadow still, rank and evil. He smelt, too, the sharp, metallic tinge of the deep magics that held Collum's parents in a captive slumber. And last, the scent—clean soap and lawn—of Esyld, lying on her bed.

The Hermit crept closer, prowling the corners and sniffing the air. The thin light of the window shone on Esyld and in that light, he saw that she was lovely with features like the Princess, but darker—there were fires in her hair and in her cheeks, where Niamh was new-fallen snow. Esyld stirred and turned, her lashes fluttering. Her eyes, pale cornflower, opened, saw the beast before her, and snapped wide with fear.

He reached forth his claw to comfort her. He op't his mouth to speak, and she to scream. In that fateful hesitation, the shadow struck, grasped the girl from behind her bed, where it had patiently lain, and wrapped its hands about her face until she could not breathe.

Snarling and snapping his teeth, the Hermit sprang upon the shadow, wrested its hands from the girl, guarding Esyld with his own body. *A pinprick of blood upon a snow-white bosom, the endless starry eye of the slain unicorn. How many innocents should die?* Esyld fell sideways upon the bed, as though lifeless—but the grey shroud of death had not yet seized her. Or so it seemed in that uncertain light. The Hermit could not spare moment to look more.

For the shadow, bereft of its prey, turned to clutch the Hermit's furred throat, its hands lengthening until they locked behind the Hermit's neck like another damnable collar. The Hermit replied with a fury of tooth and claw, ripping at the neck and breast of the demon. But though he rent the shadow fatally, no solidity save the hands the shadow proved, and all the Hermit's flailings were for naught. He gasped for breath now, and scrabbled at the shadow's hands that slipped like water away from his grasp, so that Gethin only damaged himself further, scoring light gashes at his throat and around the collar. No matter how he struggled, the shadow's grip did not falter. Only one course might save him; two breaths only remained to him. Stretching forth his claw into the very heart of the shadow, he gasped, "Niamh."

The shadow laughed. "Thou hasst named wrongly," it hissed.

All at once, the Hermit perceived his mistake. With vision swimming, a purple turmoil of fading inner light, he op't his mouth to name the Count. But the shadow, faster still, cried out the Hermit's true name: "*Gethin!*"

The Hermit felt himself collapse, felt the vile shadow scrabble at his chest for the lock of golden-haired Niamh, and snatch it in its skeletal hand. Near death, all his breath expended, the Hermit—Gethin as he was once—smiled and thought, "Ah. I should have known thee, old friend, Envy."

As though he had spoken aloud, the shadow shrieked and dropped the lock, over which it had been fawning. With a hiss, it clawed Gethin across his breast—three welts, for three dealt to the Count—and with a chill, it was gone.

The lock, seven strands woven together, floated gently to the floor, wafting on the night wind through the open door. Bemused, Gethin watched it fall and felt that perhaps it was not so bad to die in such a fashion and with such company. The strand landed on his half-human hand and coiled about the fleshy palm, like a lover against the beloved's bosom. Gethin smiled and closed his eyes for the final sleep to take him.

But lo! The lock grew warm within his hand, and its colour grew, glowing like premature sunrise. Light glided over the Hermit's face revealing for a moment only—and seen by no one save, perhaps, He who sent it—a young man's face, pale certainly, worn before its time, but human, frail and mortal. The vision faded but the effects did not, and Gethin found his life returning, felt breath shuddering into his lungs again, vision filling his eyes—pure, sanctified almost, sweet. Glancing at his hand, he saw with a joy that he had long not felt, that the monstrous deformation of feather and talon had far receded to his elbow.

Springing to his feet, he felt those too—human once again. His left arm had not changed, though, nor had his pinions shrunk. No time had he to consider these—Esyld sprawled upon the bed, her head and arm half-lolling off it like a child's doll. Her parents still lay in their unnatural slumber—quiescent, but in no further danger.

Hastily, Gethin gathered Esyld in his arms and lay Niamh's golden hair upon her bosom. Waiting not a moment more, he strode outside, crouched, and sprang upwards on his wings. Back over the Wyvern's Steep they flew, away from the dreadful sightless eyes, ever west after the fading moon.

Gold glimmered on the eastern horizon, the barest strand of flaxen light, enough to draw forth a faint responding glow from the Princess's hair—enough to give the Hermit hope. Did the girl yet breathe? The Hermit thought so— Gethin prayed so. Did her lashes flutter? Did the fires blossom in her cheeks again? Did they course through her veins once more? He beat his wings with mighty strokes, despite the pain upon his breast and neck and the weariness of his limbs that naught save sleep could cure. Yet he reached the Garrison before the sun did, and was at once admitted and his charge taken from him to the Commander's own bed.

Gethin longed to follow, but those men who sometimes served as physicians must treat his wounds, despite all his protestations. And when at last he hurried to the Commander's quarters as the cock crowed, he found there a grisly tableau. Esyld lay dead and Collum too—and all eyes held only reproach for the beast they had let into their stronghold.

"What is this?" the Hermit cried, rushing towards the deathbed. But soldiers, stony-eyed, barred his path.

"Well might we ask *you* that, sirrah," Séamus said. Gethin had not seen him before, mistaking him for an exhausted physician resting with head in hands at the foot of the bed. But now the Hermit saw grief etched into every line of the Commander's face, as though the greying at his temples had at last completed its course down his cheeks. Indeed, they were not tear-paths down the Séamus mac Tighearnach's stern face—they were twin graves.

"She is dead?" the Hermit asked.

"As is Collum—as well you know. Get you gone from us! Bring us no more grief! It is daylight and all your powers are fled! Begone!"

"Nay!" Gethin growled, pushing aside the nearest soldiers. But more took their place, and still the way was barred. His skin pringled with the first warning of transformation. He must temper himself, or surely some greater misfortune would befall them all. This was not the place to spill blood. He needed no further deaths heaped on his soul. So lowly he said, "Tell me how Collum comes to lie here, too. Then I shall depart and trouble you no more."

"You cannot convince me you do not know," Séamus said.

"Yet for all that, I maintain I do not."

Long time the Commander looked at the Hermit; long time he regarded him. And beneath that cold gaze, the last vision of so many evil beasts, Gethin did not falter. And that was his salvation.

"When the moon flew westward," Séamus said, "in the sixth hour of the night, Collum stood watch upon the tower, awaiting your return. Then restless, he betook himself to the gate when his watch was relieved and at the gate remained sentinel. But you did not come and you did not come and he—anxious, sleep-deprived—stepped fatally out of the gate and away from the wall. He stepped into the fields. Those on watch saw him go and can testify to my words. They shouted down to him, but he replied, 'No! I see him coming on his white wings! He bears Esyld living in his arms! See where he comes, this stranger saviour! Ah, let us go and meet him!' And then they all did see—no white wings but black. And a shadow swooped down upon him. When the soldiers found him, he was dead."

The Hermit bowed his head and crossed his arms within his sleeves. "He was a good man and true," he said at last.

"Twice good and more true then *thou* knowest," Séamus snapped—and Gethin flinched. Then rising, the Commander said, "Now thou hast all thou couldst want, sirrah. Betake thyself elsewhere, as sworn. And may the shadow follow thee out!"

The Hermit's eyes flashed with anger at the man's impudence, but he withheld his rage and meekly let the soldiers usher him away. If he felt the talons on his left hand dwindle, he perceived it not. And that was the last of his transformations for many a day.

It had been some years since any denizen of the forest had escaped the watchful eyes of the soldiers upon the wall overlooking the Dark Wood. Nor did the dusk bring exception—for no beast flew out from its murky eyrie, although quite another beast, flying high and at night, slipped into the woods with only an arrow or two trailing him to mark his passage.

He had travelled to the Dark Woods before, of course, years ago and in quite another fashion. He had not looked like *this*, then. Not outwardly. That had come later, in secret, despite his master's teachings. Landing with a flutter of wings among a copse of sinister trees that leaned in like a great green spider spinning webs of shadow, the Hermit sniffed the air, tasted the wind, and pushed off above the treetops once again.

Inward and southerly, the Hermit travelled, making short flights, always testing the air, watching the shadows, fancying they moved. He searched, he knew not for what. He did not know what form Niamh might take, although he well knew the shades that stalked him. The song he had learnt, he dared no more than hum: *Where hast thou gone, my lady love? O, where o'er the earth hast thou gone?* The music grew desperate in his throat as days turned into a week, then two—and no sweet voice replied *I am here, I am hidden.*

Twice he wrestled with the shadow: on the second night of his entrance and ten nights later. Twice had he won his freedom from the shadow by calling its name—yet for all that, he still sustained wounds from both encounters. The last, a rip across his leonine chest, still throbbed three days later as he stumbled to the Lornloch, known in times past as the Moon's Eye, and fell down by its mossy shores to drink.

Something gibbered in the treetops; something else laughed a reply, a soft squeal—and the world returned to its normal soft susurrations. The Lornloch by the Suirebàir was quiet, cool—its waters making a second lake in the sky—blessedly free of the twisted, malevolent trees. The Moon, who was said once to have melted herself into silver in this very place, rose to make that myth true again, shining in sea and sky at once, smiling at her own reflection.

Gethin sighed from where he lay prone on the banks, lapping the water, applying the mud and water to his hurt, and looked up at the far shore under the canopy of the trees. Did another moon glimmer there? He blinked his eyes free of water, ran his human hand over his eyes, blinked again—and froze. Silently, he drifted to his feet, padded along the shore to a low wall of shrubbery, and crouched in wonder.

There stood a unicorn.

Older even than the Moon's Eye, perhaps older than the world, were the unicorns. Born, some said, when a need was great. Born, still others wrote, to bear witness to a child's innocence. Both were true, but neither wholly. A lonely gleam of light within the forest, they were a strand of hope in the bleakest times. And this thing of myth dipped his head and drank from the waters of the Lornloch, his horn touching the surface of the waters and cleansing them.

Raising eyes of liquid light, the unicorn looked across the shore, and met the Hermit's gaze. The water turned upon the shore, seeming to whisper *Wander, wander I, Over earth and sea, Over sea and sky.* The world was very still and beautiful.

And then the unicorn stepped on the water—white against white, foaming eddies around silver hooves—and walked towards him.

Can words describe wonder? Or catalogue the parts of beauty? No—nor can sight, even by so clear a light as moonlight and starlight upon a shimmer of white flank, fully encompass the entirety of loveliness.

All the stories said that unicorns would come only to innocents and to damsels—to virgins. Did legend lie? God only knew how much he lacked the requirements. But the great, peaceful eye never blinked and the waters bore the creature up, even to where Gethin hid.

Upon land once more, shaking his hooves free of water in shimmering arcs of prismed droplets, the unicorn bowed, sank to his knees, and lay his head in Gethin's lap. With trembling hand, the Hermit touched the spiralling, silver horn, and when the unicorn did not stir, he dared to stroke the silken mane. And although the man remembered his vision, although his heart told him the beauty before him was doomed to die, still the heart of Gethin softened and he might have lost himself in that star-strewn eye forever.

~ *I know what hunteth thee,* ~ the unicorn said, almost within the Hermit's mind.

The trees rustled overhead; Gethin's wound throbbed anew.

~ *And I know whom thou seekest.* ~ The silver hairs seemed to glow golden for a moment and almost the Hermit could fancy that he saw Niamh again, resting upon the bear's head carpet. But he blinked and the unicorn returned.

"I know not where to find her," Gethin said at last. "I know not where to look. I have called and she doth not answer."

~ *Thou hast not looked for answers from he who surely hath them.* ~ Gethin started and the unicorn shifted upon his lap, raising his head until their eyes were level. ~ *Thou knowest of whom I speak.* ~

"I do. But I would give half the world to find some other way."

~ *There is none.* ~

"I shall find one."

~ *Thou shalt fail.* ~

The blue eyes hardened; the black lip raised. The Hermit snarled. "I will not crawl back to Urdür. There is nothing more the Shadowless can teach me."

~ *Is there nothing more thou canst learn?* ~ the unicorn asked and rose to his

Urdür

feet. The voice was like a rush of wind through the trees and again Gethin seemed to see Niamh standing before him, her long hair unbound, her feet unclad, her veil about her shoulders, her sweet instrument commanding, "Speak."

He reached forward, Niamh's name on his lips, but the creature shied and shook his mane. ~ *I am not she.* ~

"I know it," Gethin answered and let his hand fall to his side. "What would you teach me?"

~ *Death,* ~ the unicorn said, and lowered his horn until it touched the Hermit's wound.

"Would you kill me? Are you another shade come to haunt me on this hopeless quest?"

∼ Not thy death, Urdür's heir. Mine. ∼

Gethin shivered and stepped back. "I am no monster."

∼ Thou art no monster, but thou art not what thou wert. And thou hast taken many lives. ∼

"None innocent."

∼ Wast that for thee to judge? And how canst thou speak with confidence of those things done in thy first fits of rage, when the lion and the eagle ruled thy mind and thou knewest not whether thou hadst ever been a man? ∼

"I swear by God, I have never willingly harmed an innocent," the Hermit barked, those very beasts contending for his thoughts.

∼ Yet thou hast harmed thyself, over whom were poured the waters and the oil. It is enough. Come, unsheath thy hand and in thy mercy make my ending swift. ∼

Still the Hermit did not move. The unicorn stepped closer.

∼ Thou wilt not do it? ∼

"I cannot. I have seen myself kill you, and yet I cannot do it."

∼ All creatures are born to die. ∼

"Not you."

∼ Yea, even I. Dost thou not know our ways, Urdür's heir? I shall tell thee. We are born from air and water, from the Sea of Memory and the Lornloch, from the cloudy sky paths and the Mountains of fair Morning. We are born full-grown into this world and knowing for whom we have been born and for whom we are to die. Thinkest thou our horns can do such wondrous deeds—cure ailments and purify— merely for to taunt thee? To burn within men's breasts niggardly desire? To tempt the huntsmen to our trail? Nay, we bear our horns proudly for as long as we are their masters, until he for whom we have been born receiveth his inheritance. ∼

"Not you," Gethin whispered again.

∼ That is why thou must, ∼ the unicorn brayed, pawing the earth. *∼ Oh, beloved son of Urdür, noble Lord of Eyre, what good hath all thy studies done thee? When the moment meeteth thee, where is thy strength? ∼*

"Why do you torment me?" Gethin cried, his hands closing in fists by his sides, retreating from the figure of wind and light. "Oh, you are a thing of impossibilities! A figment of dreaming and desire, no more true than thought." And with that, he turned—and from that another thing was born.

The unicorn whinnied like a shriek of air and whirling around, Gethin saw a thing of fire and shadow—like and unlike the shades that had trailed him from the garrison, like and unlike a dragon's breath—rise and descend upon the unicorn. Silver horn flashing, silver hooves flailing, the unicorn replied, seeming to grow even as the Hermit watched. Wings and mane, claw and tooth, light and shadow, wind and fire met and clashed, roiling to an overwhelming pillar of pure elements. The stuff of nightmares and dreams collided and within that dark, imposing wood, Gethin closed his eyes and hid his face until with a final sear of heat, the moon reasserted her place and only the pleasant lappings of the Lornloch could be heard.

Opening his eyes, he saw the world full of stars—residual embers of white light, drifting to the ground, buoyed for a moment like dustmotes on a lazy afternoon. Crawling forward, he could just make out a white flank, hidden within the reeds. In the wondrous light, the water shone red.

~ *And so the deed hath been done for thee,* ~ the unicorn said, raising his head but a little—for a wide gash, like Gethin's own, ran down that noble beasts' breast. Indeed, every harm that had come to the Hermit marred the creature's glorious pelt. And in that moment, Gethin knew that he had slain the unicorn.

No pride could contain the Hermit's tears now, for they were not for himself, and freely they flowed into the unicorn's damp mane.

~ *Hadst thou obeyed, thy reign wouldst have been a peaceful one, and thy finding of the Princess swift. Now...* ~ the eye blinked slowly as though a great effort were required.

"What must I do," Gethin whispered, cupping the bloody waters and washing the white hide free of stain.

~ *Even what thou shouldst have before. Break my horn from off my head and catch the blood within it. It mayeth avail thee someday.* ~

Reaching forward, Gethin touched the magnificent spiral. "When thou art gone," he said.

~ *Now, son of Urdür.* ~ And when the Hermit hesitated again, the unicorn whickered, and rolled his eye back to the Hermit, and said, ~ *I will tell thee a thing, son of Urdür, and it mayeth ease the doing. On the day thy mother first held thee in her arms was I foaled.* ~

"And that—demon?"

The unicorn made no answer, but sucked in air noisily through his mouth. ~ *Now, son of Urdür. I have but one breath left. It is thine.* ~

And so the Hermit leaned forward and broke the horn from off the unicorn's brow and held it beneath the creature's bleeding heart and caught all the blood within. With Niamh's hair he stoppered it. Bending over the still, impossible form, he kissed the lifeless cheek. And with that kiss, the unicorn dissolved and joined the earthbound stars that hang even to this day where the Lornloch and the Suirebàir meet.

That night the shadows fled the woods to return to their master within the castle's cell. And the next dawn Liam—who had guarded like one sleepwalking, lulled by the Count's incessant chatter—started and cried aloud, for in his hand was a key and he had just fit it in the lock.

CHAPTER VIII

hand pounded on Donell's door the next morning. Pounded until the skin bruised. Pounded until the door flung open and the youth who had pounded near collapsed within the Captain's room.

"Liam!" Donell cried as he opened his door to the wild-eyed youth. Yet if Liam looked near distraction, the Captain had fared no better —for all his days and nights were filled with this dreadful matter, as well as the ever-thinning search for the Princess, the security of the remainder of the castle and city, and the welfare of his dear Sovereigns. Thus are the joys of true authority. Yet even with so much weighing upon him, the Captain did not turn the youngest of his guards away, but bade him enter, seat himself, and be refreshed with wine. "What ails thee, lad? Tell me only the Count hath not escaped!"

Liam gulped and shook his head. "Naught so dreadful, sir."

"Then tell me, what can I do?"

"Oh, Captain!" cried the youth, gripping the wine glass with trembling hands, "release me from my post, before I betray us all!"

"Betray us? Ah, I had feared it wouldst come to this. Tell me, with what dream hath he seduced thee?"

"No dream," said Liam. "Would God he bent his mind towards me again! No, I cannot bear to say how close I have come when I have guarded alone, when my companions have fallen all around me—all strong men and true!" He cast his hands over his face and shuddered, rocking back and forth with fear of remembered words.

"Calm, now," the Captain said, laying a hand on the youth's shaking shoulder. "What hath he done?"

"Naught. But he has *said*."

"Said what?"

"Words!" Liam cried, standing to pace about the small chamber. "And what are words but light and air—tremulous and nothing? Why care I so for *words*? What ails me that I cannot think in blood like my brothers? Yet all their manly ways have unmanned them and here I stand beardless to rave like a mad coward about *words*!"

"Peace, Liam! Peace! Thou mayest rail against light and air, but I see it hath affected thee more than I like. Canst thou recall aught that he hath whispered in thine ear?"

"Every word, but tumbled together—as drops may be picked out in a water-fall—and lost again in foam."

"Their tenor, then?"

"Aye. Ever the same as that first day." Slumping wearily, Liam told the Captain all that had happened since the Hermit quit them, going on to add, "But that was not an end on it. How subtle are his arts! I no longer wonder at our Princess's fall and dread only my own, for he seeks to trip me by pride. 'Come,' says he, 'be my son. Let me tell you woes and joys and what I know of the world.' And though my heart rebels and my memory of my true father's face rise up before me, it is not long before he has weaned some little news from me.

"'Is there no girl you like?' says he. 'Has none caught your fancy?' I remain silent. But he continually couches the question in new form: now reminiscing about his own youth, about his late wife, now lauding the virtues of every lady with whom he has even a passing acquaintance, now whistling love airs, now sighing like a lover himself, now whispering the question in my ear again, and again—until I answer to silence him, 'Mayhap there is one.'

"Alas that I ever sought to silence him! For he must know whom, of what birth, what village, what complexion, what dimensions, and always what her name. While all about me, my companions—men made of harder stuff—col-lapse almost upon entrance! I have been standing guard alone for much of each day and some of each night and not a moment does the Count relent. 'Is it a fair name? Is she coy? Have I kissed her? Does she care for me? What is her name? How is she called? Does she remember me? Is she honest? Who is her dam? What is her name?' He does not cease but assails me with every possible dis-traction, asking questions to burn my ears—questions I never thought to answer. In vain I say, 'You do not know her. She is from my village.'

"And the villain's fires are fully flamed. 'What village? How long since I'd seen her? Did she write? Is she peasant? What is her occupation? Had I made advances?' Oh, there is nothing he does not ask! And worse, at length extract. And no sooner answered, than glutton-like he seizes on another train entire. 'Who has my sweetheart married? Who are my parents? My siblings? How came I to your employ?' As though he would gobble me. My companions do but fall asleep, while I am consumed! And each hour I find it easier to speak—almost a pleasure, for he speaks now in such a way as to seem a sort of currish flattery.

"But Captain, I fear to what end he picks my brain, ravenlike, wormlike, burrowing through my mind like a maggot. I beg you—*I beg you!*—release me! Send me on an embassy to the edge of the world, but spare me a traitor's name. Lord!" Pacing again, he bit his knuckles and grabbed his dishevelled hair. "Speak I of words? I am stuffed full of them! And all of them senseless. But I have yet some dignity. I beg you—better a coward than a traitor."

"This is fell, indeed," the Captain said at length, passing his hand over his short beard. "I only sorrow I did not know before."

"Then you will release me? You see the danger?"

"Aye—but also I hear his subtlety. Tell me, Liam, who canst take thy place? Dost thou think that to remove thyself is to remove all peril?"

"He does not long for escape!"

"So he sayeth into thine ear. Like a snake about the throat promiseth not to bite. He mayeth *not* bite—he mayeth squeeze thy neck instead and leave thee just as dead."

"You will not remove me."

"Not yet," said the Captain kindly, touching the dejected youth's arm with fatherly concern. "Not yet. Bear a while, stuff fingers in thy ears, bind thy tongue—or better, bind his. I give thee leave to do so. But bear a while yet."

So Liam took his leave of the Captain, unsatisfied but dutiful.

So things continued through to winter. Gwrhyr and Gwendolyn had gone to Gwendolyn's father to break with him and marry and honeymoon under his roof. Gwrhyr's feet had begun to heal, due as much to the ministrations of the Hermit as well as the spiritual council of Father Cadifor. They would not return 'til spring. And many more comings and goings had happened, as they always did before the snows set in.

But this year, the Christmas revels were meagre, the new fashions tending towards black and mauve, rather than the wild crimsons and ultramarines of years past. The mummers came and went to polite applause and a sprinkle of excess coins, and the Princess's name had all but dropped from conversation. The usual pantomimes were played, of course, and the Nativity brought about a few smiles, but no one danced the Annunciation—that had been the Princess's part in happier times.

Elowen was coaxed out of hiding to at least sit stiffly at the banqueting hall, and when they brought her to the vigil, she refused to leave but prayed all through the night as if she, and not Ewan who stayed with her, were the one preparing for the golden spurs.

On Christmas Day, King Gavron himself girded Ewan, with a belt made of braided brown leather—a gift from Findola. Present, too, was Ioan Ys, the Lord of Houndshelm, who had arrived too late for Mass the night before, his poor horse worn with the hurried travel. But although he must surely have required more rest than the night could give him, the Lord of Houndshelm was the first in the Great Hall the next morning when his son was Knighted. And after mass and a hearty breakfast, wherein Lord Houndshelm seemed determined to lift the spirits of the court entire with his loud, hearty laughter and frequent toasts,

Ewan fetched Findola from one of the lower tables and brought her, hand in hand, before the court.

"Majesties, Father, Lord Mackelwy, nobles, friends, all. Today before you, in your worthy witnesses, do I ask the Lady Findola, daughter of Lord Branaugh, steward of Cadwyr, for her hand in marriage." Then kneeling before his beloved (and alone seeing her expression of girlish glee overlaid with mortification), he took her hand in his and said, "Lady, wilt thou have me?"

Findola kept herself one breath away from a blush, and said, "Sir Ewan, I will."

"That's my boy!" Lord Houndshelm roared, standing and stomping his feet upon the floor.

It was now Ewan's turn to cast his eyes down in mortification. When he at last he gained courage enough to look into his beloved's face again, he found an open amusement at his expense within her dark eyes. Had they thought to look about them, they might have found the same amusement mirrored everywhere. There had been far too little to laugh about this autumn—strange that winter should bring joy, but who would gainsay unseasonable levity?

"Hath the lady's father been broke with?" Gavron said at last, when Lord Houndshelm paused for drink between calling for cheers.

Now the newly-minted Knight did blush in earnest and admitted that he had not.

The King laughed, not unkindly, and said, "Well, sir Knight, fortune is with thee this sacred day. We have some embassy to our cousin, Cadwyr, touching a matter dear to all our hearts, and it pleaseth us to send thee, with thy lady, and a reasonable escort, to his leafy keep. What sayest thou?"

"Your Majesty is most generous with my foolhardiness," Ewan replied.

Gavron waved his hand. "Every Knight shouldst begin his career with one mishap to avoid them later on. Thou hast merely shown foresight in committing thine within the hour and for a noble cause. Many a man here can attest to broken limbs earned just after the golden spurs."

"Majesty," Lord Houndshelm said, rising. Gavron acknowledged the great burly lord with a nod of his head. "You spoke of an escort. I should like to go."

"Gladly," Gavron said. "Wilt thy wife approve?"

"If I send her a message, she will yell a little less."

"Then by all means, send thy messenger. And God speed you all there and back safely."

The court raised their glasses to this and cheered, even as Ewan kissed his lady's hands.

When the meal had done and folk dispersed until that evening's feast—which would be replete with jugglers, jongleurs, dancers, musicians, and the presentation of the Mystery of the Rose—Ewan and Findola sought out Pwll, who had been waiting on his Grace, Lord Mackelwy and Lord Houndshelm during the meal.

"So," the squire said, emerging from the wine cellar to find the lovers sheltering from the brisk wind in the lee of the filigreed arcade leading to the Great Hall. "You have won title and lady in one, Ewan! My felicitations. And lady, my condolences."

Findola laughed and pulled the fur of her cloak closer around her. "You shall not dampen my spirits, today, sirrah," she smiled. Then with a haughty sniff and a twinkling eye, she added, "No more jests from thee, I prithee."

Pwll bowed deeply, flourishing his soft hat a few times. "By all means, my lady. I am ever yours to command. Ewan, perhaps I should have offered my condolences to *you*. Your lady seems to have already gained the disposition of superiority natural to a wife."

"Thinkest thou to insult my lady?" Ewan bellowed, squeezing snow into a ball.

"Thy lady, churl?" Pwll grinned, likewise snatching a handful of snow.

Findola laughed and stepped between them. "Gentlemen, please. Your doublets will be ruined."

"Doublets be hanged!" yelled Pwll, and hurled his snow.

Quickly, Ewan thrust Findola to one side, taking all the brunt of the attack full on his breast. "Knave!" he choked out a laugh, beating his chest with his fist and causing Pwll to drop the new snow he held and Findola to race to Ewan's side. Ewan sat on one of the benches, gasping. "A scratch, a scratch."

"Oh Lord, Ewan," Pwll said, drawing closer. "I did not harm thee!"

Ewan motioned for the squire to lean down—and stuffed Pwll's face with tight-packed snow. "A hit," he said, before dodging from that place.

Pwll waisted no time running after, and Findola after that—in vain hope of dissuading them. And the result was that at the end of a half-hour, Pwll's feathered hat was a ruin of slush and velvet, Ewan's braided belt in need of a new buckle, and Findola's rabbit-lined mittens soggy.

"When do you leave?" Pwll asked when all three had caught their breath from exertion and laughter. The steward, who considered himself more important than was strictly true, had even now passed by and looked disapprovingly at the guilty trio, which had resulted in a consumptive coughing fit to cover another round of laughter.

Ewan mopped his brow and leaned against a pillar. "My father goes with us."

"Ah," Pwll said, rubbing snow against his burning cheeks. "As soon as he's well-fed, then."

Ewan nodded and wheezed hoarsely. Findola handed him her handkerchief, miraculously dry. "I trust you'll keep your sword in your scabbard while I'm gone?"

Pwll only grinned and flicked snowflakes from his doublet. "I'd give half the world to go with you, but my grandfather has no intention of travelling in winter merely for my whims. Ah, well. Did you want help packing?"

Ewan shook his head. "No. Most of my things are already in trunks, waiting to be moved into the Griffon's Wing, although I daresay I don't deserve the honour and would be much happier remaining in the Rookery."

"And you, lady?"

"I return to my father's house. There is little that I need," Findola said, her eyes shining now with thoughts of a home not seen for nearly ten years. Ewan took her hand, stripped it of its damp mitten, and kissed the cold, rosy skin beneath. Pwll turned his eyes away.

At length, Findola crossed the width of the arcade and joined Pwll, laying her bare hand upon his sleeve. "Thou art still my champion, Heir Branmoor. And thou still hast a charge within thy care." And with this she looked up to the Lyon Rampant wing and to Elowen, buried alive somewhere within that grand mass of stone.

Pwll grinned, although not with the mercury of a few minutes before, and bowed low, pressing his bedraggled cap to his breast. "At your service, my lady."

They parted ways after that—Pwll and Ewan to the Rookery, Findola to the Lyon Rampant. The steward had returned, his eyes half lidded so that he might be subjugated to only half the merry scene, and informed them all that Lord Houndshelm had protested he couldn't eat a single mutton leg more.

That evening, as Liam took the guard, he started in surprise to see the prisoner talking lordly, like a king, to one of his shadows crouching before him. The other guards seemed awake, although that did not guarantee their sentience nor their ability to perceive the shadow. Liam pressed his lips together and advanced.

"Gil, rouse yourself," he said, shaking one of the guards, a youth just a few years older than himself, also from Findair, and just come to his first tawny down.

Gil stirred and blinked his eyes, swearing as he realised that he'd fallen asleep.

"Soft, soft," Liam whispered and turned the other guard around to look into the cell. "Tell me what you see."

Yawning, Gil protested that all he saw was the villain raving at shadows, as he had all afternoon.

"Shadows? What shadows? How many?" Liam hissed, his gloved hand digging into Gil's shoulder.

Gil shook him off impatiently. He had never been good at waking. "An expression, Liam. The man's mad—he must be, to have done what he did."

Liam let Gil go, and turned to rouse the second guard, Ceallach in fact, who had been nodding and starting from sleep and muttering to Gil to go fetch replacements. When Liam woke him, he swore too, for this was the second time he'd succumbed and it meant night duty on the parapets. If that weren't a wretched thing to do to a man with a good chance of arthritis by his fortieth year, he didn't know what was. Liam didn't bother to respond, but pushed the two guards away and took his place on a three-legged stool he'd brought down a few months ago when it seemed apparent to everyone that he'd be pulling long stints before the villain's door.

He closed his eyes—although not his ears—and rested his head against the bars, and his sword across his lap. A month ago, days after he had spoken with the Captain, he had discovered the shadows could be hurt by cold iron—a valuable lesson. And from that day on, when he had plunged his sword victorious into a shadow's side and seen it and its master double in pain, he had kept his sword unsheathed ever since.

"Nowhere?" the Count was asking, his voice carrying through to Liam, despite the Count's attempt to keep it low.

"No, masster," the shadow responded. Liam looked around. He saw only one shade, the first since the last new moon. The conversation seemed to be the same.

"And where is he?"

The shadow hesitated, before answering, "Dark Woodss. We followed him there, but he carriess ssomething with him. We dare not touch him."

The Count paced the length of the cell, running his hands through his draggled hair. His proud, handsome features were grey, drawn, and in the dimming light he looked very much like one of his shadows. At length he waved his hand impatiently. "Go. Go."

"Where, masster?"

"After him, I care not. You know for whom you search. Go."

The shadow did some grotesque obeisance and unfolded itself from the floor. Liam gripped the hilt of his sword and tensed his arm to swing.

"We need ssusstenansse," the shadow said, its head barely bent in a practised gesture of servility.

The Count looked away from the small window with a frown. "I fed you at the moon's rise."

"The way iss long," the shadow answered, drawing a step closer. "And we are thirssty."

Almost, Liam fancied, the Count blanched beneath his wan, corroding skin. "Very well," he said at last, with a little strangling sound that Liam hardly hoped was fear. "Your master allows you. Step to the everlasting spring."

He need not command twice. With a leap, the shadow was upon him, drinking blood from the Count's throat. When the Count fainted, the shadow threw his master upon the meagre bed and disappeared into the twilight, with no more than a rat-scratch skitter of claw and wing.

An hour passed and Liam did not move—no, not to help the Count, for if the shadow had killed him, it was only just. And this was not the first time Liam had witnessed the gory ritual.

By midnight, while Liam partook of bread and cheese the Captain himself had provided, the Count stirred. Groaning, he pushed himself up on shaking arms, his face older, with more lines and seams along the skin than a girl's first sampler. The smell of food made him turn to Liam; the desire for good, plain, honest fare prompted him to lurch towards the bars before his legs were ready for him. He stumbled and fell hard against the stones. With a sigh, Liam lowered his dagger and the cheese and cursed his heart for its pity and its strength. Reaching within the bars, he helped the Count to at least kneel, grasping the bars. One arm around the Count's back, the guard fed his captive with his own hand, as if the once noble lord were no more than a stray dog, eating from the hand of a kindly stranger. When the Count could kneel on his own, Liam offered him some of his wine, which the Count eagerly accepted, spilling not a single drop, as if the wine were consecrated blood instead of cheap vintage from Viviane.

"Ah, my lad," the Count said when he had drained the first glass. "Ah, ha, ha—did your fine eyes see that?"

"They did," Liam said, filling the glass again.

"Ah, ah," the Count said, licking his lips, and sticking out one gaunt hand through the bars to take the glass. "It's—it's a good—good thing that you're not afraid of them. The others think I'm mad. We know better, eh? You aren't afraid of them, are you?"

Liam pressed his lips together. Was this the inquisition for the evening? He would give the Count no satisfaction. The captive must have seen something of this in the boy, for he leaned against the bars, his head practically next to Liam's own, as if he should like to rest it like an aging father against his son's breast.

"Well, nevermind," he said. "We'll withstand them together, you and I, my fine, brave boy. Do you hate me yet, my lad? Hmm? Do you long to see me dead? Is that why you let the shadow drink? Or do you care anymore? Ah," he sighed, and drained the rest of the glass. "What does it matter? We all grow old. We all die. We all become a feast for worms. And no one's name is remembered past his last breath." He laughed, choked on the bile, coughed, and laughed again. "Some of us are not remembered past our first breath! Is that the way with you, my lad? Is that how you want your name to be recorded? Another feast for worms? Another meaningless scrawl in the family Bible? For memory is everything, Liam. What we do and what we are, are nothing next to how we are remembered. But for you? A shame. You might be Liam Shadow-slayer. Liam Somebody. Lord Liam. Do you like the sound of that? I could show you how, you know. Ah, but that would contradict your fine, sturdy Findair morals. Forgive me. I would not be known as a corrupter of youth."

He looked sideways at Liam, but the guard was biting the inside of his cheeks, intent on cleaning out the glass with a bit of cloth.

"So silent tonight, Liam! What's brought this on? Why, only last night you were telling me about the girl you loved—oh, what's her name?"

"Tarra Lambing's daughter," Liam said without thinking. The Count smirked beneath his neat beard and Liam bit off a curse—a bad habit. Speaking with the captive was worse.

"Ah, yes. The lovely, false Tarra. Whom did she marry?"

But Liam would not be fooled in the same fashion twice.

"Nevermind," the Count said. "He is not important. You said she had hair like fleece. I wonder what you meant by that. Was she an albino? Did she have Wydoemi blood in her? Surely her mother didn't copulate with a ram!"

Liam's ears and neck burnt, but he kept his peace, even if his memory of the lovely, false Tarra Lambing's daughter grew fouler with every word the captive uttered.

"I once knew a girl with hair like flax. She was a countess actually and a distant cousin of mine. She lived in Aldhairen, on the shores of the Ice Floes, but her arms and legs were warm enough. Oh, dear me, there I go upsetting you again. Let's find another topic. What's the news of the outside world? I suppose the Princess hasn't come home yet, or else my head would be on a platter, eh? I wonder if they'd choose you to cut it off. I can't think whom else they'd trust. I can see your brave companions now, falling asleep mid-chop! Oh, my poor, aching neck! The axe handle would fall on me! I'd be bludgeoned to death!" He laughed, a hopeless, desperate sound, clearly meant to be joined by someone more drunk or desperate than he. Liam remained mute and wrapped the remaining bread.

"I wonder," the Count continued, when it became apparent that his guard had no intention of replying. "I wonder whether you'd have the guts to kill me. Oh, don't think I've been deaf to the few things you've let drop. 'I pity him,' 'Poor soul,' and all that rot. That's just a coward's way of sounding noble." He laughed at that, a sort of hiccup, like a child after crying. "I wonder, heh, I wonder whether that Donell knows whom he's assigned to guard me. 'Go down to the Count, Liam. Go guard that emaciated, emasculated Count. You're the only one who can do it.' The only one, Liam! All alone! While your companions wench, and drink, and fight battles you don't even know are happening. And they look at one another, and say, 'Thank God that coward Liam isn't here! Thank God the farmboy is locked up with that delusional Count! Seeing shadows— paugh! The boy frights at the least thing!'"

Liam

He paused again to see whether that had evoked a response, but Liam's face had turned to flint. And so the Count said, "But let's not think of them. Let's not think of beautiful, lovely Tarra. Let's not think of her in another man's sweaty bed. Let's not think of *our* beds—large featherbeds with feather pillows, and breakfast brought in by a fine, round wench, who'd sit with you, and butter your bread, and maybe let you kiss her and forget the adulterous Tarra. Let's not think of sleeping and dreaming of great campaigns, and of Donell himself owing his life to you for some great swordplay. Let's not think of that windswept plain in, oh, say Islendil, where the Necromancers once lived, where they say Ruthvyn of the Silver Hands still lives, awaiting his noble conqueror. Let's not think of our sword held in our capable hands, sweeping through the living dead bodies like so much lawn, your shoulders shifting as easily as the swing of a scythe upon the farm. Let's not think of the roar and cry of battle and of your own part in that great good—better, surely, than sitting mum beside a madman. Let's not think on it.

"Or if within the Necromancer's tower there happened to be a maiden— we'll give her hair of blood for variety—who, watching the great, handsome stranger lead the assault against her captor, finds her own heart captive from afar. And on reaching the tower and doing single combat with Ruthvyn of the Silver Hands, who has already mortally wounded the Captain, let us not think of that victorious death-blow, the sword plunged through his black heart up to the bloody hilt. Let's not think of how you, being the resourceful lad that you are, bring back the Captain from the brink of death with Ruthvyn's own arts. And no sooner has the Captain breathed again and his eyes opened in gratitude and, more, apologetic realisation of your strengths and his blindness to them, our lovely red-headed girl...what shall we name her? Oh, let us name her..." he cocked his head and seemed to listen, and Liam—fully intent on the Count's vision, so near the desires of his young heart—paused in the polishing of his sword, waiting for the name of his dream maiden.

Perhaps the Count realised his own power, for he waited until Liam's patience wore to the breaking point and then the villain said, with a private smile, "Esyld. Let us name her Esyld."

Liam took a breath, caught the name, liked it, and set about inspecting the sharpness of the swordpoint. The Count settled more comfortably against the bars and resumed his tale.

"Lovely, flame-haired Esyld comes down the tower steps as graceful as a willow, in a dress of olive drab and her feet are bare. 'Brave Knight,' says she and puts her hand on your heart. Then, before you know what has happened, you are kissing her and all thoughts of Tarra disappear, and there is only Esyld of the fires, and her willow arms about your neck, and her soft hair falling over your hands.

"Ah, why are you not *there?* Where are the great deeds you dreamt of? What good is a man like yourself mouldering in the dungeons? Where are the fields of Findair? Where are the brave men of Findair? Are they all so overlooked? Are your countrymen less valued than the vain men of Viviane and Malinka? Are they less hearty than the men of Dalfínn and Goewínn? Less clever than Urdür and Cadwyr? Less wise than Aldhairen and Islendil? Are they cowards to hide in coves or lighthouses? Although you are sober, are you not brave? Although your skin is fair, does not your blood run red? And yet you sit here—and worse, you do not fight against sitting here. Sitting *mute* here. Sitting mute and inactive in the *night*—when all the world's asleep and no one's to notice if you do anything worthy or not.

"Was this what you came here for? Was this your goal? To lose all the colour from your cheeks and keep company with a madman? When was the last time you even practised with your sword? No, I know well you sleep through the day. Who would not? Who would not hide his face in shame to be the nursemaid to the most villainous man who ever lived? Who would not beg for the night to hide his nannying? For what can you say to the others, hotblood Ceallach, for instance? 'Last night, while you were settling a private duel over some chit, I was cleaning up after the Count's own shit.' Is that what you write home about? 'Dear mother, I cleaned up after some madman's piss the other day and didn't puke this time. God's blessings and my last brass coronet, Liam'?

"Hells' bells! Even at home, you weren't the stableboy! Where would they put you if you went to war? Would you follow the train, sweep in hand? Esyld would not run to you then. Look! Lordly Liam knocking zombies down with his broom! Oh, a dashing sight indeed! Put away that sword, boy. You dishonour it."

Liam had gone very red with the effort of not answering. But, as if by biting his tongue, his ears opened, the Count's vision—distorted, as everything he saw became—grew too awful, too close to Liam's own restless ruminations. Thoughts that came unbidden, like droning bees, as he lay upon his thin bed, staring up at the ceiling, gilded with the morning light and longed for and dreaded sleep. The sword gleamed in the young guard's lap. He could do naught with it unless he ran it through the Count and then cleaned the guilt away.

The captive leaned forward, his eyes hungry, staring at his jailer's hands upon the hilt. "Do you hate me yet, boy?" he whispered, and his eyes flicked up to Liam's with a dreadful sanity.

Liam looked at him and answered, "Yes."

Although the Lord of Houndshelm, his son, and his son's betrothed were prepared to take their leave on Christmas Day, King Gavron forbade it, insisting that they stay at least until the New Year. "For," he said, "I have yet to write my embassy to Cadwyr and more to the matter, I have not consulted with Donell about which of his guards he shouldst like to send with you." Despite Lord Houndshelm's protest that he was protection enough against vagabonds and inclement weather combined, the King's word held sway and the expedition delayed.

New Year's came in an excitement of speculation, mainly concerned with the possibility of snow and what effect that would have on Lord Houndshelm and his party. Discreet bets were placed with a reliable squire, who had acted as broker in these matters before. Even Lord Houndshelm placed a bet—although loudly, as was his way—saying to the flabbergasted youth, "If we leave later than noon, never trust me. And you might as well bring my winnings to the gate with you. I could use the expenses." This change in events, naturally, sparked another bout of bets with considerably altered odds. Indeed, the gambling became so reckless, that Father Cadifor took it upon himself to offer up the New Year's vigil Mass entirely for the ruination of such sport. Lord Houndshelm approached the good Father afterwards, so several witnesses attested, saying, "Ten to one God'll hear my prayer before he answers yours." Father Cadifor had apparently disdained to respond.

But as predicted, at nine in the morning precisely, the entire entourage had mounted and rode to the gate, Lord Houndshelm at the lead, calling all his debtors to pay before he left. Ewan's face was very pale as his father loudly clapped several notable lords on the back with a hearty consolation, even while pocketing their money. Pwll, who had accompanied them on foot as far as the gate, beckoned for Findola to lean closer and said, "Ewan's mother is a saint. Take solace."

Findola glanced up at her future father-in-law and sighed deeply. "A pity this isn't a pilgrimage."

By ten all debts had been collected, and the King and Queen descended through the snow-dusted courtyards to the gates. Both embraced and kissed the young Knight and his lady, and whispered private greetings for various Cadwyr lords in their ears. Rhianna held Findola a long time, saying something to her that elicited tears and a fierce embrace. Then, with a final blessing from Father Cadifor, and a hearty oath from Lord Houndshelm, they bade farewell with many a long look behind.

Pwll watched until he could see them no more for the bending of the road and the curving of the hills. The rest had left long ago, for despite Lord Houndshelm's hardiness, the wind was still bitter cold, and not even Gavron and Rhianna remained. Pwll watched until the guards shut the gates and then tugging on his fur mantle absently, he turned and walked back to the Rookery. But when he rounded the Watchtower of the guard House, the curve of a dark hem caught his eye and he followed it as it wove a fleeing path around the

Practice Field and the Armoury's tower, headed towards the Lesser Labyrinth. Pwll was quicker than whoever eluded him, and by the Armoury's tower—the Halberd—he managed to snag a bit of black velvet, and then a waist, and eventually all of Elowen, kicking and scratching.

He sustained several welts before Pwll pinned her arms behind her back and pressed her up against the Halberd wall. All the fight went out of the Handmaid and she slumped against his chest although she did not weep. Surprised, Pwll could do no more than keep hold of her wrists. She would not flee again. His hold softened, became gentler. He let his hands twine around her back, while her own groped upward, about his neck. Against his shoulder, she whispered, "I had to see her go."

Memories of five days ago, of a mitten stripped and a palm sweetly kissed, of a pledge made and accepted, swam before the squire's suddenly intoxicated mind. He held Elowen more tightly and let his head drop and gently kiss her hair, her brow, her ear. She did not protest but clung to him, as he had dreamt so many nights she would. His kisses became more adventurous: he tasted her cheek, her neck, her shoulder—and didn't notice when she pushed against him, struggling in his arms, until she slapped him across the face with a hand raw from wind and weather.

It was almost comical. For she had hit him a blow harder than her hand could stand, and so while he staggered backwards, Elowen nursed her palm, groping for something appropriately stinging to say. She was woefully out of practice. Not so Pwll of Branmoor. "How long have you been standing out here, Elowen?" he asked, pressing his hand to his cheek and touching his jaw gingerly. "I swear, you've turned to ice incarnate!"

"You were warm enough," Elowen retorted, kicking herself as soon as she said it for ever stooping to something so worn and plebeian. Mustering her dignity, she tucked her hands under her arms and said, "I trust that will not happen again?"

"Not outside anyway," Pwll answered.

Elowen sniffed and stalked off towards the Great Hall and the Lyon Rampant. Pwll cracked his jaw and ran to catch up with her. "Wait for me. I will walk with you."

"I know the way. Thank you, good my lord."

"I should be surprised if you did. Have you ventured outside this past month? Have you eaten or slept? Have you thought of anyone but your own self?" He had to run again to keep up and was sorry when he did, for Elowen's cheeks had grown red with the exercise and some of the old fire filled her eyes. He longed for nothing more than to sweep her up in his arms and kiss her. The pain in his jaw advised him against it.

"Lord Pwll," Elowen said. "If you have something you would like to discuss with me, I pray you do it in a civil, gentlemanly, and *customary* manner." She waited a beat and when the squire found no words said, "No, my lord? Bid you good day, then."

Pwll watched her go, as surely as Ewan and Findola had left for the longer road that morning. When she had quite left his sight rounding the gallery, he found a convenient wall and kicked it.

The air was wrong on Twelfth Night.

Down in Brenna Housewife's tavern, Malcolm Tater complained of his gimpy leg and said a snow was coming—he could feel it in his bones. John Carpenter sneered, but kept his peace—Malcolm Tater's knee was rarely wrong, even if his eyesight was questionable. Gimpy legs were not in vogue in the castle, although languishing was, and so many a dowager lady languished with a passion, and kept the maids and pages running back and forth all night.

The mummers felt it and their dances and songs were mechanical, as though they were looking always over their shoulders, waiting for a storm to catch them. Rhianna felt it and perhaps guessed at the portent, for she ate little and listened less to the conversation around her. Gavron felt it but also felt it was his duty to keep the respite of the season, and so made merry with his lords and Knights, plying them with riddles and laughing hardier than any of them. Elowen, made to come to the feast by her father's request, sat stiffly next to Pwll and kept her hands clutched around a napkin, so that she would not cling to him like a child. Pwll might not have noticed if she clung to him—he kept looking to the doors, as though expecting a summons. Donell shifted continuously in his seat and often touched his belt, to feel that his sword was still there.

And so everyone suffered the feast, distracted by the wrongness of the air. It was not poetry returned, nor beauty restored—although it was the story come to life once more, like a dragon slow uncoiled within the belly of the castle. It was not the songs of yesteryear that mystify, nor the elemental songs that enchant. But it was the dark, subterranean thrum, the weighty rumble of the geyser's heart, the massive footsteps of a bleaker age. Something had revived—but it was not life.

The snows began by the second hour of nightfall—thick, wet, sticky wolf snow. Snow that made mountains of plains and filled a footprint within a moment. Snow that muffled sound, dimmed lanternlight, made flight a simple possibility. Snow that distracted the guards, beckoned them to the windows, and covered the sleeping form of Liam, curled around his bloody sword—the keys left dangling within the swinging lock.

chapter ix

tall, gangly guard named Rowyn from Dalfínn was the first to find Liam, who shivered under a blanket of snow. Rowyn had been unlucky enough to draw the short straw which required that he trudge out in the snow to the kitchens and the wine cellar to beg more food for the guards' own revels. His path took him past the Count's cell—all the guards on rotation had made it a habit to pass by the cell either coming or going from the guard House, in case one of their companions had fallen asleep—and had been shocked to see no guard at all at the post. All thoughts of pilfered brandy fled him as he ran down the corridor calling out, "Hey there! Hey there! Anybody, come!"

The stool, he saw, was turned over—dented from where it had hit the wall. Blood stained the floor—not enough to warrant a death, but enough to proclaim some sort of struggle. The sleeping figure within, curled on the floor, gave Rowyn some pause. Could it be the Count had taken a fancy to the unnatural snow? Could it be that Liam had a scuffle with a would-be rescuer and had left for a moment to incarcerate that man? The keys in the lock belied that. A little moonlight filtered through and shone on a bit of blue cloth and metal.

"Oh, God," Rowyn whispered and wrenched open the prison door. Liam would be too heavy for Rowyn to lift himself. He was wiry and clever, fine with a weapon, but no good in wrestling. Taking the stairs back three at a time, Rowyn summoned Gil and another green guard, Ned, and rushed back to carry Liam up the stairs and into the warmth of the common room. The Lieutenant, the capable and debonair Adrian of Castell Doon in Islendil, younger son of the Baron of that estate, immediately sent out two guards to summon the Captain, another to fetch Father Cadifor, and a fourth to get that damn brandy. The rest he banished to another room to await his orders.

"How did you find him?" the Lieutenant asked, rolling Liam onto his stomach to undo the breastplate. Rowyn quickly told all he knew, himself removing Liam's stiff black boots, while Gil rummaged around for a second blanket. Ned poked up the fire. "And the blackguard?" Adrian asked, swearing as they stripped Liam of his damp shirt and found the side bloody.

"Gone," Rowyn answered.

Adrian glanced upward and favoured the silence with another expletive. At least some of the blood belonged to Liam—a wound in the side, expertly chosen.

The Count had been known as a fine swordsman in his time. The Lieutenant set the lesser guards to making rags of the shirt sleeves, which he stuffed into the wound—flowing anew with the bump and jostle of the journey from the cells to the common room. But the wound would not be stanched. With another curse, Adrian grabbed the poker from Ned's hand and held it in the fire. "Thank God he is not conscious," he muttered and took away the useless bandages.

Gil grew a little green watching the flesh burn and sear. The stench filled the whole room. Without waiting for orders, the Findair lad ran and opened the window, breathing in the cold air deeply. Wordlessly, the Lieutenant finished his awful duty and handed the poker back to Ned, who nodded and ran it down to the washrooms.

Gil's heavings caught Adrian's attention and the Lieutenant nodded to Rowyn saying, "Take Gil down. Come back immediately." The lanky guard saluted and left with his arm under Gil's shoulder. The Lieutenant watched them go and swore again. Tearing open an adjoining door to the other room, he bellowed for someone to fetch a clean shirt from Liam's rooms. Several jumped to their feet and the one closest to the door went, just as the guard Adrian had sent to fetch the Captain returned.

"He's coming," that guard panted, leaning against the doorpost.

Adrian nodded and dismissed him to the other room. Ten minutes later, Donell himself arrived with the second guard in tow. One look at the shambles of the room spoke better than any testimony. Passing a shaking hand over his weary eyes, the Captain issued orders in his low, steady voice: "Take twenty men yourself, search the countryside toward the river. Leave Hamish with the city—he can choose how he wants to split his attention between the wall and the Count. Have Ifan search east with twenty—no, thirty men."

"And north?"

"I'll take north. Give me Gil, you take Rowyn. Was there anyone else who saw this?"

"Ned. His father's the caretaker of Saint March's on Plume Street."

"Ah, yes. Assign him to—blast. He'd do better guiding Hamish, but I'd never hear the end of it after his last blow-up. Give him to Ifan. Ah, God, God! What am I to tell his Majesty?"

What the Lieutenant might have said, no one but himself knew. For Father Cadifor, Rowyn, Ned, and the brandy arrived together. Looking at the cauterised wound, the good priest muttered that here was a case that could have used the Hermit's touch. Nevertheless, he ordered the boy brought down to the rectory and sent a messenger to the chatelaine to have someone make up the sickbed.

Outside, the snow continued, softly sifting over the ragged remnants of hope.

The search continued for three long days, spreading out mile by mile into the hills of slush and mire, until every guard's cheek and lip were chapped and many beards hung icicles. On the third day, Liam broke his fever; by the week's end, he could sit upright and stomach mild soup. Before he found his strength, he found his voice and called for the Captain to be sent to him—with no delay. The Captain could not be had, Father Cadifor patiently explained to his charge, as he wrung out a wet cloth. His Lordship was still several leagues away from the castle and expected every minute. Donell was doubtless making a slow, searching progress back. Then their Majesties must be sent for, Liam insisted. And since Father Cadifor knew that neither ambition nor falsehood could be listed among the youth's vices, he himself went to the King.

Gavron arrived immediately, still in his robes of purple and ermine, which he wore when he held audiences. Indeed, Father Cadifor had interrupted a rather heated debate between two lordlings on either side of the Gwyrglánn over property rights. For one lord, Eoden Aî, made his living by rather hefty trade, on which the other lord, Sir Ulf of Ulvin Manor, imposed taxes for use of his side of the river. Sir Ulf was a known wastrel who squandered his income as soon as he earned it and had recently married his daughter Teresia to Eoden Aî, giving a substantial dowry that had depleted what little savings Sir Ulf had left. But this could hold little legal sway. The records did seem to show that his property extended right into the very depths of the Gwyrglánn. Needless to say, the King had been glad for the excuse to leave the haranguers to their own devises for half an hour.

"Majesty," Liam said, as soon as Gavron peered his head into the room. The young guard struggled to sit, but his arms could hardly support him and the wound on his side tugged, despite the Lieutenant's surgery. Father Cadifor stepped forward and assisted Liam, bolstering him with pillows.

"Easy lad," Gavron said, accepting a seat beside the bed. "Speak thy mind in peace."

Liam swallowed and nodded. Father Cadifor brought him a stoup of water. "Majesty, he is yet free," the guard said after these ministrations.

"The Count?" Gavron asked. "We do not know. Not all the guards have returned. One mighteth have found success."

"*I* know it," Liam said. "The Count has not been caught."

"And how didst thou come by this knowledge?"

Liam shifted upon the bed and shook his head when the good Father would lay a compress across his brow.

"By dreams or visions?"

"He hath suffered no delirium," Father Cadifor interjected.

Gavron raised his brow at that, but said no more.

"I know, Majesty, because," the guard winced as he touched his side, "he left a bit of himself within me, when he dealt me a blow with my own sword."

"And how didst he come to lay hands on thy sword?"

Liam chortled and collapsed against the pillows. "By the simplest means, your Majesty. One of his shadows came to him and perhaps had given him strength—I do not know—for as I sat, so intent on closing my ears and mind to his plague of words, he came to the bars and simply took up my sword himself. All I knew was the gash on my side. I stood to do battle and collapsed immediately—such was the wound. I think I must have dealt him a few blows—I hardly know—and then the world went dark. When I woke, I was in the Father Cadifor's care."

Frowning, the King tugged on his beard and considered. His private thoughts were bloody and a red glaze shone before his eyes. At last he said, "Claimest thou, thou canst feel the villain's motions?"

"Yes, sire."

"Where is the demon now?"

"Going south by inches. He has not yet passed the border into the Dark Woods."

Gavron considered this too, covering his mouth as though to cover his counsel. Then rising, he laid a gentle hand on the guard's shoulder and said, "Thou hast done more than any man could ask for, Liam mac Hwyach. Take thy rest now. We shall visit thee anon." To his page waiting in the next room, he said, "Inform me the moment my cousin arriveth. We hunt the demon in earnest."

"Majesty!" Liam called, when the King would go. Gavron turned, a too-patient smile on his lips. "Majesty, your pardon. Do you mean to seek the Count?"

"As surely as ever I sought my eyesight when I was blind."

"Majesty, pardon." The guard struggled to sit up, managed it, and grit his teeth against the pain. "I am told by the Captain that you granted me a boon."

The stiffness in Gavron's face faded as he came back to the guard's bedside. "Oh, I am sorry, Liam, for none deserveth the right to hunt this beast more than thee. But I have been in many campaigns and know a hurt that wilt last a lifetime. No, Liam mac Hwyach—thou mayest not ask to go with us."

"I do not ask that, Majesty," Liam said, daring to stare his King in the eye. "I ask to follow the Count alone."

"Alone!"

"With one other, then. No more. Majesty!" he cried when Gavron would speak, "you are the King and may command where you will. But your word binds even your whim and you promised me a boon. This is what I require. No—do not think me mad. I shall not go until I am able to walk and ride again. But I am sure, with the surety that I breathe, that only by this means can all be made well."

Gavron sunk back into the chair. "Ah, God," he sighed.

"It is a world for the young," a voice agreed. The door creaked open to reveal Donell, still in riding gear, with helm beneath his arm. "Majesty— cousin," the Captain said, going to kneel before his King, "you shall hear no better counsel than that from Liam's lips. Let him go. I would trust my very life to him."

Liam choked back a tear—the words were so very precious.

"So be it," the King said, rising once more. He looked very stern and reckless, cheated once again of his vengeance. "Pwll of Branmoor shalt go with thee." At the Captain's questioning glance, Gavron replied, "If it is a world for the young, cousin, I can think of no more eager blade. I shall speak with the Duke immediately." And with that, he left.

Donell waited until he had gone before turning to Liam and saying, "And before God, lad, see that thou *dost* kill him before he dealeth thee another blow. I had thy family's letter of condolence already penned—I'd leif not write it again."

The Duke at once agreed to the King's request for the release of his nephew for this quest. "Marry," that noble lord said, over his glass of mulled wine, "the lad hath been like a stallion too long kept in stable since New Year's. The activity wilt do Pwll good. And although I have not told him so for fear of inflaming his pride, he is as keen with a blade as ever the Count had been—better. Thus mayeth he put his time to more worthy uses than knocking stuffing out of pells or brooding about the Princess's rooms."

Accordingly, the squire was acquainted with his fate and replied in courtly fashion that thinly concealed his excitement. Begging to be excused to make his arrangements, the squire galloped down the corridor, whooping in the manner of the Dalfinn hunt.

"I hope he is, indeed, as skilled as thou claimest," Gavron sighed. "I would not lose such vigour to the empty god adventure for half the world."

The news spread through the Rookery like sunlight through the Golden Valley, as fleet as the wings of the Wydoemi, whispering the secrets of the wind from bud to bud. Pwll was congratulated and plied with cakes and ale, as though he had been chosen to lead the dances of Syrilm, rather than track down a villain thrice over.

But in Elowen, Pwll found a colder reception. Entering the Princess's rooms, he found her polishing Niamh's wedding jewels. When he opened his mouth to speak, she smiled, took him by the arm and led him out the door.

The next day, he lingered at a side altar whilst she prayed and caught *her* by the arm. "Will you not speak with me?" he asked, pulling her toward the stone garden depicting the Way of Sorrow.

"Have you found civil words yet?" Elowen retorted, twitching away. "I have work elsewhere."

"What work? Elowen, the Princess is gone, the bridegroom likewise."

"Never say that to me," Elowen hissed—and Pwll was surprised to find tears glistening on her dark lashes. "Never say that to me." Lip trembling, she fled, and Pwll let her go.

A fortnight passed before Father Cadifor proclaimed Liam fit to return to his rooms; another week before the youth extracted from the Father his reluctant permission to travel. The final arrangements were made with none of the excitement that attended the excursion that left at New Year's. Indeed, they were all but secret.

The Captain oversaw all the provisions as though he were sending his own sons on their first quest—and perhaps he was. Donell's daughter was all but dead to him. For Elowen had not emerged from her rooms again since her last interview with Pwll—no, not even for all her father's pleading.

The room was always cool now: the fire banked, the curtain drawn, all light and sound extinguished. In this self-made sea, Elowen kept herself employed with memories and needlework against her mistress's return—a return that grew more unlikely with every passing day. And it was in this place that Pwll found her on the morning he and Liam were to depart.

"You are driving your father to distraction," said he, standing black-framed against the distant light without the door.

Elowen did not so much as look up from where she sewed pearls onto one of the Princess's gowns.

"I know you do not favour me," he said when the silence grew too heavy, "but I thought you at least capable of intelligent rudeness."

"If your hope is to taunt me out of my misery, you have chosen poor sport. I'll none of it," Elowen said at last, still not meeting his eyes.

"I do not come to taunt you. I am sent."

"By whom? My father, who so o'erworks himself in the service of the King, that he forgets his bounden duty to himself? Or Findola perhaps, who has left her duties?"

"Speak not so rudely of my mistress, nor so harshly of your father. I think you must be mad to speak so."

"If I am mad, it is only because myself did go with my mistress's banishment."

"Ah, now we come to the matter," Pwll cried, stepping into the room and pacing about it. "Lady, I had long suspected you had forgot yourself. And now I see it is true. Embrace me, then, as men parting on the battlefield—I see I have long pined after a shadow of yourself. Here is no Elowen to love, but the ashes of Niamh!"

Leaping up, Elowen struck Pwll against the cheek. "Speak you of my mistress so?"

"Did I speak of your mistress, Lady? No. Nor did I insult your memory. But as for your present state—aye, I do despise it. And well you may strike me again for that discourtesy. But strike me in your *own* colours—not Niamh's."

Elowen's face grew as white as her fisted hands. She looked at Pwll, and felt the truth of what he said. "Did you come to say you did not love me?" she asked, voice low and trembling. "It is no great news to disturb my solitude."

Pwll looked around the room, as though to unmask her employment. She followed his eye and seemed to see with them her futility. She clutched the pearl dress to her bosom, before he could look at it and steal its glamour, too. "Why did you come?" she demanded.

"For Findola, partly. She weeps, Madame, although she is too proud to water your neck. I wonder you did not see her tears upon the Queen's bosom the day she left."

Elowen

"She begged you to come. You certainly took your time about the message."

"She did not. I took the commission myself," he said.

"You have done what you set out to do, then. You have been answered, which is more than any else have got of me. Are you contented?"

"No. I confess I came on my own business as well. I go to seek the Count, Elowen."

"Alone?" she started and hid her heart in needlework.

The movement was so small, Pwll almost did not see it. "No," he said, leaning against the wall. "I go with Liam."

"He is a green companion."

"It is I who am green. He is a guard thrice over—I have yet to win my spurs."

"You are afraid." At last, she did look up; the needle paused in midair.

"I am afraid. But I should fear less if I knew thou didst live."

"For what should I live, if all I love is lost to me?"

"*All* you love?" kneeling before her.

She could not help but smile. "It was 'thee' a moment hence."

It was a simple thing to do, to lean forward and kiss her lips. It was not their first, nor last, nor longest nor most passionate—but it was sweet and that was enough.

Once upon the open road, the crisp cool wind in their faces and the sounds of the castle far off, Pwll urged his horse into a brisk canter, up to the edge of the hill. Liam joined him at a trot, a furrow between his brows and his hand held ever to his wounded side.

"What is it?" he asked, drawing up next to the squire.

Pwll grinned into the horizon and ran his fingers along the side of his jaw. Then with a wild shout of joy, he galloped down the hill, with poor Liam obliged to follow.

Three weeks saw the companions to the edge of the Dark Wood, on the border between their own country and Viviane's. Despite their differences—for Pwll's glibness was only matched by Liam's grim purpose—the open road agreed with them, two youths adventuring for the most noble cause. It was as if they had escaped a room full of steam, and only now breathed fresh air. Liam's wound had brought them southerly in such a straight path that Pwll asked more than once whether the Count might not have made the following *too* easy.

But Liam shook his head and stirred up the campfire. The sparks flew up to make second stars before them as the guard said, "His mind is set on one object alone. All his revenges overwhelm him so that he no more minds us than you or I might mind a worm. It is his shadows I fear, for they are not completely ruled by him, although he may think his power absolute."

"And these…shadows…fear iron?"

"They are not creatures of this world. Iron will harm them as surely as iron hid the shadow-blade."

"Ah," Pwll said, leaning back on his elbow and flicking an apple peel into a cloth. "But Deirdre's blade was deadly to we mere men."

"And so are the shadows. It is a match."

"There is no death for them?"

Liam shifted and touched his side as though it throbbed anew. It might, for often he called out in his sleep and woke with a fever in his eyes and a longing to follow the preternatural trail. "In the Count's death, perhaps."

Pwll nodded and grinned into the firelight. "That, Sir Liam, will be my pleasure."

Liam coloured and sucked in his teeth. A week had made them companions, but not yet brothers and well Liam knew his station.

The Garrison of Viviane reflected that Fairy's coral-sided dome and her love for outlandish resplendence. The original stony tower that Gavron and his men had erected was all but lost within the newer, higher keep and the multifarious outbuildings hedged in by a wall so delicate and filigreed that a porous winesack should have held more in. Panels of rose quartz and jade adorned every surface, emblazoned with the tamed wyvern, snapdragon in its mouth.

The soldiers, as well, wore plumes upon their helms and sashes above their breastplates and tassels on their swordhilts. Beside them, Pwll and Liam looked very plain—and dangerous.

"We seek to enter," Liam said to their Commander, holding out a letter with the seal of the King.

The Commander hastily agreed and led them to the original stone wall that barred the forest from the frippery. Very few would think to meddle with a lad with eyes like fire and another with a wolfish smile and a ready blade.

Before the Commander gave order to lift the portcullis, however, Pwll stopped him and asked, "Have you heard the news from the court?"

The Commander proved to be well-informed and the companions' opinion of him rose. "Let me stay your next demand," said he. "You wish to know if the Count entered here."

Liam nodded. "We know he did."

If the Commander wondered at the youth's adamance, he showed it not, but said, "Yet I will swear to you upon any oath you like that we did not let him pass. The Commanders before me were foolish men and led their men foolishly. Six months have I been at this post and much has changed, although to the proof of your eyes it may seem differently. Not all that is outward is truth."

"But the Count?" Pwll pressed.

"Aye, my soldiers did see him pass, riding a horse of shadows. We shot at him—silver crossbows and bows of fire—but they passed through him and his shadow-steed and harmed him not. You seek a thing of legend," the Commander said, staring at Liam.

"A man who longs to be a legend," Liam corrected. "And so he may be, but it will be a black legacy and cursed by babes still in the womb."

"Our thanks," Pwll added with a salute.

The portcullis lifted and the companions led their horses through to the wild wood beyond. A thin path through which the soldiers sometimes journeyed to do battle with the beasts of the forest promised that they might ride for a little before the road lost itself in tangles. Pwll mounted his horse and settled his sword. Liam grasped the pommel and the back of the saddle to heave himself up—he was not quite the graceful chevalier Pwll was—but the Viviane Commander stayed him, saying, "Our silver and our flame did this thing no harm. Have you a weapon that will defeat him?"

"We have not," the Findair guard said.

"Nor have I aught to give you—unless you desire tassel for your sword to encumber all your combats. But this I will tell you: if you see a tree marked with heraldry, you may follow its path and reach the next garrison. But if you see an eye, then seek another path, for some fell creature dwells beyond."

Liam nodded and hauled himself into the saddle. The companions set off and the portcullis closed. And as one soldier said to another, leaning over the parapet and watching the two adventurers ride into the Dark Woods, "It may be a blessing, after all. They look eager enough to kill a monster each, and eat the anatomy too."

"I like not this place," Liam said some days later as they led their horses through the close-set trees.

"You are not meant to like it," Pwll replied. "Or if you did, I should slay *you* for a bogey."

Liam grimaced. He had caught Pwll singing twice now—in the early morning, when the squire thought the guard asleep. When Liam had chastised him, though, Pwll had said that he sang songs to fright the beasts away—for if the sound of merriness were not enough to alarm them, then the atonality of his voice should surely daunt. Still Liam maintained that it did no good to speak too loudly, much less to sing, in that prickled web of twigs and bones.

As though to verify the guard's discretion, something snapped to the right of them.

"What is that?" Pwll breathed, swinging out his sword, even as Liam advanced, his own weapon at the ready.

Brittle leaves, crusted with dirt and frost, rustled. The horses pawed and rolled their eyes, tugging at the reins held in their masters' hands. Pwll threw Liam his rein and crept nearer the thornbushes. All heard a snuffling, wet and slobbery, and a skittering here and there with sharp nails upon peeling bark. And then a strange and savage cry that chittered and brayed and howled to the moon.

Dead leaves exploded outward as a cwynadd, as long as a man full-grown, pounced upon the horses' backs. The chargers reared and kicked, trumpeting nervous warning. Liam held tight to their reins as they rushed away from the creature that bared its sharp teeth and hissed. Pwll set about him with sword, but the cwynadd leapt upon a tree, lashing its poison monkey-tail. Again the squire swung and his sword bit deep, slicing the sleek brown pelt. But before he could raise his arm, the cwynadd fell full upon him, anger in its black dog's eye.

Squire and cwynadd rolled, wrestled. The creature shrieked and lifted its head to bite the human's shoulder with fangs that darted venom. Shriek turned to whine as Liam beat the cwynadd with the flat of his blade again and again until the cwynadd fled, its wounded tail between its legs.

"My thanks," Pwll said, lying battered on the ground. "Where did you strike it?"

"I did not. That thing is part dog, part monkey—all fury if you bite it, all coward if you beat it. Have you never studied your bestiary?"

"No," Pwll laughed, accepting Liam's hand. "Except perhaps for horse-manship or hawking, or the care of a bloodhound." Then, stopping to stare at the tangle of reins around a birch's trunk, the squire exclaimed, "What have you done? A simple knot would have sufficed had you calmed them!"

"I have never had to calm a horse in peril of more than shoeing. Findair plough horses are more even-tempered than these beasts."

The horses whickered and twitched their ears as though they understood.

Liam bent to undo the intricate constrictor's hitch that he had learned at his father's knee. "Next time," he said, although not unkindly, "let me to the monsters and tend the horses yourself."

A month later, they came upon quite another adventure. The fachan man and the phooka horse they had avoided with help of the eyes inscribed upon the tree trunks, the demon dog of Cadoc they heard braying upon some distant hill. But not all that inhabited those woods was outwardly foul.

Rhianna had once lived within the tangled briars, when her sister, Malinka, cursed her with the weight of time and sleeplessness. And within the Dark Wood, the Fairy who would be Queen had made a kind of dwelling until Gavron came and set her free at the cost her wings, and brought her home to marry her. Those things a Fairy makes can never fully fade, for Fairies do not live in time as men do, but let it pass them as a wind rushes by a firm-planted oak. So Rhianna's cottage remained a graceful oasis, untouched these twenty years and more.

Pwll saw and recognised the place first, for he lived closer to the Fairies, being of noble birth and so closely aligned with the Spires of Sunset. A slow and winding bridlepath made its way to her cottage and this they rode as quickly as their horses were able, which was not quick enough for Pwll's eager heart. As soon as they came to the low wooden gate, he slipped from off his mount's back and ran into the modest lawn and knelt in the grass and said a *Pater noster*. Liam followed after, surprised by Pwll's sudden piety, but for respect of such a place of legend, he crossed himself.

"A tributary of the Gwyrglánn runs behind her home, or so the stories tell," Pwll said, rising from his knees. "There the Queen's pinions lie buried. Those who drink from such a stream surely will be healed of all their wounds and those not wounded will be strengthened in mind and in spirit."

Liam raised a brow at this, but allowed the squire to lead him around the house. When they reached the stream, however, they saw an old woman with gibbous back and uneven eye bending over the rushing water and pulling feathers from it. She carried a sack full of golden hooves and spiralling horns, butterfly wings and cwynadd teeth, shards of roc's egg and claw of griffon.

"What do you here, woman?" Pwll said, even as Liam whispered, "She is not whom she appears to be."

The scavenger looked up and seemed to melt. Her grey and matted hair smoothed, lengthened, until it fell in black waves to her waist. Her gnarled bones straightened, her eyes evened, her withered skin bloomed like cherry blossoms, her pruned lips reddened and became full. She stood and her rags dissolved into a gown of sheerest silk, shifting colour as she swayed towards them.

"She is under enchantment," Liam cried, to which Pwll hissed, "Stand back."

"But she is in her true form. I can feel it," the guard insisted.

"Stand *back*!" Pwll yelled and pushed the guard behind him.

The woman sang, a song with no words, a song of fire. Blood rushed in the companions' ears, roiled through their veins, made their very breathing torrid. Her hand unfurled, touching her breast and reaching outward to the youths. Her hips swayed like a snake advancing. Her dark eyes glimmered.

The words took shape. *"Come to me."*

"Leave this place," Pwll ordered.

Dark eyes flashed then softened. They melted into liquid pools and turned their depths upon the guard. "Come to me. Free me."

Liam stepped forward but once more Pwll pushed him back.

The song had changed. The trees swayed to its rhythm, their roots thumped out the feral beat, the creatures of the Dark Wood took up the part of whining flute and reed and the wind rushed all together.

"Come to me," the lady said, her raven hair billowing like the great sails upon the Gulf of Barges, her dress twined closely about her form. "Come brave Knight and drink of my lips. And thou and I shall reign forever and a day."

"Listen not to her. Back away, I tell you!" Pwll cried, pushing Liam onto his horse and smacking that creature's flank so that it bolted back onto the bridlepath.

His vaulted into his own saddle and drew back his heels to kick, but the woman caught hold of the squire's leg with hands like claws. Long they looked into each other's eyes, until at last the woman said, "Then your son shall be the first to fall, when I have strength to claim my guerdon. Remember me, Pwll of Branmoor. And let all your sons and your sons' sons remember me—that I, Imórdda, shall come for them."

With that, she let him go with full smile on her broad, red lips that bore more wordy venom than ever mortal cwynadd.

Their path tugged the companions toward the Lornloch, past the place where the unicorn fell, past the glowing lights upon the eastern bank, and then southwards once more towards Findair, Liam's home. Hard-bristled boar and black-eyed stag they fought during their travels. And once they met Garrison soldiers far in from Sirena, who gave them gifts of crossbows and better, water from the deeps of which one drop could soothe a man's throat for a week. The companions stood beside the soldiers against a cockatrice and helped to bury its body in six separate graves so that it would not be reborn. And yet not all the days were dark, for they witnessed the white-wingèd swans flying to the Moon and for three nights the bright birds lit their path.

Two months and half again had passed since they had set out, but they saw no tangible sign of their prey, the Princess or her bridegroom anywhere. And when they at last emerged into a valley clearing, muddy with the melting snow and warming rains, their faces were older, grimmer, set before their time. Pwll's laugh had become a bray of triumph when his blade ran through a wild bull; Liam's longed-for quest had become a thing of habit. And yet that evening within the clearing, their faces cleared—smoothed back into boyish vigour—as they looked up and saw the evening sky free from the oppressive forest. They had reached the Dark Wood's edge at last and their hearts lifted with their eyes.

"Shall we make camp here?" Pwll asked, stripping the damp cloth from his neck and shrugging his shoulder to loosen a cramp. "Or press on until we find the Garrison?"

Liam sighed and leaned against his mare's neck. He had learned how to tame her under Pwll's tutelage and had even given her the name Mellián for her swiftness. His fair skin had browned and his cheeks burned crimson, as with a fever. "Had I a choice, I should lead you to my home. But it is far from here and," he touched his side gingerly as he had not done for many a day, "our quarry is close at hand."

Then Pwll looked upward and saw what Liam had already witnessed—for upon a hill some half-mile distant, a figure stood surrounded by three crouching shadows, his arms outstretched, calling curses to the sky.

"Our time is come," Pwll said, his hand flying to his sword.

Even Liam's eyes lighted and he swung into his saddle, like a young lord returned at last to his homeland. They had no further need of speech, but led their horses as closely as they dared to the shadowed foot of the hill. There they tethered the horses loosely to a tree and began the ascent.

The Count's voice echoed down to them as they climbed. "Where has he gone?"

And the shadows' whined response, "Many wayss. Too many. Together we cannot track them all."

"Silence," the Count commanded, his voice whipping through the night and making the earth shake.

Pwll touched Liam on the shoulder and held up his palm—blood lay on the earth.

Liam murmured, "Necromancy," and climbed on.

The Count began chanting in an ancient tongue that snarled and groaned and crashed like rocks ground together. The earth rumbled once more, shaking loose stones and dirt in small avalanches so that the companions must needs dig their fingers into the very soil to keep from falling. And even as the chant continued, they saw thin, smoky forms rise up from beneath the hill—men with drawn faces, men with swords and armour of a latter age, men with crowns and axes—and they knew this was no hill but a cairn for souls that lay unhallowed, awaiting the Judgement Day.

Then they watched amazed no longer but rushed up the hill as quickly as they were able, running with hands and feet despite the tremors of the earth beneath them.

A shadow turned and saw them, hissing, "*Masster!*" as with an ululation Pwll swung toward it with sword and dagger whirling.

The spirits wailed aloud as the Count turned, his dagger raised over a small girl-child upon a crude altar who bled but did yet breathe.

Shadow and man leapt together, setting about with sword and magics all at once. Pwll's blade was everywhere, he fought with every scrap of iron about him—sword, dagger, the toe of his shoe, the buckle on his cloak. Liam ran one of the shadows through and advanced on the hapless Count, who grinned and threw wide his arms, saying, "Ah, my boy, come home at last."

"I am here to slay thee," Liam answered, his swordpoint never wavering from the Count's heart.

"Slay me? And go against the King?"

"It is the King's will."

"Then by all means, lad, attempt." And with that, the Count lowered his own weapon—a dagger inscribed with swirls and symbols of the Necromancer's art and gleaming sanguine despite the moonlight.

Liam thrust and touched, the sword digging far within the Count's breast. But the Count did not flinch or fall. With his own knife, he lunged at Liam's side and scraped the youth across the arm still holding the sword. Yelling, the guard pulled out the sword, parried several swift attacks, and drew a line of blood across the Count's pale throat. Still the Count did not fall. Another blow defeated Liam—a backhanded fist across the jaw that sent him sailing to an outcrop several feet beyond. Distantly, he heard the continued wail of the imprisoned spirits and the clash of battle between Pwll and the shades—failing rapidly as Pwll proved a veritable iron mine—but soon all his vision filled with the Count, holding Liam's sword again, weighing it casually within his hand.

"How long has it been, I wonder?" the Count drawled, flashing the blade into the moonlight. "How long since we last spoke? Do you remember what I said to you that evening?" And when Liam did not answer, he laughed. "Still silent, I see. A prudent course. One never knows what I will do. Should I kill you now?" he whispered gently, resting the swordpoint against the boy's flushed cheek. "You would make a stronger sacrifice—for I know you are an innocent and yet you are courageous. Or should I show mercy? Don't think me entirely ungrateful. Although, as you now know, I am not mad either."

"I would thou wert mad," Liam said between his bruises. "For then thou mightest have some hope of salvation."

"Do you think to catechise me, boy?" the Count laughed, pricking Liam's skin.

But at that moment the shadows shrieked in one voice and roiled over each other until they were a single body, like an unseelie stallion with coal for eyes. "FLEE! FLEE!" they cried, and swooping, they scooped up the Count and flew off into the darkening sky.

"Liam? Liam!" Pwll's voice, battered but triumphant rose over the echoed screeches. He ran over to his companion, taking up Liam's sword as he went. The tip he cleaned quickly with some grass—his own clothes were too bloodied and dirty.

"The child," Liam managed.

Pwll looked over to where the girl lay. Her chest rose and fell almost imperceptibly. Her fingers had each been pricked and shallow whorls of blood covered her arms. She was no more than eight. Pwll lifted her from the altar, cradling her within his arms, but he had naught with which to clean her wounds.

"What happened? What frighted them?" Liam asked, rising to his knees and pushing upon his sword to stand upright.

"I know not," Pwll answered, glancing nervously to the sky. "A roc? Or a griffin?"

They looked at one another, each naming the Hermit within his mind. And as they watched, a shape did grow in the distance—no eagle's wings, but owl's; and no animal-headed creature, but the Fairy Maelgwenn.

Silently Maelgwenn landed upon the hilltop, his own face lost of all its laughter. The variegated eyes were hooded; his body stripped of all its usual finery. The moonlight haloed his russet hair and shivered down his wings as they fluttered in the night breeze.

"Are ye grievously hurt?" he asked.

They shook their heads, too much in wonder to properly respond.

The spirits crowded around the Fairy and the kingliest of all knelt, drawing his sword up in salute. "Sire," said he, and his voice was like the sussurations of bare branches in a night of rain. "Put us back to rest until we are worthy to walk the Mountains of Morning."

The Fairy nodded and stretched out his hand and spoke a word of power that cannot be translated into mortal tongue, for it contained more than mere idea, but reality. And with a sigh that rattled the earth's foundations, the spirits slipped one by one into the cairn.

Then Maelgwenn turned to the girl-child that Pwll still held and he lowered his brows and held her hand. "This is black indeed," he said. "Know you to whom she belongs?"

"No, my lord," Pwll said.

"Give her here," the Fairy commanded, holding out his arms. Pwll obeyed and watched as Maelgwenn bent and breathed in the child's mouth until she stirred and squirmed closer to his chest. Red-rimmed eyelids lifted as she looked at him and smiled before falling into a deeper slumber. "She is very like my godchild, is she not?" Maelgwenn remarked, touching the girl's pale locks.

"What did he mean to do with her?" Pwll asked.

"To cut her stomach open and read her guts therein like a map to see where the Princess or the Hermit have gone," Liam answered.

Maelgwenn looked up sharply at that, his wonderful eyes searching the guard's soul for some taint of darkness. "Thou art in the right," the Fairy said. "How didst thou know the villain's mind?"

Liam shrugged and gazed with pain toward the western sky where the shadows had fled.

"There is a Garrison to the south of here," Pwll interjected before the Fairy could question further. "We could surely reach it before the dawn breaks and then continue on our quest."

"I shall take her," Maelgwenn said, his eyes still on the guard. "Remain here until I return."

"As you will, my lord," Pwll answered with a bow.

The Fairy rose swifter than thought, cutting through space and time together.

"We must be on our way," Liam said when Maelgwenn had gone. "We must be after him before we lose his trail again. He is headed into Islendil, to the fortress of Ruthvyn Silverhands, there to confer and make sacrifice." The guard turned his terrible, tormented face to the squire whose heart ached with sorrow for the burden Liam's slim shoulders bore. "We must go," Liam whispered.

"Nay, brother," Pwll said. "All things in time. Should we race after him, we will not catch him before he reacheth Ruthvyn's keep. And should we meet him twice, I cannot think thou shalt live. He hath marked thee again."

Liam twitched aside and hid his arm where the sorcerous blade had drawn blood. But even then the Fairy returned, hovering in mid-air with mighty beatings of his wings.

"Come with me," Maelgwenn adjured, offering his hands to each. "For your tasks have only just begun."

And with that, the Fairy lifted them from the ground and flew eastward over the woods, garrison and wall, over and into the Wyvern's Steep, and to the wooden Feasting Hall of the laughing twins—in no more time than it takes a constellation to swing from one side of the sky to the other.

chapter x

n iamh woke.

She had dreamt again of those who'd fallen. *She journeyed through the Cauldron Fens. Swirling pools of mist obscured her vision, tugging at her legs, crawling snakelike around her body. And in the stagnant pools lay the reflections of those who had died for want of her, their mouths open and screaming, their eyes wide and bloody, their hands upstretched to grasp her ankles and pull her down into their Hell.*

"No," Niamh whispered, touching her heart as though to calm it. And, "No," she said again to the world that could not hear her.

Three months she had travelled north, over the Green Mountains and into the river valley, light-bedecked with the New Year's snow. Three months she had woken with the scent of wolf upon the air and the black bread within her arms that filled but never satisfied. Three months had she dreamt of the damned, until she longed to lead another life, one that held no beauty but only the common sort of ugliness.

But worst of all, three months she had woken with things that in her sleep she'd stolen: a strand of pearls, a bunch of keys, a new-baked scone, a spool of thread—even the memory of a kiss from a shepherd boy who had long sued the reluctant milkmaid's lips. She did what she detested and did not know she what had done until she woke and found the proof beside her. She began to fear she would lose herself.

And yet one thing gave the Princess hope: she had seen her reflection in a mirror and that reflection had also been seen by one other than herself.

The first frost had bent the long grass and sent the geese winging south-westerly to the Golden Valley that never knew winter's touch on the night Niamh found new hope. The scent of caramel and of toffee and the sound of cracked nuts and laughter had drawn her to a large red farmhouse that stood well within the parish lines. The family had just returned from the evening Mass for the lighting of the third Advent candle, their voices raised in tripping carol that fell over itself in *Jubilatos*. They did not notice the intruder shadow that slipped outside with fistfuls of dried fruit, but strew their wet mittens and plaidie scarves over iron pegs near the kitchen fire and tumbled into the parlour room with golden dogs yipping at their heels and calico kittens walking primly behind.

Their voices, young and old, crept over Niamh as she huddled in the lee of the woodpile, devouring her meagre feast. But at length two girls emerged and hurried over to the water barrel with many a giggle among them. On silent wolf-paws, Niamh followed.

"Think you to see Diarmad Miller's face?" the younger girl asked, standing on tiptoe to look over the barrel's rim. "He has oft looked at you, Fanwy."

"He may look as often as he pleases. I seek my true love's name."

The younger girl sighed and rolled her eyes as Fanwy and Niamh bent over the barrel and looked upon the new-formed ice—and gasped.

"Ilsa," Fanwy said, groping for her sister. "Tell me I am mad!"

Once again Ilsa stood on tiptoe and peeked over the barrel's rim—and shrieked and ran inside the house. Fanwy pulled her shawl close to her breast and looked about with troubled eyes. "Before God," she cried aloud, disturbing the owl's ruminations, "I shall not look again!" And with that she fled into the house and locked the door behind her.

From that day forth, Niamh took care not to let herself be seen in any mirror unless she was alone. And then she stared deep and long at the haggard she had become, searching for any part of her that once had been. For well she knew her own mother's tale and that of her false sister Malinka that mirrors could steal a soul or hide a shadow in its heart—but likewise by mirrors could a thing be found and what once had been restored.

The snows lay deeply now, a white sea upon the land, a flood of foam, a cloud on earth. The soil beside the Gwyrglánn was good for farming, and few were the copses to canopy Niamh's path and shelter her from the endless snow. The Princess did not feel the cold without, but rather the cold within. The wind rushed past her and played havoc with her hair, but could not compare with the daily moaning gale that scoured her very being.

Her hunger turned to desire for shelter and the Princess began to look for a home to claim for her own. The emptiness of the black bread overwhelmed her, the scent of wolf maddened her, the snow that confused all direction oppressed her. Slowly, she was losing reason.

On Twelfth Night, Niamh came upon a cottage, all run down and seemingly long abandoned. "There is no one here!" she cried. "I shall take the cottage and claim it as my own. And if the tenants return, I shall pretend I am a ghost and frighten them away."

This she did with not the least compunction and all day she pretended to be mistress of a place not rightfully hers and when night fell, she laid herself down upon a bed of old rushes. Sound did she sleep and well into the deepest part of night, paying no heed to either the whisperings of her buried conscience, or to the howl of wolf and owl fighting without the house, or to the footsteps that drew near her.

"Ah, my heart!" the old crone cried, to whom this house rightfully belonged. "There is someone in my bed! Up, rise you, vermin!" she said, shaking Niamh's shoulder.

"Who speaks?" Niamh mumbled, for she was barely awake.

"Your mistress, slave," the woman said, with hands on hips.

Niamh rose then, her astonishment at the crone's words warring with her astonishment that she could be seen at all. "I am no slave," she managed at last, adding with tearful ferocity, "Nor *thee* my mistress, biddy! I own this house, I'll have thee know—I claimed it just today!"

"Claimed it, did you? And who was there to hear you claim it?"

"Thou left no offering for me," Niamh said, her black eyes blazing, "so I took what little thou couldst offer."

"What *little* I could offer!" the woman screeched. "So you took all that I own? I'll give you what *little* I have and give it you with interest!"

With that, the old lady grabbed Niamh by the ear and boxed her about the temples, until Niamh would cede her sometime ownership of the hut.

"There, now," the old woman said, "we have come to terms. And I'll knock some sense into whatever beast whelped you, too, for giving you no better manners!"

At this, the Princess remembered who she was and curled up in a corner and bowed her head in shame. "If she who bore me beneath her breast knew what I had become, she wouldst chide you for your generosity. But please," said she, lifting her head, "I have travelled long and would beg shelter for one night. You can hear me—I know not how—so hear me now and find within your heart some pity."

Something of what Niamh had been must have shone through, for the old lady blinked and looked elsewhere. "Yes, well," said she, "have you no home of your own, then?"

"I have nothing," Niamh said, gesturing to her naked state.

"Ah, I see," the woman said. "Well, then, since you like this house so well, I shall strike a bargain with you—stay in this house and serve me and I will provide for you."

"I can pay you with nothing *but* my service, unless you would have the loaf I carry with me."

"What loaf?"

"I left it on the table."

"I saw naught but crumbs when I came in."

Niamh sprang past the old woman to the table, upon whose surface there remained only scratch-marks and a lingering scent of wolf's blood in the chill night air. Niamh shuddered, then, and wondered what else she had missed while sleeping.

The Princess turned slowly to the old woman, and just as slowly got to her knees before her. "What shall I call you, mistress?" she asked.

"You may call me Ogrin. But I shall not ask your name, for it seems you have a destiny upon you which I would be happier not knowing! But come, it is nearly dawn and for the bother you have been, you may bake the morning bread."

So Niamh lived with Ogrin all that winter, serving her and learning the craft of the home. She learned to skin and cook the white winter hare, to tend potted herbs with boiled snow, to mend the rag that served as her gown with threads made of willow bark and goosefeather down.

One day, as Niamh sat plaiting a rug of old bits of string and rags, Ogrin stirred and sighing out a ring of smoke against the green-leafing window, said, "I am minded of a thing I lost."

Niamh raised her brows but said nothing. In one brief season, she had learned that Ogrin preferred the sound of her own voice best.

"Aye, aye, when I was young and the world was green. I had a mirror, silver backed—aye! Silver! For he who gave it me were rich, and a silver mirror were naught to him. But it pleased me—and it saddened me to lose it."

With this, Ogrin lapsed back into silence and did not speak again that evening.

But the idea could not leave Niamh's mind. Surely, she thought, the Providence that had shown itself in so many mysterious way since she had left had not abandoned her now. All that night, and the next as she continued plaiting the rug, Niamh thought of the mirror, and as she thought, she longed. Finally on the third night, she asked, "Why is the mirror great? What properties did it contain, that you want it now?"

Ogrin chuckled and knocked out the ashes of her pipe upon the floor. "Because you have sommat strange about you, must all I speak of be as wondrous? It were silver-backed. Is that not enough for you?"

Niamh could not contain herself. "But how," she pressed, "came you to lose it?"

"Ah," Ogrin said, "Now that *is* a tale. Although, like you shall be disappointed by it, my ashputtle girl. When I were young, as I said, the Baronet of Udinë's son fancied me and as proof of his love, he gave me the mirror that you

122

wonder about. *For the beauty whose beauty has captured me,* were graved upon its rim—but it never had no magic, for it reflected the dirt as well as me.

"Now, Moira Blacksmith's daughter longed for the Baronet's son, and so contrived to win the mirror from me, and thus his affection.

"'Give it me!' she said daily as I passed her in the market.

"'No!' says I. 'If you crave my mirror, then court the Baronet's son yourself and win one from him! You'll not have mine!'

"'But,' pressed she, 'he cares naught for you and has been seen stealing kisses from Sally Milkmaid.'

"'Has he now?' quoth I. 'Well, let him. It is nothing one way or t'other to me. I have his mirror and have given nothing else away, while like pretty Sal shall give all herself, and get worse for her pains in nine month time!'" Ogrin laughed and rocked merrily in her chair. "She did, too! But I like my mirror better, for it does not constantly reflect my folly."

"But how came you to lose it and where?" Niamh pressed.

"Ah, *where* I should dearly like to know, myself. But calm yourself, and you shall know *how.* As I said, Moira Blacksmith's daughter were a cunning fool, but not an idiot like some I know. And she knew a prize from a curse and had no use for flesh when silver were at hand. Cruel, Moira was, make no mistake. She had no love for anything she couldn't sell, and contempt for all small pleasures. And where has it got her, I wonder? Mute for a year, when she finally spoke ill of a body we all fear round these parts. It's only a wonder she lived at all with the poison of her tongue. If you'd know, no man would have her—and you're only lucky it were my cottage you claimed! Had you gone half round Loch Corraigh, you should have found yourself in worse straits, for mean Moira mishandles her superiors and doubtless would have driven *you* to death, if you hadn't taken your own life first."

"But that is nothing to the point," Niamh said, snapping a thread with her teeth.

"Isn't it?" Ogrin cried with a jab of her pipe. "How can you know a story proper if you don't know who I'm speaking of? But enough. I can see you'll unravel more than that rug if I wander again.

"Well, then, hear this. I had come near to my wits' end what with Moira's heckling and besides that, I was a little put out by stupid Sal—who'd been boasting she'd just snared the Baronet's Son for good from all of us. So when Moira challenged me, all my pride said, 'Aye!'—and that has been my grief.

"'Let us put his love to the test,' Moira said to me, 'and let us see who his true love is. I have an aunt who is a witch, my father's sister, and my father is himself a man of great renown, for he works in iron which has properties of its own. I shall have him make for me a mirror, and ask my aunt to weave spells over it to see truly into his soul.'

"It was a dreadful proposition, as I know now, meddling in affairs we did not understand, not to mention squabbling over a heart as dull as iron. Nonetheless, I agreed out of curiosity and also the thought that even if she convinced her aunt to cast such a wicked spell, the blacksmith mirror should still not show Moira.

"Two months passed before the glass were finished and by that time, the Baronet's Son had left off fondling old Sal and had turned his roving eyes to Peghain, the Innkeeper's daughter. She had an eye for business and so soaked him for a pretty pence, but gave him biting words in return that only sparked his passion more.

"Well, now, Moira would have this in the black of night with candles by the shore of Loch Corraigh—I with my silver mirror and she with her iron one—and her dancing about and chanting in some heathen tongue she claimed was the lect of old, afore any kings come to tame the Dark Woods, but I fancy even now 'twas no more than gibberish.

Ogrin

"'Come now,' quoth I, when the mist began settling white in the moonlight, and creeping into my every bone. 'Do you hope that capering will attract his eye towards you? If that were *e'er* to work, it'd take more'n *you've* got for all your shimmying when he so much as condescends to mingle. If your swivelling hips had no effect in broad daylight, what good'll they do now when none can see you?'

"'There are others,' huffed she, 'who have eyes beyond mortal men. It is for them I dance that they might aid me when I look.'

"'The Fairies, you mean?' scoffed I, blowing hard upon my hands to warm them. 'There's none but old Maelgwenn about and he'd as soon laugh as join you!'"

Niamh blanched at the sound of her godfather's name, but held her peace. She did not bear to think how her own story should run from Ogrin's wagging tongue.

Ogrin continued heedless, fully caught up in her tale. "'I do not speak of *Maelgwenn,*' Moira said.

"'Then of whom?' I asked, grown impatient. 'Do you truck with demons?'

"'Not demons but angels and powers misunderstood. I call upon the gods of passion!'

"'Call 'em demons and have done,' said I. 'But look in your mirror at any rate, or I'm stomping home!'

"Moira let fall her hands at that and joined me on the gorse. 'The gods are satisfied,' said she, to which I replied, 'Hallelujah! I'm freezing!' I could never pass up a chance to rub her widdershins, I confess. A failing, and one I should do penance for no doubt, except that my rotten heart's not sorry.

"Well, may be there were some magic woven in that glass of hers and mayhap some heathen with a bit o' fae in him saw her jumping, for we *did* see sommat in her mirror. But if so—and I'm not saying 'twasn't still some trick from that devious girl and that's all—if so, it were a fiendish sprite that took pleasure in dissension. For when we looked, we saw a great blackness. Quickly, light appeared as though the stars were shining, but these grew and twisted until we seemed to see dogs and horns and boars and deer. Then we saw the Baronet's son himself upon his dappled mare, riding home victorious from the hunt. Across his saddlebow lay a slain doe, with Peghain Innkeeper's daughter's face. Peering out of the saddlebags were two hares, one with Sal's face, the other with a bairn's. And when he arrived at the manse's gate, we finally saw ourselves: two fighting cats with nary an eye between them!"

Niamh could not help but laugh at that, for well the image suited her sometime mistress. "Mayhap," said she, not unkindly, "the vision was indeed divine—for doubtless, it told truths!"

"Yes," said Ogrin with a sigh. "But there are nasty truths that are sometimes best left silent. And there are truths told in twisted way, so that the telling is a lie and the truth received is tainted."

"But sometimes," Niamh persisted, "the hearer is herself so wicked, only a truth told in sad cruelty can be understood."

"That's as it may be," said the old woman. "But I still say mean truths may be used in the service of lies, although never lies in good's employ."

"Have done!" Niamh cried, causing the small peat fire to jump.

Ogrin's face blanched, as though the girl had hit her. She settled with the fire, blowing slow smoke rings with her wrinkled mouth. "Shall I finish?" she asked at last.

Niamh nodded sadly, her thoughts much distracted from the mild lure of a mirror.

"Well, then," Ogrin said, taking up the methodic rocking of her chair again, "this, at last, is what happened. No sooner had we seen the vision, and saw where the false Baronet's son's true heart lay, than Moira Blacksmith's daughter took up the iron mirror and smashed it against a rock. 'It lies!' cried she. And I remember the blood streamed from her shard-ridden hands like tears.

"'*It* lies?' said I. 'What did you expect? Consorting with witches and fae.' I spoke so, although I confess my heart was aflutter and I knew not what to think. All I could see were the broken glass and whisper to myself, 'Ill luck!'

"Alas for me my mind were not clearer! For Moira Blacksmith's daughter turned on me in rage and spat, 'Speak you so? Speak you *so*! *You* have done this thing to me! Well, I'll none of your wicked tricks! But I will have your mirror for all my pains this evening!'

"'You foolish thing!' shrieked I, as she tugged my hair. 'What good will my mirror do you? You saw—he no more desires you than I! Take up your quarrel with Peghain Innkeeper's daughter. Pull *her* hair—but leave off me!'

"Such a wailing and caterwauling and screaming and scratching ensued then, I scarce can tell you! We might have spoken but it sounded in spits and hisses and is not worth recounting. And as we tussled, each grappling more for each other than for the mirror, the glass slipped off the shore and right into Loch Corraigh. We both saw it go, for we had paused in our fighting to breathe heavily and glare at one another. *Plop!* It sank just as merrily as can be. Gone. And I've no idea if it lies at the bottom of the lake still, or if was swallowed by a fish, or found by some wanderer upon the further shore. But some days I long for it, for I am a miserable creature and have no one to keep me company."

Long time Niamh pondered her mistress's words, and many nights she dreamed of the mirror floating within Loch Corraigh for she was sure that within this mirror lay her salvation. So much did the thing possess her fancy, that oft she pressed Ogrin to repeat her tale. But Ogrin, who knew nothing of the minstrelry of the Court, would bat Niamh playfully about the head and tell her that what was needed more was a good supper made than bad tales, and would proceed to speak long on the crispiness of sausage skins and nothing more of silver mirrors or Baronet's sons.

But Niamh could not be so easily dissuaded. Though as the months wore on she could forget all the Court and her own place in it and believe herself no better than a vagabond, still, she seemed to feel the call of the mirror, as though the call of long forgotten days. Her chance for exploration came most sudden and unexpectedly—indeed from the hand of Ogrin herself, who although frequently coarse and silly, nevertheless knew a great deal about how to deal with headstrong girls. So with spring fully in blossom and the spring chicks and eggs, which were Ogrin's main income, tucked nicely within a basket and a wicker cage, the old crone set out to the village for the first market day.

"I'll not ask you to go with me," she said to Niamh, as the Princess helped Ogrin tie her brown shawl about the breast and waist, and the black knit shawl over that, to keep the chill from her mistress's back. "For no doubt you'll only cause a stir with your strange looks, and you'll go pestering decent folk for stories, like as not, and ye'd certainly scare off anyone what'd buy my wares, so I'll chance you to stay here.

126

"But I'll tell you this," taking Niamh by the shoulders and staring her in the eye. "Sure as I'll breathe, I'll not be two steps out of your sight afore you go nosing about the Loch in search of that mirror, and there's no way I can stop you. But if you go near Moira Blacksmith daughter's house, you'll mind I warned you not to. And when you're scrubbing pots for the likes of her, and your fingers run red, and your eyes run blue, and you've welts from her nails across your scrawny back, you'll remember what I told you then and mayhap your heart will break with sorrow for someone nother than yourself.

"For sure, my girlie, I've grown fond of you, and if you walk eyes open to her clutches, it'll be two hearts you'll have broken and no mistake. Now off with you. Pretend you'll be staying safe within the cottage, mayhap, and think nothing of my foolish tales."

And Niamh started to see giant tears washing over her mistress' face, although never down her bent nose. Ogrin kissed Niamh then, her white bristled chin scraping Niamh's cheek and her broken nails scoring the Princess's shoulders with the embrace. But Niamh did not mind, for she had not known affection for so long—even when a Princess. For only two could touch her, and as she grew they sometimes forgot to hold their child as fondly as they did when she was small.

Ogrin left the Princess then, and slinging the empty pack over her shoulder and taking up the basket and the cage, she set off through the fir trees with not another glance behind her.

Little did Ogrin think that her fumbled kiss, more than her words, might affect her strange charge—but little do we ever know what may move mountains. For several moments Niamh stood speechless—gazing at the fir trees, and the beech trees just coming into leaf, and the early spring grass, dotted here and there with stubborn snow and rivulets—and it seemed to her that all her world narrowed to her cheek and the rough indentation the crone unwittingly left upon her soul. Much did the Princess touch her face, worn a lighter colour—although not yet white—from Ogrin's touch, and much did Niamh wonder at herself.

"Here!" said she, laughing. "I recall, distantly, dancing when young, with nobles twice my age. And the last kiss upon my hand, from the Count's wide-eyed, solemn son. I even seem to remember an eagle's eye, and a deep beloved voice, that seemed to me like embraces, but never did they confound me so! Ah, me," said she with a winsome sigh that once expelled, mingled with the breeze and rustled the rosemary. "How can I betray my mistress? Yet I shall look for the mirror, or else I know I shall never give my mistress a moments' rest with all my questions."

So saying, she wrapped a shawl as black as her skin about herself and walked away from the cottage, down the southern path, which wound by fits north again at last to Loch Corraigh. At first the bank was pleasant if a little muddy and cattails and tiger lilies grew upon its mossy shore as the Gwyrglánn gave way to the Loch proper. Much did Niamh delight in the swirling tidepools formed by errant rocks, slicked with age and periwinkles. But though she loved to watch the ebb and swell of the water, something within her still recoiled from even the merest drop touching her skin.

Niamh had not bathed at all since that fateful night and only drank water when she might hold it in a cup—never in her hands. Little did Ogrin think of this, for she was an earthy woman and held it a proven fact that water killed more often than not and so had never questioned Niamh's strange aversion. In fact, Niamh had herself almost forgotten it, so long had she lived quite comfortably without stepping near either lake or river.

But very soon, no further than a woman may walk in half an hour, the Gwyrglánn yawned wide into Loch Corraigh. There some claim the greatest of the Giants had fallen and still slept below the water, turning restlessly in his sleep and making the waters wave. The grassy bank gave way to a shoal-ridden shore—bone white, except for where the waters lay when the moon drew them upwards. Here Niamh stopped, for the wind was strong and it blew her long hair all about her. She could see clearly across the broadening lake—could see the winter trees stoutly climbing the rocky land; could see the occasional chimney smoke; could see the great birds of prey who favoured these harsh climes spread their wings unmoving above the winds. One bird, white of wing and tail though blue of breast, called out as he flew, and Niamh wondered at it, and pulled her shawl about her shoulders, and walked on.

How long she wandered she did not know: traversing white beaches and white rocks, stepping carefully along narrow, dew-slick trails, hugging the steep hillside, ducking under fallen trees, and inching on her side, clinging to vines and tree roots to keep from falling into the waters. Several times she lost her footing—for the early spring had brought the rains and the ground was unsure at best and her own feet but poorly shod—and once only the thinnest of roots kept her from plunging down a treacherous cliff. After that, Niamh vowed to seek out surer paths. But these paths held obstacles of their own—a brook, broken from the Loch, pleasantly shallow, but unhappily wide ran across her path with no dry means across.

Long time Niamh stopped here, looking uneasily up and down the verdant shore for some bridge of wood or stone. Twice she ventured toward the brook, thinking she saw a trail of rocks that might bring her safely to the other side and twice she returned to the moss, for both bridges proved false. "But perhaps there is a way further up," she thought, and so westward she walked, deeper and deeper within the trees, even as the ground rose around her, until she stood in a narrow valley that terminated in a waterfall.

The light had been falling and now shone almost level with the brook. It glimmered off the crystal waters and haloed the Princess's hair—and did one thing more: reflect upon the faintest hint of a mirror, buried deep behind the waterfall. Niamh jumped to her feet with a gasp. "I have found it!" she cried, adding quickly after, "I have found it and I know I fear to take it. Ah, that the sun would burn up the water that I might retrieve it! Oh, that I dared to touch the water at all! The very thought of it seems to burn me, like another fire!"

Her eyes, dark and deep, grew red but did not tear. The fire she had passed through had burnt away more than just her skin. Softly, Niamh pressed her cheek. "I shall brave it," whispered she, and those words proved more courage than anything she had ever done before.

Her eyes on the far shore, Niamh raised her foot and held it over the running water. She pressed her lips tight, until she could feel her teeth against her skin. Her nails dug into her palms, even through the thick homespun shawl. She stepped forward.

Steam and bubbles burst forth, mingled with the Princess's dreadful cry and filled all the woods and echoed over the Loch to where the eagles held their council. They looked at each other, these dread birds, clacked their beaks, and nodded each to each. *It is she,* they said, and others replied, *It is not she with whom we spake,* but the eldest replied, *Who will go to our Master?* And the youngest of all flew up and bowed before the eldest eagle and said, *I will go.*

So be it, the eldest eagle said, plucking a white feather from his thin tail, and placing it before the youngest. *Seek for the master, and if you find him not these three weeks, then seek you his master, within the Shadowless. Go.*

And so the youngest of all the eagles took the feather within his claws and set forth, south, with the cry of the Princess ringing in his ears.

Niamh did not see the eagle go—nor would she have known the purpose of its flight. The water had burnt her badly and she had fallen, collapsed upon the bank.

"*Who disturbs my waters!*"

The Princess turned, pulling herself away from the bodiless voice. But the voice called again, "Who disturbs my waters! Who pollutes my keep? Speak—be ye man or beast!"

And then Niamh saw within the waterfall, as though it boiled along with the waters at its feet, a huge bearded face emerge. His fierce eyes were darker patches of moss mixed up with water and his beard continued to flow even into the brook.

"So please you," Niamh gasped, "I am Ogrin's girl."

"She hath no child."

"She took me in. And within your beard is her mirror. I have come to claim it."

"Oh ho! Hast thou, ashputtle? And what wilt thou give me if I let thee have it? For I see that thou canst not take it as thou art—thou shouldst lose thy arm in the attempt."

"Yet I must have it."

"Then thou must pay for it."

"It is not yours to keep."

"Nor is it thine to demand."

Niamh twisted a lock of her hair, still golden despite her skin, and said, "What would you? I have little I may offer, for I came to my mistress with nothing but my service."

"Then thy service I shall require. Know of me who I am—I am Ydulhain of the waterfalls."

"Your pardon, my lord!" Niamh said, sweeping a curtsey. "And your servant. What would you?"

The waterfall twitched, as though perhaps their King remembered a bit of news rippling from Castell Gwyr to Loch Corraigh about the Princess lost. But aloud the great merman said, "I have a daughter, Ariana by name, lovely in my eyes and dear to my heart. She is lost to me by a vile witch with small powers and a wicked soul. Some do call her Moira, but among ourselves we call her Mara of the Weeping, for she keepeth my daughter enchanted within a basin of maiden's tears and so none of us canst come to her aid."

At Moira's name, Niamh had blanched and said, "Your pardon, lord, but my mistress has forbidden me to go near Moira Blacksmith's daughter's house. And yet, for the mirror...." She stopped and standing straight like a soldier at attention, she asked, "What must I do?"

Nightfall saw Niamh returned once more to Ogrin's house. But this night she did not sit docilely plaiting rags into a rug, but paced about the cottage, gathering travelling things within a satchel. As she paced, she spoke—hurriedly so that her mistress might not naysay her. At last the Princess stood before the old lady, who had seemed to shrink and age since the afternoon, and she leant forward and kissed her mistress's brow. "I shall return," she said.

"Return," Ogrin said. "How shall you do that? How high you sound! Are you a Knight upon a quest? Why not dig up one of them and send them in your stead?"

"I am promised to this quest."

"You've broke promise before."

"No," Niamh said quietly. "I have done many vile things, but my word is still good. And there are promises I have made that I still hope to keep. Leave me this one goodness."

"Goodness! You're breaking promise with *me*!"

"But I go to seek your mirror!" Niamh cried, kneeling before Ogrin and taking her hands.

"My mirror, paugh! It's your own vanity, belike, you mean to seek."

Niamh laughed. "When once I had reason to be vain, I did not care for mirrors. But I swear yours has a hold upon me that I cannot understand and must obey. Do you not see? Once I refused to look within myself and men died for that. And now, methinks, I must seek out my true reflection. You yourself said a mirror showed the truth of things...."

"But not my mirror. Not the one you seek."

"Then Moira's mirror. Moira to whom I go."

"And if I do not want it sought?"

"I have promised this for Ydulhain. I *must* go."

"You'll forswear yourself, sure, if you keep promising the least little thing to any who ask it. Ach, child! You're sworn to break my heart, aren't you? I know not why Heaven sent me such a wild shadow girl for my old age. I should have brought home a pup rather than a girl that's now thief, now lady, now Knight, now insolence herself. There's naught I can say to keep you by me, my ashputtle girl?"

Niamh shook her head, playing with the folds about her mistress's wrists. Then looking up into her mistress's eyes, and seeing the milky tears there, the Princess said, "I will swear one more thing for all your kindness to me. Should I return, I shall tell you of myself. And should my quest lead me to what I seek, you shall be rewarded."

"Tell me all, so I shall mourn you more when at last you remember all and to whom you truly belong? Ah, be off child," Ogrin sighed, pushing Niamh from her skirts. "You've a few hours left before dawn, enough to sleep in. But here, take this," and she handed her a little ivory comb. "Now, mind you, it has no great properties, no hint of magic within it, other than sticking in the hair like any other comb. But with luck, you'll remember to return it to me someday, and then I'll keep you beside me, my ashputtle girl, until I pass away. Now get you to bed. I've no mind to sleep myself."

And so Niamh left and as she lay down on her pallet, she thought she heard her mistress weeping.

chapter xi

Ven as Niamh set out for the witch's hut and Gethin wandered the earth, Maelgwenn flew with squire and with guard, landing just upon the Green Dragon's wings, near the twins' Feasting Hall. The Fairy had spoken little as they flew, and neither Pwll nor Liam dared to question him—although Liam looked ever and anon westerly.

Grim-mouthed, Maelgwenn landed and stretched his arms and wings. In that moment, the youths saw scores and welts upon the Fairy that the night's faint gleam had hidden. How many more did his robe conceal, they did not know, but the wounds they could see were still red and raw although several months old. Pwll looked at Liam as though to ask whether he sensed the Count's doing in this harm, but Liam shook his head and touched not his side.

Then Maelgwenn turned to the youths, saying with something of his old humour, "I would have thought a trek through the Dark Woods would have lightened you, but I should have suspected that young men will never truly lack for nourishment."

Pwll laughed politely, but Liam said, "We did well for ourselves in the Dark Wood, yes."

"You live, and that might be said to do well," Maelgwenn said.

"We fought and were oft victorious."

"If you please, lord, why are we here?" Pwll asked desperately.

"Because you were on the wrong path," the Fairy said, turning hooded eyes to the squire. "Because I have need of you elsewhere."

But Liam flushed at this and blurted out, "Your pardon, lord, but we had even come to the moment of all our questing."

"And acquitted yourselves nobly. Let no one deny that. But though you fought valiantly, thou knowest as well as I that one minute more and the Count shouldst have slain thee. I am only sorry that I did not arrive before you reached that awful moment. I might have spared you much grief. Alas, although I know much, I do not know all and had only just learnt of your journey."

Liam opened his mouth to speak again, the fever burning in his eyes once more, and his hand upon his wounded side as though upon a sword. But Pwll did not let Liam address the Fairy, fearing that his companion might put them in worse straits. "You spoke of another quest," Pwll said.

Maelgwenn nodded his russet head. "I did. My cousins guard many things from their Feasting Hall—the Caves of the Dragon Prince, the petrified heart of the Wyvern's Steep, the Gateway of the Worlds—and the Sea of Memory."

"What is that to us?" Liam cried, unable to withstand the fire of his wound. "We are sworn to hunt the Count—no more."

"Sworn?" Maelgwenn said, turning from the dawn so that his face was all in shadow. "*Sworn?* Nay, that thou art not. A boon wast given, not an oath. Do not confuse duty and desire, Liam mac Hwyach. Thy duty is to the King, as is my allegiance. My words are not idle, and thou wouldst do well to heed them."

Liam flushed again and stepped backwards, calling, "Your pardon, lord, but graver matters press upon me. You snatched us from our path, as well as from our horses...."

"Your horses will fare well without you. I have asked the men of Findair's Garrison to tend to them."

Maelgwenn

But Liam did not listen. "Pwll, you and I must part company it seems. Be contented, Maelgwenn—he will remain. My duty calls."

Then Maelgwenn's many-coloured eyes narrowed and he looked—not at Liam's face, set like stone—but at the space between Liam's fingers, to the cauterised wound beneath. "Ah," he breathed, "I see now what hath transpired." And leaping forward to touch the guard's brow, he said, "Sleep," and caught Liam when he fell.

Pwll's face had gone deathly white as Maelgwenn returned, Liam in his arms. The Fairy stopped just beside the squire, raising a brow. "And thou?" he asked, very low. "Wilt thou also flee?"

"No," Pwll said, bowing. "Although all my heart is fearful, I will trust you."

"Even though I may prove to be no better than the false Malinka?"

"You have the Queen's trust."

"So did our cousin, before she fell."

"You are not she."

"And yet I once loved the false one. Thou knowest what it is to have thy heart rejected, even for a time. It mayeth drive a Titan to ruin and despair."

"The shadows fled before you, lord," Pwll said. "Lead me on."

Maelgwenn did smile then, the quicksilver at once restored to his ageless face. "Come," said he. "And all things shall be answered."

The Feasting Hall of Dalfínn and Goewínn nestled deep within the forest and seemed to grow out of the trees themselves, as though one of those massive trunks had thought to hollow itself out, dislodge a few boles for windows, and twist upward a sturdy chimney branch. The first buds of spring garlanded the hall, a few leaves—a remarkable shade of green—already unfurling upon the bough. Only the door, bolted by strong bands of copper and steel, with giant handles—molten brass like the spiralling horns of a gazelle—proved evidence that some mind beyond Nature's had a hand in the making of so strange and wonderful a palace.

Although the light was just rising as the Fairy and the two companions made their way down the hill and up another to the Hall, the household was already awake. Dogs, cats, pigs, cows, horses, sheep, chickens, ducks and all manner of bird and beast ambled abroad, speaking each in their own manner to the morning. Their human counterparts were not far behind and no less quiet, although Pwll suspected that many of them had been up late the night before, if the empty barrels twelve boys rolled down the eastern side of the hill were any indication. Upon seeing Maelgwenn, all the denizens laughed and clapped and called out his name. Some of the younger children trailed paths of forgotten birdseed in their wake, so glad were they to see Maelgwenn again. Apparently, not all Fairies were as formal as Aldhairen and Islendil in their double spires.

Maelgwenn's mouth split into a smile as two of the children grabbed him about the knees and sat on his feet while he walked. Seeing another tow-headed lad racing towards him, his own bucket of slop dribbling the earth, the Fairy's tone changed again and he said, "Are thy master and thy mistress within?"

"Yes, lord," the boy answered, somewhat taken aback by the laughing Fairy's gravity. "Shall I fetch them?"

"Tell them I am coming and that I bring ambassadors from Rhianna's court."

The youth's eyes flit to Pwll and then to Liam still sleeping. Without another word, he fled back to the Feasting Hall, barely pausing to lay his bucket down in the yard—unfortunately several feet away from the irritated pigs.

A few strides brought them to the twins' door. Gently shaking off the children, Maelgwenn stepped inside, even before Dalfínn approached.

"Cousin," Dalfínn said, shrugging on his cape of forest green over a loosed doublet of silver-shot vert, his hawk wings twitching anxiously. "He requireth aid?"

"A soft bed, a hot knife, and a cool hand and cloth for when he waketh," Maelgwenn replied, pulling aside Liam's shirt to reveal the cauterised wound beneath.

Dalfínn gestured to one of his servants, who ran into another room, calling out as he went. "I had hoped thou hadst come on a happier occasion," Dalfínn said, as they walked down the corridor after the servant. Pwll noticed that the floor, like the walls, had been polished until it gleamed like dark gold and then engraved with patterns of leaves and vines.

"For the first of spring? Alas, I wish that hadst been the list of my voyage," Maelgwenn replied. As he followed Dalfínn, he stumbled and had to lean against a wall. But when the Lord of the Hunt would question him, Maelgwenn shook his head and said, "Goewínn hath not returned?"

Dalfínn nodded and invited them into a side room that looked west and was still cool in the early morning. A breeze wafted in through the glassless window, carrying with it the smell of heather and herbs. "She is with the maidens and hath been since midnight."

"Ah, I had hoped to employ her hand in this affair."

"The wound cannot wait, even for her ministrations. It hath too long festered. Who did this?"

"Dost thou mean who inflicted it, or who sealed the shadow within? I can name the first only," Maelgwenn said, laying Liam upon the bed.

"No need, cousin," Dalfínn replied, "I can guess that name too well. We have used it oft in curses this winter. But I shall send one to the door to bring my sister when she arriveth. In the nonce, thou mayest use my blade, Soul's Peace—thou shalt find it sharp enough for thy purposes."

Perhaps the fairies had forgotten about Pwll, so caught up were they in their arcane surgery. But though he had dwindled from their minds, he still remained within the room, hunched in a corner whilst Liam cried out in his enchanted sleep; whilst Maelgwenn took the knife from the fire and placed it again in the guard's wound; whilst the sun shifted until it streaked through the roof of twisted roots and dotted the floor. Within his corner, Pwll hid his face in his arms and prayed. And so acutely aware was he of all the sounds around him, that the squire was the first to note a new sound—laughter, turned to silence and the patter of bare feet against a patterned wooden floor.

Noon had come and brought brown Goewínn with it—brown Goewínn and several of her other maids, dressed likewise in earthen hues. Like her brother and her cousin, Goewínn's attention narrowed to the patient, now sweating as though he would melt, stretched out upon the bed of heather. She whispered a few words to her Handmaids, who all ran off—except one. Her hair that hid autumn leaves perennially within it; her eyes reflected the bottom of forgotten wells, and her skin shone like new-foamed cream. This one dared to step into the room, and up to Pwll, and give her hand to him.

"Come," the Handmaid said. "It will be many hours until your friend will wake, and you will only burden your heart more if you stay. Come, take your rest. You have earned it."

With one last glance at Liam, Pwll nodded and stood, crossing himself as he did so. "I will come, lady," he said, "but I will not rest."

The Handmaid cocked a brow at him and then smiled. "Bathe and eat first. We shall see whether your body agrees with your mouth after that."

Hours later, as the Fairies still toiled, Pwll at last took his ease, his eyes swimming with the vision of Graithne, as the Handmaid was known. "Hast thou magic?" he murmured, even as exhaustion pulled at his eyes.

"No more magic than any housewife has," Graithne smiled, resting a slim hand upon Pwll's shoulder. "Sleep now."

Reaching up, Pwll grasped her elbow when she would leave. "Go to him," he said. "Then I will sleep easy."

"As soon as you let me go, I shall," said she, passing her cool hand over his brow. Beneath the thin wool blanket, Pwll shivered and thought desperately of Elowen's soft lips. "Sleep now. Your friend shall not wake until dusk has come. I shall be with him."

No more could be said, for sleep—more persistent than all of Pwll's protests—triumphed, even as the parish bell rang nones and the sun warmed the room where Liam lay, unconscious.

The feast that evening was sombre and not at all fitting to the season, for the people of Dalfínn and Goewínn tended towards merriment, even when it was not a holy day. But the first days of spring had always been dear to these hunting folk and week-long celebrations usually attended the revelry. Not so this mere second day—Pwll and Liam had brought the shadow of Gavron's court with them and it hung like an invisible pall above all within the twins' dominion.

But even as the feasting—listless as it was in comparison with years gone by—made its way to the spit pigs and whole roasted venison, Liam's eyelids flickered, closed, shifted, and opened into crescent moons.

Graithne, who had been stirring up the small fire, came to his side at once pressing a damp cloth to his eyes to rid them of their yellow sleep. The loose strands of her hair hung in tendrils about her face and her touch seemed the sweetest thing that Liam had known in a long while.

"Do I dream?" he asked.

"All men dream," Graithne replied, pausing in her ministrations to look piercingly at the guard. "But you are not dreaming now."

"I think I must be," he said, and might have said more except that his time with the Count and as the youngest and the greenest of the guards had taught him caution. Instead he asked, "Where am I?"

"In the house of my lady, Goewínn, and her brother. You are safe here."

Liam looked up then and around and saw the strange, curving room he was in, like the inside of a rosehip, or the shell of an acorn. "I remember," he said and touched his side, closed and stitched—clogged with blood, not fire. His head turned upon the pillow and he shut his eyes again so that the lovely maiden might not see him. "Ah, God," he whispered, "I remember."

The cool cloth slipped off him. He heard it dipped in the water, heard the excess dribble back into the basin, and felt it against the back of his neck, behind his ear, upon his temple, and his jaw. And Graithne's voice, as smooth and clear as water, saying, "It is over now. Whatever has happened is past. Your fever has left you. Let your memories go with it."

Liam laughed then—brittle and dry and old. "Forget, lady?" he said, turning his head to look at her. "Nay, that is one thing I shall carry with me always, though my wound now heals. There is nothing that can cure me of my remembrance of my sins."

"If it is confession you seek, Father Damien is here hard by. I can call him if you like."

The guard sighed heavily and let Graithne turn his head towards the fire so she could press the cloth upon his other cheek and ear. "Perhaps hereafter," he said. "Though I have been shriven for my blackest fault already, it has not expunged my memory. Nor have all my battles cleansed me of my guilt—no, not even when I ran my blade through my tormentor's breast. But even his life I should not begrudge him, if I could but forget what I have done." The cloth stilled; Graithne hid her face in shadow even as Liam said, "There is naught that can do that."

Dark green eyes held his as the Handmaid touched his jaw and made Liam look at her. "Perhaps there is," she said. But of that hope, he could draw no more from her that day.

That night, the Fairies held council whilst the mortals slept.

"We have tended to the one thou brought to us, cousin," Goewínn said, "but he hath not the only wound. What hath befallen thee? Wherefore come thy injuries?"

"I would not speak of them," Maelgwenn said, twitching his wings irritably. "They are of the moment."

Twins exchanged glances, slender fingers that held the bowstring in the day tapping their white birch glasses.

"Art thou mortal, cousin?" Dalfínn said. "Hath time a claim on thee?"

"Do you ask if dread-lovely Malinka hath laid curse on me? Nay. I have not tempted the Perilous Strait these twenty years. She hath no hold on me."

Maelgwenn mumbled this last into his cup and by this the twins knew that indeed he bore a wound, but not one that balms could salve. Still the twins regarded Maelgwenn with the weightlessness of those to whom time is nothing, until at last he said with a rueful sigh, "Pride alone stoppeth my mouth. I have found the Princess."

"Where?" Dalfínn demanded as Goewínn started from her carven chair.

"Better to say at what price. She fell into the Wolf King's snare—although that might have been a Providence. For long had I searched for our godchild to no avail. I had thought the cause a hopeless one when word came to me from the foxes and the jackdaws that the Wolf King had left the Green Mountains and travelled up through Urdür."

"Didst not our cousin waylay him?" Dalfínn pressed, fine brown brows lowering over nut-brown skin.

Maelgwenn shook his head and the shadow of a smile played about his lips although his eyes did not laugh. "He seeketh wisdom from the stars and hath forgotten all that liveth beneath him."

"Yet the Wolf King is bound to the Green Mountains," Goewínn interjected. "We twelve bound him."

"We twelve are no more," Dalfínn said and rested his hand upon his sister's own. Then turning to Maelgwenn, he said, "I fear thou shalt make us nine."

"I fear the same," Maelgwenn breathed.

They were silent for some time. The lonely nightingale sang her song as though she, too, lamented their passing. Dalfínn rose and stretched his wings, looking outward through the slender trees that served as columns and as gateways to the outside world. Perhaps his far-reaching eyes rested on the Mountains of Morning, wondering at their rosy peaks shot through with streams of light. Maelgwenn did not look eastward to those mountains, but deep into the red wine in his chalice. And Goewínn, lovely Goewínn, fiercesome Goewínn of the Bow, who hunted earth and sky-path, gazed at Maelgwenn whom she loved well, and stifled tears that shamed her. At length, Goewínn said, "Dawning cometh. Wilt thou not grace us with thy story?"

The laughing Fairy nodded with eyes far distant on the day he had begun to die. "Long I tracked the Wolf King, for he stalked that which I could not see— something blacker than himself. Many days I followed after, and many's the time I thought myself gone mad to follow with no proof that the Wolf King didst not merely lead me on a merry chase. But when Faunden gave his place to Hintev, that very night I saw a thing that gave me hope—I saw a haggard reflection within a basin of ice, the reflection of Niamh, much changed from whom she had been.

"From that day forth, in windows and in glasses, in icicles and water's depth, I saw her. And when the snow began to fall, it blew everywhere—but caught upon Niamh, within her hair and upon her shoulders, so that she appeared like wind with form, like untameable Voro whom Hintev has long courted. Then on the day most wretched, when that snowy-bearded Vertumn showed his greatest wrath at the Wydoema's coquettery, a cottage seemed to rear out of the snows, the door open and then close again, and the Wolf King snigger and wheeze his lust.

"Wily Wolf King waited—howling to the moon at last, when he knew Niamh wouldst slumber. Then that villain, whose very being hath long polluted all elements, shifted into human shape, and raised the latch and entered. Swift as thought, I followed after, and hid myself within my wings as oft we've done before to conceal ourselves when mortal eyes are prying.

"I watched him walk up to that bread he maketh with bones and excreteth again; I saw him swallow it entire. I watched him slink to the Princess's side and sit upon the bed beside her. I watched him smile and stroke her hair then open wide his mouth again, with tooth grown long into a fang and tongue grown dry and raspy. And when he came into this state—not man, not beast, not anything—and all enraptured by his prey, then I struck with wing and arm, lifting him writhing from the ground, my hand about his throat.

"'What dost thou here?' growled I. 'How camest thou, O fell and foul creature, into all of grace's presence?'

"That creature didst not answer but whined and wriggled within my grasp. And so I summoned all my power to lay another binding upon the Wolf King's soul to leash him once again forever round the Falcon's Folly. But as the strength welled in me, the Wolf King's eyes shone yellow slits, and within one heartbeat and the next, he'd changed into his lupine shape and freed himself and sprang on me.

"His claws raked my shoulder, his teeth ravaged my wings—and I returned him blow for blow, buffeting him with wind and ground upheaved, speaking words of power to hurl him to the ground again. But my hurts were nothing, as well you know when the nervous mare will bite you or the teething puppy gnaw. Even as we fought, I felt my wounds fresh healing. I raised my hand and op't my mouth to speak, but even as I did—forming words to spell him to imprisonment—he changed his shape and said, 'Well fought, Maelgwenn. Well fought indeed.'

"My hand still raised, I said not the magic word but spoke in mortal tongue, 'Tell me all thou knowest and it may go well with thee.'

"'Wherefore should I tell thee?' said he. "What wilt thou give me in return?'

"'Naught but what thou deservest.' I replied.

"'Then I'll not parlay with thee.'

"'Yet thou wilt speak all, villain, or thou shalt die.'

"At this, he snarled and wavered in his form, shrieking as he changed, 'Then thou shalt *know* naught, Maelgwenn. Nor shalt thou trap me again. And the secrets that I and I alone know shall die with me: eyes to see the Princess with, eyes to make her pure again.'

"'Thou liest,' said I, folding my arms within my cloak—for I confess it amused me mightily to see the Wolf King foam. And more, I had some thought to trip that creature into telling all, as I had done before. 'Come, come,' said I, in gentlest tones. 'What dost thou know that we Fairies do not?'

"'The way the dark things go,' said he, 'and secrets of the dark.'

"''Tis naught but riddles,' said I. 'The dark shroudeth those which are the merest commonplaces and calleth them secrets. But I will tender this to thee: let us ask one other a single riddle each, to see whether the dark shroudeth all.'

"'And if I win?' the Wolf King asked.

"'Then thou shalt rule right soon enough, for all will then be lost. But should *I* win as I think I may, then thou shalt live no more.'

"'This is no bargain,' said he, shaking his fur and pacing about me. He blew hard through his nose and sidled to a fallen tree and sat upon it. And as he sat he flowed back into his human form. 'Let me offer another, since thou art so eager to take my blood. Shouldst *thou* fail to ask a riddle that I know nothing of, then thy blood also shalt be forfeit. Then thou shalt live no more.'

"'Done,' said I—for I had no fear. What harm could he bring me, powerful though he is and long-lived through vile enchantments?"

"The gravest harm, cousin," Goewínn said. "Didst thou not see thy doom?"

"Had I seen it, coz," Maelgwenn said, taking her hand and pressing it, "then sure I should not sit here as I do now with time weighing upon me. We all looked strangely at Rhianna when first Malinka cursed her. What could we know of that which did not touch us? What could we know of sleep, much less of sleeplessness, much less of that final sleep from which no man awakeneth? Nor," said he with the weariest of shrugs, "do I see thou comprehendest me, fairest Goewínn." Then reaching forward to touch the tendrils of her hair that hung all entwined with ivy leaves, he said, "Believe me, were it within my power, I shouldst see that thou of all our kin shouldst remain untouched."

"Beware what oaths thou makest," Dalfínn said, turning from the mountains. "Even those oaths thou but beginnest to whisper. Thou art not yet full mortal, cousin, and that which thou bindest on thyself or on any others wilt still hold."

"Too late hast thou counselled me," Maelgwenn replied, rising. "I swore my life to Niamh and bound it in men's writing. I did not think it shouldst be called upon—no, not even when I faced my doom. Thou mayest once more berate me for my foolheartiness—but do not chastise me for my charity."

Dalfínn knit his fine brows and fluttered lashes like moth-wings upon his high and beardless cheeks. "What black magics are these to demand so high a bloodprice?"

"What deep magics, coz?" Maelgwenn chided. "What deeper magic is there than noble sacrifice?"

"If men speak true, then true love's kiss," Goewínn said, her voice easily lost within the morning mist that wound throughout the chamber and made all the world still and wonderful.

"Perhaps," Maelgwenn said in voice so low that only Goewínn, longing for such a hope, heard its faintest echoes.

The Dawn rose his multihued mantle from off the world's very edge, tracing in his wake the brilliant colours of the True World, and heralding his father whose majestic golden brow rose in splendour to spill over the fields and mountains in pools of molten light. The cock crew, the animals stirred, the church bells rang the matin hour to call the faithful to prayer. Men woke and did not marvel at the wonder of their waking, and fewer still recalled their dreams and held them, chrystalline, before their eyes.

"'Tis no hour to linger on such foul deeds," Maelgwenn said, breathing in the scent of lawn and dewdrops on the air.

"And yet, as thou wilt, 'tis the very hour," Dalfínn replied sternly. "Thou hast not many remaining to thee."

"And each more precious than the last," Maelgwenn said, never turning from the dawn. "I am loathe to lose them."

"They shall be lost if thou fearest to grasp them as the mortals do. Speak. Or doth pride stop thy mouth again?"

Then Maelgwenn laughed aloud and all about him glowed a whiter parti-coloured, as the invisible light by which we see will sparkle into its separate parts when twirled through a prismed glass. "Well-aimed, Dalfínn!" Maelgwenn crowed. "Thou art indeed most worthy of thy eponym, for thou speakest like a very Arrow!"

"And thou, O Fox, doth ever me evade," Dalfínn said, although not harshly.

"Then hear ye both our riddle game and be ye then contented. He spoke first, since I had laid the challenge, and put to me this riddle, which doubtless you shall guess before I did.

> *'Grasp me, I'm already gone,*
> *Look, and I've already come.*
> *Use me and I fly away,*
> *Mourn me but I'll never stay.*

> *'Search for me, I am not found,*
> *But for your heart, I have no sound.*
> *I am the order in the void,*
> *By me are all things destroyed.*

'I, the day and night divide,
I, the future from you hide.
Before me, mighty mountains bend,
Within me die the race of men.

'I, that creep o'er hill and dale,
I, that make the red cheek pale,
I, that rule o'er field and glen,
I, beginning, I, the end.

"'What am I' chuckled the Wolf King, concluding.

"'Without imagination,' said I. 'Thinkest thou to trip me by a children's riddle? A babe squalling in a nursery, the grandfather in second infancy, both could name thee those verses and many more.'

"'Then answer,' said he. 'Or bend thy neck for my teeth to bite. And I shall howl from hill to hill that the Fairies are but charlatans who know not all that lies within the veil.'

"I confess, I had not known immediately the answer to the riddle—but as he gloated, I understood, and yawning I answered, 'Time.' Without waiting for his reply, I put to him this riddle:

'Within a land no foot can trod,
I met a man who was not there.
He spoke, as though with voice of God,
Of long ago and places fair.

'He spoke of lands of never-been,
He spoke of times that never-were,
Then took my hand to visit them—
Though from my spot, I never stirred.

'What wonders flashed before my eyes!
Though naught but woods stood in my way.
And though I'm told he told me lies,
'Twas only truth I met that day.'"

"Thou speakest of legend," Dalfínn said.

Maelgwenn nodded. "Specifically of that of which men have writ."

"And didst he guess so?" Goewínn asked.

"Yea, for well he knew those legends writ of him. 'Thy life is forfeit, Maelgwenn,' said he, rising.

"'Forfeit!' cried I, astonished. 'Hath thy word no honour?'

"'We have both won,' said he, shrugging, and as he shrugged, shifting ever restlessly from one form to another. 'Both lives are forfeit.'

"'That is not the nature of the game,' said I.

"'What matter? We are the rule-makers, thou and I. We are not bound by what we decree. We bind on other men.'

"'Dog,' spat I, and gathered light within my hands, so that he whined and backed away, 'thou hast no power but what is allowed thee. Thou hast no more than the bone without the marrow.'

"Then I threw at him that ball of light, which pierced his heart and cracked his skin so that he seemed to be a new-formed star within the sucking void, exploding and imploding all at once. Yet he hadst voice for that one moment, and caught my eye with his dread eye, and whispered through his gleaming teeth, 'Blood will tell.' And with a final howl to the moon so long his mistress, he fell.

"His final riddle worried me. What didst he mean by those three words? I bent over his body—as pale and grey and wolfish as the day his mother whelped him. He mighteth have been but another creature, grown gaunt with the harsh winter storms. But his side wast slashed where the light hadst slain him, and his blood slugged out, thick and viscous. This I touched and knew all his mind, for he hadst lived and died by blood, and in his blood still fresh-flowing, what one mighteth call his maddened mind remained in part.

"And terrible things I saw—too terrible to relate. But last I saw within his mind the answer to the riddle I had sought. Simple wast the answer—so simple, I should have thought of it myself, but perhaps it wast held from me so that I should have the strength to bear it. Twofold is the Princess's redemption: the loss of herself and—"

"The bloody sacrifice of another," Goewínn finished softly.

Maelgwenn nodded.

"But thyself, cousin?"

"Whom else shouldst it be? He who wouldst marry her?"

To this Goewínn had no answer. Dalfínn bowed his head in sorrow. Maelgwenn closed his eyes and leaned against the warm trunk of a twisting tree. "My wounds were closing fast. A pinprick remained on my finger alone, where he hadst bit me. This I dipped into his blood—and felt time crash upon me."

The sun rose. And he said no more.

On the third day of their stay, when Liam was able to walk without wincing, Maelgwenn called together his cousins and the two companions and addressed them thus: "Not all men are made for the same purpose. Some are created to rule, others to serve; some to write ballads, others to till the land;

some to wrestle demons, and others to aid angels. This, gentlemen, is your task and no other, although in the moment it may seem petty.

"To the south and east of this place lieth a bay from whose waters not even animals dare drink, for anyone who so much as toucheth a drop to his lips wilt lose all remembrance of his life, even to his name, and for this there is only one cure and that is hard acquired, but will be found, in time." The Fairy shifted and the companions remembered his wounds and wondered at them once again. The twins said not a word. "But this water carries another property, for they say that from these waters were the unicorns first begot, and something of their purity still lieth within the waves.

"This, then, is your task and no other: gather for me a cupful of this water, taking care not to drink any part of it. And this you shall bring to the Princess to offer her to drink—not withholding from her its nature or its properties, for the thing must be done in knowledge or its effect will be null and beauty lost even to herself."

"Your pardon, lord," Pwll said. "But no one knows where the Princess has gone, nor where the Hermit has fled. How are we to find her when all else have failed?"

"Nay, she hath been found," Dalfínn intervened. "She is by Loch Corraigh and hath been for this whole Winter. She is…much changed."

The companions looked askance at Maelgwenn who clenched his fists and loosed them. When he spoke, he addressed himself to Liam and spoke in mortal voice, "I wouldst thou *had* slain him the night I found thee. My mind would be at ease if I knew he were in Hell."

"He is in Hell, lord," Liam said, his own voice distant, as if remembering the long, cold nights locked up within the prison. "You have no need to wish a greater one upon him. But he cannot yet be killed. I ran him through twice and still he lives. They feed off one another, his shadows and he. And until a shadow may be slain, the Count will live in this earthly hell of his own devising. I say live, and yet he craves death at any man's hands."

"When shall we set out for this water?" Pwll asked when the silence grew too deep.

"Tomorrow morning," Maelgwenn said. "We have all delayed too long."

The next day, even before the cock crowed, Graithne roused Liam and Pwll from their slumbers and bade them dress and eat—they would start out with the rising sun. The two did so and met the Handmaid by the door, surprised to find within her hand a walking stick and upon her back a sack. "I shall go with you," she explained, "at least as far as the edge of the Wyvern's tail, where the water is visible. Take this," she said, handing the sack to Pwll, "but do not open it until you come to the waters and then lift the lid but a little. The waters shall flow into it of their own accord."

"What is it?" Pwll asked, looking within the sack at the golden horn ringed with precious gems. A dragon curled upon its back as though upon its treasure hoard. And looking at it once again, Pwll wondered if he beheld not horn but tooth.

Graithne shrugged. "It has many names, but here we call it the Dragon's Maw. Whatever element the rim touched—be it earth, air, water or fire—will be drawn in and never released until the one who bears it gives it willingly to another. I have drawn air into it and so give it to you. You may draw the waters into it and so give it to the Princess. But come," she said, swirling a light cloak, the colour of the sky in the late hours of a cloudy night, about her thin shoulders. "It grows light and it were best to return before nightfall in the lands of the Wyvern's Steep."

They travelled for about three hours, coming at last to where the trees thinned into a rolling, grassy hill which terminated in the Sea of Memory. Pwll set off at once, eager to bring good news at long last to the King's court, but Graithne stopped Liam when he would follow saying, "You must promise me not to drink."

Liam started and looked anywhere but at the Handmaid. "And what if I do not heed you? Is there any harm in solace?"

"Aye, if it be sought in things that bring you greater sorrow."

"Sorrow, lady?" said he with a grin just short of a grimace. "What sorrow can there be when naught is remembered?"

"Greater sorrow, sir, for that which cannot be remembered."

"But one would not sorrow if he knew that the memory which is lost were bitter and far better bled from the mind than allowed to cloy?"

"But if all is forgot, how can that knowledge of the goodness or the illness of the lost memory be remembered? Nay—its virtue is recalled indifferently by the mind, but not the heart that ever and anon longs for wholeness. And those memories lost long to be named, with all their joys and sorrows still attendant. We are more than the sum of our memory, and yet if it be stripped, we are less than who we should be."

"You speak in riddles, madam. Too clever for a poor farmboy like me."

"Then listen with thy common reason, if thou hast wit enough to argue."

"No argument, but that you shall not sway me."

Then Graithne took Liam's head in her hands and made him look at her. "Tell me my name," she said.

"Graithne," he replied.

"So I am called. Tell me my name."

"I have said it. If it be not Graithne, I do not know it."

"Nor I—and that is my sorrow." She let go of him then and stepped away, as though he had burnt her hands or bruised her heart. "Go," she whispered. "But remember." And then she fled into the forest.

Pwll was already half-way down the hill when Liam joined him. "She is a fine girl, that Graithne," the squire essayed when it seemed clear that Liam did not mean to reveal the content of their conversation.

Liam did not answer. His thoughts were on the waters, lapping pleasant white foam upon the sandy bank. Pwll he hefted the sack more comfortably over his back and descended the grassy hill, Liam walking after like a man within a dream. But even as they approached the waters, the guard grew agitated and refused to come closer than twenty paces from the beckoning sea. When Pwll would question him with look, Liam replied with that not-quite-grin, "We have but one cup between us and one hand only required to hold it. It was given you—what need have you for me?"

"None," Pwll replied truthfully, "except to keep me from falling in. I have been known to topple into rivers fully-clothed before this, albeit only when my mother were absent."

"Fear you to touch this water?"

"With all my heart," Pwll said, glancing at Liam's wound. The bandage beneath the shirt was clean and no fever raged in Liam's eye—but a pallor lingered, like an invisible shroud. "As you say, this is a task for one hand. I do not know how long the Dragon's Maw will drink, but if weight is any judge, I am like to be a while. I think I saw some mushrooms to the east of here, between the trees where the tail descends. Perchance there is also a stream from whose waters one *can* drink. Would you take such a commission?"

Liam nodded, looking back up the hill where the tail of the Green Dragon bordered the Sea of Memory. A few autumn leaves still lingered beneath those trees, all but ground to dust. He wondered if the memory of autumn would die with the waters, too. "Farewell, brother," he said, clasping the squire's forearm in the manner of guards at war.

"Shall I see thee in two hours' time?" Pwll asked anxiously.

Liam only released the squire's arm and set off northeast, following the curve of the water rather than heading into the wooded hills.

So for the second time since coming to this country, Pwll prayed without words, even until he could no longer see the guard. The waters he collected without incident to grace ballads of a later age. Although the songs we hear now account variously a hydra, a merman and a phooka with whom the valiant Pwll did single combat, and the famous riddle of the *Lay of Branmoor* answers that he is the man who neither drank nor drowned, but held the Dragon's Maw to his mouth, breathing in the air until he hit the hydra at its heart and swam upwards to the surface with memory still intact. But these are the invention of poets, no matter how cleverly writ, and the simple *fact* is that Pwll of Branmoor spent an hour at the water's edge, as the Dragon's Maw let out its air and breathed in the waters of forgetfulness, with nary a frog croaking let alone a hydra roaring, to mark the event.

Liam had not returned within that hour, and so Pwll waited an hour more, wandering the side of that hill—and then the next hour, and the hour after that, stretched out upon the new-sprung grass and basking in the sun—and the next two hours, climbing eastward through the trees, now truly hungry and uneasy as well, always in view of the Sea of Memory, always looking for the tall, thin, beardless form of Liam. The promised mushrooms he found unplucked; a stream he found later on. A few of Dalfínn's men saw he riding through the forest surrounded by their barking dogs, with spears under their arms chasing the tusked boar.

Come terce, he found his way back to the Feasting Hall—but no Liam greeted him at those wooden doors. An hour later, the hunters returned with the boar and several pheasants upon their shoulders, and soon after that the fires roared and the whole household gathered in the Hall to celebrate. Still Liam did not come. The minstrels sang and asked their riddles, the jugglers plied their trade, the fruit passed round the long wooden tables, the women retired and the children with them, and the men passed flasks between them until the fire died. But Liam did not come.

And so into the last ember, Pwll whispered, "Farewell, brother."

That night, as the squire lay sleepless upon his bed, a stranger stumbled out of the woods into the clearing of the Feasting Hall. His shirt fell open at the neck, stained with water at the collar's end. His short hair stuck out in odd directions, as though a bird had made his nest upon his head and then wet fingers had tried to brush the result into order. He walked like one distracted, as madmen do by the pull of the moon, or drunkards returning from the tavern— his path was never very straight, nor always forward. Often he stopped and leant against a tree, and covered his face with his hands to muffle the sounds of his sobs. So crumpled against one maple, just without the light of the Feasting Hall, the strangers' shoulders shook, with laughter and with tears equally commingled.

Graithne, pacing the long gold-gleaming halls and dressed in a gown of white—trimmed at throat, sleeve and hem in patterns of green and gold, vainly arrayed for her long-neglected bed—heard the stranger and heedless of her bare feet and unbound hair, went out to see who came so late to the twins' keep.

"Liam," she whispered, as the figure unwound himself from the base of the tree and allowed the moon's rays to touch his face.

She ran towards him on feet more used to chasing the hind than a human, and checked herself even at the shadow's edge. Liam turned to look at her, his eyes as dark as night—and Graithne felt something within her die.

"Stranger," she said. "You are well come to this place."

"Lady," said he, "I thank you. Lead me on."

Graithne smiled, a dim, murky reflection of latter days before the wounded guard had op't his eyes and asked if he still dreamt. Turning, she said, "Then come with me, good sir. And you shall find a bed already made for you, a fire laid out and bread and wine awaiting your arrival."

Meekly, the stranger followed the Handmaid past the doorway, over the gleaming threshold, down the curving hallways gently lit by hanging lanterns of filigreed iron that cast shadows of birds and beasts and leaf and vine upon the walls in a pattern as wild as the twins' own hearts. Into the room, he followed her and watched her as she lit the beeswax candles upon the mantle and beside the bed, lighting fires in her hair as she bent and breathed life into each flame. She stood and passed him, as noiselessly as a ghost, as the soughing wind Areal. Her lips barely found the strength to wish the stranger a good slumber.

Past the half-closed door, she put her fist in her mouth and choked back the salt tears that threatened to well from her eyes, run down her cheeks, and down the hills to drown in the Sea of Memory. Silently, the door opened to reveal the guard, his hand outstretched to take the Handmaid by her elbow and turn her pale face to his.

"Thank you," he said, gravely, taking her hand and pressing it.

She stuttered a breath and blinked. "'Twas no less than...."

But he stopped her mouth when he kissed her hand and said, before slipping back into his room, "Thank you...Graithne."

All the tears caught in her throat, and her face lit as though it were already dawn.

chapcer XII

he Princess crept out of the cottage before dawn so that she might not encounter her mistress, for she feared that the old lady would talk her out of her oath to the Lord of the Waterfalls. As for Ogrin, she stayed abed for much the same reasons.

Three days the Princess travelled, following the path past the village and back into the woods where Moira lived on the north-west shore of Loch Corraigh. There the waters begin to narrow before they make their way into the Ice Floes of the great Giants, whose backs turn always away from men and their doings. And some say among them sits Östrung the Giant, looking ever upwards after his *gvennik luv*.

Moira's house stood lonely, black, and crooked atop a hill sparsely grown over with spiky yews and bracken. Thick smoke belched from the chimney and all looked as desolate as ever anyone said the threshold of a dragon might be. A few mangy cats, a dog or two, and a slit-eyed goat wandered about the blasted yard, hissing and nipping at each other, as though to drown out the sound of the lake beneath.

Niamh wrinkled her nose at the acrid stench that coiled from the hut, but steeled her soul and said, "That way lies my course. I must go." And so she set up the hill, although her heart was loathe. Roots and stray pans tripped her, half-filled with half-spilled rainwater and residual mud, so that she arrived with stained petticoat and matted hair.

Three times knocked she upon the door, strangely tight shut despite the dilapidation of all the house around it. At last a lady opened the door. She was worn and thin, with sharp, bagged eyes, and puckered lips. A rough burlap shawl barely concealed gnarled white hair dyed in patches a tattered black. When she saw Niamh, her whole face shrunk like a pumpkin hollowed and rotting, but her sharp, murky eyes took in everything about the Princess, from her bare feet, to her singed skin, to the golden wisps peeking out from under Niamh's simple mantilla.

"Who are you and why have you come?" asked Moira in a voice like crackling sticks.

"My name you shall have not, but I come for Ariana, Ydulhain's daughter, whom you hold captive here."

Moira did not laugh, nor frown, nor do anything more sinister than open the door a little wider and courteously invite the Princess inside: an act that caused Niamh to shudder more than any other answer might have.

The inside of the witch's house was as decrepit as the exterior, for the whole hut drew to it drafts that even chilled Niamh's burnt skin. Moira closed the door and bolted it tightly, and then paced across the floor where she gestured to a hole in the ground. She had no need for a cane, Niamh saw, although age had bent her a little. Obediently, Niamh followed, and looked within the hole to find it full of water—but no Hydoema maid. So dark were the waters that Niamh did not even see her own reflection—and for a moment the Princess feared that her quest was in vain.

"I do not see her," Niamh said at length. "Or have you captured her reflection, as the Wolf King hid Deirdre's blade?"

Moira laughed deep in her throat and said, "Nothing like, my sweet. Do you see nothing but water there?"

So Niamh looked again, and this time she saw the distant shadow of fish milling below the deeps, for a pool ran beneath the whole of the house.

When the Princess said what she saw, Mara of the Weeping smiled narrowly, as though someone had taken a knife to the old woman's face. "Then you have seen she whom you have come to rescue, and you have seen all those whom the Lord of the Waterfalls sent before you—as well as three fish who are…legitimate."

The Princess's eyes widened. "All those who have come before? Do you mean to push me in among them?"

"If you guess wrongly, aye. For I must let you guess three times, once a day. Those are the rules and not made by me. Had this magic been mine own, I should have made a meal of the Hydoema's daughter, though Ydulhain rise up the lake and drown me. But I do this for Ruthvyn of the Silver Hands…."

"I have heard of him," Niamh said, shortly. "You mean Ruthvyn Necromancer."

"Yes," Moira said, caressing the tawdry fringes of her shawl, "the same. The girl would not have him, I believe. Although she gave him the secrets of the deeps, and these he turned against her. But that is naught to us. It is enough that he did me a service once and lifted from me a muteness, and now I repay him. Thus you may live for three days as you are, but within my house and under my whim. There is bucket and cloth about the room, and I have lost a speck of gold somewhere underfoot as well. When you have found the speck of gold, shall you guess."

The bucket and cloth Niamh found easily enough, but looking about the room, Niamh despaired of ever finding *anything* other than dust. "Were I other than I am," Niamh said as she brushed the floor, "were I Rhynn or Faunden, were I born of earth or air, I might call upon birds or mice to aid my search. But I suppose those things are only in tales, and naught for the likes of me."

All afternoon Niamh toiled, but found nothing for all her pains. As the sun set Moira returned, smiling her thin, awful smile. "Have you found it?" she asked.

Niamh stood, all her joints aching and sleep already overwhelming her. Her gaze wandered to the hole in the floor and she shivered at the thought of her fate. But when she opened her mouth to speak, a ray of sunlight chanced between some crack in the stone, and so Niamh smiled back and said, "Aye, mistress, there! I wonder that you had not eyes to see it for yourself."

Moira's eyes crinkled, and her nose flared, and she leaned forward as though her back pained her more, but she said, "Well then, shade, tomorrow may you look and make your guess." Then, leaping forward, she grabbed Niamh's arm and pulled her into another room filled with straw. "Two more nights do you have. Sleep well, while ye may." And with that she bolted the door, leaving Niamh alone in the darkness.

Around midnight, a little light from the moon crept through the poorly thatched ceiling, high, high above the Princess's head. In that spill of moonlight, Niamh looked almost as she had years and years ago. Within her hand gleamed the little ivory comb.

Above, a bedraggled magpie looked in, and seeing the comb, gave a screech of jealousy.

The next morning, Niamh woke to someone pulling on her hair. Her eyes still blurry with sleep, Niamh lashed back, sinking the teeth of the comb into her invisible assailant's arm. With a shriek, the tugging stopped. Niamh rubbed her eyes to see Moira who pressed her crooked back to the wall, nursed her hand and sneered. But as the witch saw that she was regarded, her sneer became a smile and she said, "What a pretty thing you have there. If you give it to me, I shall release you from me and—although you may not guess—yet you will have your life."

Niamh clutched the comb to her breast. Quickly, the snarl returned to the old woman's face and she said, "So be it. But remember, I have been generous with you as is not my way, as any will tell you. Go now and guess. Although I do not think you shall choose aright."

Niamh went to the water hole and bent and looked, until she could make out all seven sleek bodies of every rainbow shade. Of Ariana, she knew but this from the lore of Lady Marien: that the Hydoema's fins, when she took that half-form, were so lustrous as to seem purple in one light and white-silver in another.

"Surely what little I know, the others who came before me also knew," she thought. "And doubtless, they guessed that one that sits ever in the middle, like a lady in her court, for her behaviour, if not her colouring. So I must not choose her.

"Who, then? Which? Shall I choose the plainest of them all, thinking that the enchantment might have robbed that lady of her beauty? Shall I choose the one of gold? Yet four still remain—the blue for water? But blue may still be sky. The crimson as water's opposite? Yet again, others might have made such mistakes of logic before me. And here yet is another conundrum! For the two remaining are as like one another as two peas in a pod!"

Behind her, Moira tapped her hardened foot upon the packed earth and cleared her throat in a rasp of dry lightning.

"Ah, well, I have two more chances, should I fail, and perhaps Providence will remember me." And so thinking, she rose and said aloud, "I choose the crimson."

"You have chosen wrongly," Moira said, quietly. "And so gained yourself another day's work. Unless, of course, you concede your bagatelle?"

"You know my answer."

"You show your strength—but I shall beat it down. In the valley westward does Connela herd his golden sheep, which feed on buttercups and are guarded by the red-eyed dog, Guleesh. Anyone who draws even within a hundred feet of Connela's flock does the dog harry and maim, and so Connela and all his ancestors have grown wealthy and made much of themselves, marrying even into titles, although they themselves are naught but farmers.

"Connela today will be wed to Lord of Udinë's daughter, Gwenhyfarch, and some say that Cadwyr and Viviane may attend, since Cadwyr first gave over the golden sheep to Connela's family, and Gwenhyfarch's mother served as Viviane's Handmaid before she married Baronet Udinë's son. Thither must you go and pluck double handfuls of the golden fleece. And this all done and returned by nightfall, or your life shall be forfeit and you shall beg me to enchant you into a fish's form rather than what else I may devise."

Niamh listened to the whole of this, standing so straight and still, she might have been the post of a door. For she feared that if she moved at all, she would faint of fright. When the witch had finished, she stood silent a little and then said, "Show me the path westward. I shall delay no longer."

The land to the west of Moira's cottage fell slowly, even as the land to the north rose into the Ice Giants. Between the pines and the new-leafing trees, over fallen trunks and always beside the diminishing Gwyrglánn, Niamh walked as quickly as her feet could take her. But though she walked for hours upon hours—past small, neat cottages, over treacherous rivulets, across a gentle plateau dotted with proud birches and surrounded by prouder oaks, and beside a forgotten well, overgrown with ivy and moss—no plain opened before her, no sheep did she see, or barking of dog, or merry epithalamion. One hour had already passed the sun's zenith and perhaps seven more hours of daylight remained.

Sitting on a large stone and rubbing her calloused feet, the Princess laughed sadly. "Thou art doomed to be a wanderer, Niamh! Ah, well, thou canst do no better than to continue on the path before thee. Mayhap some new adventure shalt befall thee and then thou *shalt* be foresworn."

No sooner had she said this than she heard the bell-chiming of a running stream—barely more than a hand across when she found it—that ran downhill and wound its lazy way around the trees. Its song seemed to call her and she followed it, thinking that it might lead her as well as the wider Gwyrglánn. Stepping lightly over mushrooms marking the water's edge, the Princess followed the strange trail until she found herself standing before a small pond covered in part by water lilies, their broad pads inhabited by jewel-like frogs and dragonflies, the water itself smelling strongly of iron and minerals. Looking up from this enchanted pond, she saw the promised valley, patchwork emerald green and gold.

"Now all the saints be praised and our Lady look kindly upon me!" Niamh cried, holding onto a branch to steady herself. "Perchance some sheep should stray to this pond to drink, and I may take the fleece before another hour passes."

But no sheep came near, although she waited ten minutes together. And as she peered through the hanging vines of the double willows before her, she saw that her hope was vain—for Guleesh prowled around the herd, and a sheep strayed no more than a yard from the fold before the great bloody hound nosed it back. Worse, as the Princess stood there, she saw Guleesh raise his muzzle often and sniff this way and that, as though he caught a whiff of her cinder-smell.

Even as she despaired, she saw coming from a distance a cart and horse driven by a russet-haired lad who smoked a pipe, humming a tune the whilst. Within the cart were several bags, and from one of the bags poked a tuft of golden fleece. Niamh quickly clambered up into the willow tree and waited—unsure whether she might be invisible to the lad or not. For something had changed the night she had come to Ogrin's hut, and though she knew those who were not wholly good could now see her, she knew not if those virtuous were still blind. As the cart passed under the willow, she dropped lightly into the back of it and hid herself between the giant bags.

The lad did not seem to mind, although he cocked his ear as Niamh landed, but with a puff of smoke, he turned his eyes forward again, and took up his tune in earnest.

One day in the spring, when the world was new,
I saw a maid sitting by a yew,
And such a sight I ne'er did see,
As the silver hair of that fair lady.

"Oh mistress mine," I whispered low,
"Oh swear to me thou hast no beau.
Oh swear that thou wilt e'er love me,
And be my own sweet, fair lady."

Said she, "My love, my love thou art,
And nothing ever shall we two part.
But if thou wouldst have me, then this thou know'—
I am the Maiden of the Snows.

"My father lives on yonder hill,
While I am his, I do his will.
And he hath set this sad decree:
That none but beast shalt e'er have me.

"Thou art no beast, if my eyes see' true."
"No beast," said I, "no more than you.
But I love thee so, I'll thy father dare,"
Said I to the lady of the silver hair.

The Maiden of the Snows

To yonder hill I set my way,
And upward walked all night and day,
And when I came to the snowy crest,
Before the gates I took my rest.

"Where is the master of the house?" I cried.
"For I am come to claim a bride.
Listen well, all ye, unto my woes:
For I love the Maiden of the Snows."

Three days sang I before the keep,
Three days sang I, and ne'er did sleep.
Until her father, giant tall,
Did come outside, and to me call,

"Leave me, leave me, mortal man.
But one shall have her—but one can:
He that doth not melt the snow,
Only with him shall my blessing go."

"Then tell me how," I made so bold,
"To chill my heart and keep it cold.
For my palm is warm with lover's sighs;
Myself shall melt into her eyes."

"Turn back," said he, "if thou hast will,
Keep thou thy sighs and warm heart still.
For if thy love thou chance' to freeze,
Then thyself shalt be that beast."

"I do not fear," I said aloud.
And ah, my heart, I was too proud!
"But tell me whither I shall go,
To wed the Maiden of the Snows."

The song ended abruptly there and Niamh, who had paused with double fistfuls of golden fleece in her hands to listen to the song, felt all the breath go out of her as if the song had held her tight within its spell and only now released her. The russet-haired driver turned his head slightly, took a puff from his pipe and sent a fine ring of smoke into the air, saying, "Do you know how it ends?"

Niamh gasped. The lad chuckled and flapped the reins over the pony's back. "You might as well come out and sit more comfortably. And *I* might as well tell you that should you try to run, Guleesh shall lame you at the least. And if you make it back up the hill," pointing with his pipe, "the fleece shall melt like butter in your hands. Few people know that, for thieves do not like to nose about their misfortunes much."

The Princess could no more than answer, "You—you can see me?"

The youth laughed, a merry sound like trumpets in fanfare. "Are you invisible?" Before Niamh could explain, he continued, saying, " I beg your pardon. I had no idea I carried a sprite with me! I quite mistook you for a maid too long travelling. But you have not answered me: do you know how the song ends?"

"No," Niamh said, "I have never heard it before, although I have heard similar tales."

The youth laughed again and puffed on his pipe for a while. "Good, good! For you see, I made it up. And so my question was not entirely honest, just as you were not with me. But what did you think of the song?"

"I liked it," the Princess answered, finding that as she said so, she thought that she very much liked the youth, too.

"But it is not great literature."

"It kept my interest."

The youth flicked the reins to turn the pony, saying, "The two are not always the same. But if it entertains, that is good enough, I suppose. I have promised to sing it for my brother's wedding banquet tonight and have been worrying over the last two verses considerably. Would you like to know how it ends or would you like to guess?"

"Well," Niamh said, her full hands lowering into her lap, "I suppose he must win the Maiden in the end."

"Ah, ah! There you are wrong!"

"Then he does not achieve the task?"

"Oh, aye, he does that. But he becomes so cold, he forgets all about his love, until years later, when he happens upon that very pond we passed, where his lady love wept herself to extermination."

"But how horrible!"

"Hmm, I do admit I stole a bit from the tales of the Moon's demise...."

"No," Niamh interrupted. "The story is tragic. I cannot think why your brother should want such a song at his wedding feast."

"Not all stories end well, as my brother knows. It's our tradition to remind ourselves of the dangers of pride on happy occasions. You, for example. I suppose there's a reason why a girl like yourself dropped into my cart? Unless, of course, you *are* a sprite, in which case I shall have to lay hands on thee, if I want to marry thee."

Niamh blushed which made her ashen skin glow like embers on an autumn evening, and although she was not beautiful as she had been, she was yet for a moment quite handsome. Quietly, she said, "How do you know I am not already promised?"

"Oh," said he, shrugging beneath his coat of tweed, "as for that, I was hoping that my luck would hold and even if you *had* a beau, you should give up him in a twinkling for my easy charm and grace. I'll let those bear me out for now while you tell me why the willow trees are raining women."

At this Niamh shifted between the sacks and twined the golden fleece about her fingers, wondering whether she dared to chance running away, despite the lad's warning. "Will you let me go if I tell you?" she asked.

"*Let* you go?" cried he, turning full around on the seat to face her. "What story do you have that you fear that I'll imprison you?" She did not answer at once and so he said, "Well, as you will. By this hand and by my name, Padriac mac Connivar, if you tell me true, I'll see you safely where you will myself."

So Niamh told Padriac of her bargain with Ydulhain, and of the tasks Moira had set her. To all this Padriac listened with stony silence, puffing smoke from the corner of his mouth and lowering his ruddy brows until they fair met in the middle.

When the Princess had done, he said, "Then why did you not come directly to the hall and tell your tale? Gladly would my brother give you double bags of the fleece—oh, aye, and men as well to guard over you as you journeyed back."

"I—I do not know. The thought had not crossed my mind. Much has happened since I last entered any court."

Padriac quirked his brow at that, but held his peace. They ambled on at a leisurely pace south-east to the Connlach Manor House, upon whose double turrets two flags flew: a red boar passant upon the baronet's crown flanked in fess by the two twined black oaks upon a field of erminois for the Baronet of Udinë, and a golden ram's head upon a simple verge ground for the sons of Conn. Garlands of early crocuses and honeysuckle hung from the rooftops and surrounded each post and lintel. Just within sight of the wide lane leading up to the great oak door, Padriac pulled the pony to a halt. For some time he sat hunched over, staring discontentedly at the traffic upon the lane and glancing up occasionally to the position of the sun. The pipe he tapped against his teeth, in time to the song he had sung before.

"Tell me your name," he said.

Niamh bit her lip. "Would that you had asked anything else."

"But I have not. What is your name."

"You do not know what you ask," she replied, queenly.

"I will not aid you unless I know whom I aid. If you will not divulge your name, as I have to you, then you may run empty-handed and late to the witch. But if you will have my aid, I ask your name in return."

"Will you renege on your word? You have had my story, is that not enough?"

Padriac smoked out a waft of sweet weed for answer and looked with a shrug at the golden fleece within her hands.

An eagle flew above, and Niamh's heart lifted and fell at the sign. "So be it. But I must swear you to secrecy by your name, Padriac mac Connivar of Connlach House. She who begs thy aid is Niamh, daughter of Gavron, son of Aidhen, son of Beorn, son of Olwen, daughter of Rhys, son of Siawn Shieldbearer."

As she spoke, Padriac's pale green eyes grew wide and frightened, flitting from the black homespun garments to the charred skin, to the long golden hair, matted with dirt and time. But her voice was untainted gold, and she had not finished before he leapt out of the cart and knelt on the ground.

"Your pardon, Princess! The news was so old and so fanciful that on a winter's evening amidst so many strange stories of yesteryear, I did not credit it. And our country, so full of wonders to supply us with many an impossible tale, has brought queerer folk to our herds than one I thought merely in need of a bath."

He stopped and seemed to weigh his words and find them wanting, and so he added with a courtly flourish, "Your servant, Princess, to command."

"Command?" Niamh laughed, rising. "Nay, Padriac, son of Connivar, I am not who I once was. Had you seen me six month ago—or rather, had you fallen at my doorstep, plagued by my beauty—then might I have commanded you. But I have been deceived, banished under deception, and become a deceiver myself. If you will not rise, then tell me at least how I may fulfil my awful quest."

Standing then, Padriac reached into one of the sacks and took out two handfuls of fleece. Bidding Niamh to replace her own, he then gave her the fleece, saying, "Blessings and good fortune be thine." He sighed and looked once more at Niamh, and she realised with a start that the good lad looked on her with longing and sorrow that he could look on her at all and was not blinded by her beauty. The moment passed and he shrugged and knocked out his pipe. Climbing back up to his seat, he flicked the pony's back and turned its nose towards the stables on the southward side.

Once there, he jumped down and hailed an auburn-haired lad, who looked near enough to Padriac that he might have been a cousin. They held short conference and the auburn-haired lad nodded and then went about saddling up a lean saffron mare with a star upon her brow, whom he introduced as Liseva, after the Lord of Radiance. Padriac turned back to the cart to help Niamh down—his heart sinking again as she touched him without burning him (besides that of his own cheeks)—and said, "Can you ride?"

Niamh smiled and put the fleece into the pockets of her apron. "I can hold on."

158

Padriac nodded, "Then I shall take you to Moira's. And if you are success-
ful, I pray you return some day to Connlach."

"I will," she said and allowed him to put her upon the saffron mare.

Native to the soil, Padriac knew the way to Moira's house across the plains
where a mare could gallop for two hours and trot for one through the last stretch
of forest. Thus they reached the witch's hut with an hour of daylight to spare.
Padriac let the Princess down at the bottom of the hill, hidden within the circle
of trees and said, "I dare go no further, but if ever you wish to summon me, then
take this," and he pressed into her hands a small whittled cross, twined with a
length of braided fleece that also served as chain, "and give it to anyone you see
passing by, and tell them to bring it to me, and I shall find you."

"Will any do this?"

Padriac smiled grimly and set about refilling his pipe that had lain in his
coat pocket while they had raced together. "But mention the destination and
any man will come. An errand to Connlach is promise of gold. There is no man
yet who has said nay."

"I thank thee," Niamh said, and touched her hand to his.

"Oh, do not, Princess," said he, drawing back as though suddenly weary.
"Perhaps you no longer drive men mad, but they are sorrowed for their loss."
He shook his head and turned to mount. Once upon the mare, he lifted his rus-
set head to the wind and breathed deeply, smelling all the promises of spring.
Grinning, he looked at her and said, "Perhaps I shall change the ending to my
story. Should you like that?"

Niamh hung the cross about her neck, and said with a laugh choked by
tears, "If you please."

Padriac lit the pipe and held it between his teeth. "Come to my brother's
house, and I shall sing it for thee." Then with a "Heyup!" he disappeared
among the forest branches.

Niamh wandered up the hill touching each tree as she passed it, as though
to gain some of the ancient strength that made them stand even when the tempests roared. The sun danced upon the treetops as she walked into the hut and
found Moira boiling blood in a pot above the fire. Wordlessly, the Princess
removed the handfuls of fleece from her pockets and gave them to the witch.

Moira wiped her eyes with the back of one tattered sleeve and plunged her
hand into the rich stuff. Her nostrils flared and she looked angered enough to
throw Niamh into the pot. Instead she gestured to a loaf of bread saying, "If you

are not worn out enough, you may stir this pot until the salamander burns blue and then eat your fill."

"What is it?" Niamh asked.

Moira gave the ladle to Niamh and said, "There are means to take the youth from another." Then holding the fleece to Niamh's hair as though to compare the colour and richness, she added, "This is one of them."

As the witch moved her arms, stroking the fleece, Niamh saw the edge of Moira's shawl fall away to reveal a belt set with shards of glass and iron. Her reflection distorted weirdly within them, showing at once herself kneeling by the hearth and again herself as once she was. But of Moira, she saw reflected dessication.

Niamh smiled to herself and hummed Padriac's tune. Moira looked sharply at her and then down to her belt. With a jerk of her fingers, she pulled the shawl over the ruins of her mirror and did not let the Princess sleep until the moon began her descent.

The next morning, Niamh woke to see the witch sitting in the corner of the closet upon an uneven stool, like a raven come in from the rains. "Make your guess," Moira said.

Niamh pressed the heels of her palms to her eyes, for her thoughts were all still on the peacefulness of Connlach and she had quite put her quest out of mind. The wooden cross shifted against her breast and so she said, "The plainest of all."

"Wrong again, shade," Moira said.

Niamh groaned and lay back upon the straw.

The stool creaked as Moira stood and hobbled over to the girl, leaning on the wall for support. Within the folds of Niamh's shawl, the head of the ivory comb peeked through.

"You are weary," Moira said in a voice as close to kindliness as a jackdaw's hoarse cry. "You needn't subject yourself to more toil today. But give me the comb and you may walk free, whither you will. You might walk to that fine lad's arms, where waterfalls will ne'er pursue you."

Niamh pushed herself up on her elbows and looked amazedly at the crone, but Moira only smiled back and pawed the girl's shoulder—perilously close to Ogrin's gift.

"You have only one more guess," the witch continued, when Niamh rolled away from her. "One more guess and I can guess that you shall not guess aright, for none before you have and they were all more clever than you. But none of them had a dainty as fine as that comb, and so none of them escaped their punishment. What say you?"

"I say that I am recovered of myself and do not fear a corpse." And she gestured to Moira's belt.

The witch grimaced and then softened, saying, "Perhaps you will make exchange with me. Give me the comb and I will give you one shard from my belt, which will tell you anything you desire to know. What say you?"

"That I have long learned the dangers of accepting gifts from those whose hearts are villanous. What employment have you today? I shall gladly do it."

Moira snarled and stood up suddenly straight and tall, as though she were a young girl again. Loudly she said, "There is a magnificent bird that lives in a nest of fire in the foothills of the mountains above my house and its plumes are so long that when it flies, men point to the sky and wonder at the comets. Long have I desired this Firebird—for so it is—but I have been unable to catch it. Had I but one plume from its tail, I should be happy, for whoever owns but a single plume shall immortal be. This you must retrieve by nightfall—and the mountain is a day's journey away. So you see, I have given you an impossible task. Would it not be better to give me the comb and spare yourself death? For even if you reach the bird, you must pass through its fiery nest, and then bear a living brand back, and all this before the sun sets in the sky."

"I shall seek the bird," Niamh said, "for fire does not fright me now."

Fire did not fright her, but water still held sway, and so Niamh stood helpless before the Gwyrglánn only three hours upon the road. Before her she could see the Firebird's mountain rising in the distance—its sides slicked with ice, its peak crowned with flame. Gladly would she adventure either of those, but flowing water she could not abide. No bridge either did she see, nor any boats going across, and although the worn sides of the cross played across her burnt skin, calling upon Padriac—himself four hours away from her destination—could do no good.

Even as she stared into the restless depths, the Princess felt anger rise within her like an ember fanned into a blaze. Falling to her knees, she looked into the rushing river, looked past her distorted reflection, and cried out, "Thou hast done this, Ydulhain! Thou hast done this! I begin to believe thou art in league with this witch and thy daughter safe at home, whilst thou makest sport drowning any who cometh thy ways! What wilt thou do now, Ydulhain? Wilt thou allow another to fail thee? For thou hast chosen the only one willing to attempt this foolery, and now keepest her from thy task! Answer me, Ydulhain! I shall scream until my throat is raw, but I shall be answered! Answer me, Fool of Waterfalls!"

She had barely time to pause for breath when the man himself rose up before her, this time in his fleshy form, his broad chest ringed round with a sash of seaweed, his scaly fins thrashing the water. His terrible blue-green brows were lowered, but he said no word although clearly angered. Gesturing to the river, he called up a great white horse made entirely of foam, with eyes of coral and teeth of sea ivory. The horse reared and drops of water flew from his mane. The Lord of Waterfalls spoke a word and the horse grew calm and bowed in his fashion before his master.

Then, turning to Niamh, Ydulhain said, "This I shall do, but only this once. Aüngiadd wilt carry no one twice. Thou must find thy own way back."

Niamh closed her mouth and bowed profoundly. When she had looked up, Ydulhain had gone and Aüngiadd stood by her side. She mounted the strange horse, although the little drops burnt against her hands when she held onto his mane. As they rode across the Gwyrglánn, the great stallion's hooves barely touched the top of the small waves, and so Niamh was spared that too. They reached the far shore in four score strides that passed so swiftly that the Princess seemed to have no sooner mounted, than Aüngiadd was kneeling again to let his rider off. Niamh's feet touched land, and the water horse reared and plunged back into the waters, becoming swirls of foam upon the river's surface.

Now the harder task loomed before her, and the Princess realised how hasty her desire to climb the mountain rather than traverse the Gwyrglánn had been. For, as Niamh neared the mountain and saw how terrible its icy sides, she felt how hopelessly impossible was the task Moira had given her. And even as she began the long climb—now half-way into the day—even as the ground became more steep and the paths more narrow, the Princess wondered if it were too late to return to the witch's hut and relinquish the ivory comb. "But where would I go from thence?" she said aloud, pausing in her climb to wipe her brow and look at the green foothills eastward. "If I break faith with Ydulhain, I shall not cross the Gwyrglánn again, and then friend and foe will be barred from me. Unless I travel south, to my father's court, where I am sure I am all but forgot." A cool breeze, carrying the scent of dandelion and loam from the far-distant earth, drifted by and tugged on her skirts. Niamh smiled into the wind and turned her back to it, so that it might help push her up the mountain.

By the hour of mercy, she had reached the snows which burnt first her naked feet and then upward to her knees, despite her sturdy dress. The wind too, heretofore so pleasant and amiable a companion, grew bitter and sharp and ravaged her from every side. Still Niamh pressed on, clawing her way upwards with her hands and feet, crawling to the top. More than once did she look behind her and think of sliding backward to the lands in springtime. But then memories of the river and proud Ydulhain would rear within her mind, and again she would set her face northwards to the nest of fire.

Three more long hours by the sun spent she climbing that strange and magnificent foothill, and after a time the burns became less, or else she made less of them, and the coldness of the snow and wind impressed themselves upon her—bruising her cheeks and making her poor body quiver with chilled fever and fatigue. Padriac's song sounded in her ear, echoed from this hour in a golden yesterday, and new verses seemed to reach her, singing harshly in the very winds themselves:

> *Up to the mountain's peak I climbed,*
> *Past frost, and hail, and cold cold wind,*
> *And with every step, I whispered low,*
> *"I love the Maiden of the Snows."*
>
> *But all the winds, they stole my song,*
> *And, ah, the road was fearsome long!*
> *And soon I had no breath to blow,*
> *The name of the Maiden of the Snows.*

Her head she kept bent down, her eyelashes near frozen together, her breath turned to ice within her mouth. She knew not whether she lived or died or moved or slept or felt hot or cold, or even whither she was bound. And each step seemed like the one before, for the wind blew the snow about so much, that even looking behind gave no indication of where she had been. The snow burnt, or else her skin did; her flesh froze, or else the ice did. How could she know a nest of fire when she did not know the natural elements?

But at last her fingers found purchase upon barren rock and the road levelled so that she could walk upright without falling back. When her eyes could open again, she saw before her the wondrous nest and the great fiery bird within it.

The Firebird's eye was very black—but not the empty, hollow blackness of Moira's hut, or the ugly darkness of a nightmare, but rather within that eye shone the watery reflection of all things combined. To look within it was to see one's own self, one's home, one's land, and all within that—birds and beasts, friend, foe, kin, cloud and field, and all of history besides—of ancient wars, so old they are all but forgot, of Titans and Fairies, and of times before and between these, of the memory of the True Earth, and the Pillars of other worlds. One could be lost in that eye and never desire to leave again. It was, indeed, a very pleasant fate for those strong enough to brave it. The eye held constant although the body shimmered, more like the aurora than fire—refracted light, a mirage to cover a greater glory. But the fire that surrounded the great bird was no illusion and the heat of it burnt worse on Niamh's face than ever the small, fatal hearthfire of her home.

Thou hast come at last, the Firebird said, turning her head to better gaze at the bedraggled Princess. Her wings flapped once and the flames rose in response. Niamh shielded her face from the sparks that flew like stars dropped towards earth. The Firebird seemed to chuckle—although such an action seemed far too earthy for such a creature—and she said, *At one time thou longed for nothing more than to wrap thyself within the hearts of the Ice Giants. Hast thou forgotten?*

Niamh shook her head, but could find no voice. The wind still held it.

The awful eye blinked. *What wouldst thou, Princess?*

"I am come for one of your tailfeathers," Niamh replied at last, catching the words out of the air.

And how shouldst thou hold one of my feathers? Art thou incorporeal? Art thou spirit?

"Neither," the Princess said, her shoulders slumping even as she looked upon such majesty. "Ah, me! I have travelled so far for naught. Is there no means for a mortal?"

For one willing to enter through the nestfires, aye, the Firebird's voice of everywhere and nowhere ran sweet and high about the mountaintop, heard below as perhaps no more than a softer soughing, but upon the summit, an intelligible chorus of chimes.

Niamh looked then to the fires, asking, "Will it hurt?"

Yea, but thou shalt not burn.

"Will it," she stopped, gasped for air, found the wind tamed once more, and all the promises of hope within it, "will it reverse this enchantment?"

Thy skin? That is no witchcraft, and only that which thou fearest will save thee.

"I have many fears, lady."

With all the same root.

"That I will lose myself entire."

The Firebird nodded. *And for that reason, thou seekest Ogrin's mirror, although she hath told thee nothing but the truth. It holdeth no charm, nothing but glass. It wilt not bring back what once was.*

"Then my quest is in vain."

Nay. It hath reached the very moment for its being. Come, child. My fires may giveth thee comfort, if thou canst bear them.

"And if I do, may I have one of your tailfeathers, and so complete my lesser task if that is all allowed me?"

The Firebird did not answer, but blinked her eye, shifting the images that rested there.

The Princess nodded. "So be it." And stepped forward.

Colours engulfed her—red, white, yellow, and all those in-between— molten gold, old roses, the deep purple of cloudy evening. She seemed to sift through light incarnate—dandelion puff, white-jaundy daffodil, moth-wing, swan-breast, sea-foam, iron. Her fingers spread as though to catch the light within nets of air and memory; her arms spread, her head lolled, her eyes looked to the heavens and saw only light. Her back ached with the strain of beauty weighing on every side, at once pushing and supporting her arms, her legs, her back, her head. Colours poured through her open mouth like faceted mist—red, white, and yellow grown liquid on her tongue. The ache had spread to her limbs now, even to her eyes. Her mind spun, kaleidoscoped the world, broke it in twelve places and spun it like a top. And the brand in her back spread outward to her limbs, until she thought she must be passing through that other fire so long ago.

Did she walk? Did she live? Had she fallen into the Firebird's eye? Once more the colours shifted, lifting until she saw rising from the cold flames themselves the Firebird's brow, crowned by three plumes that glowed as brightly as the Dwarfish Swords made for the heroes of old. The vision shifted, changed, from bird to lady—wings became veils, plumes turned to diamonds, those diamonds to stars and stars to white roses—and Niamh felt tears well up in her eyes. For in the lady were all the colours of the fire, all the colours but combined and so beautiful that to see her were terrible for the knowledge of the smallness of the self. But the lady only smiled and seemed to say, "Bear yet a while," and then she disappeared, or else melted back into the fires.

How long Niamh remained suspended, she did not know. But as she ceased to count heartbeats and gave herself up wholly to the fire that did not burn, a sweet sleepiness overcame her, like honey slow-melting on the tongue or the laziness of summer upon a bank of thick, rich grass. The colours still shifted, but now Niamh could pick out patterns within them, could see the gradation from sable to snow, could trace the subtle graceful weavings where the colours touched and kissed, and took something of each other. And when at last she might have closed her eyes and let the colours carry her where'er they would, even to the world's edge, she felt herself drawn out of the fires and back into the cold drifts of Time.

Before her sat the Firebird, smiling. *Well met, Niamh.*

Niamh curtsied profoundly. "Lady."

What didst thou see, Niamh?

"I hardly know. Although I looked long, I cannot tell you what I saw."

The Firebird nodded. *So many a man hath said, standing without my nest, when I have asked the same of him.*

"Is that how I appeared?"

At one time, yes. To those fortunate few. I am but a servant to the fire; He revealeth what He will. The features shifted once more, the wings settled in a graceful fall of shivers, the great eye blinked. *Thou didst come for a purpose. Is that so soon forgot?*

Niamh shivered, although the air was anything but chill, and wondered whether she ought to knee'. "Lady," she said at last. "I am come to beseech a tailfeather from you on behalf of Moira Blacksmith's daughter."

And what wouldst Moira do with this gift?

"She says it will prolong her life."

And so it mighteth, although not in the way she supposeth. But this she shalt not have.

"Then what am I to do?" Niamh cried, looking to the heavens, already crowding over with Dusk's dark hair. The sun was nearly a memory, merely another star far, far in the west.

Speak for thyself. Think, Niamh, for we shall not meet in these guises again: what wouldst thou?

"Wisdom, lady," the Princess said, the answer flying to her lips as though another spoke for her.

A goodly choice, and one I shall grant thee. Come hither, Princess.

Niamh approached the Firebird trembling and stood with hands clasped, so far out of her element. The great bird bent and kissed the Princess's brow, which glowed brightly for a moment as though a star had fallen upon her, like Guilian Silverbow's fabled coronet. Within a heartbeat the glow faded a little, so that now one spot shone white, as though cleaned with soap and water, and to look closely at it was to see that it formed like petals newly opening from the bud. The Princess smiled, as she had not done for many a season, and it seemed her spirits lifted with her mouth.

Tonight, the Firebird said, drawing back, *thou shalt wake when the world groweth darkest. Creep to thy door and listen to what thou shalt hear. Riddles shalt be solved and all promises kept. Now turn thy back to me and I shall blow thee straight to Moira's keeping. And when thou speakest to her, give her a handful of the ashes from thy skin and say, 'This is what the Firebird granteth thee.' It shalt avail thee well. Now go, little one.*

And within the space of one blink and the next, Niamh found herself outside the witch's door, with the sun just glimmering through the high and twisting roots of the trees.

The Firebird's word was good, and the witch accepted Niamh's proffered ashes with dislike, but no word gainsaid. The Princess was given bread and made to gather worms' eggs until Moira locked her in her closet for the night. And when the darkest hour came, which for the past two nights had come and gone amidst a worn-out slumber of Moira's canny devising, Niamh rose as though her name had been called. Remembering the Firebird's words, she crept to the door and waited silently.

After a little time, she thought she heard a muffled sobbing, a hushed conversation, a final plea and a door slammed. The cries returned, and then a sweet voice rose and sang with a voice that shifted between and over itself, so that to hear it was not so much to listen, but to see:

> *Sing softly, sing.*
> *Hear me, all ye who wake, my woes:*
> *Three years am I enchanted;*
> *Three years by love betrayed;*
> *Three years am I imprisoned;*
> *How long, oh world?*
> *How long?*
>
> *Folly-fallen, to the Silver hands,*
> *To Ruthvyn, mad for power.*
> *The secrets of the deeps I gave him;*
> *The secrets of the deeps he owns;*
> *The secrets of the deeps now keep me;*
> *How long, oh world?*
> *How long?*
>
> *Choose ye the great one?*
> *Nay, she is in true form.*
> *Choose ye the least one?*
> *Nay, she is my sister.*
> *Choose ye the gold one?*
> *Again, thou hast the truth in hand.*
> *How long, oh world?*
> *How long?*
>
> *Choose ye from the colours?*
> *Blue once was a peasant,*
> *Pretty lass, and promised to*
> *A great sea lord,*
> *If I would be her dowry.*
>
> *Crimson was a poet,*
> *Languishing for love long lost,*
> *Fancy-filled, but heart of gold—*
> *And so he fell.*

Twins remain, and these two twins,
The last to come, ah sorrow!
One is maid, and one is true,
And nothing apart can tell them.

Tomorrow another joins us,
Tomorrow another falls.
Ah, hear my song,
All ye who wake!

I am not maiden,
I am not fish,
I am the secret of the deeps.
Tears have I shed, me,
Tears do I weep, me.
How long, oh world?
How long?

At this, the song grew silent. The weeping took up the strain, until this too died and all the world was silence. But Niamh bore the mark of the Firebird, and so she crept back to her bed and slept with prayers full on her lips.

"Make your guess, shade," Moira cried, throwing open the closet door with a crack as loud as doomsday. "I am weary of your deceits."

Niamh did not roll over to see where the witch stood—well could she imagine the great ragged shadow—but she kept her head in her arm and made sounds as though weeping.

"What, girl? Do you think that after all the pains you've given me I'd take your comb now? Not one jot—make your guess. I'll take your comb after."

"Alas!" the Princess cried into the hay. "How I am beguiled! What a wretch am I! A wreck past hope!" Then turning to the witch and grasping her hem, she said, "Ah, wilt thou not reconsider? Wilt thou show no mercy?"

"None, shade," Moira said, black eyes glimmering quite unlike the Firebird. "Make your guess."

"I will give thee my comb!"

"I will not take it whilst you live."

"I will be thy slave!"

"You will be that anon."

"Wilt thou nothing grant me? No reprieve? Not one request?"

"Not one! Make your guess!"

"Very well," Niamh said, lowering her head to cover her smile. "Although thou speakest so to the perdition of thy soul, if I guess aright."

"What care I for that? I've the Firebird's ashes and Connlach's wool. You dissemble; speak!"

"As thou wilt. I choose the water."

Moira's eyes grew wide, as large as saucers, and her lips spread horrible thin like a fish. *"How…?"* she managed to shriek, before the very foundations of the house rumbled and groaned and began to split apart as the waters who were Ariana, Ydulhain's daughter and her sister Anwen, rose and rumbled and seeped through the patchwork wood and mortar. A great hand, entirely formed of water, reached up and grasped the crone about the waist until she bent nearly in two. With a splash and a shout, the witch disappeared, dragged under the breaking flagstones and perhaps dragged even further down to Hell.

Water flooded the house, spilling over from the hole in the ground as though it were a spring and not a well. And from the hole, came two maids and a youth, who looked about them astounded. Niamh grit her teeth and strode forward, hopping through the rooms, stepping on any elevation she could. "Come with me!" she cried, and hastened through the door, followed by the unenchanted rescuers.

Down the hill they ran until they reached the small valley where Padriac had left Niamh, half a world ago. The house burst asunder as water spilled down the eastward slope, to the Gwyrglánn, rioting in a joyful splash of violet waves and met by a return spray that seemed to be both man and element. All stood in wonder at the sight, but less wonder when the water resolved itself into Ydulhain and his two daughters stepping lightly on the riverway, hand in hand and smiling with delight. Ariana stepped forward onto the dry land, her body shifting shape to accommodate—and any looking upon her then would have only thought her a handsome lass and plainly dressed.

"Thou hast saved me," Ariana said, curtsying before Niamh and holding out the silver mirror that had been the goad and goal of the journey. "And it is little that I can repay thee. But ask of me what thou wilt and know that thou and all thy descendants shall ever have the love of the Hydoemi."

"Only one thing I ask," Niamh said, accepting the mirror, "salve for my burns."

Ariana, her broad, open face before near glowing with gratitude, now grew troubled and dark, like the restless tides between sharp rocks. Looking back to her father, she said, "That I have not within my power to give thee, although it shalt come to thee by and by. Is there nothing else?"

It was all Niamh could do to keep from crying and burying her face in her hands. "No," she said, very quietly. "No, Princess. I can think of nothing else I require."

Ydulhain's daughter sighed—a sweet sigh, like lawn after rain—and said, "Then let me do thee this service. Thou hadst a lady well-beloved of our country, who taught thee when thou wert young, didst thou not?"

"I did," Niamh said. "Lady Marien. She is long departed from me now—the first to go."

"Then let me tell thee of her story. When she quit thy side, she travelled to her home, and when she came she couldst scarce lift her hand in greeting, and all her kisses were weak with contagion. She wast ever too good for this world. But on the day her soul wast looked for, Aldhairen himself came, and turning to us he said, 'Choose three among yourselves to come with me.' And turning to the Lady Marien and gathering her in his arms, he said, 'Beloved one, thou shalt have thy heart's request.' 'Shall I to the sea?' she asked. 'Aye,' said he, 'to the sea and beyond, to where there is no horizon.' And I was one of those chosen to go with the King of all the Fairies, and this I can report: that Aldhairen brought the Lady Marien to the Mountains of Morning, and on their rosy shores didst a young man greet her—the like of which I have never seen before nor since—and when she saw him, her eyes glistened more brightly than ever sun danced on rippling wave, and he took her in his arms and said, 'I am the sea that hath no shore, and long I have waited for thee.'"

Ydulhain

Niamh wept freely then, sitting with her back against a tree and her knees drawn up to her breast. When at last she found words again, she dried her tears and smiled up into the Sea-Princess's sweet face. "Thou hast done me the greater service, lady. And salved my heart, I knew not was bruised."

Ariana smiled too, and indeed Niamh's salt tears had wiped clean some of her ashes, for Ydulhain's daughter looked otherwhere. "It shalt not be long, I think, Princess," she said, and curtsied low to Niamh. Then turning, she came to her father and said, "Where is my brother? He is promised to a maid hereby."

Ydulhain quirked his brow and stroked his beard, regarding the quiet girl in blue who stood with the other maid and the poet. Then with a snap, the Gwyrglánn stirred again and out from it rose mighty Aineiron, of the iron scales. With a cry of delight, the girl (whose name was Elisa Viner's daughter) rushed forward and into the merman's arms.

"She hath no fins, my son," the Lord of Waterfalls remarked, when the lovers had quite done kissing.

"But I have feet, sire," Aineiron replied, stepping onto the shore as his sister had done before him.

"Wilt thou become a mortal for this lass, Aineiron?"

"And give my crown in one. I do love Elisa. And have died a thousand deaths since thou cast her from thy foaming hall, on Aüngiadd's wild back."

"Then my blessings go with thee; my sorrows I shall keep for myself. I have regained my daughters and lost my son. But go thou and be merry. And thou, oh newly-made daughter," he said, taking a strand of seaweed from around his chest and giving it to Elisa, "fear to lose this gift. For each leaf shalt grant thee one day beneath the waves for thyself and the grandchildren thou shalt doubtless carry with thee. There are two score—guard them well."

"Sire, I will," said Elisa.

The Lord of Waterfalls sniffed haughtily—although Niamh thought she saw a tear glisten on those high cheeks—and addressing the two rescuers who remained, he said, "Where'er you shall go, my steed shall bear you."

So Ydulhain summoned Aüngiadd once more from the deeps, and the maid and the poet sat upon his broad, white back. The maid looked to Niamh, turning hazel eyes like sunlight through a leafy canopy upon the Princess. "We owe you our lives, lady," she said. "Will you not ride with us?"

Niamh shook her head. "I have ridden once and may not again."

"Then is there any embassy we may make for you?" the poet asked.

"Yes," Niamh said, and took from around her neck the wooden cross. "If you will bear this to Connlach and to the very hand of the younger son of Connlach, Padriac, pray tell him that I am alive and all has come out happily. Tell him—tell him what has happened. It may be he shall put it in a poem."

The poet started and had the gall to look a bit affronted, but the maiden smiled and took the cross about her own neck. "That we shall, lady. And if ever you have need of us, do but call upon Aoife of Yew Manor...."

"Or Terence Songmaster," the poet put in with a flourish of his crimson hat.

"...And we shall requite you well."

And with that, the company split, each his own way.

chapter xiii

he Shadowless had once housed the Dusk, so the stories ran. Standing on the very edge of Urdür's lands, where the Gwyrglánn opens up into the Ice Floes, its towering walls curved upwards like another white mountain, filigreed to let in the natural light. As tightly constructed as a rose before 'tis bloomed, the ancient keep was as distant as the True World, as desirable and terrible as a the Tree of Knowledge. Steps circled without and within. Separate spires, added over the passage of time, sprang out from the central keep, connected by thin spanning bridges of different heights and curvatures. Below, gardens of every variety thronged—wild, tamed, herbs, spices, flowers, fruit, vegetables, trees, stone, sand. Each was dotted intermittently with graceful statues of marble, many-hued, depicting again and again the same lovely lady, draped in simple robes that hung in folds over the curves of her body as she inspected a jasmine leaf, raised her arms to the sun, or looked down upon the Hermit striding between the massy gates and to the tower proper.

One could tell time by the Shadowless, Gethin had often thought. From the upper stories, the gardens took on the shape of the hours: the wilds of the night tempered by the order of the day. The observatory, the laboratory, and conservatory reared on their westward wings, balanced by the library, gallery, and music hall easterly. Northward to where he could not see stood the chapel— replete with stained glass windows rising three stories high and ten feet wide, its grandeur humbled by the small herb-house beside it. Southward, where Gethin trod, lay the lesser buildings: kitchen, laundry, all the essentials to any life, particularly those of a scholar, for the master was like to forget to eat or wash unless reminded.

The long months since Gethin had met the unicorn had not been idly spent. Findair had he searched, and the length of the Rhún and the Suirebàir. To Sirena's coves had he travelled and dove beneath the waves of the Emerald Sea and the Serpent's Sea, and seen the remains of the beast that Guilian Silverbow had conquered so long ago. The Golden Valley he wandered, among the fields of buttercups and marigolds, even into the Ivory Citadel where the Moon had once made her home and where the Sun had wooed her, forgetting all else, until the world grew dark except for in her valley. He did not go into the Spires of Sunset, although he saw their gleaming towers and the never-ending waterfall flowing between and beneath them and saw them gilded with the dying sun. But the King and Queen of Fairies made their court there, and Urdür—often made journey to his cousin's keep. No, Gethin would not go there.

To the Well at the End of the World he had travelled and looked into its molten depths. Within the curve of the giant Östrung's footsteps he had slept, but found not Niamh. So south and east once again he went, to Malinka's bleak castle where he prowled without the grey and dismal walls, hiding beneath the faded buntings and looking within every black window for a glimpse of golden hair. And from there he sojourned gratefully to Rhianna's long-abandoned lighthouse, where he was greeted cordially by the honest scholars who guided ships past the deadly coral reefs. Then upward he travelled, over the coral reef and past the Sea of Memory, to the Gate—a stone edifice lonely on the windswept extremity of the Wyvern's Steep, unadorned and unattached, through whose portal the sea seemed to swirl. But that was illusion; for this Gate, like all the others that touch world to world, led only to the great Coliseum in the land of the Paladins, leading into and out of all the other worlds that dotted the True Earth. He did not pass through the Gate—if she had gone through there, then truly all hope was lost.

Gethin did not yet despair.

And ever he sang his portion of the song, as he wandered from one corner of the earth to the other, futilely. Come the first days of summer he had no other place to search, no other to consult than the place—and the one person—he had no desire to seek.

Urdür.

Second born of the Fairies. Lord of Learning, Lord of Mysteries. The Cowled, the Bearded, the Grey, the Ancient, the Solitary. All of these, and yet none of his titles could fully encompass the entirety—the majesty, the awfulness—of Urdür.

Of Gethin's sometime master.

And now all things had conspired against him to drive him back to the one from whom he had fled ten years before. No one impeded him or challenged him as he came, just has none had when he had left. Those who travelled to the Shadowless knew the risks full well; Urdür had no need for soldiers.

Once set upon his task, the Hermit would not be swayed, would show no weakness. Down the white gravel path, up the stairs, through the high white-domed hall and up the gilt spiral staircase he strode, as arrogantly as though he were still heir to this great tower. He followed the path left when it split, westward, up to the sixth story, and across the Swan Bridge to the observatory, past the ceaseless orrey of the True Earth, and to the great telescope. The round room seemed empty, but Gethin knew better.

Aloud, he said, "I have come with a petition."

"A petition?" A shape that had seemed no more than yet another shadow cast by the telescope stepped forward into the light, revealing the very edges of the Fairy's mottled wings and silvering hair. "I had not thought to hear that word from you ever again, Lord Eyre."

"I had never intended to utter it."

"Perhaps time has changed you after all. Step forward, boy, to where I can see you."

Gethin complied, letting the full light of the sun gild his lion's head, his eagle's wings, and all his deformities.

"You still wear the collar, then," Urdür said. "I would have thought you might have taken it off, at least for your wedding day."

"I am not wed," Gethin answered, growling deep within his throat.

"Is that why she fled you?" Urdür's lips twinged—the closest he ever came to smiling, and held up one hand when Gethin would step toward him. "No, do not attack me: I know the truth. As do you. It is the one thing my poor teaching could give you."

"And you see what pursuit of truth has wrought in me," gesturing with his claw to the mane and the tail. "I wonder that you did nothing to stop me."

"Stop you!" Urdür exclaimed, his shaggy white brows rising. "With every breath I warned you what you sought, but you had no ears to hear me. Paugh," turning away, with a snap of his own wings, "my words are still wasted. Leave, Gethin. You have not yet learnt the object of your fifteen years' lesson."

"I came with a petition."

"And why should I grant it?"

"You have not heard what it is."

"I have no need. Twenty years ago, a young strapling of a boy came to my door, stood where you do now, and asked to be my student, to learn the mysteries of the world. And I—more the fool—let him come. No matter that he was the only son of Eyre, no matter that the Lord of Eyre was dying. I turned my eye away when he abandoned his duties in favour of study, and when his father passed away, I was *pleased* that he did not take up the responsibilities of his title. 'He is a scholar,' I said to myself. 'My only king is wisdom,' he told me. And the more fool I—*I*! Urdür! I, who foresaw the doom of my cousins. I, who conspired with Aldhairen to put Siawn Shieldbearer upon the throne. I, Urdür, who first saw the blackness creep into Malinka's heart, when the star shone over Gavron's crib. *I*, Lord of Mysteries, to be taken in by a proud, arrogant, selfish, capricious thief! For that is what you are, my Lord Eyre, a thief of knowledge. For what do you have that I did not give you? Nothing—except your present wretchedness, which is none of my doing. Leave me, Gethin," the Fairy said, pacing wearily to a window made of marble lace. "You have stolen my anger and I have nothing left now to bind myself to you."

But Gethin did not leave, did not move. For several minutes, while the orrery softly whirred in the outer room and birds newly nesting chirped their songs in trees far below, no word did the Hermit and his Master speak. Until at last the low voice of Gethin—usually overlaid with something of the beast, now stripped of that to a common human baritone—rose within the room. "When I first put on the chain, Master, do you know what I expected?" Urdür did not answer. Gethin did not expect him to, and so he said, "I thought I would look like you. This...frippery. This masterpiece of sorcery, slaved over in the small hours of the night, small hammerings of blacksmithing accompanied by the incessant patter of rainfall, this *thing* to show the true form of a man, I thought would turn me into you. I could not be my father's son—that frail man? He could not have begot me—no. Nevermind the slander I put on my mother within my mind, I knew immortal blood flowed illicitly within my veins. And when my wings began to sprout—I can still feel the pains within my shoulder blades with the new-formed hollow bones—all my sleepless nights seemed justified. I impatiently waited for the morning—and yet I restrained my joy. I would not run like a schoolboy to his mother's knee, with his scrawled and simple figures upon the slate, so soon to be washed away by indulgent kisses. I would wait for my wings' maturity, and greet you when the sun rose as your equal in image and in likeness."

"I woke to find you gone," Urdür said.

"You see why," the Hermit replied, lashing his tail. "I saw the true measure of myself by false dawn. I left with the rising sun. I have never looked back."

The Fairy turned to look at his pupil, and the word *until* hung unspoken between them. It was not quite a reconciliation—they were both this side too proud, for a Fairy is not an Angel, and man, alas, is fallen. But they both stepped away from the shadows they had hidden in and stepped forward to look better at each other, as men who are about to fight, or who have just concluded and now need only to salute the King until their next exchange.

"Will you hear my petition?" Gethin said at last.

"Speak it."

"I seek the Princess."

"To what end?"

"To woo her."

"And if she be dead?"

"To mourn her."

"And if she be married?"

"Whom should she marry?"

"Anyone it pleases her. There are none, now, who cannot see her. And it has been nine months and more moons since she fled. It is two Easters since you were first summoned. Why should she not make a new life, since she had been banished, mistakenly, from her Father's court?"

"I—I cannot think she is married."

"Think what you will," with a shrug, "I do but name possibilities to test your resolve."

Gethin laughed hollowly. "For that you need not fear. Did I not walk when I might have flown the long road down to Gavron's court? Have I not, these pregnant months, sought even to the very ends of the earth? Have I not come here? What more can be asked of me? What further trial can be put to me? Shadows have pursued me every day since I have quested and were I to disrobe now, you would see as many livid scars upon me as rivers upon the earth. I have come so far; I will not now be dissuaded."

Urdür touched his beard and his lips twinged again. Then, snapping his fingers and holding out his arm to the glassless window, he called a great eagle to him, like in colouring and form to have been one of Gethin's own. The eagle bowed twice, once to the Fairy and once to the Hermit, stretched his wings, and settled upon Urdür's arm.

"Two months ago," the Fairy said, "this one came to me from across Loch Corraigh, from the forests where you make your home. Within his claws he bore a white feather. This one here." And he took up from a desk a bedraggled plume and gave it over to the Hermit. "You can read what has been written."

"Yes," Gethin breathed, even as he saw the rune for HOME shine like quicksilver upon the hollow stem. "But what drew her, of all places, there?"

Urdür laughed—a sound the Hermit had heard only twice before from those stern lips—and said, "Where else could she go but to the land of your home? Almost to your very step? Where else could she go if her father's house were denied her, but to the house of her bridegroom?"

"Yet you said she mighteth be married to another."

"And so she might be. I did not say she knew her own promptings."

HOME. Gethin shook his head, blinking his eyes as though to clear his sight. "It seems so long. I had not thought to ever return to that place."

"It seems there are many things you never meant that nonetheless you do."

"Home," Gethin whispered again. "Such a strange word. I wonder if I truly ever made a home. Of my own lands I have scant remembrance—the Shadowless was a laboratory, my cottage a retreat." He took a breath and tucked the feather within his cincture gently. "I wax philosophical. My thanks, Master, although it is but little. What can I offer you in return?"

"I have said—all bonds between us are broken."

"All ancient bonds, those of a youth misspent, aye," the Hermit replied. "But what of the present?"

"What of it? The present becomes the past as soon as it is named."

"The future, then."

Urdür's face grew bleak and he paced restlessly to the end of the observatory, where the charts of the stars hung like a second sky upon the wall. "Even

I cannot see all ends, Gethin," he said. "I may speak in riddles: joy and sorrow mingled shall be thine. But what doth that vain prophecy portend? Naught that canst save our land and keep strong the line of Kings." His hand traced the line of stars that formed Elena's Lyre, whose strings melted into the tail of the Southern Lion, slayer of Elena's love, Oisin, whose blood lay strewn in diamond drops across the southern sky. Softly, Urdür said, "Doff thy collar."

"Your pardon?" Gethin asked.

"How shalt thou woo in that form?" Urdür replied, turning to face his sometime student. "When thou hast need of the collar, it shalt be near thee. But go to my godchild as a man and not a beast. Woo her in thy human form—too long hast thou hidden."

"But that were to woo her falsely," the Hermit said.

"No more falsely than this proud glamour of thy soul. Come, remove it. Or dost thou linger upon the words of prophecy? Then I tell thee, Lord Eyre, she wilt not be won now, until thou showest her thy human face."

The black lip curled, as the Hermit looked down at his human hand—the measure of how pitifully far he had redeemed himself since that last fateful morning he stood within these walls. That same hand he reached up and undid the chain around his neck, fumbling—for the link was intricate and long unused.

His body wrenched sideways as his old form tore out of the bestial skin, exploding like an arrow from the bow. He raised his muzzle to the sky to howl and heard only his old, meagre voice cry to the Heavens. He lashed his tail in impotent fury, but now he had no tail, nor claw, nor great golden mane, except the wild locks that streamed down his now-smooth back, and the tawny human beard upon his chin. He stumbled forward, lost all balance upon the hem of his robe and collapsed upon his hands and knees, coughing as his heart pumped dizzily. His wings hung limp around him—and it was several minutes until he realised he still possessed those wings.

"What is this?" he asked, touching one of them with wondering hands, feeling the soft down of the inner plumes, the rigidity of the outer. He looked up at Urdür, the old wild hope rising in him. "How did this come to be?"

"There are magics other than ours," the Fairy said, although slowly, as though he too were surprised at the outcome. "The transformations of nature that Cadwyr deals in daily."

And then Gethin remembered Gwrhyr's bull's-feet, and wondered whether his wings were a blessing or a curse. But the Fairy interrupted his thoughts, saying with a cough that passed for a chuckle, "Perhaps they are granted thee to fly thee to thy love." Then growing stern he said, "For this have I seen: if you meetest her past Midsummer's Eve, she wilt not remember thee."

"Doth new evil befall her?"

Urdür shrugged. "An evil for a time. A greater evil if thou arrivest not by that day. The greatest if thou hesitatest longer. Go now. I shall see thee anon."

"I thank you," Gethin said, standing on shaking feet, like a colt new foaled. His face lit with pleasure at the feel of skin and not fur upon cloth. His very smile seemed to light the room, and for a moment, but a moment only, he shone as brightly as ever Niamh did the morning woke to find Gwendolyn and Gwrhyr fallen at her doorstep. "I thank thee, Urdür!" He cried, leaping up into the air on his wings and hovering near the high-domed ceiling. Urdür's hooded eyes twinkled as the man—a spoiled youth no longer—swept down, grasped his master's hand and kissed the veined and spotted back. Gethin soared once more, out the delicate window, over the Swan Bridge, skimming the golden dome of the Shadowless, and flying eastward across the Gwyrglánn.

But the light in Urdür's eyes faded and he turned his back to the sky that told him of things to come and things that were, for there he read of Maelgwenn—and his hidden heart grew heavy.

In vain had the twins cajoled and pleaded with Maelgwenn to stay at the Feasting Hall—but he refused their obtestations. And even when Goewínn sought him out the morning he departed and took his face in her cool hands and kissed his mouth, he would not be swayed. But he said to his cousin, untangling her arms from around his shoulders, "Do not do this thing."

"Too late thou hast spoken, Maelgwenn," Goewínn said. "My heart was thine when first we met, the day I was created."

"And thou said naught to me?" Maelgwenn said.

"I spoke with words that transcended mortal tongue. But too long thou hadst lived among men—thou didst not see what I would say."

"I have been a fool," Maelgwenn said, looking truly at his fair cousin—for both the first and final time.

"Thou hast been as thou wert created, oh Trickster."

"And fallen prey to mine own devices."

"So it ever is."

And this time he bent down and kissed her lips and tasted them mingled with salt tears. "I do not know if I am worthy to return to the Mountains of Morning," said he against her brow, "but if the Guardian of the Gates doth not turn me back, I shall meet thee there."

"Thou shalt be worthy of those lands, beloved," Goewínn said fiercely. "Thou hast made thyself so."

"I shall wait for thee in the foothills," said he. "And we shall climb the way together."

Soon after, Maelgwenn had flown northwards with Liam and Pwll, faltering but a little as he took to the air. Dalfínn came to his sister as she watched them recede into the sky, and said, "Dost thou not grieve?"

"Nay," said Goewínn. "This is our home but for a while. My heart is lifted, brother."

Dalfínn raised his brow and looked over to Graithne who sat within a tree and also watched with her heart held in her eyes. Then, having no part in such affairs, he shook his head and took up his bow and set off with his huntsmen.

Maelgwenn flew as swiftly as ever from the Wyvern's Steep, over Llewellyn's lands and Viviane's Dome. But when he passed beyond Castell Gwyr, his wings failed him and he began to reel along the sky paths. He set his jaw, and held the youths more firmly, and flapped his mighty wings, but though he flew as strongly as any owl, he could not conquer Time. It drew him back, like a current beneath the ocean waves, it pushed him into the past like winds atop the mountains, it snagged his feet and drew him downward, ever downwards, to the earth below.

He had but landed, the guard and squire had but risen to their feet, when the Fairy collapsed. The companions ran to him, and tried to help him to a fallen tree, but the Fairy cried out in pain when they touched his arms, and again they saw the ever-raw wounds upon his wings and arms and back and legs, and wondered at them.

"Let me rest an hour," Maelgwenn panted, adding, "By the Lord, lads! My cousins fed you well!"

The jest could not comfort the companions. They let him rest an hour exact, watching anxiously to see if he slept. But his eyes remained open and his breathing steady and his skin as pale as the clouds above. When they called to him, he stirred himself and tried to stand, but fell back again against the grass that seemed to whither and die beneath him, as though he brought winter in a rush. And as they watched, they saw snow drifts form and melt, and the grass grow again with daisies and with dandelions and then whither and so on—and then they realised that the Fairy bled immortality.

"You can carry us no longer," Liam said, kneeling beside the Fairy. "But we may bind your wounds, and carry you up to Castell Gwyr or whither you will."

"Nay," Maelgwenn gulped. "You carry the Dragon's Maw. That is your task, as I told you."

"You did not tell us you were ill," Liam said, removing his jerkin and taking hold of his sleeve to rip it into bandages.

But Maelgwenn put his hand upon the guard's and said, "It wouldst do no good, Liam mac Hwyach. My wounds cannot heal like thine. Take up thy sworn duty."

"You have made yours my duty, lord," Liam said. "I am in your debt, for you cured me when I knew not I required aid, and you saved me from my death."

"No," Maelgwenn said, when Liam would move to tear the sleeve of his shirt again. "Thou canst not right this wrong."

"You add another burden to my soul should I let you perish," Liam cried. "How much more my soul can stand I cannot say. I have failed in every particular. I shall not fail in this."

Maelgwenn closed his eyes and chuckled. Then touching his fingers to the guard's forehead, he whispered, "May thou findest peace, Liam. May thou findest peace." To Pwll he said, "Journey across the Gwyrglánn at this point, then northwest 'til you find a village. There you shall discover Niamh."

"Where shall we meet you again, lord?" Pwll asked quietly. He had been raised with too much respect for the Fairies to argue with them as Liam did.

"You will find me here. I do not think I shall ever fly again. Fear not," said Maelgwenn to the guard, "I shall live, though barely, until thou returnest."

With a bow, Pwll took Liam's arm and the companions set off as Maelgwenn commanded. And that night and all the next and for as long as Maelgwenn lay there, the creatures of the forest and the Vertae and the Wydoemi gathered around that grove, and bowed in sombre silence.

"Ah, my heart! Ah, my heart! Ah, my black, ungrateful heart! She is returned!"

Niamh looked up from the path before her, and a broad smile threatened to split her face in twain, for here came Ogrin, all bush and bristle, leaping toward her down the path. The old woman embraced Niamh breathlessly, crying, "I have waited too many days for you, my ashputtle girl! I have barely left the window this fortnight and I burnt the bread twice. Is this the way you come back to me, as though you had just been out a-wandering? Ah well, nevermind that now, but come in and I'll wait on you. And don't forget you owe me all that has transpired, missy! And your whole story besides. I have not forgotten, not me, not old Ogrin. Peghain Innkeeper was by just the other day, plying me with a bit of cheese as if I were a mouse, but I told her that I'd not budge from my chair, and the latch wasn't done up if she wanted to come in. But not a word she got from me the whole while she was here. And so you can trust me with your secrets, my ashputtle girl, never fear that. I'd have waited 'til doomsday for you, and may have set out against the mouth of hell if another day had passed. Och, but my tongue does rattle! Come here again, child. Ah, my black heart!"

And so they went inside, and sat with mugs of warm milk in hand. Ogrin forgot she promised to wait on Niamh, but Niamh was happy although tired after so long an ordeal and did not mind that there was no more was to be had but the mug of milk, which had never tasted so sweet in the Princess's mouth, although she had once drunk honeyed elderflower wine. Nor could she take more than a sip before Ogrin plied her with questions, which Niamh readily answered. By and by all was revealed—including the Princess's name, and all that had befallen her from the day the Hermit had been sent for to this very day.

When it seemed clear that Niamh's tale was done, Ogrin sat silently for quite a while, her empty mug within her two wizened hands. The silver mirror, reflecting nothing more spectacular than the dun roof, lay on a low table next to the old woman's chair. Niamh had glanced in its depths as she had walked the long way home, only to find what she had been told from the beginning. But this the plain glass reflected: the lightening of Niamh's skin in places, and the delicate mark upon her brow. She had laughed when she had looked—laughed loud and long so that her voice rang from one end of Loch Corraigh to the other. She had laughed and noticed not that where she stepped, small white flowers bloomed like lace upon the riotous grass.

The ivory comb Niamh wore in her own hair; Ogrin would not take it back. The Princess played with the steel prongs that peeked out under the curls, waiting for her mistress's response to so strange a story. Occasionally, Ogrin would smack her lips and mutter a word or two, as though trying out the taste of a word. Finally, putting down the mug with a little clink, the old woman said, "Well, that's quite a tale. And I daresay you've had enough time between that witch's and here to dream up something interesting to tell old Ogrin, but I'm not so much of a gull to believe more than a word or two of it. Do you remember how to salt my stew? I'm famished."

Thus life continued happily through the remainder of the spring and even to the first days of summer, when all the world was green and warm, and every hill held at least two types of flower—whether on the ground or in tree—and small birds filled the air and seemed to be another flower ever rustling in the light wind, while mice, rabbits and badgers brought the secrets of the earth to the surface. Lambs bleated, colts found their legs, goslings paddled aimlessly within the swelling ponds, adding their high-pitched honks to the metreless melody.

And Niamh journeyed for the first time to the village, her head covered and bent, her arms clothed up to the wrist, her fingers lost around the edge of a basket. A few paid her mind, for the village was small enough that any stranger, even one as unassuming as the Princess, caused a mild stir. But Ogrin snapped at those who would try to peek under Niamh's veil, and when they asked whether Ogrin had found herself a daughter within a walnut, as the nursery tales ran, Ogrin would jut out her chin and raise her hoary brows and say, "And what if I did? A woman grows old and her bones are brittle. A walnut girl might be a blessing. And what's this I hear about that old witch, Moira's cottage?" Invariably, this would turn the conversation to wild speculation, hushed words, liberally strung with "Well, *I* heard's...", twinkling eyes and fingers laid significantly along the nose.

Many times Niamh returned after that, and a mere month before Midsummer she went alone and traded chicks and eggs for bread and milk and pork and lamb. She was subjected to no greater inquisition than where old Ogrin had got herself to, to which she truthfully replied that Ogrin was lying abed with a cold from the goldenrod that had sprung up that year closer than ever to their house.

"Ah, well she's a tough old bird," Peghain Innkeeper said, slicing some cheese for Niamh and adding on a little more for Ogrin. "No doubt she's sniff-

Peghain Innkeeper

ing more now that she has you around to work for her, Brighid," (for so the village folk had named her. Some had first called her Nut or Shell, but these had not seemed quite right for the quiet, dignified stranger, and so Brighid Scrivver's daughter, all of five and terribly important, had bequeathed her own name and the village had nodded). Peghain, a grandmother herself now and matriarch of the village, as her father had ruled before her, set about wrapping up the cheese and said without so much as a raised eyebrow, "There's a lad that's come down from northways to see you."

Niamh started and dropped her own cheeses on the floor. "A man? Whom?" she asked, stooping.

"A comely lad, if that's what you're after."

Niamh's brow furrowed further as she placed the recovered cheese into her basket. "Comely? Not—not...." But she had no idea how to subtly ask if his head were that of a lion, or if he had wings, and so she said, "Has he a name?"

"Aye," Peghain said, wiping her hands on her apron. "And one well known around these parts. He came riding a saffron mare with a star upon her brow, and smoking a pipe, and his saddlebags were full of gold." She allowed herself to glance knowingly at Niamh, and then turned to the state of her stew, adding onions along with advice, "He has come down before, usually with his brother, but marriage has made Connela quite the homebody." She laughed and tasted the stew, nodding to herself. "The boar has tamed the lamb—but stranger things have happened." She paused in what she was doing to look back at Niamh, saying, "He'd make a fine beau, Padriac mac Connlach. I saw him last at Peter Tailor's, ordering things for Udinë's daughter, Gwenhyfarch. Connela spends a fortune on her; his brother might be like to do the same if ever he had opportunity."

Niamh blushed and pulled her veil further over her head. With a short thanks, she scuttled out of the inn, through the yard, and past the gate. She had not got farther than Farmer Demmit's cart (so called for his notorious cursing when chasing out vermin from his cabbages), than she heard a laughing voice behind and the pounding of hooves. The great saffron mare reined before her, and Padriac slipped down from her back and bowed elaborately, sweeping off his soft green cap. He was dressed, she saw, as one come wooing.

"Princess," he said, and then checked himself when he saw that she ducked her head at the title. Standing, he replaced his cap, saying, "Sprite?"

"I am called Brighid now," she said.

His fingers fumbled for his pipe, thought better of it, and bent towards her. "I hope I have not mistaken you?"

She smiled. "No, Padriac mac Connlach. You are not mistaken. But I told you that I am not who I once was."

The news seemed at once to please and to sadden the youth, as he offered his arm to her, and said, "My own commissions are all but done. May I walk you about on yours?"

"I will walk with you," Niamh said, taking his arm, "but I was even now on my way back."

"May I walk you home, then?"

"You may walk me as far as the forest line. I can make my way from there."

"Give me just a moment," and calling to one of his men, Padriac entrusted his remaining obligations and Liseva to his care. "Now," said he, as they started off, "Aoife came, and you sent a dreadful nuisance in Terence Songmaster, and nothing would do but he would sing for us four-hundred and fifty-two verses of the lay of himself before we could persuade him to depart for Viviane's court. We threw at him a whole bag of fleece mid-song, but he would not be stopped until he were finished."

"And your own song?"

"Unfinished. I had hoped—that is, I thought you might tell me its true ending."

She stopped, and looked into his eyes. The Firebird's mark upon her brow shone and glimmered off the comb within her hair. "I am promised already," she said.

"Niamh is promised. To whom does Brighid give her heart?"

"Brighid is a shadow. She has no heart."

"Even the giants have hearts, although they hide them."

"Will you not tell me of Aoife?" Niamh countered, noticing the turned heads as she walked by arm in arm with one of Connlach's sons. Apparently, Peghain was not the only one to think him a fine catch.

"Aoife? I know little of her. She came and left soon after. Lucky her—she escaped the would-be poet. Perhaps she had heard him bubble his verses whilst they were both imprisoned. But you have not told me of your own adventures since we last parted. Will you not now?"

"Gladly," Niamh said, and proceeded to describe—in brief—her meeting with the Firebird, and the song Ariana had sung that night. Padriac replied in suitable fashion, although it seemed that his mind was still on other matters.

They had just reached the first trees of the forest that lay thickly along the border of Loch Corraigh, when Padriac turned to Niamh and swept off his cap again, but without the bow. "Here we must part," he said. "But I hope, Princess, I may come and see you again? Connlach Manor has seemed the emptier since you left it. And," grinning, "no other woman has dropped from the willows for me to set my eye on."

"Perhaps you have not been looking," Niamh said, not unkindly. And then, "You may come visit me. I shall return to the village in two weeks' time."

"Do you go to Mass? Shall I meet you there?"

"I do not. I dare not. Not like…" she gestured to her face and arms, the constant burning of her skin. "But if you wait for me by the innyard, I shall come by and by."

"Take this," Padriac said, pressing the wooden cross back into her hand and adding when Niamh protested, "so that I may know you again. You're paler than you were."

"Truer," Niamh said, and turning, left him.

A fortnight to the day, Niamh came out of the woods, basket on arm, and onto the well-trodden path that wound among the several farms and came eventually to the village. There she was met by Padriac, who was leaning on the saddlebow of his saffron mare and grinning into the sun. Seeing Niamh, he urged the mare up to her and reached down his arm saying, "Will you ride with me into town, Brighid?"

"I cannot ride," Niamh answered, switching her basket to her other arm.

"I think you can hold on," he said low. Then, squinting down the road, "Come, it is three whole miles, and my horse is not like to run off with you, as a phooka might."

With that inducement—and with Padriac already leaning down and grasping her about the waist—Niamh found herself pulled up before the Connlach boy and sitting within the circle of his arms while they trotted their leisurely way down the road, past the emptying Church, where all the departing faithful could see them and speculate.

That same day, Gethin soared over the ruins of Moira's hut, and over Loch Corraigh, and at last to his own long-abandoned cottage. Weeds and tender saplings had sprung up near the firmament and the wild vines had gone unchecked. Moss covered the rim of his well and cobwebs the corners of the two gables. Sitting on the plain pilgrim's bench of carven stone, was a boy with his hat in hand.

When Gethin arrived, his wings spreading a shadow over half the yard, the boy jumped to his feet, nervously twisting the hat every which way. He opened his mouth to speak, but when he saw the human head, he stopped, puckered his mouth and brow, and considered a different speech. "Begging your pardon, lord," said he, bobbing a bow, "I don't know which Fairy you are." When Gethin did not answer at once, the boy added, "I am waiting for the Hermit they call Duncan."

"Haven't you heard he was bidden to the King's court to wed his daughter?" Gethin asked.

"That's as it may be, sir," the boy said. "I don't know about that. But the Hermit's been here forever, and mayhap you know where he is and when he will return? I've been here three days now, and I've et all my bread already. And I don't much care for the goat's cheese m'mum gave me, but she says it'll make me grow."

"And why do you seek the Hermit?"

The boy was silent for a moment, sizing up the giant before him and finally answering, "Well, I don't know that you can be of any help. There's Fairies and then there's folk what knows what folk need, and this here Hermit's one of that sort. But my sister's fallen ill and there's nothing that can bring her out of her cold sleep that we know of. She had caught chill like always this early spring, but then everything grew too heavy for her, and now she can't even open her eyelids, it's that bad. Farmer Brandon's daughter, Anna, fell ill the same way about the same time, and she died just three weeks back. Her father came here but couldn't find the Hermit, and so he just held Anna, weeping, and now they say he grows a patch of rue among his carrots. But I told my mother that I'd wait until I found him, and I've waited three days, and I haven't seen hair nor hide of him. Do *you* know where he's gone?"

"I do and I will tell you if you answer me a question."

"A riddle?" The boy's eyes grew wide and terrified. "I can try, sir. But I'm no good at faults. The best I can do is sommat like *Blue eye, green eye, I love best*, and that's not even a proper riddle."

"No riddle," Gethin grinned, stooping until they were of a height, "but a

185

question. And if you cannot answer, I shall not be angry and shall tell you where the Hermit is, nonetheless."

"Right-o," the boy said, nodding. "I'll do my best."

"Thank you. I am looking for a lady with black skin, like embers come to life. Have you seen her?"

The boy furrowed his brow and tasted the idea. And then looking up through brown lashes, he said, "Black skin? Like an unseelie, you mean?"

"Something like."

"Well, I haven't seen any such thing about, although Tom Greenfield says that he saw one once, but I don't believe him because he's always making up stories to scare us."

Gethin sighed and stood again, crossing his arms in front of him. Then smiling, he said, "Well, you have fulfilled your part, I shall do mine. You seek the Hermit; you are speaking to him."

The boy's eyes, already the proverbial saucers, widened if possible further and he stood with mouth open. He took in all of the Hermit, from the sandalled feet to the ragged hem, to the folded arms within the deep sleeves, the wings held loosely around the Hermit like a second shroud, the fabled blue eyes, and the singularly human mouth and hair. "Um," the boy managed after a time. He crushed the hat between his hands, rocked back and forth on his feet, shuffled them in the dirt, tapped one clog against the stone bench. "Um," he essayed again, "I had heard that, um, that he—you—um, looked...."

"Did you now?" Gethin asked not unkindly, quirking lip and brow. "You have also heard that I am a magician." The boy nodded and so Gethin continued, "You spoke of your sister. Where do you live?"

The lad indicated a place south and east, beside the Giant's Crook, where Loch Corraigh ran widest. Gethin nodded, and scooped up the lad over both his arms, before taking to the air with joy in flight.

While Gethin ministered to the boy's sister as best his altered state allowed, Padriac took his leave of the Princess by the edge of the forest, extracting from her as he helped her down from the gentle mare's back the permission to return on Midsummer's Night.

Niamh walked pensively the rest of the way to Ogrin's cottage and barely noted the old woman's inquisitive eye or any remark about golden wool. And when she lay upon her bed of rushes and looked up to the thatched ceiling, the world of her father's court seemed farther away than ever, and the Niamh who had once been seemed an impossibility of the past.

186

The boy's mother did not know of any girl that fit Niamh's description, but she did know of two more children struck down by the spring malady. So Gethin went to their bedsides, and fed them mixtures of herbs and holy water. And from these commissions came five more—although still no news of a strange, unseelie girl. This, in turn, led to an inquisition of the wells and the ponds, and the discovery of a great, grey wolf's body, tied to a rock as curved and smooth as a loaf of bread, drowned within one of the small pools where the children liked to play and bathe.

A faint smell—delicate like the shy perfume of violets—hung to the mangy fur and brought to mind the Princess and the letter come to him a year ago by eagle. But even more, the last, crusted drop of blood Gethin had touched and seen faintly the last months of this wolf's life.

A red mist clouded the Hermit's eyes, and he quietly ordered those around him back, back to their homes, back to their lives. And when they had gone, he tore into the beast, he tore into the King of Wolves, although he had no tooth or claw now, no talon, no stomach for raw meat. With blunt fingers he ripped the engorged stomach wide, strewing entrails upon the shore. The jugular he bit into, spitting veins away. The heart he crushed underfoot. And when the rage had passed, he looked about him in fear and loathing and ran his hand through his muddy hair, and thought fondly of his collar which had kept in check the beast, even while portraying it.

"I am not worthy of her," he whispered to the world. "My aspect may have changed again, although my heart hath not."

He touched his arm, feeling the coiled muscle beneath the skin, and squeezed it as though to assure himself of his humanity. The warmth of his hand brought back memory of Rhianna and of her geas—which he felt, now, must still lie upon him despite the King's decree. There were things in the world, he well knew, over which even Kings had no command.

The humble parish bells chimed out the compline hour. Families left their homes and streamed to prayer and raised their voices in response to the clear tenor of the cantor.

Heavily, Gethin stood and set about collecting the carcass into one pile, over a small pyre of sticks and twigs. That twilight, even as Niamh closed the door of Ogrin's hut and lit the candles, and set about the homely task of braiding rug, her betrothed burnt to ashes the mortal remains of the Wolf King, ancient hand of evils, ambassador of the Dark Woods, Deirdre's bane, Maelgwenn slain, far from the Green Mountains.

The day before Midsummer's Eve, two strangers came to the village where, with their courtly attire, still fine yet much travel-worn, they caused a greater stir than even Brighid's coming or Moira's demise.

"Belike it were another messenger from the king," said Farmer Demmit, leaning over the bar in Peghain Innkeeper's.

"You're daft," said Thomas Cooper, touching the side of his nose. "If it were a messenger, why should he stop here? Why not go up to Connlach Manor? Or over to Udinë?"

All speculation was cut short however by the arrival of the two gentlemen in question.

"Good masters, a moment of your time," the darker of the two said. He carried with him a sack that he held as closely as a newborn babe. Several sharp eyes glanced suspiciously at the shape of the satchel rather hoping that it might look something similar to a bottle of wine. Rich men, they had heard, could often be induced to share.

"Well, I don't know about *good*," Farmer Demmit said. Someone elbowed him in the side.

"What can I do for you gentlemen?" Peghain asked.

The one who had spoken before answered, "We are looking for a lady."

"We have our fair share of those," Peghain answered. "You might take your pick, unless there is someone specific you had in mind."

The one who had not spoken—taller, fairer and with a dead weight in his eyes, behind which the smallest ember of hope newly flickered into being—now spoke. "She with golden hair."

The Inn erupted with laughter. When at last Peghain regained herself, the first of all the room to do so, she came up to the stern-looking youth, patted him warmly on the shoulder and said, "That alone is worth a drink. Come in and sit."

But the guard did not move. He opened his mouth as if to remark that he saw nothing at all humorous in his statement, but the squire grinned, clapped his arm around his companion's shoulders and steered him firmly to a table, saying, "You have read our mind, good mistress. And for your generosity, let it never be said that Pwll of Branmoor could not return in kind. Pray fill up the glasses of those about me. I would not drink alone."

Smiles of mirth became smiles of greed and many lips were licked. The general opinion of the strangers from that day to this has always been of genial conviviality, even though for the sake of their purses neither Pwll nor Liam ever returned to that place.

"Now," Peghain said, "if you've no more than gold hair to recommend her, you might try Jane Dyer's daughter, or then there's Nellie who minds the goats up Connlach's Way, or Brandy Viner's girl who's vintage you're drinking now, or two or three dozen others. Myself, I'd pick Brandy for you, sir, but mayhap quiet Jane for your stern looking friend."

"Do none of the others have names?" Pwll asked.

"Oh aye," Peghain said, "but all of them mere variations on Jane, Nellie and Brandy. We've none of your courtly ways this far north and have stuck to good solid ones so that those as can spell can spell 'em."

Pwll laughed good-naturedly and raised his mug in salute. "Well then mistress," said he, "perhaps this will put you in mind of a certain Jane, Sallie and Brandy. The one we seek, they say, has skin as black as night."

The room grew suddenly silent.

"Oh aye, does she," said Peghain carefully. "Well now that would be something even Blind Yorick might take notice of. That would be a thing, it would."

Several men shifted on their benches and stools and wicker seats; the room grew darker as men turned brown-coated backs toward the strangers.

"And what would you be wanting with such a girl, eh?" the Innkeeper continued, raising her greying brows and covering her mouth with an age-spotted hand.

Pwll's grin became stiff, his eyes darted around the room. He seemed to weigh several answers, all of them politic. But then Liam spoke, like a king himself, quiet and full of authority, "Maelgwenn sent us. We do his bidding now."

Peghain blinked. "Old Maelgwenn? What's *he* want with her?"

"Mayhap he wants her as a servant," someone suggested.

"Or his eye is set on her," someone else winked. "He's a strange one, he is, and they say he once loved black Malinka."

"Nevermind that," Peghain answered, never moving her eyes from the strangers' faces. "What do *you* want with Brighid? For I tell you now, she's all but engaged to Padriac mac Connivar."

"Engaged?" Pwll smiled, even as Liam asked, "Brighid?"

"Did you not know her name before you came?" Peghain asked in her quiet voice.

"We knew her by another name," Pwll answered.

"Be that as it may," the Innkeeper replied. "She comes down here tomorrow. You might speak with her then. But I'll tell you she'll come on Connlach's arm and will not be speaking with you alone, no matter how you coax her."

"As you say, mistress," Pwll replied, with a nod. "But let me assure you, that we do not mean the lady harm. Indeed," with a sigh, "she has come to too much already."

The next day as promised, Brighid herself arrived, again riding Padriac's saffron mare. They went about their business for an hour, before stopping by the Inn for Ogrin's cheese. As Peghain unwrapped the wheel, she said so quietly that the girl almost didn't hear her, "There's two men looking for you staying upstairs."

Padriac's hearing was not at all impaired and tracing the grain of the bar with one finger he pleasantly asked, "What sort of men? Relations?"

"I should think not," Peghain answered cutting a wedge with as much precision as she chose her words. "But one of them calls himself a lord and spends his purse as freely as if he might be one. Although I've known stupid men to do the same. But then who says that one who is called His Grace may have all the graces of a good wit?"

"You said there were two," Brighid inquired.

"I did, aye. But the second was short of words but long on meaning...if you get my point. Has a wicked, desperate air about him, that one."

"What did they want?" Padriac asked.

"You might ask them yourself. My granddaughter, Emma heard them stirring half an hour ago. I can have her fetch them down, if you like. You might speak here—I don't expect anyone to come until midday."

Niamh's cheeks burned red and her fingers quivered as she placed the cheese in her basket. "Did he give a name?" she asked.

"Something of Branning. No, no that's not right. Bran...Bran...Branflake... Branfield...ah! That's it: Branmoor."

"Branmoor!" Niamh exclaimed. "Pwll of Branmoor?"

"It might be that. You know him them?"

"If he is who you say, then yes, I knew him once." Then quietly to herself she said, "Although it was not he who I expected."

"Shall I have him fetched then?"

"Yes, please. I'll give you tuppence for your leman."

A nobler soul would have refused to take the money, but Peghain Innkeeper was not so much noble as practical. Emma was dispatched and returned some few minutes later preceeded by Pwll of Branmoor, followed a little after by a guard Niamh knew by sight but not by name. Pwll skidded to a stop before Niamh and gave a deep bow, more practised and less showy than Padriac's had ever been. "Brighid, I presume?"

"Some have called me that, sir," said she.

"Then you have known a different name?"

"In times long gone by I have. I feel sometimes I have forgotten who that other woman might be."

"If I said her name, would she remember?"

"I think she might."

"Then well-met, Princess. Long have many who love thee sought for thee."

Tears stung Niamh's grateful eyes and seemed to burn more sweetly than ever fire did. Something else burned in Padriac's eyes. But it was not love.

"Thou didst say," she whispered, "that thou didst know her Christian name. It hath been long since I have heard it. Wilt thou speak it now?"

"With all my heart. Lady," said he, taking her hand like a brother, "thou art Niamh."

"And so I am," the Princess said and then could not speak more for weeping.

Two hours later, when Pwll, Liam, Niamh and Padriac gathered in Peghain's own chambers—moved to the ground floor since her legs had refused to walk upstairs—Pwll acquainted the Princess with all that had transpired since she had been deceived: of the many doings at court, of the Count's escape and the Hermit's arrival, of Findola's engagement, Gwrhyr's recovery, and his own modest adventures. When at last, he came to speak of the flight to the twins' Feasting Hall, and the gathering of the waters of the Sea of Memory, his narrative faltered.

"Doth something ail thee?" Niamh asked, resting her hand on Pwll's flushed cheek. He started and pulled away—perhaps afraid that she still possessed the powers of beauty, perhaps truly touched by something awakened, though dimly, within her.

Taking a breath he said, "I have been told how you may be cured, Princess."

"Is the remedy so awful that thou fearest to speak of it?" she asked.

"It is," Liam said speaking at last.

She looked up at the guard's shadowed face. "Ignorance is worse. Do not fear to speak thy mind."

"It is ignorance that you must fear, Highness," Liam replied, "for you will regain your beauty, but lose all that is yourself."

Niamh looked from Liam to Pwll, her heart sinking. Lightly she said, "I fear I have been too long from the court, for I do not understand his conundrum."

"He means that you will lose your memory, Princess," Pwll explained. "All that you have been, all that you have known, all that you have cherished will vanish. That is the price of your restoration."

Dost thou know the price? Art thou willing to pay it? The words of the Wolf King echoed in Niamh's mind, joined then by the Firebird's *Only that thou fearest will save thee.* *

"I will not know even my name?" Niamh asked.

Liam shook his head and stared again into the shadows.

"Nor why you took the waters of the Sea of Memory, or that you ever drank," Pwll added.

"Nor anything you have done," whispered the guard.

"Nor anything..." Niamh echoed. The Firebird's caress, the long hours listening to Ogrin's tales, her Mother's smile, her Father's laugh, her Handmaids—the memory of Gethin. And the memory of those who'd died, whose spirits never truly left her. And were there not others? Had not the past months been so many times a type of Hell? Moira, Wolf King—a different losing of herself. And those years before it. The wails for Gwrhyr, the Lily Spire, the fire—the unquenchable fire—that clung still to her skin like a lecherous lover, never to be shaken off...but for this small sacrifice? Why should she not? What but sheer perverseness prompted her to cling so closely to that which was destroying her? It was fear merely.

"I will take it," said she.

"You do not know what you do," Liam said.

"She is no fool," Padriac retorted. "And might not she be reacquainted with her memory, as some are recovering from a fever?"

"It is not time alone that will cure her," Liam replied.

"But there is an antidote to the loss of memory?" Padriac asked.

"I know it not, although I do not know all."

"Then why offer false hope by speaking of such a spell at all," Padriac countered, standing.

"Pray!" Niamh cried, "Do not speak of me as if I were not here." Then turning to Pwll, she said, "Lord Branmoor, shalt thou tell me who I am once I have tasted these waters?"

"Aye, Princess."

"Then let me drink."

The guard and the Connlach man moved as if to speak but Pwll stopped them both, saying, "This is Maelgwenn's command and her Highness's wish. Your servant, Princess, in this as in all things."

Hands more accustomed to drawing blood than healing unwrapped the satchel, and offered her the golden cup of the Dragon's Maw. Brown hands received it: charred lips drank. Liam turned his face away and so did not see how like a veil slow removed from statuary on Easter day, the blackness of the beauty's skin melted into the woodwork at her feet.

Niamh glowed whitely, the Firebird's brand the whitest of all. Her hair uncoiled itself, fell loosely to her feet. Her cheeks bloomed light blushed roses, her lips a deeper red like one who has eaten strawberries. Her fingers held a radiance, her feet did not fully touch the floor. Like a star, she shone to fill the room, as resplendent as the nestfires. The men stood in awe, unable to speak or look away, overwhelmed in the presence of loveliness. But the lustre faded, sighed, and dissolved into the air. No lilies sprang up beneath her feet, no perfumes filled the air, no music wafted from the celestial spheres to greet returning beauty. Niamh descended. Her toes touched the floor. Her eyes retained their blackness.

No longer did she burn.

"Lady," Pwll said, kneeling before her, "do you know me?"

She smiled with an abstracted glow, like light harmlessly diffused by dust. "Should I, sir?" she asked.

Daring to reach out, he took her hand and pressed it. His heart did not convulse for want of her. His pulse did not speed or skip. His mouth grew not dry nor desirous. And he mourned the beauty's loss. The squire opened his mouth, but it was not he who answered her.

"We are none of us strangers," said Padriac. Then turning the Princess to himself, he said, "You have forgot yourself, Brighid, Ogrin's girl."

Niamh blinked and cocked her head to the side. "Am I Brighid?"

"Aye," Padriac said, also kneeling and daring to do more than press her hand—to kiss it. "And I," he said before even Liam or Pwll could interrupt him, "am Padriac, Brighid's love."

The parish priest, newly appointed and much in awe of the Hermit, nonetheless found courage enough to hear his confession and place the host upon the Hermit's tongue—grateful that the mouth was not as terrible as he had heard, nor that eagle's claw made the sign of the cross. Eagerly would the priest have bade the Hermit farewell then, but Gethin stayed that good man and once more inquired after Niamh. The priest blinked and smiled at that, grateful for more certain ground. Indeed, he had seen such a girl upon Connlach's horse when saying Mass across the Loch a fortnight past when Father Bartholomew had complained of croup.

Gethin laughed when the good Father had done, and bowed to kiss his hands. "Thus are all debts fulfilled," said he, whispering, "Niamh, I am come."

So, even as Padriac rose to be the first to kiss the Princess tenderly on the lips, Gethin spread his wings and flew to his beloved.

chapter xiv

moment of your time, sirrah."

Padriac, riding northward to Connlach Manor late in the day, followed by his guards, barely flicked a glance at the two horseless men barring his path.

"My Lord Branmoor. Sir," he said, a quiver of the eyelids sufficing for a bow. "How may I help you gentlemen?"

"I think you know what we require," Pwll said, touching his sword. Liam had already unsheathed his. Padriac's men, ten in all and brawny, touched their own weapons, loosening them from their sheaths, producing daggers from their sleeves.

Padriac smiled ruefully. "You see I am not an unreasonable man, my lord. I have no desire to match you in battle—I bear you no grudge. Take some friendly advice and walk away from here, back to the King's court. You have fulfilled your commission, and no one could ask more."

"Our commission was to return the Princess to her home," Liam said, quietly.

"The Princess?" Padriac asked, cocking his head. "She has no home. And, you will pardon me, but what sort of *home* can it be when she is banished from it for no fault of her own? Believe me, I desire nothing but the best for the Princess. Good day, gentlemen."

And with that, he urged Liseva forward, but had not gone a few steps before the horse whinnied and pranced backwards—away from Liam's sword held casually at the mare's breast.

"I'm afraid we are not quite finished, sirrah," Pwll said, pleasantly.

Liam did not smile. "Dismount."

"Dismount?" Padriac mildly exclaimed, raising a russet brow, and rifling in his pockets for his pipe. He leaned back in his saddle as he lit it, gave a few thoughtful puffs, and then shook his head. "No, I don't think I will."

"Then you will die," Liam said and thrust upwards.

Padriac pulled Liseva to the side, unsheathing his own sword and swinging down towards Liam, who parried, forcing Padriac's blade perilously close to the mare's neck. Padriac withdrew his sword and aimed again at Liam's right shoulder, tugging on his mare's reins to swing her around until he might wield his weapon more easily. Several of his men leapt forward, and were met by Pwll who slashed across three horses' breasts, and hamstrung a fourth. Six mounted remained, and three of the fallen still capable of walking.

"Parlay!" Pwll shouted, his back to his companion, as he fought two at once and watched seven more circle around them.

Liam arched his sword and hit Padriac across the thigh.

"*Parlay!*" Pwll cried again, even as he hit one opponent in the face with his elbow, and scraped his sword against another's collarbone. "*For the love of God! PARLAY!*"

"*Agreed,*" Padriac called, grasping his thigh. "Stand back."

Both sides regarded each other and then very slowly sheathed their weapons.

"Do you think me a villain?" Padriac asked as soon as his own men and the companions stepped out of sword's length.

Pwll of Branmoor

"Would we not be justified?" Liam asked. "You are not the first to prey upon her."

"*Prey* upon her?" Padriac laughed. "I? I, who alone in all the world showed her favour when she looked…other than she does now? Are not *you* in the wrong for demanding she return to the tyranny of her beauty?

"She chose her own end," Padriac continued when the companions did not speak. "Do not forget that, although she may have forgotten—she *chose* this life. None other. Now, pray you gentlemen, stand aside. If you wish to press the matter further, come to Connlach Manor when once all wounds are healed."

And with that, Padriac and his men passed without further challenge, excepting Pwll's muttered oath.

Peghain saw Niamh—Brighid now—safely home to Ogrin, and herself explained the whole of it to Ogrin's ear when once Brighid was safely sent to rest.

"You've picked yourself a strange one, and no doubt," Peghain said, shaking her head, and tapping her neatly pared nails upon the rough wooden arm of her chair. "Showing up out of nowhere, disappearing to nowhere, showing up again, courted by Connlach—and now without her memory. You've taken in a shadow. Why didn't you take Brandy before Owen Viner got her?"

"That clump?" Ogrin retorted, chewing on the end of her pipe. "What good would she have done me? Two of my new-hatched chicks have more sense than she has, and they're as dumb as rocks. Besides, I've taken a fancy to my ash-puttle girl."

Peghain looked pointedly at her friend.

Ogrin squirmed in her seat. "Well, I hain't accustomed to her lilywhiteness yet. And leastways her eyes haven't changed." When Peghain raised an eloquent grey eyebrow, Ogrin bit on her pipe and stuck out her hoary chin. "And anyways, what mind is it of yours what that girl does? You'd sell your cheese to the Devil hisself if he'd come up and pay you. Are you thinking of getting your hand on that boy's fleece? Good luck! And may that demon dog bite your bum for trying."

The Innkeeper sniffed delicately and folded her hands. It was a truth with Ogrin that if you kept quiet enough, eventually she'd talk herself into a different argument.

"And as for coming and going to nowhere, I've half a mind that I know more than *you* as to that. She told me everything, she did, and I can repeat it all right back to her, if need be. If she ever asks me, that is. If she's ever curious. If we've got nothing better to do an evening. If that damn Connlach boy doesn't come around too much. At any rate, if you have even the wits of that imbecile girl Owen Viner's got, you'd have thought of some answer of where she came from to begin with, what with those fancy folk showing up at your door all of a sudden. Leastaways," Ogrin said, thinking that perhaps she'd said too much and not really sure what *she* believed about her ashputtle girl, "if you had any imagination rather than a moneybox for brains, you'd be able to think of some story. But you've never had the blarney, Peghain, and that's a fact. And so I don't wonder that *you* never wondered where she's come from."

"*Are* you going to tell her?" Peghain asked, while Ogrin blew angry puffs of smoke.

"No."

"No?"

"Are you deaf?"

"I still hear Lester snoring and he's been dead these ten years."

"Then there's your answer."

Peghain nodded and stood, her beltpurse jingling. "Well, that's good then. I'll worry less. Because I'll tell you frankly, Ogrin, she's got a way of stirring hearts, that one, and I'm not ashamed to say it. And no, I don't say that because I've got an eye on acquiring sheep. And I can see she's stirred your black heart and I'm glad for it, for I've often thought you should have married and had children, rather than wasting up here. But you were always too proud for our menfolk and that's your sin. Well, good night to you, Ogrin. I'm glad to find we're of a mind about this."

Ogrin hrumphed and didn't bother to see the Innkeeper to the door.

Brighid could not sleep that night. Her mind was calm, but her heart was restless, as though it longed to be about on some quest left unfulfilled. She turned upon her pallet a few times and kept her eyes closed as best she could, but always when it seemed she might drift into the realms of slumber, she thought that she heard singing.

> *Where hast thou gone, my lady love?*
> *Oh, where o'er the earth hast thou gone?*

But even in her dreams, she had no answer.

"Are you my mother, then?" Brighid asked the next morning, as Ogrin once more taught her how to make the morning bread.

"I am not," Ogrin replied. "But I'll do for now. Keep kneading."

Brighid did as instructed. But very soon, her mind wandered again and forgetting the soft dough within her hands as white as the flour upon them, "Are you my aunt?"

"Lord, love you! Do I look like any relation of yours?"

The girl shrugged. "I don't know. I can't see my face."

Ogrin poked the fish cooking in the ashes and scratched her chin. Her wrinkled eyes flit to the drawer where the silver mirror lay and then back to the fish. "Believe me," she said at last, "you en't."

After some time, Brighid spoke again. "I saw this morning that I have two knicks on my ribs. Was I in war? Or a prisoner? I have a knife-wound upon my hand, too. See, just here."

"I don't know about those," Ogrin said, amending, "You had them before you came to me."

"Then who did I live with before?"

"Will you take all day, Brighid? Or shall I make the bread myself?"

Brighid sighed and punched the dough.

Pwll and Liam took their leave of the Inn that afternoon. They had left in curious standing—Pwll well-liked for his open hand and the magic he had brought their Brighid; Liam a bit more feared for the little that he spoke. A few had thought to question the squire about the transformation and had received full cups and hearty laughs but no answer. Only Peghain had thought to ask Liam what had happened in her apartments—the answer she received was no more satisfactory. "We failed, Madam, and now return to Maelgwenn," the guard had replied, carefully rolling the spare shirt he had purchased that morning into his pack. "There is no more to be said."

There were many to help the travellers to the door, and at least five who thought it worth their while to travel with them up the road to Loch Corraigh, and two who had no wives thought it might be time to visit some relations on the other side for a day or so. As for Peghain, she saw them no further than the yard, her arms crossed, her iron hair immobile even in the breeze that blew the travellers' cloaks behind them. She had not been deaf to the name the squire had called their Brighid, but what need had the Innkeeper of princesses? But a hard worker and an extra pair of hands, particularly for that fool Ogrin, could be valued. Nevertheless, as Peghain watched the travellers depart, she thought she felt something twist within her breast, something akin to guilt.

Something else twisted within a heart long corrupted—it was not guilt, but life.

The Count lived, more wretched than Damhain Leanblade, Deirdre's false brother, when in exile. The Count sat alone, huddled, miserable upon the soft sandy shore of Islendil's lands—far from Ruthvyn Silverhands, abandoned by his shadows. The green water, thick with seaweed, lapped his greying, bony feet. He had sat there so long with no sustenance but the occasional crab or snail, that the moist sand had gained the permanent impressure of his body upon it. The sea swelled, rushed up to cover his shoulders with brine, and lapped salt water in his face with every wave, which he drank as eagerly as though it were pure. The sea receded and left him shivering in his once-fine rags, open to the stinging air that raced across the edge of the world like invisible darts.

The fight upon the hill with that damn boy had weakened him, although he still lived. A wound to the heart, a slit throat, and yet he still lived. Day after day the sea consumed him, abandoned him, the wind barraged him, and yet he lived. How many times had he taken his own life, had he made ropes of seaweed, plunged his ensorcelled dagger into his belly, let the shadows feed on his blood until not one drop remained—*and yet he lived!* Mortal man has long desired to cheat death. The Count longed only to cheat life.

The sun set, the tide rose, the gulls flew overhead, calling each to each, circling above him like white vultures. He looked up, seeing with sunken eyes the brief companionship of the seagulls. Three flew, then suddenly ten, twenty—the eye blurred with the rapidity of the wing-beat spiral. Dodging, diving ever closer and closer, until the first one nipped his ear, the next his hair, his neck, his shoulder, his elbow, his fingers, his nose, his lip, and every extremity within reach. The Count did not move, but allowed the strange embrace, enjoyed—if such a word can be used to describe the mild salve his hollow soul received—the fluttering touches of black-tipped wings battering his arms, back and head.

Smiled as the seagulls screeched within his ear. They took nothing from him he would not more willingly part withal—except his life. And when they had done with him as they fled from the rising tide, he sat like he had for these many months since the shadows had abandoned him here to search out the Hermit, to search out the Princess, to search out fresh blood and revenge—the Count sat whole, every part of him intact and wretched.

When at last he dreamt, he dreamt of death. And when he woke, he screamed.

Two days later Padriac returned, riding right up to the clearing before Ogrin's door. He dismounted, took a deep breath, ran his fingers through his curly hair, and knocked. The old woman answered him with a squint. "She iddn't here," Ogrin said before he opened his mouth. But she could see as well as anyone that he wore clothes for courting and gold crosses were embroidered on his surcoat's sleeves.

"May one inquire where Brighid has gone to?" he asked with a small bow.

Ogrin sniffed and eyed the bright-faced lad. "She might have gone down to the water's edge. But I wouldn't know and wouldn't tell you if I did."

Padriac bowed again, even as the door slammed shut upon him. Shrugging philosophically, he took out his pipe, lit it, and made his way to the Gwyrglánn. He found Niamh humming a tune he didn't know, and so lovely and haunting it was that he stopped for a moment to simply listen. Humming gave way to half-words, half-words solidified, gained shape, seemed to form the song mid-air, like music evaporated to the atmosphere.

"*Over earth and sea, over sea and sky*," Brighid sighed and wrang out the last drops of water from the laundry.

"That's quite good," Padriac said, leaning against a tree.

Brighid jumped and looked behind her. "Oh! I didn't hear you coming."

"I didn't intend that you should," he answered, going to her. "May I help you?"

She shook her head. "I am done here."

"You are always finished when I arrive."

"If I am, I am sorry. I wouldn't know."

"No, forgive me." Then sitting beside her and looking over the river, he asked, "Where did you hear that tune?"

"I don't know that I *heard* it quite," Brighid replied, folding the cloth. "Not the way you mean, at least." She placed the dress in the basket silently, as though weighing her words. And then, very quietly, she said, "Might I ask you a question?"

"Ask me anything."

Her small, perfect hands closed into fists on the basket edge. She let her long hair tumble around her like a veil. "The day—the last time I saw you, you kissed me."

Padriac risked turning over on his side to touch her hand. "I did. Did I offend you, Brighid?"

She shook her head and her cheeks dimpled. "No. At least...." Suddenly, she stood, her basket in her arms like a shield. "You must forgive me. Please believe I do not mean to offend you. And I am very glad you came today, for I do like you but I do not think I can love you. At least, not for a little while. Not until I know more."

"What do you wish to know?" Padriac asked, scrambling to his feet. "Ask me—I promised to tell you anything."

Her eyes grew very fierce and terrible at that moment, and although she wore humble plainspun, for a moment she glowed so that Padriac flinched and saw his heart not wholly pure. "Tell me who I am."

With that, she left him and he did not dare pursue.

Some time later, the clouds began to gather, crowding out the sun and rumbling deep within their bellies. Brighid looked upward and saw the lightning flickers and drew her things together and set back to the house.

The air misted, trickled rain like drops flung from Ydulhain's beard. Thunder clapped like the beating of great wings. Brighid began to run.

"Your pardon, Princess?"

Brighid started and looked around, but saw nothing but the forest. Tucking the basket more firmly beneath her arm, she set off again for Ogrin's cottage. But the leaves sounded strangely, and the voice she had heard before whispered a name—*Niamh*. Nervous now, Brighid hastened her footsteps until she skipped awkwardly over root and tree, skirting gorse and blackberry bush and pools newly forming. Only when she came upon a swath of unfamiliar stumps—she had once known them to be the border between Alf Forester's land and Ogrin's—did she stop, and realise she had lost her way.

Her mind whirled. How far had she come? Might Padriac hear her if she screamed? Dare she face whatever pursued her? She risked a glance back the way she came, and so she almost missed when the Fairy-formed man landed softly.

"Niamh," he said, for it must be she, he had *seen* her through the eagle's eyes and in memory ever since. "*Niamh*," he said again, stepping closer. She clutched the basket like a shield; Gethin's heart ached. "I mean you no harm." And then in softer tones, over which Padriac had no mastery, "Dost thou not know me?"

"I do not," Brighid replied. "Nor am I like to desire better acquaintance." She raised her chin—although Gethin could see it tremble—and added, "If you please, sir, let me pass."

"Niamh!" he cried, catching her when she would flee. He had never held her before—had imagined it a thousand times—but never in such a manner, never with her struggling to be rid of him. "I have traversed earth and sea for thee, I braved the terrors of the Wood for thee, I brought a man back from the brink of death, took life from an unstained creature, fought shadows everywhere that I have travelled, all for *thee!* Four long months did I journey on foot for thee, five more have I sought for thee." Then with a rueful laugh, "My throat is sore from singing for thee. Remember—Niamh! Thou answeredest my song but a moment hence." He let his hand run through the glory of her golden hair that had saved him when he lay dying in Goewínn and even now kept the unicorn's blood within the alicorn. "Hath it been so long, Niamh, that thou hast forgotten?"

"I do not know the woman you seek," Brighid answered, her struggles ceased, only to be replaced by an awful stiffness. "But I am not she." The look of pain within the stranger's blue eyes unnerved her, and she felt her heart soften for the desperate plight of the man who held her. Fortunate the girl this Fairy sought. For a moment, she considered answering to the strange name—but, no. Brighid could not bring herself to such a deception. Gently, she smiled and said, "Release me."

"No," he whispered, although Brighid was not quite sure she heard him speak. And bending forward, he kissed her. White wings enfolded them, hid them from the world, and time, and gentle rain, and the fumbling words of poets.

And when at long last he drew back, it was only to see twin tears running down her lovely face, like spray from a dolphin's back. Her heart pained her more than she could say—she knew not why. Would Padriac brave flood and fire for her? She knew not. But the stranger before her was warm and strong and she longed to tell him of her woes, and ask of him who she truly was. Something spoke deep within her, like a Firebird's voice, that made her doubt the words of those who said they knew her.

She did not say this, but laying her hand upon his heart, she whispered, "Let me go."

So that third time, he released her, watching as she walked away with his heart held in her hand. And so Gethin did not notice when in the trees, a patch of shadow moved, blinked a coal-red eye, and grinned with a hiss. Scuttling into the air, it crawled southeast to its master.

Farmer Demmit rushed into Peghain's Inn, yelling. When once they sedated him with slaps and mugs of ale, he regained some of his composure, gripped his heart as though to pump it back into steadiness, and then looking Peghain in the eye, he asked if she were in bad standing with the Fairy folk.

"Bad standing?" Peghain said, irritably, pulling away his mug and handing it to her grandson Cormach to wash. "I've never met a one of them. I wouldn't know."

"Well, there's one coming, lassie. You'd better find out quick."

And with that, the occupants of the room rushed as one to the windows and looked up. They weren't disappointed. For no sooner had each one jostled for a view, than he was among them like a bright and angry cloud. A few attempted bows—most stepped back.

"I seek the Princess," the Fairy said, his blue eyes dark and terrible. The great wings spread and snapped shut, which caused several to edge toward the door. "Or rather," he added, quietly, "what hath become of her."

The poor customers looked uncomfortably at one another and wondered what devilry had come their way that so many travellers disturbed their quiet.

"Your pardon, lord," Peghain said, stepping forward. "The Princess is not here."

"Peghain Innkeeper's daughter, isn't it?" the Fairy asked, turning his piercing gaze upon her. She nodded calmly—nothing could outstare Peghain. "How is your lame goat? And your knee? You have been using the poultice I sent you?"

At this Peghain did blink, and although she did not move, her lashes lowered nervously.

"And you," the seeming-Fairy said, looking at Farmer Demmit crouched against the counter. "Still troubled by rabbits?"

Farmer Demmit shook his head, looking very like a rabbit himself.

"Ah," the stranger said, "and young Cormach! Does your bow still shoot straight?"

The youth in question nodded, a full froth of foam upon his downy upper lip.

"Your pardon, lord," Peghain spoke again, her wits recovered her. "But are you known to us?"

"Well known," the Fairy said and then took from off his belt a fine chain that caught the afternoon sun and glimmered into the patrons' eyes. He put it on. And perhaps it was the ale, or the summer light, or something deeper than these two combined, but when they could see again, a golden glow surrounded the man so that they had to blink away tears and avert their eyes just so. The halo lasted but a moment only. A few said that they thought they saw his right hand looked like the leather of an eagle's claw.

"Who are you?" Peghain asked, covering her eyes with her upraised arm.

The stranger felt for his face and wondered whether he would rather laugh or sigh that no leonine features plagued him now. "You know me, all of you. I am the Hermit, whom you called Duncan."

"The Hermit!" several cried at once, leaping out of their seats and squinting against his light to make out the features of tawny beard, furred chest, and double claws. But these soon sat down with headaches, as one might after looking at the sun too long.

"You look different," Cormach said meekly, before his formidable grandmother could silence him. Catching her eye, he quickly spun around and applied himself once more to the washing of mugs.

"I am different," Gethin whispered to himself, touching his jaw and arms. Only the single claw remained—ugly, certainly, but a small token and easily hidden within the folds of his Hermit's robe. Whispers rose up around him. He paid them no mind, but fixed his eyes on Peghain.

"Tell me all you know," he said so low that it reached the Innkeeper's ears alone.

"The Princess isn't here," Peghain replied stalwartly.

"But Brighid is," a small voice said, trembling, coming up close to the Hermit.

Peghain's eyes darted down to her granddaughter, Emma. But the Hermit bent down to her, took her by the arms and said, "Wilt thou tell me of Brighid?"

Emma's face split into a broad grin, for she liked nothing better than taletelling. And the whole room quieted, for there is no better tale than a true one, and a man likes to know what part he has played in the great events of history.

chapter xv

Soon after midsummer's Day, Ewan returned to Castell Gwyr with Findola and both their fathers, and their eyes were bright with love and laughter. Heralds had been sent ahead of them, trumpeting their return all through the city, so that crowds lined the street as they made their way to the King's home. And some who were new-come to the city, asked if that were the Princess that everyone kept going on about, and those were firmly hit upside the head, and asked if they had eyes to see how dark the lady was. To which the unfortunate would reply that he had heard that the Princess was dark now, and that if these were city manners, he looked forward to returning to Findair or Aldhairen or wherever he had come from.

Brenna Housewife, ever garrulous, stuck her hands on her hips as the last of them passed, and said that if the Handmaids were come home—for Gwrhyr had returned with Gwendolyn a month before—it was a sure thing the Princess would be, too. Only it would've been nicer if they'd come all at once, so that she might have only baked for one celebration. It was too hot for baking, anyway. They might have come in autumn.

Between the northward city wall and the gates of the castle lay an upward slope of rolling land, used mainly as pasture for sheep, goats and cows. The Heralds had already gone this road, and the gates stood open for the young Knight and his lady, people bubbling out of the portal and lining the road as they had in the city—led foremost of all by Gavron and Rhianna.

And so all the court was present when a shadow passed overhead, blocking out the sun. And those with keener sight said that it was a man upon a foul, winged horse. And those with more wisdom claimed that this man was the Count. And those with some imagination said that horse had three heads, instead of one.

Three times more Gethin attempt to speak with Niamh, after Emma told her tale and named the name with which Pwll had greeted Brighid. The first time, he met Niamh when she came to gather wood for the fire. Ogrin had an old axe that she rarely used, even when young and spry, and this Gethin took up and began chopping steadily and competently a large fallen branch the lightning had severed. Brighid had come to the sound, wondering who could be making such a racket—for Ogrin was sleeping. And when she saw Gethin, she stopped and swayed a little back and forth, as though her heart and her mind warred against one another for her body.

"You are very kind," she managed at last, never moving from where she stood. "Here, take this in payment," and she took from her apron a small brown bread and cheese.

He nodded and laid the axe against the side of the cottage. But when he took a step forward to take the food from her, she flushed and placed the gift upon a barrel. Then, whirling, she left him.

When she returned for the firewood in the evening, she found lying in place of the food a fine golden chain that shrank even as her hands touched it, until she saw that it would fit nicely about her own neck. But she did not put it on. And when she showed it to Ogrin, the old woman's black eyes twinkled knowingly and she tapped the end of her nose and looked northward to Connlach's lands, but said nothing more except to smoke her pipe and rock her chair back and forth.

The second time, Gethin waited by the water's edge until Niamh came with her basket of clothes to wash them. He coughed politely to announce his presence, and when she looked as though she might flee again, he called out, saying, "I can tell you who you are."

She paused, even in the act of taking up her basket, and looked long and hard at the stranger, taking in his brown robe, his tawny hair, his blue eyes and white wings, hoping that something, anything might make her remember. "What is your name?" she asked at length.

"I have many names. But the truest one is Gethin."

"Gethin," she tried the sound of it. "And then who, pray, am I? For I have been told that I am Brighid, and none until now have contradicted that."

"If none have contradicted your name, why do you hold it in question?"

Her brow furrowed and she crouched in the grass, letting her fingers dip into the Gwyrglánn, as though her answers might lie there. "I dream some nights," she said, "of fire—of many types of fire. The hearth, the heart, the wings of a bird. And a voice beckons me through the fire, but I am always too afraid." She looked up at him and smiled. "You see, I cannot possibly be the girl that you think I am. Surely, a lord like yourself must be someone very grand who never dreams of anything but pleasant things. Perhaps she dreams of you."

"I think she doth. Although she doth not know it. And I dream of her and have for ever so long. Shall I tell you a story?"

"If I may finish my task while you do so. I do not know why a household with only two women should have so many dirty things within it, as though we had shunned water altogether! And Ogrin will not speak of it...." She sighed, and tucked her hair behind her ear. "But you said you had a story. I am very rude to complain."

"It is not a new story, I'm afraid," Gethin said, easing himself onto the grass, a respectful distance from Niamh. "I have not that facility. But you may not have heard it, for it comes from Islendil, from my mother's people.

"My father, and all his ancestors were the Lords of Eyre, Earls of that name, whose lands extend along the borders of Urdür and Aldhairen. But my mother came from Islendil's lands, the Lords of Fingal, where they border on the Serpent's Sea, just before the waters rush off the edge of the world, and ever downward to the True World beneath. And oft she would tell me this tale.

"In the days before the Fairies came and yet well after the Titans had passed, grieving for their slain, in that period when the Wolf King ruled and heroes like Deirdre and Guilian Silverbow walked the earth and gave men hope, the first of my mother's line, Fingal himself, set out in quest for honour and for fame, and to see what he might make of himself in the wilds of the world. And so he kissed his mother and his father and took up his sword, Eimobhar, known as Swift Help, and set off inland. For many months he travelled, until at last he came to a castle woven entirely of rose bushes. And it was here, he was certain, that Destiny had called him.

"Confidently he approached the gate, which looked like the unhewn trunks of two trees and as immobile, fully caught up in its branches with roses and with thorns. Yet Fingal was undaunted, and raising Eimobhar, he hit the pommel against the seam of the two trunks three times, and called out for entrance. And no sooner had he done so than the trees pulled up their roots—for they were truly Vertae guardians—and stepped aside for him to enter, before settling back into their places.

"No sooner did Fingal step inside, than he was greeted by tall, willowy creatures, who looked in one light like fair women with green hair, and at another like small trees that one might find along the waters' edge."

"They were Vertae, too," the Princess ventured.

"They were. For my ancestor had unknowingly stumbled into the stronghold of those earthen kings. And when he was brought into the main hall, he saw the four great kings themselves—Hintev, stern and blue of eye and beard; Mabon, gay and mischievous; Lellemond, who had wooed Eileen with stolen kisses so that she kept the Autumn at bay a little longer; and Faunden, all brown and wrinkled like a leaf. And since this was summer, Lellemond sat upon the high throne with his wife by his side and looked gravely down at the mortal man who had dared to enter their domain.

"'Thou art well come, Fingal, son of Urthar,' Lellemond said. 'What bringeth thee to our court in these troubled times?'

"'So please you, lord, I seek adventure.'

"'Adventure?' Lellemond said, sharing a private smile with his brothers, particularly Mabon who often set traps for the unwary, and from whom, some say, came the first pathway to Auberon's court in the True World. 'And what adventure dost thou seek?'

"'So please you, lord, that which you might set for me.'

"'And what of the dangers thou mightest encounter? Dost thou think naught of that?'

"'I have wits and strength and youth enough. Challenge me how you will.'

"'And what wouldst thou in return?'

"Then Fingal, who had been well-versed in the lore of that time, let his eyes wander around the enchanted hall, which no man can find by seeking it, and if he chances there, it is only by the will of the Lords of the Earth. And his eye happened to light upon fair Sorcha, Lellemond's daughter, who stood at the foot of her father, and whose smile seemed sweeter than cherries from the bough. So raising his head, he asked for the hand of fair Sorcha, and Lellemond looked at his daughter and saw how she regarded the youth, and so agreed.

"'Then this is thy task, Fingal son of Urthar,' Lellemond said. 'There is a giant who hath strayed from the north and who walketh unchecked through the forests, doing great damage to many of our people. At first we thought him simply ignorant of where he wast, but when we sent our ambassadors to parlay with him, he chased them off, killing two and sending the hounds in such a fright that they could not be coaxed out of the kennels for many a day. And so we sent a hunting party after him, and my brother,' indicating Faunden, 'himself took the lead, but again the giant chased them away and didst great damage. And so we sent spies, the beasts of the earth, to find where he wast and hear if he ever spoke to himself. And this a squirrel said to us, that the giant hath a grievance against our kind, for his brother hadst died, strangled by the trees, and the water hadst rushed in over him'—and that is how my mother's people explain Loch Corraigh. 'Thou, Fingal,' Lellemond continued, 'must find this giant and rid the world of it. And bring back with thee his head as proof of what thou hast done. If thou returnest with this trophy, then shalt Sorcha be thine; elsewise thou shalt die, either in battle or from shame if thou findest thyself a coward when the moment is upon thee.' The King of Summer waited a moment to take the measure of the youth before him and then asked, 'Having heard our demands, wilt thou go on this adventure, Fingal?'

"'My lord, I will,' answered he. And to prove his determination, he approached Sorcha and knelt before her, and gave her his ring with his seal upon it, and kissed her hand. Then bowing, he left that very minute, and set out that very hour in search of the giant.

"Now it was not at all difficult to find the giant, for as soon as Fingal stepped outside, he could hear the brute's howls not very far away. And when he looked behind, the fantastic castle was not there. And so Fingal set off after the sound, and it was not many days before he came upon the giant, tearing up the trees and hurling them to the ground, looking within them to see if they were real or the hollow dress of a Vertumn.

"When Fingal saw the giant, for the first time he knew the cold coil of fear. But he gripped Eimobhar and planted his feet and called with all his might, 'Ho, there, giant! I am come to slay thee!'

"'Ho, ho!' laughed the giant in return, throwing aside a tree with one hand. 'And what have we here? A mouse to challenge me? Go home, bug. You are not worth a meal.'

"'And very glad am I of that!' Fingal replied. 'But I am hot for blood, and I fancy thou hast enough to sate even the thirst of the Wolf King and all his court. Come—defend thyself!'

"And so the giant swung towards Fingal, but Fingal leapt aside, and ran under the giant's legs and pricked him on the ankle. Then the giant lifted his leg to squash Fingal, but Fingal leapt upon the giant's foot, and by the time the giant had finished grinding the dirt, Fingal had climbed to the giant's belt.

"'Come on!' cried he, throwing his voice so that it sounded as if he stood within a patch of bushes. Accordingly, the giant gave all his attention to thrashing the harmless gorse, and while he did so, Fingal caught onto the giant's sleeve, and crawled all the way up to his shoulder. Again, Fingal threw his voice, and again the giant attacked another clump of bushes a few feet off, giving Fingal time to climb up the giant's neck—the most difficult part of all—and into the giant's beard, and finally up to his very nose!

"And there he cried, 'Ah, ha! I shall climb thee like I shall climb my fortunes! My thanks, Sir Giant.' And with that he ran his sword through the giant's left eye, and then the right.

"As the giant fell, dying—for Eimobhar had touched his brain—the giant put all his hatred into one last curse, and put that curse into his very blood, and that blood, having touched Fingal's arm, made Fingal forget all that had happened to him since he had left his father's house. And so Fingal left the giant, glad of his adventure, but with no more remembrance of the Vertae court or fair Sorcha than a dream lost upon waking.

"For many more months, Fingal wandered, and adventured far and near, for he was skilful with his blade and wily besides. And many more adventures did he have before he finally returned home. And when he arrived there, his father greeted him saying, 'Fingal, my son, glad am I that thou art returned! For we have found a bride for thee, lovely in form and in mind.' And Fingal, weary from his adventures, thought it well to marry and raise a household.

"But though Fingal had forgotten the Vertae court and fair Sorcha—she had not forgotten him. And often she thought of him and wondered after him, and when he would come to claim her hand. And many long days passed. Days turned to weeks, weeks to months and no Fingal came to wed fair Sorcha. So the earth girl turned herself into a fox as red as her hair and sped out from her father's house and sought for her beloved everywhere. Not a few days passed before she found the giant dead, and conversing with the animals who were under her fathers' dominion, she discovered that brave Fingal had indeed slain the giant, and about the curse the dying giant had put into his blood. And then Sorcha wept, and wrang her hands, and beat her breast, and cried to the heavens above for solace.

"But she was her father's daughter, and so she quickly dried her tears, and plaited her hair, and set out for Fingal's home. And when she finally came to that place, she found herself in the midst of Fingal's wedding preparations. Swallowing her pride, Sorcha presented herself as a simple servant, and was immediately set to work in…the laundry."

Brighid smiled at this, scrubbing a tablecloth over a rough stone. "A fitting task," she said. "Go on."

Gethin smiled too and leaned back on his elbows. "All that first day she worked until her arms were sore. Several times she caught sight of her beloved, but he passed her by without so much as a second glance. And so that night she turned herself into an ant, and she climbed up the mansion wall until she came to his window, and saw him sleeping. And then she turned herself back into a girl, and sang this song."

He cleared his throat nervously, for although his voice was not poor, neither could it compete with a minstrel's or even with Padriac's merry tenor.

> "*I loved my love, and my love loved me—*
> *Sing hey dey, while the roses grow.*
> *I love my love; he's forgotten me—*
> *Sing hey dey, life is woe.*'

"But although she sang, Fingal did not wake. The next day was very much the same, and the next night Sorcha again turned herself into an ant and crawled up the wall into his chamber, and this time she dared to sing sitting by his bed, and even touching his hand. But though her voice was lovely—as mine, I'm afraid, is not—Fingal did not wake.

"Now the third day, the day before Fingal was to marry, Sorcha contrived to mend Fingal's evening robe, and into the hem of its sleeve she put half of the ring he had given her, and she whispered deep enchantments over it. That evening, as Fingal prepared for bed, he discovered the ring and wondering who had stolen it and broken it, he pretended as though he were asleep and waited—for although he had slept deeply the past two nights from exhaustion and mulled wine, he had dreamt of a woman sitting by his bed.

"That night, Sorcha once again crawled up to Fingal's room, and this time she came straight to his bed, and grasped his hand and wept over it, kissing it, and singing her song. And as Fingal listened, he dared to peek beneath his eyelashes, and so saw the other half of his ring about her neck. Then Fingal remembered his journey to the Vertae court and his promise to fair Sorcha, and throwing back the covers, he leapt to his feet—"

"Much to the astonishment of poor Sorcha," Brighid added.

"Very much. And he embraced her and brought her down immediately to the chapel, and woke up the entire household and told them what had happened. And that very night he wed the fair maid and took her to his bed. And from that marriage came the line of Fingal, who have reigned well and prosperously from that day to this."

Brighid was silent for some time, folding the damp clothes reflectively, and placing them back in the basket. "What of the other girl?" she asked at last. "The one who was to be married to Fingal and who suddenly had her life turned upside-down? What of her?"

"The stories do not speak of her. But I have often hoped that she found a nice ostler and married him—one who never would run off on adventures where one is bound to meet the strangest folk."

"Do you think she was happy? As an ostler's wife, I mean. When she had been bound for the great Fingal?"

"I hope she was."

Brighid, her work complete, sat back on her heels and regarded the stranger beside her. He was not handsome in the way that she thought Fairies ought to be—as though a statue come to life—and yet he was not unpleasant to look at. His features were regular, his colouring tawny, his nose perhaps just this side too wide for perfection, his brows just this side too thick. And yet, his mouth she knew was warm and quick to smile, and his arms were strong—and well governed by his heart if he thought to employ them to cut wood for two lonely women.

"You said that you might tell me who I am," she said, softly. The wind rustled the tall grass at the water's edge, making unexpected ripples in the river and splashing water upon the shore.

"I have told you, in a way. You are Fingal, or rather, are like Fingal. And the fire you dream of is the cursed blood that plagued him."

"And you are…."

"Gethin," he said shortly, pulling at the grass and tossing it away. Then looking up, again with that soft pleading in his eyes, he added, "Niamh's love."

"And who is this Niamh you seek?"

Gethin closed his eyes and lay down on his back, speaking to the heavens. "I begin to wonder if she is a dream."

"But a dream of whom, of what?" Brighid persisted, moving to sit a little closer to him.

"A dream of perfection," he answered. "Have you never heard of her? The Princess whose beauty couldst drive men mad?"

Brighid laughed but the sound was hollow in her ears, for the Firebird's kiss sang within her blood. "It sounds like another tale."

"It may be one day. But her tale is not finished, yet."

"Does she still drive men mad?"

"Oh, yes," Gethin said, and in his eyes was a dangerous light and the reflection of Peghain Innkeeper and Padriac mac Connlach.

"What a terrible thing."

"Truly. And yet, is it so terrible? Or do our minds conceive perfection thus to name it terror—a word sprung from our maddened minds and not at all reality? Man has never abided perfection. Four times only has it walked the earth before this Princess. Two fell, one we slew, and one was taken into Heaven. As for the last, for the Princess—I fear she hath come to the same end the first have. I fear she hath become merely human."

"Is that so horrible?" Brighid asked, drawing herself upright. "I can name many a man who is more beast than man. Indeed, a true man is one in a thousand!"

"More true than thou knowest," Gethin answered and touched his neck where the chain once hung.

Brighid was silent for a moment. She looked over the water, letting the breezes kiss her cheek and brush her hair behind her. The edges of her overdress played in the wind; the sun slid along the lovely contours of her face. Gethin hardly dared breathe—she was like the unicorn come unbidden, and he dared not fright her away. Her long lashes fluttered when she spoke, slowly, choosing her words with care. "You said—you said that I am like Fingal. I wonder…." She hesitated, glanced only briefly at his eyes, and looked away, confused. "I wonder where you might fit into the tale. Do you fancy yourself a sort of Sorcha, to sing at my window when I dream?"

Gethin shook his head. "Sorcha was Fingal's love. I am Niamh's. And you…."

"I am not she." Brighid said, lacing her fingers together. "Although, for your sake," she added to the wind, "I wish I were."

After such an encouraging interview, it was sheer perverseness of fate that the next time he encountered his love, bearing with him a poesy of herbs that might salve Ogrin's arthritic joints, Gethin found that Padriac had come calling first.

The saffron mare was tied to a nearby sapling when Gethin arrived. The door opened and the thwarted bridegroom ducked into the cover of the trees, hiding among the shadows as though no more than shadow himself. Padriac came out first, leading Niamh by the hand; Ogrin followed after. A few niceties were exchanged, and then Padriac swung himself into the saddle, bent down and lifted the Princess easily into the circle of his arms.

With a click of the tongue and a heel to the mare's flank, they set off. But Niamh looked directly into the shadows where Gethin hid, and in her gaze he heard as clearly as if she had spoken, *Do you think she was happy? As an ostler's wife. When she had been bound for the great Fingal? If not happy, she shall be contented.* And then, again, *I am not she. Although, for your sake, I wish I were.*

Despair threatened to bear down upon the Hermit as he leaned against the trees and folded his arms against a world that did not follow the tales its people spun. But then his eyes lit upon a spark of gold dangling from Niamh's cincture—a chain that he knew well. And so he kept in the woods until they returned, and when Padriac left on his saffron mare and turned her nose northward to his home, Gethin followed after.

Liam came first to the clearing where Maelgwenn lay dying. The land beneath him changed more slowly now, passing through the final seasons of the Fairy's life, as his blood began to crust and drain. All about the glade, a white light shone in prismed rays from the Fairy's body. And though Liam's heart was moved to sorrow for the loss of valiant Maelgwenn, yet he shed tears for the beauty of his going.

Maelgwenn heard the rustle of the guard's coming and turned his head to look at Liam and smiled as though he were already far away from the heartaches of this world. "Thou seest I have kept my promise, Liam mac Hwyach," he said.

Liam nodded and stepped forward to kneel beside the Fairy, and all the creatures who attended his passing bowed more deeply still, and leaned against each other for comfort. Pwll followed closely after and stood just without the circle, feeling that somehow he was not meant to bear this grief. Silently, he crossed himself and watched in solemn awe.

The night deepened, and the creatures raised their voices and sang each in his own manner. Softly, their laments blended, overlaid by the whispering melody of the soughing Wydoemi as they played the leaves of the Vertae trees. The strain lapped over itself, swirled like mist, eddied and flew to call out to the distant stars. And in that lament, Liam raised his voice—a clear tenor, strong and sweet and full of the valour that looks on doom and finds hope yet —and he sang with words not his own of Maelgwenn's passing.

And Pwll listened to the lament and had not the heart to listen too closely or to imprison the song within the clumsy bars of mortal writing, for the song was greater than he. And as the moon sank and Liam sang his sorrow, Pwll saw himself as he was, small and humbled. So Pwll—Heir of Branmoor, scion of a line second only to the King—knelt in the high grass and bowed his head and gave honour to the guard who sang for the first Fairy's death, and of whom no man has ever sung.

Between the village and Connlach Manor, at the Inn of the Twined Oaks near the border of Udinë's land, Padriac took his rest for the evening, since he had started late in the day from Ogrin's cottage. The Innkeeper, Morris, knew Padriac well—almost everyone thirty miles around made sure to know all the scions of Connlach—and gave him the best room in the house, and the best seat in the bar, and the best foaming golden beer to go with it all. And Padriac accepted it with a smile and a handshake, and the passage of gold from hand to hand. His coming was hailed by several of the regular patrons, and the better part of the first hour was spent in the passing of news, jokes, and jibes. But soon the Connlach boy grew weary of such frivolity, so excusing himself, he went to the fire, sat himself in a wooden chair, and stretched out his legs in front of him.

His thoughts were dark although his afternoon had not been unpleasant. Indeed, Brighid had been everything that was sweet and charming and attentive. And yet—and yet....

Padriac sighed and pinched the bridge of his nose. Perhaps the Princess still possessed some of her old magics, he thought. For sure, he had thought of no one else since she touched him that day he left her outside the witch's hut. And yet to blame Niamh for his own deceptions seemed a base excuse—thin, like a whiff of cloud before the truth.

No more time for dour ruminations was left the lad. A stranger, deep hooded and brown robed, stood beside him asking if the second chair were empty. Padriac gestured toward the chair and the stranger sat, stretched out his legs, and turned his hidden features to the fire. The moment past, Padriac thought to apply himself again to the whirligig of thought, but that the stranger spoke.

"You are Connlach's boy, are you not?"

Padriac nodded. "Anyone may know so much of me."

"To know so much and yet so little," the stranger mused. He pulled on a golden beard with long fingers, saying, "I think I saw you southerly, once."

"Yes," Padriac answered carefully. "My brother has married recently and prefers to keep at home with his wife. It has fallen to my lot to oversee the buying and selling of things."

"An admirable position, to be sure. And yet, perhaps you desire your brother's happiness?"

"I have no designs upon Gwenhyfarch, if that is what you mean. Are you a Father Confessor to plague me so?"

"Not as such, not as such," the stranger said, looking at the youth so that Padriac thought he caught a glimmer of deadly blue eye. The moment passed and the fire crackled in the silence. No one came to disturb the two men—no, not even Morris who was, on other occasions, wont to hang about Padriac's chair lest the Connlach boy desire another drink.

After some time the stranger spoke again, the words drifting upward to mingle with the smoke from Padriac's pipe. "I have been travelling over the face of this earth, and yet just the other day I saw a sight that made my heart leap for joy."

Padriac made a disinterested noise and sucked in a draft of smoke.

"It was a maid," the stranger continued, staring deep into the fires, "of such surpassing beauty, that sure I thought I beheld not a maid but a vision. And yet I spoke to her and she answered me, and so I cannot think she is a dream. You have been southerly, do you know of this maid?"

Padriac was silent for some time, and let the short puffs of smoke answer for him. But when the stranger did not look away, he said, "Mayhap I do."

"Sure!" the stranger laughed, "if you had seen her but once, you would not say 'mayhap!' Tell me at least her name, that I may name my dreams."

"Are you a poet that you name your dreams?"

"I am not so wise nor so crafty. I am but a plain, honest man, although," with another glance that shot straight through the heart of things, "that may be enough."

The Connlach boy shifted in his seat, rested his weight against one arm, and then the other, bit his pipe and looked away. "Some call her Brighid," he answered at last.

"And what do you call her?"

"The same."

"And what doth she call herself?"

Padriac then looked fully at the stranger and the youth's face hardened into the lines of anger and madness. "Who are you?" he asked.

For answer, the stranger removed his hood to reveal the Lord of Eyre, Gethin, Niamh's love. "One who hath sought long for his bride, friend," he whispered pleasantly. "One who wilt not fail now."

chapter xvi

O n the night the shadows came to the land around Loch Corraigh, the usual customers crowded into the White Hind and huddled together near the fire, as though they knew the devilry afoot miles away from them.

"Tell us a story, then, James," Brenna Housewife said, chaffing her arms against the summer night.

James Bobsboy nodded solemnly and held out his mug. "What would you hear?"

"Deirdre's blade," someone said. The others gathered there silently agreed. The kingdom waited for their Princess; now was the time for the darkest tales.

The room grew quiet. Lights dimmed, pipes flared, mugs lay quietly in large-knuckled hands. They knew the tale—not a man lived who did not know the tale. And they waited for the first words, rehearsing them in their own minds as they had each heard it at his mother's knee. It was reverent; it was religious, this telling of tales.

James cleared his throat, and leaned forward, his head downcast as though in prayer. The people listened for the story voice that rose and fell in the measured waves of a monk in evensong. They listened in vain. For James raised his head and pressed his hands to his eyes.

"I cannot do it," he whispered. "The power has left me for this night," he added in surer tones, "when all may be unmade."

The room had grown too quiet, as though the shadow that even now lay in wait beside the Inn of the Twined Oaks had settled deep within the common room. Some muttered among themselves that James spoke prophecy, and James himself wondered at his words that felt as true as the stories he told.

Shaking his head, James jumped to his feet and shouted, and all the patrons blinked as though just waking up from a dream. "More ale, Mistress!" James Bobsboy cried, with a grin that dimpled his cheeks and reminded the other men of their own youths. And then with fierce determination, James began singing a rowdy tune with entirely too many verses, and a chorus that a man might sing, even when in his cups.

> *"But I'll sing to brandy,*
> *And to brandywine, aye,*
> *And I'll sing to songs that are sweet.*

And if ne'er love should find me,
Then ne'er find me dry!
Raise up O the song, boys!
Let time keep the beat!"

Above the Green Mountains, above the Gwyrglánn, a shadow passed over the moonlight, eating whole swaths of the stars and spitting them out again, to burn redly against the night. Directly west from where the Wolf King had met his end and poisoned the lake the children had swum in, the triple shadows landed, raised their muzzles to the night and howled—whether in sorrow or triumph no one could say. People shut their doors and closed their windows, even in the summer, and crowded together and told each other stories to block out the howl. Only one ventured out of the Inn of the Twined Oaks—the Lord of Eyre, his hood still thrown back, his blue eyes blazing. The unicorn's horn hung by his side like Deirdre's blade.

Raising his eyes to meet the haggard ones of the Count, Gethin smiled. "It has been long since we met, my lord."

The shadow horse reared and snorted as Gethin took out the unicorn's horn, and held it in his hand as though it were a dagger. But even as he raised his arm to throw the alicorn into the writhing black breast, he felt that hand shiver, felt his nails lengthen and begin to point, although he did not wear the chain.

The Count saw this too, and laughed. "Brave words, Gethin. I see that she has tamed you back into a handsome youth. Perhaps she has tamed you to a eunuch?"

Gethin felt the rage build up within him, but he did not let it blind him. Slowly, as though it pained him, he lowered the alicorn and stepped back. "It

Padriac

seems thou shalt live a while longer. I would not undo the good that hath been done me for all the world—no, not even for thy blood."

And turning, he spread his wings and flew into the southern sky.

The Count never moved from where he stood upon the shadows' back, for his feet had sunk into the shadow and he could not get free. Nor would the shadows pursue the Hermit while he bore the alicorn. But Gethin was not the only one who ventured out to see what howled at the moon. And in the weak light of the crescent, Padriac wandered into the clearing and within that youth, the Count found a heart tinctured like his own.

Liam woke.

The song had ended an hour past and those attendant upon the Fairy had drifted into light slumber. Rolling over onto his back, Liam could see the last light of the old moon, holding the new moon in her arms. And in the light wind, he thought he could hear an old familiar voice—a voice that whispered incessant promises and curses rolled in one, the smooth, hopeless voice of the Count. He had often dreamt thus—even after the Fairies had healed his wound, and visions of Graithne replaced the worst of his nightmares—still the voice remained with its questions, and one question in particular: *Where hast thou gone? Where hast thou gone? Where hast thou gone?* And some nights Liam thought the voice did not ask the question of him, but of a son lost forever from his side.

Every shadow cast by tree or root or cloud, every sudden adumbration from glimmering candle-flames seemed like a thousand shadows pursuing as Gethin sped over earth and sea, over sea and sky to Niamh. He did not know the shadows did not pursue him. All his thought was bent on the safety of the Princess— for if *he* could be so easily found, doubtless the Count would seek out Niamh and finish the evil that he had begun. So the bridegroom flew to his bride, flew to her very window, and called to her both by her true name and by the name the village had given her. And when she did not answer him, he summoned what remained of his magics—for every day without the chain had drawn a little more out of him—and he stepped through the stone wall, and into her room.

The sliver of moonlight through the high, small window barely gilded the curve of her body beneath the thin sheet; it silvered her hair and wrapped her in a halo, as though she were one of the Seven Sleepers lost beneath the Sea of Silence. He came near to her, and knelt beside her like a Knight at vigil, and called her true name once more.

217

Immediately she woke, and turned to see who called her. And when she saw the white winged man beside her, she opened her mouth to scream, but he pressed his hand to her lips, saying, "We have not time. I come pursued and this place is no longer a refuge."

She arched her brows and pulled away from his hand. "If you bring trouble here," she whispered, "begone. You cannot wish your ills upon us. For the kindness you did us, chopping wood to last us many months, and out of Christian charity we will give you what you need to flee from here. But you cannot stay, nor ask us to share your troubles."

"Niamh! No, hear me out, by any name you choose. You asked me to tell you of yourself, and yet whenever I speak your name you refuse it. You have not that luxury now. That which hunts me hunts you, and his hatred cannot be slacked, although every mercy has been shown him. But if you allow me, I shall return you to your father's home, and there you may find some haven, safe with those who have always loved you."

"I have not any enemies," Brighid began.

"You have no memory of your enemies," Gethin corrected and dared to take her hand and press it to his heart. "Niamh, believe me I wish thee no ill. But if I leave thee here, it wilt not be many days—perhaps a matter of mere hours, for I do not know how close he is behind me—before he findeth thee. I know," he hesitated, played with her finger ends, and tried again, "I know it seemeth that each person hath a different story, and well I know that my own matcheth in no item at all to any of the others. Thou hast no cause to believe me against such a flood that nameth thee 'Brighid.' But perchance it is they who lie, perhaps fearing to lose thee. For I see in thy eyes this doubt."

"And you seek to fan that doubt," she interrupted, although her words lacked the certainty she intended.

"I do. What canst thou think? Wilt thou believe me?"

"And if I do not? What will you do then? Will you carry me off over your shoulder to some cave, like the giants are said to do? I cannot think it of you."

"No, Niamh. If thou wilt not come with me willingly, I shall not take thee. I made thee that promise long before we met that I should not take thy hand by force or policy, and to that I hold. But if thou wilt not heed me, then I shall return and seek him out again and either he or I shall die." He looked down and released her hand, saying beneath his breath, "Both, perhaps, even if I deal him a killing blow, for it seemeth that I have not yet purged myself of all my sins, and may transform myself without use of chain." Then, looking up again, he asked, "Wilt thou come, lady?"

But Niamh's thoughts were elsewhere and reaching out in the darkness to a small table by her bed, she took up the chain and held it out to him, letting it glimmer in the moonlight. "You left this here and have now spoken of it again. Here, take it, for it is far too fine a gift."

"Nay, Princess," said he, "I will not take that up again."

"What is it?"

Gethin looked over his shoulder even as he spoke, perhaps looking to see whether the shadows flew. "It showeth the true form of a man. Many a year I wore it as a penance, and have but only recently released myself of its burden under the instruction of my better. Within it I have stored most of my magics and it mayeth shield thee for a time."

"Shield me? And yet you will not wear it."

"I need not wear it. But if thou wilt...." And he took the chain from her hands and fastened it about his neck. Immediately his right hand formed the claw as it had in Peghain's Inn, but he also felt the feathers upon his forearm. No halo surrounded him now. Grinning wryly, he held up the arm, pushing back his sleeve to reveal the full deformity. "So thou seest that which I feared to answer the night we spoke through eagles. If I kill the Count, I have no doubt my whole body shalt transform, for I see already that when I drew upon him the eagle gained a greater hold once more. If thou wilt," he added, gesturing to the clasp. "I cannot easily remove it in this state."

She did as he instructed and watched in fascination as his right arm returned to its human form once more. "Will this happen to me if I wear it?" she asked.

"I cannot speak for all its properties," he answered. "But I think it mayeth restore thee."

"You speak freely," she chided.

Gethin's heart sank, but he said, "Lady, the hour grows late. Wilt... will *you* come? I can no longer tarry."

Brighid looked at the chain lying in a pool of moonlight upon the white sheet, and touched it gently. She did not dare to look at the man beside her. He had some strange enchantment of his own that made his words seem like the merest common sense. But she could trust no one until she discerned the truth of herself.

"I am very sorry for thee," she said, striving to sound as a sister. But her simple *thee* struck like a thorn upon the soul and Gethin stood and turned his back to her to hide his grief. "For I well wont the sorrows thou hast endured and still endure for the sake of thy love. And believe me that no one more than myself prayeth that thou mayest see the end of thy sufferings and come at last to her arms. And believe me that were the circumstances different, I might myself be persuaded to...to *like* thee better than our brief acquaintance hath allowed. But I cannot allow thee to suffer delusions on my behalf." She stood, too, and taking his hands in both of hers, she pressed them, saying, "There is strength in thee to have endured so much and to return to face this enemy, even to thy doom. That must weigh heavily upon the scales of justice—believe it. But with no proof beyond thy word, I will not go with thee. Go with my prayers. Myself shall not come."

Gethin nodded, and kissed the backs of her milk-white hands. He spoke no more word, but let his eyes drink their fill of his beloved, and then stepped through the stone again with the very last of his magic and into the night.

And when Niamh turned again to her pillow, she found her eyes well with tears that she could not dispel until they had run their course down her cheeks and left her soul raw and barren.

Where hast thou gone?

The youth who wandered out of the Inn of the Twined Oaks did not look in the least like the Count's lost son, for his hair was too red and curly, and his mouth too broad and apt to smile. But tonight Padriac did not smile and his mind was all full of murderous thoughts. And it is a truth that if three shadows, hungry for blood the Count could no longer give them, had not waited beneath the oak trees, the Connlach boy might have gone home and forgotten about the Princess, and in time found his own Gwenhwyfarch like his brother had. But the Count did wait, his feet sunken into the backs of his threefold vices, and although he had not much strength left, he had his voice and he called to the lad.

"I know what troubles thee."

The youth spun to see the gaunt shape, the sharp dark eyes, the quick mirthless curl of lip.

A cloud passed over the moon as the Count quietly added, "Come, I shall aid thee."

Gethin never looked behind him as he turned his back on Ogrin's cottage and began the long walk northward, his eye ever on the sky, ready to leap up from the dark forest floor and into the night to do violent battle. He had no doubt the shadows would bring the Count to Niamh, as surely as a needle pointed northward; the Count could not help but come at last to her doorstep, to rage against the stone walls and shriek curses against her name.

And as the stars wheeled their last course westward—as Elena's Lyre fell, and the Southern Lion rose, his paw rampant with Oisin's blood upon it—Gethin was at last rewarded with the sight of the double headed horse, the gaunt figure upon its back, silver Necromancer's dagger in hand. Hesitating no longer, Gethin darted upwards, his white wings buffeting light before him as though to dispel the night before its time. The unicorn's horn came easily to his hand, as long as a sword and as deadly.

Horn and dagger met, clashed in a shower of sparks that rained for miles around, and even against Niamh's small window, so that she sat up and wrapped her black shawl around her shoulders and listened.

They spoke no word but the language of the fight. No repartee passed from lip to lip like a second barb, but the cold and crystal ringing of alicorn on silver, silver on cloth, cloth ripping, and a wound across Gethin's broad chest reopened. For the Count was a fencer, the victor of many duels with every sort of weapon, while Gethin had trusted always to his magics, and later to tooth and claw—all of which he was now bereft. Wild and deadly were his swings at the villain and to some good effect, for the shadows feared the alicorn more even than Pwll's iron, and darted wildly about to avoid a blow. But the Count, bloodless though he was and almost no more than a wraith himself, when faced against the man he hated as much as he hated himself, found new strength to rein in the shadow stallion and make clear light swipes across the bridegroom's arm, leg, and side.

Gethin bled. Every laboured breath told him he was dying by inches. His wings faltered, he stumbled in the air and onto the Count's blade, felt his pinions rend as he twisted to avoid the blow. Swinging the horn, he felt it connect with shadow and flesh, and heard a dreadful howl even as he fell backwards into the dark arms of the trees. The shadows plunged after him, following the erratic course his broken wings brought them. Through the broad trunks, and back over the leafy canopy, downward again to run along the ground, a brief tussle in a rose briar that mingled petals with red and black drops of blood, and then into the trees again where Gethin had the advantage, and cut the Count several times with the alicorn.

Each victory transformed him as he had feared. And now, fighting within the leaves, thin moonlight and starlight dappling vision, not only the right arm bore the eagle's mark, but his teeth lengthened to a lion's incisors and he felt his great tawny tail return—and with that, balance. Thrust, and the shadows reared, fell back into the boughs of a maple. Despite his wounds, Gethin leapt, felt his feet lengthen, change shape, become leonine, and he welcomed the change. Feathers sprouted on his back and along his wings, strengthening them once more. His hair grew, became a mane over ears suddenly keen and pointed.

The Count swung towards the Hermit's breast but he swiped the Necromancer's blade away, and let his claws rake the Count's pale chest where they had long months ago. The Count laughed and looked deep into his enemy's eyes. "You are killing yourself."

And Gethin knew it to be true. Already he could feel the soul of him twisting along with his body, as the lion and the eagle consumed the human within him. "If I kill myself, I shall not die alone this day," he said around his lips growing wide and black. And he raised the alicorn, taking aim at where the Count's hollow heart lay.

But even as his arm descended, he felt a knife within his back, felt it touch the edge of his heart, and twist until a small hole opened, and his life drained out like sand through open fingers.

"There's for thee, *friend*," a voice said behind him.

Then Gethin saw what he had not noted before—that the Count's stallion bore only two heads. Twisting with a stifled cry of pain he saw the third, bearing up Padriac mac Connivar of Connlach House.

"So," Gethin said, with something of his old mirth, "the Devil will reap three souls tonight. So be it. We have lost all who we hold dear; what have we to live for?"

Gethin

And though he felt the wound within his heart widen, he raised the alicorn towards the youth's breast. But even as he did so, he saw within Padriac's eyes the raging waters of madness, and at their centre the image of Niamh, and he knew that he could not kill this one. No such compunction, no fear for his immortal soul touched Connlach's boy, and wresting the knife from Gethin's back as he turned upwards to fly to another battlefield, Padriac struck again, put the knife deep inside Gethin's shoulder, near the bone. The Hermit fell, rolled between branches, and onto the soft long-grassed ground.

Immediately the shadows were upon him, and the Count and Connlach lad, too. Stabbing and rending, picking at his skin as though he were no more than carrion, and every minute bled. Clutched within his human hand—all that remained now of the Lord of Eyre, Urdür's heir—the unicorn's horn glowed, encased his arm in a shield of light that deflected every attack. With great pain, he raised his hand and clutched the horn to his heart so that the light covered his ravaged chest, and his enemies must retreat to warring upon his legs. Almost, he seemed to hear the unicorn's voice whisper with his mother's stolen voice, ∼ *Courage, child. Courage.* ∼

He closed his eyes, even as the shadows bent to gnaw upon his toes, and in that darkness, he found Niamh, waiting with arms outstretched. And behind her, the whole host of Heaven, smiling. And he saw the Virgin lean her head against her Son's breast and whisper in His ear, and he thought perhaps she spoke for him, for that is what the priests had said. But he could not think that such loveliness awaited him. And so he opened his eyes again and looked at the dying moon and found his voice too weak to whisper to the wind the last words his heart contained, *Lady, I love thee.*

Padriac, senselessly scoring the Hermit's leg, carving upon it meaningless symbols as red as the madness that filled his mind, suddenly stopped. Looking at his hands, sanguine, browning in spots where the blood had dried already, he gasped and let the knife drop. The shadows gazed upward, and their eyes glowed incarnadine, smelling the youth's doubt, the restoration of sanity. But Padriac could spare no thought for them—his hands were stained and would never come clean. He looked to where the Hermit lay, silent, still, as though already dead, the unicorn's horn glowing like a Knight's shield over his heart. Crawling along the ground, Padriac dared to reach out, to touch the horn, and the shield of light allowed him. He looked at the marks upon Gethin's chest, and put his hand against Gethin's bleeding side. But the wounds were everywhere, and Padriac's two hands would not stop them all. He could not reach in to cup Gethin's failing heart. He could not reverse time to stop his own hand.

Padriac's knife lay still at Gethin's side and the youth took it up and rushed at the Count. He scored the knife within the Count's neck, but the Necromancer's blade swept up neatly between the youth's ribs, glanced off bone, and only prolonged death. The shadows closed in, circling the youth so that he knew not where to strike. And then as one they dove, clawed arms outstretched, black lips pulled back to reveal curved black teeth. They descended upon the Connlach boy, and although he set about him with knife, against four he could do nothing.

But one of the shadows shrieked and fell to the ground—the one that had borne him—as Gethin rose behind the fallen shadow, taller than he had ever been, still holding the alicorn to his breast, and as white as his wings. His maimed feet could not hold him long and he stumbled forward into Padriac's arms. The twin shadows struck, and Gethin pierced them with the alicorn so that they rolled away like chastened dogs. But his heart failed and he sagged to his knees. The unicorn light dimmed, pulsated with his shallow breath.

"Do not do this thing," Padriac whispered, even as the shadows gathered once more and crept toward them. "Not for me. I am not worth your life."

"The boy speaks truth," the Count said. "One this night may be spared."

The shadows grinned and hissed, "Give him uss!"

Gethin did not answer. But his claws clutched the alicorn and he drew himself upon his hind legs and rushed one last time at the very heart of the triple shadows and at the Count caught among them. The netting of Niamh's hair, he removed from the base of the alicorn, and the blood he threw upon the Count and upon his shadows.

Then with a howl that rent the night air—and quailed the heart of Niamh, who struggled over root and branch, following she knew not what pullings of her heart, or to whom—the shadows turned upon their master and when they had fed upon him, they disappeared with laughter that sounded more truly of wailing.

Padriac sank to his knees beside the Hermit and put his arm around the Lord of Eyre. As the shadows left, so did the eagle and the lion from the Hermit's wracked body: a final mercy. But when Padriac touched Gethin's skin, he felt it to be cold, and when he looked into Gethin's eyes, he saw that the shadow of death had already claimed him.

chapter xvii

rustling in the grass was all the herald that remained to announce the Princess as she came upon the clearing where she saw her two loves spread out upon the long grass. Gethin seemed a pool of white lying in a cloud of white wing, and all his blood shone silver in the last rays of moonlight. But Padriac, stretched out beside the Hermit gasping away the last of his life from the Necromancer's blade, was brown, blue, green, red—the colours of the earth, the colours staining the knife that lay within his bloody hand.

Niamh ran between them, collapsing onto her knees beside them, touching their eyes, their cheeks, their lips. Gethin was cold and she drew away as though he burnt her skin. Her heart wrenched as though something died within her. But Padriac stirred at her touch, and she saw in his face more pain than ever man has right to know. She saw despair.

"Oh, God," he whispered in mingled oath and prayer and turned his head away from her.

And as he turned, she saw his hands clenched over his stomach and realised that the blood upon the knife was also his, and that he had stabbed himself in the last remnants of madness. She pressed her hand over his belly, and felt his life flow between her fingers—almost black in the fading light.

He laughed, choked on blood, and rested again in the grass. Turning bleak eyes upon her, he said, "Do not touch me. I am dying."

"Thou shalt live," Brighid answered, taking off her shawl and clumsily laying it on his gravest wounds to stanch the flow of blood. "Thou shalt live," she repeated, not daring to look beside her to where Gethin lay like an angel sleeping.

"No—no, I shall not. Nor do I deserve life. If you knew...."

"Well I do not," she replied. "And I am the happier for it." But her breath came in short little gasps, and she clenched her fists against the lump that rose within her throat. For all the wind around her seemed to whisper, *Thou hast done this. Thou hast done this. Their blood lieth upon thy head. But see, there is the knife—take it and end thy grief quickly. Die between those who loved thee. There is nothing left for thee now.*

But Niamh raised her eyes to the wind and to the black heavens, whose starlight faded even now, and said, "No. There is grief enough tonight." Then to Padriac, taking one of his hands and pressing kisses upon it despite the blood, she said, "Dost thou not feel that? Is that not life? Thou hast been kind to me, my lord Connlach. It is not meet that thou shouldst despise small gifts now."

But Padriac would not answer. He bit his lip and closed his eyes as though to shut out the sight and sound of her. So abused was his body that he could not even weep, and perhaps that was a mercy, for the shame he should have felt if she could have seen those tears. She still held his hand, cradled it against her cheek as though he were a babe and she his mother to sing him to one of a thousand sweet sleeps.

And when at long last he felt the pall of death begin to steal over him, he drew all his strength together and looked one last time at Niamh. He touched her golden hair which he had seen even that first day she fell into his cart, black as ashes between the bags of golden fleece, still lovely beyond the shallow appearance of the flesh. He drew his life together in his lips and said, "Forgive me, Princess."

And then he closed his eyes and breathed his last.

The Mountains of Morning come with the dawn, creeping over the horizon in great billows of ochre and rose. Long do men look upon the Mountains and desire them, and many are those who salute them with the morning song. And some say that those who sing to greet the Mountains are greeted with another song from those who dwell upon the gentle slopes.

Many now would deny that second song and claim it only their forefathers' fancy. But that morning as the Mountains rose and Liam, Pwll, and the creatures stirred, they heard that song—the counterpart to their lament. Joy and peace were mingled there, and all the elements combined, and trumpet and flute and harp and drum sounded like laughter made to music as the Mountains approached.

And even as they stood in wonder and awe at the song and watched the brilliant streaks of warm colours stream through the sky above, Maelgwenn closed his eyes and slept the final sleep. And the streaks of light shifted, wavered, glided over the treetops and the small glade where the mourners sat, and onto the Fairy's face. The light grew and grew, streaking down like fingers through the clouds. And when the light receded, Maelgwenn, Trickster of the Fairies, beloved of Goewínn, was gone.

Niamh wept.

The sun rose, tentative lavender worlds away it seemed, and never more than a thin golden stream through the midsummer canopy within the forest edge. And Niamh wept. She wept even past the time for tears, past all the tears within her small frame—more than the Moon when she formed the three great rivers and the Lornloch, more than Ariana within Moira's keep, more than the Virgin at the tomb. She wept until only convulsive sobs were left her. She wept past those sobs into shaking and wordless prayers.

By mid-afternoon, Ogrin found her, but when she would come within the clearing, Niamh raised her head and yelled from grief and rage, "Tell me thou didst not know my true name! Tell me that, old woman!"

Ogrin stopped, and leant against a tree as though the Princess had knocked her. She clutched the edge of her own shawl, and tried to smile. "'Twas only because I loved you. We all did. We didn't want to see you go. Now, come with me. We'll deal with the bodies after you've had sommat to eat."

"I shan't be going with thee," Niamh said, resting her head against her knees again.

"Now, now…."

But Niamh stood, and Ogrin saw about her throat the golden chain that Gethin had left her. "I have been deceived. I know now. Do not deceive me further. Dost thou not see what it hath done, where it hath brought me?" She laughed another sob and pressed her hands to either side of her head, as though to keep her new-won memories within. They had come with the dawn, even as Maelgwenn had closed his eyes. They had come like rays of the Firebird's light within her mind. And in that light, weakening with every moment, now no more bright than the last gleam of a star long receded, Niamh had regained herself.

Crouching beside Gethin's still body, she rested her hand upon his heart, upon the unicorn's horn, upon his own hands. Very quietly, she said, "I shall tell thee a tale. A true tale. It beginneth so: there wast once a girl, the daughter of a Fairy and a King, and she wast so glorious fair that any man who looked on her longed for her. And soon she hadst become a prisoner within her own household, a slave to her perfection, for there wast no man good enough to see her without running mad. And so they sent for one they thought could hold her," she stopped, raised her hand to her mouth and bit upon her finger to stave away the pain. "And he loved her and she him, although he hadst never seen her. And now he lieth here dead and I can do naught but mourn him. Is that how this tale is to end? For this is the ending we have wrought, thou and I and all who have had a part in this. Art thou contented? I hope thou art, for methinks I shall never smile again."

"Oh, love," Ogrin sighed, hobbling towards her.

"Aye, love," Niamh said, but did not let Ogrin embrace her. Instead she held out her hand that bore the wooden cross Padriac had given her a second time, saying, "Send this to Connlach Manor. Tell them that their son is dead. Tell Connela that his brother died nobly. Make it known that he died with his honour unstained. That he died for the sake of love. Tell them that."

Ogrin nodded and took the cross. "I shall get Alf Forester to bring the message," she said.

"Get whom thou wilt," Niamh shrugged, and Ogrin grieved for though the Princess lived, yet her heart lay within the Hermit's bosom.

Then Ogrin rose and left her. She returned the next day with Connela himself and a few of his men to take the body with them. And when Niamh laid her hand upon Connela's arm and spoke of all of Padriac's kindnesses to her, the eldest son of Connlach turned his head away and answered, "We did not know what had come over him, Princess. For he would not speak of you and forbade my men to do so as well. But I can see now why he loved you, and although our lives will never be fully healed, please do not be a stranger to Connlach house." And within the hour Connela had gone, bearing Padriac in state with him.

"Shall I fetch Alf Forester again?" Ogrin said when the Connish men had left.

"No, not yet," Niamh said, never looking to her sometime mistress.

"But child—"

"Come tomorrow," the Princess whispered. Once more she knelt beside Gethin, and touched his breast. "I can bear tomorrow."

So all that night the Princess kept vigil and sang snatches of songs she had known: Gethin's song of searching, Padriac's lay of the Maiden of the Snows, Sorcha's song outside Fingal's window, and songs older than that, hymns of mourning and lullabies. And when she had sung all the songs she knew, had eaten and sent Ogrin away again, she grew silent and lay down next to Gethin, upon his white wings, and put her head upon his bruised shoulders and slept.

Sometime in the night she woke and wept again, and let her tears fall upon his many wounds, and washed his body clear of the silver blood, and dried his body with her hair. And as she ministered to his still form, tenderly touching the mangled toes, the scarred legs, cleaning them with her tears, she sang haltingly—for the words came to her lips unbidden—a song never heard before that day, although many sing it now:

> *Across the earth thou searched for me,*
> *The darkness thou didst light for me,*
> *All evil thou didst fight for me—*
> *Wilt thou not wake and turn to me?*

Thy song I heard thee sing to me,
Thy love I do return for thee,
Thy death I cannot bear for grief—
Wilt thou not wake and turn to me?

Through fire have I gone for thee,
Banishment have I borne for thee,
Then let me no more mourn for thee—
Ah love, awake and turn to me!

But he did not wake, and the sun began to rise.

Soon Ogrin would come with Alf Forester and with the cart to bear Gethin away. Niamh would return to her Father's court and perhaps she would rule for a time and then name an heir, and the line of Siawn Shieldbearer would perish as though the lion had never roared. The moon turned and hid her face, the stars drifted to the grass like heavy dew, the sky grew grey and colourless. The Mountains of Morning did not come.

Within Gethin's hands, the alicorn lay dull and lusterless. Slowly, Niamh pried his hands from it—seeing for the first time the net of her own golden hair. She pressed her lips together to stave away more tears. A Queen would not weep longer. She must learn to be a Queen alone.

Reaching forward, Niamh took up the alicorn—and as she took it, the last drop of the unicorn's blood, hidden at the very base of the horn, slipped out and onto Gethin's breast and shone there like an emblem.

And he woke, and turned to her.

"Do I dream?" Gethin murmured, as his eyes drank in the glory of his beloved. "I do not think I can be worthy of Heaven."

Niamh could find no words, but drew back amazed. But even as she looked she saw the warm colour suffuse his skin, and when she clutched his hand she felt it live and vibrant. "I am no dream," she said at last, touching his face and letting her finger stray over his ear. "And there will be time enough for Heaven."

And then she bent down and kissed him. And that kiss seemed to do more good than anything she might have said, for his arms drew strength to enfold her.

"Ah, God, Niamh," he said, drawing her down to rest against his chest, for the touch of her was a better salve than any herb, "too long I had lost thee."

"Thou hast found me now, beloved. And if thou wilt have me, despite the pain I have caused thee...."

229

But he stopped her mouth with another kiss and held her more tightly, winding his fingers through her sun-glory hair. "The only pain thou couldst cause me, dear heart, would be to leave me once again."

"That I shall never do," she said.

"Then Niamh, daughter of Gavron and Rhianna, Princess of the house of Siawn Shieldbearer, wilt thou take me, Gethin, son of Ysgafin and Danae, Lord of Eyre, as thy husband?"

"I will," she said, and sealed her words with a kiss.

And when they broke apart, Gethin laughed and rested in the early morning dew-damp grass, and took Niamh's slim hand, and said, "Then before God, lady, help me to stand. For our wedding hath been too long delayed!"

Ogrin returned at noon of that day, carrying with her a small spade that she used for her own garden. And when she saw Niamh and Gethin embracing, she shouted in fright and dropped the spade on her foot.

Niamh looked up joyfully and ran to the woman who had cared for her these long months of banishment. She knelt down before Ogrin, much to the old woman's embarrassment. "Ogrin, dear heart," Niamh said, kissing Ogrin's hands, "wilt thou forgive me my harsh words?"

"Forgive you?" Ogrin said, attempting to draw her gnarled hands away. "Whatever for?" But then she saw Gethin as he struggled to rise, holding the unicorn's horn to his breast to keep closed his wounds, and Ogrin nearly fainted. "Oh, oh, oh!" she cried, snatching up Niamh from where she knelt and clutching the girl to her. "Oh, oh! It's a ghost, it is! A ghost come to haunt us! I should have known Alf Forester's land would be haunted. I never trusted him."

"No, no, Ogrin!" Niamh cried, taking the woman's hands and pulling her into the grove. "He is no ghost."

"No ghost! He looks pale enough to me. Begone, you!"

"As you will, Madam," Gethin replied, genially. "Truly, I desire nothing else, but you see that although I am alive," and he reached out his hand for Niamh and she rushed to him. "I am not yet able to walk."

"Nor able to float through walls, I wager!" Ogrin said, brandishing the spade.

"No longer."

"Ha! Then you *were* a ghost!"

"For a little while, perhaps. I broached the gates of Heaven and saw beyond them the courts of all the ages arrayed before me—but not one would let me enter." And his smile became distant, as though he saw again he who had stood before the gates—one with eyes of many hues and wings not unlike his own.

"I'd think *not!*" Ogrin cried. "Come, come girl. We'll be well off now, sir."

The old woman hobbled forward to grasp Niamh's arms, but the Princess surprised her once again, grasping Ogrin about the shoulders and kissing her joyfully on either cheek. "Oh Ogrin, thou sweetest fool! Where are thine eyes? Here is my beloved, no ghost but living! Rejoice with me...and put down thy spade. 'Twill be many a year before 'tis needed."

Ogrin squinted her eyes, then, and limped closer to Gethin, at last seeing the harm done to his legs. "Hmmm," she opined. "I don't know what but you've a way about you, as I've said many a time my ashputtle girl. I'm not saying I believe any of what you've said—but as it seems he's walking and talking and you've let off wailing, you'd better come back with me. I can't say but there's old food left, but someone chopped the wood up nice and we can get you before a fire, sir, if that'll suit you."

"Exceedingly well, Mistress Ogrin," Gethin bowed as best he could.

For answer, Ogrin snorted and led the way back. She was a tough old soul, but less hard than she appeared, and though she tramped as briskly as she dared through the forest to her cottage, she was glad that no one could see her face twisted and contorted in sadness to lose the one happiness of her small life.

A week and more passed before the happy couple quit the lands around Loch Corraigh, for Gethin's wounds closed slowly—and more, Ogrin's cottage surged full of visitors who had all contrived to hear tell the strange and incredible events that had taken place in their little corner of the world. Many were amazed that Brighid should have been the Princess, and they came to gain her blessing and the blessing of the bridegroom whom they still thought of as the Hermit, Duncan. Toasts were called as frequently as the glass could be filled to the long life of Gethin and Niamh, and as many toasts were returned from Gethin and Niamh to the admirable folk of those northern lands. Soon drinking gave way to stories, and stories to song, and songs to dancing—in which Niamh herself participated, and the simple folk watched in awe at her beauty and her grace, and not one man had to shield his eyes.

Peghain had not the heart to come until very late that week, and then only when to have remained away longer would have been a greater insult. She greeted Gethin and Niamh very stiffly, and curtsied more stiffly still—although she did not correct Emma when she flew into Gethin's arms and received kisses upon her cheeks and brow for all the good she had done, or when Cormach stuck out his hand to Niamh and gawped at the Princess before blushing to the very tips of his fingers and running away. Nor did Peghain apologise, although she wished them both very well.

On the day they were to go, they asked Ogrin to come with them, but she demurred, saying, "What's a thing like me to do in a big court? I'd speak my mind too free and that's the truth. And what's more, I couldn't smoke my pipe, and then what's there to shut me up when I'm a bore? No, my ashputtle girl, I'll stay here and no mistake. But if you comes up this ways and happens to nod your head at me, it'll not be amiss. After all the fears you've put me through! Why I'll be better when you're gone—not so worried that you'll be off gallivanting around Moira's cottage."

This, of course, meant that Gethin must hear the whole of Niamh's adventures, at the conclusion of which he opined, "Bravo, my love! I confess, I had often wondered how to rid the land of her, for half the ills I cured were of her doing."

"You struck her dumb a year and that was a relief," Ogrin muttered as she put her finger down to help Niamh knot a satchel of foodstuffs. And when Niamh opened her mouth to speak, "Now not a peep more, lassie! Time enough on the road you'll have to speak of your adventures. Although not time enough to my mind nor to yours, I'll warrant. For sooner than you'll like you'll be at that castle of yours, and then there'll be celebrations and coronations and one too many lawyers, if I'm any judge."

Niamh laughed and threw her arms around Ogrin's neck. "I shall miss thee," she whispered. And Ogrin choked back tears and patted the Princess awkwardly, muttering "There, there" to no one in particular.

"Art thou sad, beloved?" Gethin asked as they rode southward. Niamh sat on the horse before him in the circle of his arms.

"A little, yes. It wast sweet, for a time, to be rid of the burdens which are mine. I dream yet of the men who died for me. Only thou hast been returned."

"Thou dreamest of Padriac," Gethin said quietly.

"Yes. And of others. And of a face that shineth more brightly than the dawn—but I do not know whom he may be."

Then Gethin sighed and drew Niamh to his breast and kissed her brow and said, "Thou wilt learn soon enough, beloved. For I dream of him, too." They continued in silence for a time until Gethin said in a voice with too much lightness, "Niamh, *dost* thou desire to wed me?"

"Whom else should I wed?"

"Any man it pleaseth thee. Thou art bound by thy beauty no more."

"No," said she, "I am bound by something greater." And she touched his heart and he knew peace.

So it was that one year to the day since the Hermit arrived at Castell Gwyr and the Princess had fled that they returned, stopping by the White Hind to rest the night before the long trek to the castle. Every day of travel, Gethin's wings had shrunk, for it seemed, as he himself said, that their purpose was finished.

"Wilt thou not miss them?" Niamh had asked one morning, as Gethin pulled her upon the horse with arms grown strong and whole again.

"I will," Gethin conceded, as they had started down the road. "Of all my deformities, the power to fly came as a blessing. Thou wilt have to teach me how to be a man again, and not a hybrid creature neither one thing nor another."

When they came to the White Hind, Brenna Housewife gave them a table in the corner, and two rooms with no more mind than the quality of their haggling which was, in her opinion, very low. The conversation that night mainly surrounded the marriage of James Bobsboy to Agnes Baker's daughter, and many were the toasts raised to that couple. And when, weeks later, the humble newlyweds received the gift of a finely wrought rosewood box filled with a modest fortune in gold, they thought that perhaps it came from some Fairy, or that all of the patrons of the White Hind had contributed to help the newlyweds to a good start in life. And when Brenna Housewife received an invitation to the wedding, she thought it one of John Carpenter's hoaxes and did not go. She soon discerned her folly, however, and much was the laughing at her expense at the White Hind, until she threatened to throw the lot of them out altogether. And when, years later, an invitation to the coronation of King Gethin and Queen Niamh arrived, Brenna Housewife did not make her mistake twice, but put on her finery and paraded up the hill to the castle as though she were a queen herself.

Ewan was the first to see them the morning they approached the castle, for he had taken to waking early and walking the circumference of the castle's land. At first he could not believe what his eyes told him, for so many times had he imagined the scene, but never in such simplicity. Where were the heralds? Where were the retainers? Where were the crowds of people cheering and ringing the chapel bells? Even his own homecoming had more pomp than this return.

The young Knight did not wait long upon such vain thoughts, but flew from the battlements to the Lesser Hall where Gavron held his daily court. The steward, who had become even more self-important in this time of trial, was loathe to allow Ewan such an unannounced interruption. But Ewan would not be swayed, and politely pushing past the old man, he went up to the King, bowed, and said, "Majesty, your daughter is returned."

Immediately all thought of state fled Gavron's mind, and he rose—a document regarding the pasturing of cows still within his hand. "Pray God thy words are true!" he exclaimed. "Is there any doubt—this is not the imaginings of thy mind?"

"No fancy, sire. For remember, I saw her those days before the Hermit came, when she desired news of him. It can be none other."

Gavron closed his eyes and released his breath, as though he had held it that whole year until this moment. When he opened his eyes, all his councillors would agree later, he looked much the same young prince who had returned with his own lady so many years ago. "Take me to her," he said—and such was his haste that it was not until he stood at the very gates that he realised he had brought the document with him.

All his councillors hurried behind and as they walked, a few peeled off to bring others, and Ewan himself ran to the Lyon Rampant to bring the Queen and the Handmaids and all the ladies to the gate. Father Cadifor, that kind but solemn man, ordered three boys to ring the bells, even as he slipped on his sandals and ran, scapular flapping in the breeze, towards the gates. Elowen was the first of all the ladies to arrive, and immediately made her way to the front, across from their Majesties, to greet her cousin. Her father, Donell, stood beside the King and he too seemed to have shed the weight of years, and Elowen thought that all the sorrows of the past year were as nothing if her father stood a little straighter.

The great gates were pulled open, and then all the court saw that it was indeed their Princess. And if they did not immediately recognise the man who rode with her, such was their elation that they were willing to concede that something might have happened to his fine lion's head, and that they had heard of just such a transformation before in some tale they couldn't remember at the moment. The handsome couple rode through the gates smiling as though to outshine the sun, as lovely and regal as they ought to be—despite the plain homespun she wore and the bandages about his legs and chest. The court was willing to forgive the lack of ceremony that day. There would be time enough for jewelled bodices and dagged sleeves.

Gethin lowered Niamh into the arms of her parents and then dismounted himself, grateful when a page, at the instruction of the Duke, ran up and took the horse from him. Elowen was the next to hold Niamh, for though the court accepted without question their ability to see the Princess, not a one dared to touch her—the memory of Gwrhyr had not yet left them. But Elowen, having so longed pined, would have welcomed any discomfiture if only she could cover Niamh's face and hands in kisses for the first time in their lives.

"Cousin!" Elowen exclaimed, holding Niamh at arms' length. "This is a joyful day! Why dost thou cry?"

"If I cry, cousin," Niamh replied, laughing and embracing Elowen once more, "it is only because I share thy tears. Come, dry them on my shoulder. It is sturdy and wilt bear them well."

"Indeed!" Elowen added, "My tears mayeth only improve thy habit! Oh, my dearest cousin, what hath befallen thee?"

"Much that might be related at another time," Niamh answered, administering the edge of her sleeve to Elowen's cheek. "You have all greeted me more wonderfully than I could have hoped. But I should not have come at all had not Gethin brought me from my banishment and back to my true heart. Father, Mother, you have met my beloved before, but not, I think, in his true guise."

Then she brought forward Gethin. Rhianna walked to him, and lay her hand upon his arm, and looked into his eyes, and smiled. "It hath been long since we have seen thee, my lord. Thou once said that there is always hope, and to that I add that hope wilt not disappoint. Welcome, Gethin, by thy true name and form." And then she reached up and kissed his cheek.

Gavron spoke next, with voice raised so that it echoed even down the hall and over the Gwyrglánn. "Thou hast returned victorious, sir, and so doing hast won for thyself the hand—and dare I hope—the heart of my daughter. Come, sir, thy hand; and thee, Niamh, thine. Our cousin, Maelgwenn wrote us one year ago not to delay your marriage by even an hour. It hath been delayed a year. Let us not tempt fate."

"Sire," Donell coughed when Gavron would bring them all to the chapel, "although I am the first to desire this wedding, would it not be better to send messengers to the Queen's kin so that they may also bless the marriage?"

"Majesty," Gethin added, bowing, "you must know my heart and how it seems that every minute of niceties is a year of waiting, but I can safely assure you that the threat which once beleaguered the Princess can no longer distress us."

"He hath been killed then?" the King asked.

Gethin bowed again. "His own shadows, which young Liam first saw, consumed him."

His face blenched and Niamh pressed his hand. "It is done," she whispered, and Gethin smiled only for her. The court grew silent, perhaps aware that these were mysteries beyond them.

"Come," Gavron said at last, "let us repair to the castle. All will be done in time, and perhaps sooner than feared. But much hath happened since you last quit us, and we would have the whole of your story."

A week later, Pwll and Liam walked to the gates. The honour of first seeing them belonged to Rowyn, the guard who had found Liam that fateful day, and sad to say he saw no need to raise the alarum about a mere squire and guard. But he threw wide one of the gates, and Pwll and Liam came through—although the re-entrance to the place dampened Liam's spirits, and he looked about the walls as though he had returned to his prison. Pwll immediately made his way to the Lyon Rampant, while Rowyn took Liam to the guardhouse to be feasted in their way there, and to report to Donell.

The Captain rose when Liam came in and greeted the boy heartily. But he

saw the nervousness and restraint within the youth's eyes, and when they were alone much later, he asked the young guard—not what had happened, he might ask Pwll for that—but what Liam most desired. "And do not fear to anger me or shame thyself, lad. But speak honestly, like a soldier, and I shall do what I can."

"So please your lordship," Liam answered, shifting uncomfortably upon his seat, and looking up ever and anon at the masonry, "release me from my duties. I had thought, while travelling, that all my ills were cured, but I see that the Count's poison sunk deeper than any could suspect."

"Whither wilt thou go?"

"To Goewínn's court. I left a lady there with a promise to return."

"Then by all means, Liam, go and with my blessings. But I will tell thee this, and thou must remember it upon the pain of thy life: not all heroes' tales are sung. I do not think the poets will find much within thy tale—thy tale of nobleness beyond compare, of bravery in the face of odds overwhelming, of honesty and honour and duty and courage, above all courage. Such things are too commonplace for the poets, unless they be aligned with titles and magic and the stuff of dreams. But were it not for thee, Liam, and thy foolish headstrong perseverance that hath caused me more than one restless night, were it not for that very commonplaceness, the poets' tale shouldst have ended in sorrow. Go, Liam, and take up thy life again. Thou hast earned the right to joy—let no one stealeth it from thee."

And then Liam smiled—a sight no man had seen since all the troubles had begun—and he slumped within his chair and laughed and laughed and laughed.

Duty demanded that Pwll seek out his King before anyone, but Gavron's was not the face that Pwll longed to see. He knew not where to go but to Niamh's old chambers, and waiting outside the door, he indeed did hear a beloved voice, laughing. He slid the door open enough to look inside, and saw Elowen and Niamh sitting in the window seat, their hands clasped. Findola sat in a chair beside them, embroidering Ewan's wedding shirt. Pwll swore quietly and closed the door. He would have to see the King first, it seemed.

The interview with Gavron took the whole of the afternoon, carefully transcribed into the annals of history even as he spoke it. And when at last they quit the Lesser Hall, the dinner bells were ringing. Excusing himself as soon and as politely possible, Pwll raced across the lawn, around the Great Hall, and between the glasshouse and the wine cellar, so that he nearly collided with Niamh and her Handmaids as they descended the stairs from the Lyon Rampant to the Great Hall.

Elowen froze when she saw Pwll, for no one had thought to tell her of his return, and even Findola who had seen him peek into Niamh's chambers that afternoon had kept silent, not knowing what her friend's feelings towards the squire were. For although Elowen had chatted about everything between the sun and moon since Niamh's return, she had breathed not one word about the squire.

"Tell me true," Pwll said, determined to face out any embarrassment of the moment. "When I left, thou wert kind to me. Hath thy heart changed against me in that time?"

"I might ask the same of thee, my lord," Elowen retorted, her dusky cheeks burning more crimson than the combined rose blossoms in the garden. "Is thy return delayed because thine eye hath strayed upon someone else's favour since thou quittest my side?"

"We have been journeying on foot from the mouth of Loch Corraigh, lady," Pwll replied. "Moreover, our every waking hour hath been spent on one quest or another. Why, we traversed the length of the Dark Woods and fought a creature nearly every day! While thou hast been here, likely collecting hearts and locking them up where men can never find them again."

"Thou mayest search for that coffer, sirrah. Thou wilt not find it. But I wonder, if I looked for the heads of these fearsome creatures thou *sayest* thou hast slain, will I find instead a trail of footprints from where thou rannest *away* from any confrontation?"

"By all means, lady. I bid thee to search for these footprints. Thou wilt find them as invisible as thy coffer. But," he said, stepping closer to her, "thou hast not answered my question."

"Didst thou put a question to me, my lord? I seem to have forgotten it."

"Thou knowest the question I would ask."

"Do I, my lord?" Elowen said, her black eyes snapping. "I am but a silly girl, plying my needle and thread. What can I *possibly* know of thy great mind?"

"What other question might I ask thee, Elowen?"

"I repeat: no question hath yet been asked me!"

"I needn't say it before this whole company," he whispered drawing to her side.

"And yet thou art very free with thy opinion otherwise."

"Please, Elowen...."

"Aye, do please Elowen. If thou hast reason, ask thy question. If thou seekest only to make a fool of me, then I am very willing to bid thee farewell, until thou hast found thy tongue again. Which wilt it be, my lord?"

"Oh, blast it, Elowen!" Pwll cried, stomping back down the steps. "Wilt thou marry me or not? And I tell thee frankly, if thou refusest me, I'll...."

Alas, no one knows what injury the squire might have done to himself had the handmaiden said no, for before he could finish Elowen ran down the steps, took him by the shoulders, and stopped his mouth with kisses.

The Fairies arrived the following week, for Gavron had wisely sent one messenger south to Viviane's court, and bade her fly to the twins, who in turn flew to their kin, and so spread the news more quickly than messengers on horseback ever might have. But Maelgwenn did not come, and so on the wedding eve, the nine Fairies and Rhianna gathered and sang their own lament which no mortal ear has ever heard. But Goewínn smiled and looked ever to the dawn, and her part of the hymn was sweet beyond comparison and seemed to rise above the rest and give them hope that they had not known for many and many a year.

And on the Lord's Day they all assembled in the Cathedral of Saint Siawn. And there, in the sight of God and all the assembled, Gethin and Niamh at long last were wed. And when they kissed, so the poets say, a new star joined the ranks of the heavens, and this the sailors call True Light, for neither day nor night nor rain nor clouds can dispel its brilliance, since neither life nor death could part beauty from her beloved.

the end

A BRIEF NOTE ON PRONOUNS

The following is an excerpt from Headmaster Neville mac Nagle's *Gentleman's Grammary*, dated some five centuries after the events of this book. However, mac Nagle's work—written in the pretentious style favoured after the Conquest of the Gates—nevertheless sheds light upon that which actually *was* "Merest Common Knowledge" during Gavron's reign.

> *"When in Court, it is advysable for the Ambitious Gentleman to master Language. For it is through our Words that we reveal Ourselves, as either the Scholar or the Fool....*
>
> *And thence we come to Pronouns, which when employed by the Learnèd Man are more subtle than Snakes, more pointed than Poniards.*
>
> *The Common Farmer addresses his Pig, his Neighbour and his Priest equally as "you,"—reserving "Thee" for God alone, and then he "Thees" God out of Habit, not Understanding. But the Courtier, far wiser than his Agrarian Counterpart, reserves his "yous" for his Noble Peers, and most especially for his King, who is above him. When formal or distant, he employs the word. Nor does the Courtier ever "thee" a Gathering of two or more Men— which Egregious Salutation would surely find him laughed out of the Court within the hour, with the advyse to learn his Numbers.*
>
> *Conversely, the Wise Courtier will "thee" those beneath him, as a Father "thees" his Child. To those within his Close Acquaintance, he will likewise offer such singular Salutation. And in the Sweet Moments of Intimacy, he will whisper "thee" to his Beloved....*
>
> *Let this Last stand as the Merest Common Knowledge, nonetheless recorded for the Benefit of those Countrified Gentlemen who are wont to choose their Words with the same Carelessness that so admirably suits them to govern the perilous Edges of our World. The Gentleman, no matter how noble his Blood or close his Kinship to the Sovereign, is always solitary, although he oversee more than one Holding due to Marital Alliance or Accident of Birth. Thus no Man has the right to name himself "We" as a King speaks when speaking from his Throne. Therefore, let this serve as Warning to our less Courtly Brethren, that to express his Views as though speaking for more than himself is to declare Usurpation."*

Appendices

appenдix a:
characcer lisc

In Castell Gwyr

The Royal Family

Gavron &
Rhianna

Gavron (GAV-ron)—the King of the Twelve Kingdoms from the line of Siawn Shieldbearer. At his christening, he was cursed with near-blindness. Through the love of his bride, Rhianna, and his own fortitude he was miraculously cured, and has reigned peacefully and prosperously since.

Rhianna (Hree-AHN-na)—the Queen of the Twelve Kingdoms, wife of King Gavron. Once one of the Twelve Fairies, Rhianna gave up her immortality to cure and wed Gavron, her love.

Niamh (Nee-EHV)—the daughter of Gavron and Rhianna, only Princess of the Twelve Kingdoms. Since her youth, Niamh has led a life apart due to her overwhelming beauty. No one unworthy can stand a moment in her presence without dying or running mad.

The Noblemen

Duke Llewellyn (Lou-WELL-ehn) – senior of all the courtiers, the Duke hails from Dalfínn, where he rules over a large family, including his grandson and squire, Pwll.

Lord Hugh Mackelwy (MACK-ehl-hwee)—an Earl and Knight, Lord Mackelwy acquitted himself well under Gavron's reign, proving himself upon the field of battle as Gavron sought to push back the boundary of the Dark Wood, and earning himself the honor of "shieldbrother" to the King. Now aging himself, he has taken on the care of many of the castle's young squires, including Ewan and Gwrhyr.

Earl Marshall—the uncle of Gwrhyr and distant cousin to Duke Llewellyn.

The Count—an aging personage of respectable appearance, Lord of Ainsidhe in Aldhairen. The Count's only son and heir sought the hand of Niamh, before leaving her side in holy raptures to take up a priestly garment. Since then, the Count has questioned the ability of Niamh to rule after Gavron.

Ioan Ys (YO-wen YISS)—the incorrigible Lord of Houndshelm in northern Maelgwenn; the father of Ewan.

Sir Ulf —a known wastrel whose land, Ulvin Manor in Urdür, extends into the Gwyrglánn.

Eoden Aî (Ee-YO-din AYE)—a nobleman and a trader who lives across from Ulvin Manor and recently married Sir Ulf's only daughter, Teresia.

Father Cadifor (CAD-ih-four)—the long-suffering chaplain of Castell Gwyr, and sometime physician.

Sir Gwrhyr (GWEER-hir)– nephew of the Earl Marshall, he is known as "The Bull." The newly-minted Knight left the service of Lord Mackelwy on Easter day. No sooner had he won his spurs than he sued for the hand of Gwendolyn.

Pwll of Branmoor (Paul)—the son of Pwll, Earl of Branmoor, and the Countess Imelda; grandson of Duke Llewellyn and squire to the same, Pwll's pedigree, alas, does not seem sufficient to reclaim the affections of Elowen. His acerbic wit, cavalier gallantry and impetuous temper—particularly on the behalf of his friend, Ewan—may not count greatly in Elowen's estimation either.

Ewan of Houndshelm (YOU-ann)—the son of Ioan Ys, from whom Ewan's even-tempered nature could not possibly have sprung, Ewan very early on found his way into the hearts of his fellow-squire, Pwll, his mentor, Lord Mackelwy, and the lovely handmaiden, Findola.

The Ladies of the Court

Elowen (EHL-oh-when)—the daughter of Captain Donell and cousin and Handmaid to Niamh, Elowen's own snapping and merry charm has won the hearts of many of the court gallants. Alas, Elowen's own loyalties lie deep within her cousin's bosom; the handmaid will give her heart to no man until Niamh's happiness is assured.

Findola (Fin-DOLE-ah)—the daughter of Lord Brien, the Steward to Cadwyr, and Handmaid to Niamh, the dark-haired Findola no sooner came to court than she won the favor of Ewan. Although quiet and introspective, Findola possesses the inner strength, practicality and knowledge of tamed beasts common to the people of Cadwyr.

Gwendolyn—Handmaid to Niamh and newly-betrothed to Gwrhyr.

Magdwa (MAG-dwa)—the youngest of Niamh's handmaidens.

Lady Marien—native of Sirena; Niamh's childhood governess.

Teresia (Tear-EEZ-ee-yah)—the only daughter of Sir Ulf.

The Guards of Castell Gwyr

Captain Donell (DONN-ehl)—the father of Elowen and distant cousin to Gavron, Donell might have easily claimed himself a title at court, but eschewed rank in favor of serving his King.

Adrian of Castell Doon—younger son of the Baron of Castell Doon in Islendil, the dapper nobleman sought his own way in the world and now serves as Donell's Lieutenant.

Hamish & Ifan (HAY-mish, AYE-fin)—Lance-Constables under Lieutenant Adrian.

Colin Carterson—a guard on the city wall, under the command of Lance-Constable Hamish.

Liam mac Hwyach (LEE-am mack HWEE-ack)—a green guard from Findair, Liam's mettle proves itself time and again as duty and necessity call upon him for the most daunting of tasks.

Ceallach (KAY-lachk)—an older guard who has seen many battles.

Gil—another guard from Findair.

Rowyn (ROE-when)—a guard from Dalfínn.

Ned—a local guard, son of the Caretaker of St. March's on Plume Street.

AT THE INN OF THE WHITE HIND

Brenna Housewife—the proprietress of the White Hind and matriarch of all thirsty traffic to and from the city; source of the city wall guards' ale.

John Carpenter—a skeptic and general detractor, particularly of Malcolm Tater.

Nob and Rob Tanner—sniggering middle-aged twins and avowed hecklers.

Malcolm Tater—a potato farmer just south of the city, prone to dreaming visions and gimpy legs.

Farmer Cartwright—the sometime suitor of Agnes Baker's daughter and loud derogator of James Bobsboy.

James Bobsboy—orphan apprentice to Bob Cobbler and beloved of Agnes Baker's daughter, many speculate that James must be the son of a noble since he is the unanimously acknowledged poet laureate of the White Hind.

Bran Blacksmith's son—the quiet, burly apprentice of his father Branwell Blacksmith; friend of James Bobsboy.

Agnes Baker's daughter—famous local beauty, pursued by Farmer Cartwright and beloved of James Bobsboy.

Nat Younger—younger brother of Colin Carterson and general knowledge-bringer of the doings of the city wall guards.

WITHIN AND NORTH OF THE GREEN MOUNTAINS

Kieran Wanderer (KYEER-ahn)—one of the last youths to encounter the Princess and fall under her spell. He roamed the whole of the Twelve Kingdoms searching for a Beauty such as she, but found none. At last he traveled even the dangerous roads upon the sides of the world, where he passed out of history and into legend.

Wolf King—after the death of the Titans, the Wolf King—a man who could shift shape at will—took up the reigns of power by means of a pact with shadows from the netherworld. Although his reign was eventually ended by Deirdre, he himself lives within the Green Mountains even to this day, with his ragtag offspring.

Fanwy and Ilsa (FAN-hwee, IHL-sah)—two sisters who live north of the Green Mountains in Urdür.

Diarmad Miller (DEER-mid)– a young man, who hopes to win Fanwy's heart.

AT THE GARRISON OF GOEWINN

Séamus mac Tighearnach (SHAY-mus mack TEAR-nachk)—a stony-faced leader of men, the Commander has faced many a monster while patrolling the border of the Dark Wood.

Collum (COLL-em)—a young guard from the Wyvern's Steep.

Esyld (Ess-ILD)—Collum's sister, named for her beauty because of her passing resemblance to Niamh.

AT THE GARRISON OF VIVIANE

The Commander—a life-long soldier only six months assigned to Viviane's border. He bears the unfortunate responsibility of reforming popinjay garrison to something better able to bear arms.

IN THE DARK WOOD

Imórdda (Ih-MORE-tha)—once a simple farmer's daughter from Malinka, she came into Malinka's service when she was but twelve years old, and from thence learnt the darker arts of witchcraft—for this was after Malinka had strayed from her brethren. Imórdda soon felt the call of destiny upon her, and through scrying saw that her name would ring with the Kings through the ages. So when Gavron came, seeking a cure to his curse, she made advances on him, supposing her vision to mean that she was to wed kings. But when he spurned her, and when Malinka fell to him, Imórdda set her way to the Dark Woods, determined that if she could not marry into her prophecy, she would align her name by bringing down the Kings.

Mellián (MEL-lee-ann)—Liam's mare, named for swiftness.

AROUND LOCH CORRAIGH (LOCK COR-RACH)

East of the Loch

The Hermit—a healer and a holy man known as Duncan, with the arms and wings of an eagle and the head and tail of a lion, his past is swathed in mystery.

Farmer Brandon—a vegetable farmer east of the Loch; his daughter suffered a mysterious malady, symptomatic of many of the local children.

Anna—Farmer Brandon's daughter. She died of a mysterious illness.

Tom Greenfield—another farmer, he enjoys pulling practical jokes on the young and gullible.

A priest—young and still nervous in his remote parish.

A boy—youngest of a brood, general trouble-maker and message-bringer.

West of the Loch

Ogrin (OGG-rin)—an old crone who lives by herself beside the mouth of Loch Corraigh.

Alf Forester—Ogrin's quiet neighbor.

Moira Blacksmith's daughter (MOY-ra)—a witch, who in her youth stole a silver mirror from Ogrin. She is also known as Mara of the Weeping.

Terence Songmaster—a self-important poet.

Aoife of Yew Manor (EE-fee)—a restless wanderer and would-be rescuer of Ariana.

In the Village

Peghain Innkeeper (Peg-EEN)—the local grand dame and sometime friend of Ogrin, Peghain inherited the Inn from her father and will doubtless pass it on to one of her many children.

Lester—Peghain's late husband.

Emma, Cormach (COR-mack)—two of Peghain's grandchildren, hired help in the Inn.

Father Bartholomew—the local parish priest.

Brighid Scrivver's daughter (BRIDGE-hid)—all of five and terribly important.

Farmer Demmit (DEH-mitt)– a vegetable farmer with a notoriously foul tongue.

Owen Viner (OH-win)—local purveyor of wine, father of Elise

Elisa Viner's daughter (Eh-LEE-sa)—daughter of Owen, beloved of Aineiron

Brandy Viner's girl—Owen's hired hand, known for her industry, not her wits.

Peter Tailor, Thomas Cooper, Jane Dyer's daughter, Nellie Goatgirl, Blind Yorick, Sally (Sal) Milkmaid—various denizens of the village.

From Udinë

The Baronet of Udinë (YOU-deen-ay)—father of Gwenhyfarch; a notorious womanizer in his youth.

Gwenhyfarch (GWEN-hwee-fvarch)—the daughter of Udinë, allied to Viviane's court through her mother; wife of Connela of Connlach House.

Udinë

Morris—proprietor of the Inn of the Twined Oaks between Udinë and Connlach Manor.

From Connlach Manor

Connela mac Connivar (CON-nell-ah mack CON-nee-vahr)—husband of Gwenhyfarch, the eldest son and lord of Connlach House, where the golden sheep are herded.

Padriac mac Connivar (PAD-hree-ack mack CON-nee-vahr)—younger son of Connlach House.

Liseva (LEE-seh-vah)—Padriac's saffron mare.

Guleesh (Goo-LEASH)—the red-eyed guard dog of the golden sheep, a descendant of the Demon Dogs of Cadoc.

AT THE TWINS' FEASTING HALL

Graithne (GRAYth-neh)—one of Goewinn's Handmaids, she has lost all memory of her past.

Father Damien (DAY-mee-ann)—the chaplain for the Twins.

IN FINDAIR

Tarra Lambing's daughter (TAH-rah)—once beloved of Liam mac Hwyach.

IN ISLENDIL

Ruthvyn Silverhands (ROOTH-fvin)—a Necromancer who once practiced the physician's art, Ruthvyn's insatiable desire for power and quest for the Gate to the True World, drove him to seduce Ariana and draw from her the secret of the deeps. He still lives upon the very edge of the world, on the fringes of Islendil.

IN URDÜR

The Lords of Eyre (AIR)—known for their remarkable affinity with the eagles of that place. Their crest is the blue winged, white headed eagle, with whom it is said many of that house can converse. Lord Ysgafin (Is-GAV-inn) and his lady, Danae (DAY-neh) are the current nobles of that house.

Appendix B:
Mythic Characters
& Legends

The Fairies

Aldhairen (Ahl-DHAIR-enn)—the eldest and King of the Fairies, Lord of the Spires of Sunset, married to Islendil. Several generations ago, he decreed under the advice of Urdür's vision, that the passing of the Fairies was at hand, and he himself crowned Siawn Shieldbearer as King of all the Twelve Kingdoms.

Islendil (IZ-len-dihl)—Queen of the Fairies, Lady of the Spires of Sunset, wife of Aldhairen.

Urdür (UR-dyur)—second-born of all the Fairies, Lord of Mysteries, Keeper of the Shadowless, Master of Visions.

Cadwyr (KAD-weer)—Lord of Tamed Beasts; renowned physician.

Sirena (Sih-RHEN-ah)—Lady of the Hydoemi, Protectress of the Serpent's Sea.

Findair (Fvin-DHAIR)—youngest brother of the Fairy kin; Lord of the Harvest.

Malinka (Ma-LIN-kah)—once-beloved of Maelgwenn and Lady of the Perilous Strait, Malinka brought about her own fall when she cursed Gavron and her own sister, Rhianna, in a fit of jealousy. In order to restore his sight, Gavron severed Malinka's wings and then imprisoned her with the aid of the Mirror of Sight.

Rhianna (Hree-ahn-na)—the youngest sister of the Fairy kin, wife of Gavron.

Goewínn (GO-whinn)—twin of Dalfínn, Lady of the Hunt, Mistress of the Feasting Hall, also known as the Bow.

Dalfínn (DAL-fvinn)—twin of Goewínn, Lord of the Hunt, Master of the Feasting Hall, also known as the Arrow.

Viviane (Vih-VEE-ann)—Lady of the Arts.

Maelgwenn (MAYL-gwin)—the trickster of the Fairies, he once loved the false Malinka. Also known as the Fox.

The Titans

Brangwenn (BRAN-gwen)—once revered as a goddess, Brangwenn is one of the numerous Immortals who protects and guides the manifold worlds which have arisen since the Sundering. Since ceding her place to the Fairies, she resides in the Mountains of Morning.

The Sun—the first of all the Titans, he fell in love with the Moon when she lived in the Ivory Citadel and soon he refused to shine elsewhere. The people took their complaint to Brangwenn, protectress of that world, and she banished the Sun to reside in one of the flowers of the Golden Valley until his repentance. Centuries later, after the release of the Moon from her own banishment, the Sun was restored to the Heavens by Östrung the Giant.

The Moon—wife of the Sun, the Moon was once a lovely girl who lived within the Ivory Citadel far from her jealous step-mother. After the Sun left her, she herself was banished to walk the earth alone, but her sorrow so overwhelmed her that she cried herself into the three great rivers: the Gwyrglánn, the Suirebàir and the Rhún. She then melted into the earth at the place which is now known variously as the Moon's Eye or the Lornloch. Centuries later, Brigglekin the Dwarf found her, fashioned her into a great ball and threw her into the Heavens, where she regained her usual shape and earned her immortality.

Dawning—the eldest child and only son of the Sun and the Moon, Dawning allowed himself to be seduced by Cináedd of the Fires who planned to kill the Titan in return for the immortality of the Dragons. But Dawning woke when she would carry out the deed and murdered his lover.

Dusk—the lovely sister of Dawning, youngest child and only daughter of the Sun and the Moon, Dusk loved no one better than her brother and longed to find a way to bring Dawning to live in the Mountains of Morning, where his heart might find solace. Consequently, she went to her uncle Day at Castell Gwyr. For love of Dusk, he sought but was unable to grant her request. Mad for Dusk's love, he accosted her, who was rescued from her uncle's unwanted advances by her brother and her other uncle, Night, who then built for Dusk the Shadowless. In time, Dusk came to love the Night and they were wed.

Night—the brother of the Sun and Day, Night lived in the citadel by the Perilous Strait, where Malinka now makes her home and prison. After the restoration of the Sun and the Moon, Night and Day drove back the Dragons to the Eastern Caverns, killing the Green Wyrm and subduing the Dragon Prince. But the Dragon Prince blew his fire upon the brothers, making Day rich and golden, and Night dark and burnt. From this time on, the two brothers were estranged and ever at odds. After Day attacked Dusk, Night took upon himself the care of his wronged niece and eventually they grew to love and at last marry.

Day—the brother of the Sun and Night, Lord of Sciences, Day built Castell Gwyr wherein he experimented with the sciences to a success not seen before nor since, including the creation of the Elementals. Unfortunately, in his love for order and perfection, he could not comprehend why his niece, Dusk, did not return his love for himself, but instead chose Night as her bridegroom. Lunatic with desire, Day called down thunder and lightning upon the nuptual train, killing both Night and Dusk. When he realized what he had done, Day threw himself upon a pyre, thus ending the reign of the Titans.

The Hydoemi (Hi-DOE-mee)

Masters of Water, the Hydoemi's greatest gift is their song which can move the hearts of men to great or terrible deeds. The Hydoemi can take on four shapes: water, fish, human, or a hybrid of any of those three. Perhaps because of Sirena's love for the Hydoemi, these Elementals are the most human of all their kin, and frequently take on their full or half-human forms.

Yurë (Yuh-UHR-ay)—the mightiest of all Day's making, King of the Hydoemi, Lord of Frost, husband of Sylenn, brother of Ydulhain.

Ydulhain (Yuh-DOOL-hane)—brother of Yurë, Prince of the Hydoemi, Lord of Waterfalls, husband of Sylvaenn.

Sylenn (Sih-LENN)—Queen of the Hydoemi, Lady of Rains, wife of Yurë, sister of Sylvaenn.

Sylvaenn (Sill-VAY-ehn)—sister of Sylenn, Princess of the Hydoemi, Lady of the Deeps, wife of Ydulhain.

Ariana (AH-hree-AHN-ah)—the second daughter of Ydulhain and Sylvaenn, Ariana was seduced by Ruthvyn Silverhands to whom she gave the secrets of the deeps. Once he gained that power, he used the secrets to imprison Ariana within Moira's hut.

Aineiron (An-NYEER-on)—elder brother of Ariana, son of Ydulhain and Sylvaenn, Aineiron first saw Elisa Viner's daughter as she slept beside the eastern edge of Loch Corraigh. Disguised in human form, he wooed her until found out by his father who set Elisa's dowry at the release of his daughter, Ariana, from Moira's clutches.

Anwen (ANN-win)—the elder sister of Ariana.

Aüngiadd (Ah-OON-gee-ath)—the steed of the Hydoemi, he appears to be formed from the foam of the seas.

Tritons—the lesser lordlings of the Hydoemi court.

The Wydoemi (Why-DOE-mee)

Masters of Air and Wind, the Wydoemi's song is but a little less powerful than their cousins'. Their truest magic is in whispers, particularly between those who have traveled to the Mountains of Morning, and those still on earth. For this reason, they have been much pursued by Necromancers. Twelve sisters rule the Wydoemi, governing the twelve months. The Wydoemi can take on four shapes: air, bird, human or a hybrid.

Silpsm (SIL-psim)—Queen of the Wydoemi, Lady of Breath, Keeper of the Sky Paths.

Voro (VOH-row)—Lady of Tempests, also known as the Untamable, her hand has been long sought after by Hintev.

Nimainn (Nim-AY-ehn)—Lady of Gales.

Mysre (MISS-reh)—Lady of Storms.

Syrilm (Sih-RIL-em)—Lady of Dreams, wife of Fevir.

Anae (Ah-NAY)—Lady of Breezes, twin of Areal.

Areal (Ah-RAY-al)—Lady of Sighs, twin of Anae.

Eileen—Lady of Zephyrs, wife of Lellemond.

Brianne (Bree-ANN-neh)—Lady of Clouds.

Gwennia (Gwen-NEE-ah)—Lady of the Calms.

Reinstë (Ray-EN-stay)—Lady of Haze.

Isllel (IZ-lehl)—Lady of Mists.

The Pyrae (PIE-ray)

Masters of Fire, the Pyrae speak directly to the heart in words mortals cannot fully understand. Their songs must be tempered by another of the Elementals' or else merely hearing the fire's melody will make a man lose his reason. Although the Pyrae can take on four forms—fire, salamander, human or hybrid—they rarely venture out of their fire form, and are therefore rarely seen. Twenty-four brothers govern the hours.

Baone (BAY-ohn)—King of the Pyrae, Lord of Light.

Scoule (SKOOLE)—Lord of Sparks.

Fevir (FVEV-heer)—Lord of Glimmers, husband of Syrilm.

Vorur (VOH-ruhr)—Lord of Visions.

Lleve (LEHV)—Lord of the Gloaming.

Parix (PAHR-icks)—Lord of Flames.

Enver (EHN-fvir)—Lord of Hearths.

Aoish (ASH)—Lord of Brands.

Scinilan (SIN-eh-len)—Lord of Lightning.

Cinte (KINT)—Lord of Zeal.

Celve (KEHLV)—Lord of Fervor.

Sciae (SHEE-ay)—Lord of Passion.

Brone (BROHN)—Lord of Illumination.

Chao (KAY-oh)—Lord of Burns.

Sceth (SETH)—Lord of Blue Fire.

Ignae (IN-yay)—Lord of Consummation.

Kiliv (KEHL-evf)—Lord of the Furnace, Patron of Blacksmiths.

Tinys (TIN-yis)—Lord of Thaw.

Lisev (Lih-SEVF)—Lord of Radiance, youngest of the brothers.

Saright (SAH-rite)—Lord of Warmth.

Cigin (KIDG-ehn)—Lord of Cinders.

Empratë (Em-PRAT-eh)—Lord of Shadows.

Picouse (PIH-koos)—Lord of Death.

Brelev (BREH-levf)—Lord of Embers.

The Vertae (VEHR-tay)

Masters of the Earth, the Vertae keep their court within a stronghold that shifts shape as each of the four brothers takes his turn governing in season. They have domain over Day's lesser creatures: fauns, griffins and various other hybrids. They themselves have a multitude of forms—from earth to human to trees or stones, animal, vegetable and mineral.

Hintev (HIN-tevf)—Eldest of the Vertae, Lord of the Snows, long-time suitor of Voro.

Mabon (MAY-bon)—Lord of the Spring, known as the Mischievous.

Lellemond (LEHL-ley-mond)—Lord of the Summer, husband of Eileen.

Faunden (FAWN-dehn)—Lord of the Autumn, a Warrior.

Sorcha (SORE-sha)—Daughter of Lellemond and Eileen, wife of Fingal.

Strange Beasts of the Twelve Kingdoms

Bansidhe (BAN-shee)—wailers of the dead. If once one hears a Bansidhe's voice echo outside one's door, someone is doomed to die that very night.

Chimera (Shih-MARE-ah)—a creature with the head and body of a lion, the hindquarters of a she-goat and the tail of a snake. They are ferocious and cunning, and possess the ability to shimmer in and out of sight, like a mirage.

Cockatrice (COCK-ah-TREESS)—a creature born from a cock's egg, nested under a dungpile. They are related to the basilisk, although bear more physical relationship to a bird than a serpent. To look a cocatrice in the eye is to be turned to stone.

Cwynadd (KWIN-ath)—a creature with the head of a dog and the body of a monkey. They are stupid but deadly: their tail and their fangs are venomous. They will attack viciously, but are easily cowed if rapped about the head and hindquarters.

Demon Dogs of Cadoc (KAD-ock)—when the worlds were created after the Sundering, the Great Deceiver—known by many names and comfortable with none—snatched those creatures that had not been taken up to the various worlds and twisted them to obey his commands. Most fearsome were his Hounds, known as the Dogs of Cadoc (Cwn Cadoc) for the Immortal who follows closest to the Deceiver's heels. Some say that Cadoc himself became one of his dogs and worries ever at his master's heels. Others say that Cadoc dogs come from his own unnatural copulation. Often since the Paladin's fall has Cadoc sent his dogs through the Coliseum of Gates into the various worlds where they have lived and bred and become numerous. Guleesh and the Wolf King both are distantly related to Cadoc's Dogs.

Dragons—ruled over by the Dragon Prince and now confined to the easternmost mountains that border Dalfínn and Goewínn, the dragons range from their great sanguine master to the smallest wyvern who has only one set of legs to recommend him. Many believe the dragons are no more—except, perhaps, for the people of the Twins' lands, and especially those who dwell on the Wyvern's Steep, where the carcass of the Green Wyrm fell, defeated by the Titans, Day and Night.

Dwarves—dwell primarily beneath the gently rolling hills of Malinka. Their caverns extend deep into the foundation of the Twelve Kingdoms, although not all the way to the True World. The Dwarves are miners and craftsmen, and closely aligned to the Vertae court.

Fachan Man (FASH-han)—an ugly unseelie sprite with one of everything: one arm, one leg, one eye, and so on. He carries a spiked club with which he beats off intruders to his domain.

The Firebird—a creature of mystery and magnificience, she has long dwelt in the foothills of the Ice Giants, upon one of the lesser mountain's peaks, surrounded by her nestfires. Those who seek her always leave with that which they are deserve. Some have said that she is indeed Brangwenn, but those who have met her will not answer for such a claim.

Giants—a great race of men, who stood twelve to twenty feet tall, and roamed freely while the Titans slept. They were a cold-hearted race and crafty, holding grudges against any who did them wrong—even their own. Only Östrung was kind among them, and for that he was outcast. By the Fairies' coming, most of the Giants had fled to the north, where their coldheartedness had changed them to men of ice, like mountains.

Griffins (GRIFF-ihns)—noble creatures with the head, foreclaws and wings of an eagle and the body, hindlegs and tail of a lion.

Hydras (HI-drahs)—seven-headed sea-serpents who own this strange quality: that for every head cut off, two will grow in its place. The only means whereby a hydra may be defeated is the severing of the seven heads at once and piercing of its heart.

Manticores (MAN-tih-koar)—a creature with the head of a man, the body of a lion and the tail of a scorpion. They have three rows of sharp teeth with which they eat a man whole—clothes and bones as well.

Phooka Horse (POO-kahs)—an unseelie stallion that will ride off with whomever is foolish enough to mount it. Some say that those who fall prey to the phooka horse are bucked off the edge of the world to fall to their deaths. Only Auberon is ever said to have tamed a phooka horse, and together they ride from world to world.

Rocs—also known as the King of Eagles, rocs dwell upon the highest peaks of any world. Their wingspan can blot out the sun, and sweep a seventh of the stars from the sky. Their wings are the lightest gold, and their eggs and nest are likewise gold. They are wise beyond compare, but will suffer none to bring harm to their children.

Sprites—mischievous creatures made of wisps of thought and desire.

Unicorns—born from several sacred pools, including the Sea of Memory, unicorns enter the world when a soul is born who requires aid. To that one, the unicorn entrusts his dying breath, his horn and his blood, which three have healing powers. But many is the man who does not meet the incarnation of his purest soul, and those unmet unicorns die at the hands of others.

Unseelie (Un-SEE-lee)—a dark sprite who brings only mischief.

LEGENDS & HEROES

Auberon (OH-behr-awn)—originally a minor War-Lord during the time of Perpetual Twilight, his name became one of legend as he fought to defend the people in his care from the monsters that reigned in lieu of the Titans. Many times he sallied forth deep into the very heart of the Twelve Kingdoms—which was then overrun with the Dark Woods—and returned victorious, claiming a greater part of the land for his people. But once, when he went hunting alone, he rode out and never returned, although years after many of his comrades claimed to see him beckoning them over the water, over the Gulf of Barges into the Sea of Silence. From this arose the myth that Auberon had found the Gateway to the True World and there held his court, forever youthful. Popular legend also claims that Siawn Shieldbearer's line hails from this ancient King.

Brigglekin the Dwarf (BRIH-gehl-kin)—a loner with a love for silver above all other metals, Brigglekin discovered a sheet of silver beneath the Lornloch, excavated it and formed it inexpertly into a sphere—for he was no craftsman. When he called his fellows over to admire his handiwork, their hearts grew hard with jealousy and so they waited until Brigglekin fell asleep, and then stole into his house and mauled the sphere. When Brigglekin awoke, he chased the other dwarves from his house, picked up the sphere, walked to the edge of the world and cast it into the Heavens. But instead of sinking, the sphere became a lovely girlish shape, and from thence was released the Moon.

255

Cináedd of the Fires (Kin-AY-eth)—the false lover of Dawning, Cináedd made a bargain with the Dragon Prince that should she kill the only son of the Sun and the Moon, she would gain the immortality of the Dragons. But on the night she would have murdered Dawning in his sleep, he woke, turned on her, and dealt Cináedd her own fatal blow. The poets have since written that Cináedd haunts the world over, looking for Dawning to bring him down to Hell with her.

Deirdre (DEAR-dreh)—the only daughter and youngest of the house of Ainsidhe (ANN-shee), Deirdre took up the Wolf King's challenge to find and wield the Shadow Blade. Unfortunately, although she succeeded in defeating the Wolf King and freeing her seven brothers, Deirdre was forced to destroy the Shadow Blade when her youngest brother, Damhain, would have used it for his own power.

Damhain Leanblade (DE-von)—the illegitimate youngest son of the house of Ainsidhe, he was the first to challenge and lose to the Wolf King. His time within that Shadow Keep warped his mind, so when he was released he longed for nothing but power like the Wolf King's over all people. Stealing from Deirdre the Shadow Blade, for a time he did control the land, until Deirdre had forged for her the Sword of Adamantium, which shattered the Shadow Blade. She then threw the Sword of Adamantium into the sky, where it hangs as a constellation.

Elena & Oisin, Southern Lion (Eh-LAY-nah, OH-shin)—Elena lived on the northern coast of the Emerald Sea in what is now Findair, as a changeling daughter of the Hydoemi. In return for their hospitality and knowledge of the deeps, Elena was granted a lyre which would charm the most savage beasts. One day, as she sang to soothe away the storms and the Southern Lion who was said to blow them from the abandoned Citadel of the Perilous Strait, a warrior youth Oisin came to her, drawn by her song. When they saw each other, they immediately fell in love, but although Oisin sued for her hand, Elena refused him because she dared not stop her song. The next day, Oisin again came and this time asked if he could at least place his ring upon her finger, but again she refused him. One the third day, Oisin begged but for a kiss, and this time Elena granted his request. But her fingers stilled upon the lyre strings and so freed the Southern Lion, who tore over the water to the lovers, and rent Oisin limb from limb. Distraught, Elena took up a melody wild and destructive, that wrang the soul out of all three bodies and strew them in forever in the sky.

Fingal (FIN-gull)—son of Urthar (UR-thyr) and ancestor of the current Lord of Eyre, Fingal sought adventure and instead discovered the love of a Vertumn, Sorcha. His sword Eimobhar (EEM-o-vahr) remains one of the treasures of the Lords of Fingal, for its blade is ever sharp and true.

Guilian Silverbow (Julian)—also known as the Savior of the Civil Wars, Guilian was not so much a soldier in those days when man fought man, as a merry-maker who brought peace in a time tranquility was sorely needed. The Dwarves gave him his silver bow, quiver and arrows—which, when used together, never failed to hit their mark. With these, he defeated the Emerald Serpent, that now lies in the Serpent Sea, and gained himself an emerald crown and the friendship of the Hydoemi. But best known of all is his love for a Wydoema, cursed by a Necromancer to wander the earth in the shape of a White Hind when the Necromancer was displeased, as a lady when he was mirthful. Guilian accidentally shot the Wydoema in her animal form. No sooner had the arrow pierced her breast than she turned back into a woman—a saving grace, for the arrow would only kill that which Guilian intended. In order to save the Wydoema, Guilian sought out the Necromancer and presented himself as a jester. Once in the Necromancer's favor, Guilian was able to discover where the Necromancer held the Wydoema's breath which would release her from the spell. Using his arrows, he pierced the steel of the cage, releasing the breath, and then shot the Necromancer. Such was the Wydoema's gratitude that she married Guilian Silverbow that very day.

Östrung the Giant (EUR-strung)—one of the few kind-hearted Giants, Östrung was ostracized from the Ice Giants for his gentle nature. When wandering one evening, he found a young boy who begged the Giant to take him to the edge of the world to catch his love. Östrung did so, but could not bear to cast the youth over the edge of the world—for he did not believe this youth was the Sun. Thinking the youth had died in fruitless pursuit of the Moon, Östrung sat and wept the Well at the End of the World. When he woke, Day had dawned, and the Sun with him—and Östrung saw the child he had carried in all the Sun's glory.

The Seven Sleepers—King Beorn (BEE-yorn), grandfather of Gavron and son of Queen Olwen (OHL-when) lay dying, and all expected him to name his eldest son, Rhys (REESE) as his heir. But Beorn saw that Rhys, although named for his excellent grandfather, was unworthy of the throne, and so he named his younger son, Aiden (ADE-ehn) as King. But when Beorn passed, while Aiden mourned his father, Rhys stole the crown and proclaimed himself King and Aiden traitor. Thus, the true King was forced to flee for his life, and seven of his truest friends sailed with him over the Sea of Silence and to the cloister that hangs off the edge of the world where Olwen kept her peace. Aidhen was safe delivered to his grandmother, who warned his friends that they should not sail again to the mainland or they would die—but the lordlings paid the Dowager Queen no mind and bravely sailed into the turbulent seas. As they sailed, they were beseiged by a storm from all sides, called up by a Necromancer allied to Rhys. Seeing this within her glass, Queen Olwen prayed that the lordlings would but slumber beneath the waves, until such a time as they may be required. This happened, and Rhys—astounded when his Necromancer told him that the lordlings yet lived and yet were not visible to his eye—ordered a ship readied for himself and set out into the Sea of Silence to search for the lordlings and to slay his brother himself. But when he sailed over the place where the lordlings slept, a great whirlpool opened at his feet, at the bottom of which were the seven lordlings. Rhys was drowned, the Seven Sleepers returned to their slumber, and Aiden restored of his inheritance.

The Walnut Girl—A nursery tale, frequently told to unruly children. An old nursemaid had long desired to have a child of her own, but she had never wed and was getting on in years. So she prayed everyday for a child and one day as she sat down with a bushel of nuts, she cracked open a walnut and found a perfect tiny girl curled up inside. Soon after, the lordling to whom the nursemaid was employed took a second wife who thought to do away with all of the old household—the lordling's children, the nursemaid and all! The Walnut Girl heard this and climbed into the lordling's ear and whispered to him in the night what his new wife intended to do. The lordling listened in astonishment, and when his second wife rose to poison the household, he crept after her, and caught her just as she held the poison above his eldest daughter's ear. The lordling grabbed his false wife and forced her to drink her own poison. Thereafter, the Walnut Girl and the nursemaid both enjoyed the lordling's favor and lived happily and adventurously ever after.

Appendix C:
General Timeline
to the Present

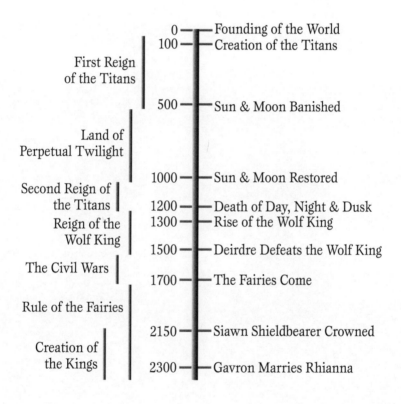

First Reign
of the Titans

Land of
Perpetual Twilight

Second Reign of
the Titans

Reign of the
Wolf King

The Civil Wars

Rule of the Fairies

Creation of
the Kings

0 — Founding of the World
100 — Creation of the Titans

500 — Sun & Moon Banished

1000 — Sun & Moon Restored

1200 — Death of Day, Night & Dusk
1300 — Rise of the Wolf King

1500 — Deirdre Defeats the Wolf King

1700 — The Fairies Come

2150 — Siawn Shieldbearer Crowned

2300 — Gavron Marries Rhianna

maps

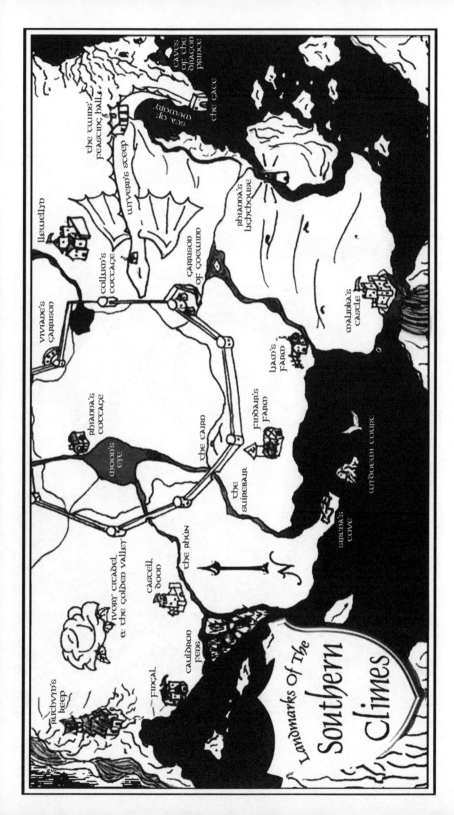

Landmarks of the Southern Climes

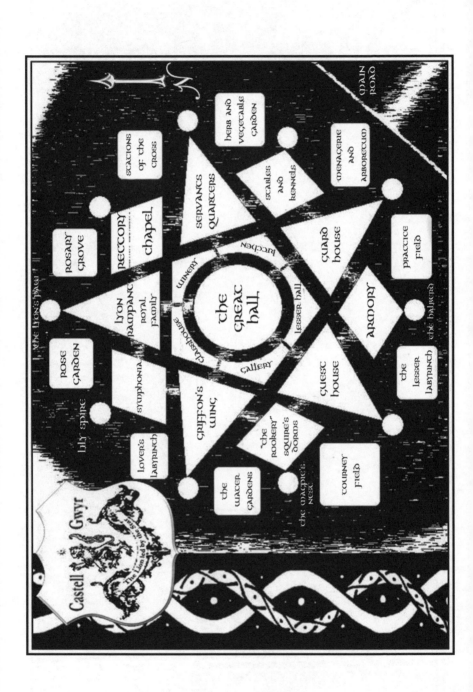

a note on the hydoemi

THE FOLLOWING HAS BEEN RECEIVED *from the collected works on the* <u>Elementals</u>, *stored at the Southern Lighthouse in Rhianna, and written over the course of several centuries by the Dòbhainach Scholars who serve as Stewards to that place.*

The majority of the information regarding the Hydoemi is recorded in the form of first-person narrative, interwoven with so much tale-telling and myth that it is nearly impossible to separate the factual from the fantastic. Indeed, the task proved too daunting for Scholars of a later age, who prided themselves on anything devoid of imagination and so resolved the issue by ignoring it completely.

However, despite our modern Scholar's grave misgivings on the subject, most honest historians agree that the bastard Prince Iorwrydd the Navigator's (2179-2235 f.w.) accounts may be generally accepted, at least on the basis that Iorwrydd certainly *lived*. Although his *Maritime Diary* still contains much that is unbelievable—such as his granddaughter, Arianrhod's supposed siphoning of Iorwrydd's life, which is far more readily explained by his own declining health—yet his notes regarding his travels are meticulous to the point of tedium, and may therefore be credited.

EXCERPTED FROM THE JOURNAL ENTRY DATED
The Hour of Brone, The Season of Syrilm,
The Rule of Mabon, In the 16th Year of Beorn's Reign

In the first watch of the fifth day passing the Perilous Strait, while we were still some twenty-three leagues from the easternmost tip of the Serpent Isles, [and] nineteen leagues north of the Lesser Fall…I happened to find myself unable to sleep. My mind kept wandering the hidden path to the Smuggler's Cove, where I had journeyed so foolishly in the days of my passionate youth. And now I would pass that path again, although I would not take it. I am bound north-west to Ruthvyn's Keep, there to live or die. As I sit upon the leeward side of the Emerald Eye, where once I sat with Wynne, I cannot help but think I shall die there.

My thoughts were much the same as I paced about my cabin, and then outward to the night to take solace in the stars which have ever guided me. Some say they still sing, the stars, although I have never heard them. Yet that night, as I stood staring upward at Undulië Morprianto, that solitary southern giant, I heard a voice distinctly, from beneath me, from the very waves.

...I looked down and saw a full dozen men and women in the sea, their hair strung with pearls and shells and delicate strands of seaweed, their skin like foam, the tips of their tails dazzling colours into my night-accustomed eyes. They sang a song strange and yet familiar to me—and I realised with a start that they sang every ripple beneath the stern and gave them words and form....

Two hours by the moon they stayed beside us. Many of my men petitioned me to throw over the anchor and stay in that place forever, so enchanting was the Hydoemi song. But I rebuked them...[and w]ith that rebuke, the Hydoemi shook their heads and began to leave us. Alas, that I should have spoken! In that moment, I knew my folly, and mourned that I had never truly loved the sea.

Yet, one Hydoema, a female, did not depart. "I am Yrina," said she, "sworn to Sylvaenn, over whose court you are now passing. She bade me follow you until these waters mix with the Serpent Sea, for she knows the sorrows of your heart and would fain comfort you in your last hours." When I pressed her wherefore the Queen of the Deeps cared for me, whom she had often barred from her deeps, Yrina answered, "My lady bears no love for Ruthvyn who ever seeks to learn her secrets."

Three days Yrina journeyed with us...[once even] coming aboard our ship in human form. On that last night, as we approached Sirena's Cove, Yrina sang for us a final song, which she told us was the Parting Hymn among her people. Although she had sung for us before, we were all amazed when her voice parted two, then three, then ten, then twenty ways, until it seemed that all the voices of every Hydoemi that had ever lived since their first creation sang with her.

When Yrina had done, she laughed at us all and asked us whether, because she was in human form, we thought she was bound to human abilities. "We are water," said she, "and no voice ever truly dies beneath the waves."

"Then you are never alone," said I, "if you may conjure other voices to you when you will."

"Nay," said she. "We may sing with any voice, true. Just as you may summon memory and smile fondly on a long-forgotten face. But though we may sing our memories and so make them true for as long as we can sing, so we are fleshy, too, and may die in time."

"And have you souls?" pressed I.

Again she laughed with a dozen voices, and in that laugh, I was answered.

Unfortunately, Iorwrydd's singular encounter with the Hydoema Yrina only enlightens us to their practice of music, but not to their form of preservation. In fact, until recently it was thought that the Hydoemi maintained an entirely oral form of music, since Iorwrydd and others seem to imply that the sea itself carries the memory of songs.

But a thorough search of the library at the Southern Lighthouse, led by the Scholar Xu-Tang from Djō-Khai, has yielded the interesting insight that far from spurning written music, the Hydoemi developed such an intricate system of recording that it has long been mistaken for mere illustration. Hundreds of the volumes at the Southern Library contain hand-drawn replicas of Hydoemi artwork, which Xu-Tang now proposes may actually be Hydoemi *music.*

The breakthrough picture, which Xu-Tang is calling *Illumusation*, is the full orchestration of "Ariana's Lament" which figures prominently in the legend of Queen Niamh (2307-2393 f.w.). Written during the sixth year of her reign,

Ariana's Lament is a collection of these Illumusations along with the well-known lyrics. The curious thing, Xu-Tang points out, is that the lyrics run *backwards*— that is, one begins reading at what would typically be the last page of the manuscript, and then progresses by turning the left-hand page.

Once this discovery was made and measured against more traditional forms of written music as well as local oral traditions, it was possible to decipher Hydoemi musical notation.

A sample of the first Illumusation for
"Ariana's Lament."

ARIANA'S LAMENT

[Editor's Note: In classical fashion, Xu-Tang organized his narrative by the Thirteen Noble Khai. However, for the sake of printing space these have been removed.]

Translated by Xu-Tang, Clan of the Jade Tortoise,
Counsellor and Ambassador of Djō-Khai,
Visiting Scholar to the Twelve Kingdoms

In Hydoemi Tongue:

Ari uŋë
Bri ǫllë, vɽ Urdë
Ll Ariana

In Mortal Tongue:

Sing, softly sing
Hear me, all ye who wake
My woes.

Literal translation:

Sing, Hydoemi, the lament beneath the still waves
Attend to me, living world
My sorrow, myself

Notes on Translation

Ari: a command, everyone (meaning in this case Hydoemi) is to sing. Also the root word of "voice."

uŋë: literally "beneath the waves," from *un* "beneath" or "below" and *në* a dimunative form of "wave," such as in smooth waters. Together the two *n*'s form a velar nasal ŋ. This conjunction also has the connotation that the wrong done Ariana must not be forgotten.

Bri ǫllë: again, the command of "listen," better translated as "heed" or "attend" because of its imperative form. *ǫllë* is simply *ǫ* "to" with the attendant stroke to the object, in this case *llë* or "me."

vɽ Urdë: *vɽ* is short for *vra* which means "all" or "every." The mark beneath the ɽ merely indicates a contraction. In this case, the use of *vra* emphasises that the singer is addressing not only her own kind, but any creature who may aid her. She is admitting the desperation of her plight. The singer might have as easily begun the song with *vɽari*, that is "all creatures sing." That she did not is simply a restatement of the power and sacredness of Hydoemi music. Curiously enough, *Urdë* is a word the Hydoemi adopted from humans during the Fairies' reign. It literally comes from "Eden," with the specific sense in this case of "living" or "waking"—that is what we would call "awareness." Casually, it has come to mean merely "world."

Ll Ariana: *Ll*, as may be discerned, is merely the contraction of *llë* (cf. *Bri ǫllë*).

Ariana is a compound word of *aria* "voice" (cf. *ari*) with *ana* "fading." Together, it is best translated as "sorrow" or "woe," with especially dire associations for the Hydoemi. [Editor's note: see also Iorwrydd's Maritime Diary extract above.]

Let it not be said that the Hydoemi lack the curse of puns. The singer, Ariana, well knows what her name means, and uses her name in the third line to several ends:

First as a pun—the song, were it not a Lament, would be titled the "Lay of Ariana." The singer indicates that such a change in title, and thus in situation, would be welcome.

Second as a clue—the final stanza, *"tears do I shed, me/tears do I weep, me"* are, of course, those which must put the listener on the correct path to answering what is, essentially, a riddle song. However, the singer gives a hint at the very beginning of the song to any knowledgeable in Hydoemi philology. Niamh, with the Sirenean Lady Marien as a tutor, might well have been known that *arii* are shared through the very water itself.

The Illumusation

All Hydoemi Illumusations do not read right to left as originally supposed. Rather the *composition* of the Illumusation as a whole expresses the nature of the song itself. That "Ariana's Lament" is meant to be read from right to left indicates that the following song is one of sadness or regret. Comments here will be restricted to "Ariana's Lament" only. Further research may be found in my book, *The Art of Illumusation: An Exhaustive Study*. In Illumusation, the pictures serve not only as companions to the music, but as the lyrics themselves.

THE MOON
"Pointing" left denotes in which direction the reader is intended to peruse the manuscript. That it is quarter-full reveals that the singer is in a fading state—neither one thing nor another. Since the moon is used to indicate this rather than the sun, it further implies that the singer has no control over her state, but is in the power of another. Again, the use of puns is evident even in the first symbol. By using the moon to show Ariana's powerlessness, the singer likewise comments on her captor: namely that Moira (Mara of the Weeping) is a lunatic. Yet the moon, although pointing "backwards," nonetheless is moving towards the new moon, which proves that Ariana still hopes that her prayers might be answered after a time of trial.

THE TREE
Like the moon, the tree is a dual sign of sorrow and of hope, of entrapment and liberation. Its branches are nearly bare, the outermost limbs just beginning to show buds. It is out of its element also—its roots plunge deep beneath the waves, while its branches rear heavenward into the sky. It is trapped in an element not its own, while breaking free and sheltering that very element. The tree also serves the purpose of "pointing" the reader in the right direction by acting

as a beginning border. The tree, in conjunction with the Vertumn indicates *Urdë*, and specifically *vɾUrdë* because of its spreading boughs (cf. *Urdë*).

THE WHITE HYDOEMA

Also known as the Gwenglánngil in the Mortal Tongue, the White Hydoema is the herald of the mer-people. She commonly appears with the lyre, the most sacred of all the Hydoemi instruments. Here, she is invoked and represents the very first words both by her presence and by her quiet and literally sibilant posture: *Ari uŋë* (see above). It need hardly be mentioned that she is both beneath the waves and above the earth—the meaning of which should be clear, given her direct association with the Moon and the Tree.

THE RISING HYDOEMA

This, too, is a common symbol in Illumusation. Frequently Hydoemi themselves are portrayed—either as witnesses or participants to the song. In this case, the Rising Hydoema may be meant to represent Anwen, Ariana's sister who first came to Ariana's rescue. This may be ascertained by her darker coloring, as well as by her modesty, and finally by the indication that she failed in her attempt since, she, too, is separated from herself via the tree. Regardless of the identity of the Rising Hydoema, her posture is meant to represent the second phrase, namely *Bri qllë* (see above).

THE VERTUMN AND THE WHALE

The man in the Illumusation is meant to represent a Vertumn, or Earth Elemental who with the tree symbolises *vɾUrdë*. He may be discerned by his staff and his clothing made of leaves. That the Vertumn is not turned to face the White Hydoema does not mean that he cannot or does not listen, but only that the singer's attempts have thus far fallen upon either deaf ears or upon those unable to help her. This latter conclusion is literally upheld by the presence of the whale, which again figures into the whole schaema of inbetweenness, but which also indicates the watery fate of those who have failed Moira's challenge. This image, in various forms, is naturally repeated later in the Illumusation.

THE MARTLET DISCLOSED, DESCENDING

Any student of heraldry is aware of the legends surrounding the martlet—that it has no feet and therefore may never rest upon the ground. The presiding image indicated in nearly all the other pictograms need not be repeated. Had Ariana chosen a mortal life, she might well have added the martlet to her arms, since she is the youngest of all her kin and perhaps therefore felt the need to prove herself. This led, obviously, to her falling into the Silver Hands of Ruthvyn and from thence to Moira. That the martlet is descending shows not only the singer's sorrow, but literally *LlAriana*.

The Music

As may be expected, the musical line is interwoven into the essence of the Illumusation, hence setting this artform aside from all others.

THE MELODY
This is typically found as an unbroken line on the page, frequently at the bottom as the line of earth or sand, although a very few Illumusations use clouds or fire or other elements nearer the top or the middle of the page. As is also customary, the melody line begins at the very "feet" of the White Hydoema. Although this woodcut is imprecise regarding the melodic line—as the original painting would not be—the basis for the traditional form can still be seen. [Editor's note: the melodic line for "Ariana's Lament" can be found on page 273.]

THE HARMONY
Beginning with THE WATER, we hear what might be translated into the strings or woodwinds as a series of turbulent arpeggios. Likewise THE SKY acts as the brass and timpani (the latter indicated by lightening in later Illumusations), which in this section is very chordal in nature, almost exactly following the line of melody.

THE KEY
Given the nature of the Hydoemi, it is not surprising to discover that the concept of "key" has almost no meaning to them, since any given Hydoema may sing with any voice in, effectively, any register.

THE TEMPO
Hydoemi music, as Iorwrydd observed, resembles nothing so much as water given voice. Any who have listened to the sea know her rhythm as well as her anarchy. So, too, is the tempo of Hydoemi music. There is a greater beat than may be found in sacred chant, yet also a greater fluidity than folk music. In Illumusation, the tempo is not formally demarked, but rather indicated by the state of the sea itself.

ARIANA'S LAMENT

Emily C. A. Snyder and Elizabeth van den Enden

The Maiden of the Snows

Emily C. A. Snyder
Copyright ©2002 by Emily C. A. Snyder

One day in the spring, when the world___ was new, I saw a maid__ sit-ting by a___ yew. And such a___ sight, I ne'er did see, as the sil-ver hair___ of that fair___ la-dy. "My love," said__ she, "my love_____ thou art, and noth-ing ev-er shall we two____ part, but if thou wouldst__ love me then this_____ thou know, I am the Mai-__ den of the__ Snows! Leave__ me, leave__ me mor-tal man, but one shall__ hold her, but one can. He who does___ melt the snows,___ on-ly with him shall my bless - ing go.

NOTE: *The Maiden of the Snows* follows the oral tradition of changing the music according to who is speaking or who is being spoken of. Thus, any verse which ends with "Maiden of the Snows" takes on the second system of music, while those which are about or sung by the Father take on the third. The remainder of the verses are sung in the first form.

Song of Searching

Emily C. A. Snyder
Copyright ©2002 by Emily C. A. Snyder

Wan - der, wan - der I_____ Wan - der, wan - der I_____ Where hast thou gone, my__ la - dy__ love! Oh, where o'er the earth hast thou gone? I have ___ wan - der I_____ Ov - er been to the moun-tains, I have delved in the sea, I have sung in the air, "Sweet__ love, come to me." I have

earth and sea_____ ov - er sea and sky._____

been in the mount-ains I have swum in___ the sea. I have flown through the air,___ I have not found

thee. I am here, I am hid - den in the heart of the flame, nor___

fly_____

wan - der, nor flee shouldst___ thou___ call___ my___ name.

wilt thou not wake
niamh's lament

Emily C. A. Snyder
Copyright ©2002 by Emily C. A. Snyder

A-cross the earth, thou sear-ched for me, the dark - ness thou didst light_____ for me, all___

ev - il thou didst fight_____ for me, wilt thou not wake and turn to___ me? Thy song I heard thee sing to___ me, thy

love I do re - turn_____ for thee, thy___ death I can - not bear_____ for grief, wilt thou not wake and

turn to___ me? Through dark - ness have I gone for thee, ban - ish - ment have I borne_____ for thee, then___

let me no more mourn for thee. Ah, love a - wake and turn to___ me.___

The complete sheet music for
Niamh and the Hermit
is scheduled to be published in 2004.
Please check the Arx Publishing website for details.
www.arxpub.com

If you enjoyed this book, you might also be interested in these other high-quality works from Arx Publishing...

Mask of Ollock by Robert F. Kauffmann
Embark on an intelligent and captivating foray into a fantastic world of powerful wizards, demonic spirits, desperate battles and political treachery. Olgo the elderly mage-king of Umbra fashions an enchanted golden mask for Ollock his beloved heir. But tragedy soon engulfs the storied kingdom as the awesome power of the mask swells the ambitious prince's arrogance and dooms Umbra to an all-out war of conquest.

Dream of Fire by Nicholas C. Prata
Kerebos Ikar, the nihilistic commander of the ruthless Black Legion, carves a swath of terror across the Pangaean landscape. But from the holy city of Kwan Aharon rides a lone priest from the Order of the White Flame, armed only with an apocalyptic prophecy about a soldier of hell who will be forged into a herald of salvation. *Dream of Fire* combines the intensity of a modern battle narrative with the intellect of classical allegory.

Angels in Iron by Nicholas C. Prata
Over 200 years ago Voltaire wrote "Nothing is better known than the Siege of Malta." *Angels in Iron* is a riveting historical novel recounting the valorous deeds and terrible privations surrounding the Great Siege of Malta in A.D. 1565. Wonderfully written with crisp and visually intense prose, *Angels in Iron* brings the heroism and horror of combat sharply into focus.

The Laviniad: An Epic Poem by Claudio R. Salvucci
An epic in the classical tradition, the *Laviniad* relives an ancient legend of the Trojan War cycle. The quick-tempered Ascanius assumes command of a city in crisis as the tyrant Mezentius lays waste to the Italian countryside and strangles Lavinium under a bitter siege. While the city starves, a divine omen suddenly impels its beloved queen to flee the city to meet her own mysterious destiny in the Latin wilderness.

For further information on these titles, please visit our website:

www.arxpub.com

Arx Publishing, LLC is a new imprint specializing in fantasy, adventure, and epic fiction. From our small press located in historic Bristol, Pennsylvania, the Arx Publishing program blends forms such as the classical epic with modern genres like fantasy and action/adventure. The unique character of the books in our growing catalog will attest to the innovative and highly original results.

As a small company, we depend on our readers to spread the word about our books to like-minded individuals. If you enjoyed this book, we encourage you to review it on your favorite internet book sites, discuss it in online forums, and mention it to your local bookshop owner.

Thank you for supporting independent publishing!